THE REASON SERIES - COMPLETE COLLECTION

Zoey Derrick

THE REASON SERIES - COMPLETE COLLECTION

Zoey Derrick

Reason Series Reading Order:

Give Me Reason - Reason #1

Give Me Hope - Reason #2

Give Me Desire - Reason #3

Give Me Love - Reason #4

The REASON Series - Completed Collection

Other Works by Zoey Derrick

Finding Love's Wings

The Struggle Anthology

"Give Me Reason is a story full of heart, pain, doubt and learning to trust again. This story is about a woman who doesn't immediately run off with the man who offers her the world. She has seen the ugly in the world and trusting someone again isn't a price she is willing to pay."

★★★★★, Emily, TheSUBCLUBbooks

The entire Reason Series is dedicated to all the men and women around the world who are or have been a victim of Domestic Violence.

CHAPTER ONE

Give Me Reason

PROLOGUE

An angel is he
Alone in this world
With the wealth of three
He'll meet his true love
Answering her song
His wings he will grow
His heart will respond
Him she will follow
His wife she will be
Two joined making three

What had at first appeared to be a faint birthmark slowly morphed into something more. The lines became more defined. Smooth to the touch but appearing shadowed, three-dimensional. And they seemed to flicker, to dance, to be alive.

In the beginning, the lines grew quickly. It took his mother years to realize that they weren't merely random, that they appeared to form a shape or pattern. Of what, it was hard to tell.

Doctors could never explain it because they could never see it; the lines remained a concern with his mother throughout his childhood. Then, when he was eight, the lines stopped changing.

They remained the same until tragedy struck: He'd been helpless to save his family. The changes began anew, with the lines morphing and becoming more pronounced over time. Soon they started sending tingling sensations across his skin. Sensations that were rare and seemingly random.

Until today.

Normally he'd be able to go about his day without too much trouble from the markings on his back. But over the course of today's celebrations — groundbreaking on a new condo project his company has invested in — the pulsing prickles have gone from an irritating nuisance to downright painful. Finding the sensation to be too much to handle around other people, he leaves the cocktail social he's been attending.

When he steps out the front door, he finds his driver.

"G'day, sir. Done so soon?"

"Aye," he says, looking at his driver. Just as the car door opens, the left side of his body hums harder and faster, pulsating, and a strong tugging sensation pulls on his arm. He stops, unsure what to make of it. The tugging has him curious. "I'm going to go for a walk."

"Sir," the driver says and closes the door.

"Stay close, though," he says, and turns to his left.

The moment he takes a step in the direction of the tug, the hum across his back dims slightly. After a couple of pulses and another step, the sensation spreads across his back in a starburst from between his shoulders. Another step and the pulse increases – marginally, but it's stronger still.

Another and another.

With each passing step the sensation gradually increases. After about three blocks it's starting to become painful. He sags under the heavy weight of the pain he is beginning to feel, which forces him to slow down.

Up ahead, the word *diner* is shadowed backwards across the sidewalk. His eyes flicker up to the source of the shadow: light pouring through the windows behind large letters stickered on glass. Normally he wouldn't have even noticed the rundown restaurant, but the hum in his back has turned to pulsing again, as if in excitement or anticipation.

With each step he takes, the pulse radiates across his entire body, the sensations across his back pushing him forward.

He glances up the sidewalk, and there's a flash of bright white followed by ghosted stars. Rubbing at his eyes, he sputters, "What the hell?" He opens his eyes again, looks from side to side to check that his vision has returned to normal. His gaze lands upon what he'd subconsciously seen the first time.

Bright white light surrounding a red-haired, blue-eyed angel. Gorgeous.

The pulsing turns to a pleasurable buzzing sensation as the young lass walks toward the diner and goes inside. Her shoulders are slumped protectively around her body. He cocks his head, puzzled.

Suddenly his mind fills with a quick series of images — blurred and unrecognizable, but he has a sense of what he needs to do now, though it's not clear to him what's driving the need.

He takes a step and the hum ceases. Feeling the need to test his invisible guide, he takes a step backward. It roars across his skin in response. He turns around, takes a step away from the diner, and there's a stab of pain between his shoulder blades so sharp it causes his knees to buckle.

Quickly, he turns and heads back toward the diner. The sensation levels out to a pleasurable buzzing as he closes in on the restaurant.

He can see *her* through the window. She's heading toward a door in back, bright blue and white light engulfing her form. It's beautiful. And so is she.

ONE

The chilly October air has me huddled inside my hoodie. My feet are swollen and sore, and I'm flat-out exhausted, but I slowly stagger into the diner that I started working at about a month ago.

Waitressing at Garrison's Diner is far from my ideal job, but what can I say? It's a job, and the tips are...well, they're tips. I've managed to survive. For now. It's Tuesday, usually a day off for me, but Nyssa, one of the other girls who works here, needed the evening off, so I stepped up to take her shift. Right now, every little bit helps.

"Hi, Viv," Laura calls from behind the counter as the bell on the front door announces my entrance.

"Hi, Laura," I say back, fake enthusiasm in my voice.

"How are you doing today?"

"Fine, I think." She gives me a quizzical look. The same look she gives me every time I give her that answer. I just nod slightly at her.

Laura is in her mid-fifties and has been working in this diner for at least the last thirty years. Her hair is nearly all gray, and the wrinkles in the corners of her eyes only appear when she smiles, which makes me

14

think her smiles are genuine. She is very warm and motherly. Maybe this is why I find her so hard to handle some days.

I head toward the back to stow my bag, shed my hoodie and change into my stark white tennis shoes: a uniform requirement to go with your typical diner garb of a pink and white smock that flatters no figure.

I slide my hoodie off — not that the sweatshirt does much against the chilly Minneapolis rain — and notice the small bump rising from between my hips. I shiver. I've lost so much weight since the trip to the hospital two months ago that everything seems bigger and more pronounced on my body. My knees seem huge compared to the rest of my leg. My collarbones, shoulders and ribs are eerily prominent.

Looking back down at the bump, I realize that my boss, crabby old Bartie, is going to have a field day when he figures this out. He's quick to think about the impact his staff may have on him and his precious diner. Thank goodness it's covered by my apron. For now.

I take a seat on the bench in front of the four lockers in the employee area and sigh. "How did we get here?" I say to no one. I can't believe that it's been two months since that asshole put me in the hospital. With each passing day going a little more quickly than the last, I'm finally beginning to feel more like myself, but the overly friendly, bubbly personality that I used to have after I got away from my mom is still lost inside.

But I don't want to dwell on it anymore; I know I'll just end up in a crying heap on the floor. I take a deep breath and stand. Tying my apron around my waist, I stuff my hoodie and bag into the locker and head back out to the dining room, grabbing my timecard along the way and punching into the ancient time clock. It's four in the afternoon. I can already tell it's going to be a long night.

When I step back out into the diner, I'm greeted by the classic fifties diner décor in black, white, chrome and red. It no doubt looked great at one time, I suppose. Red faux leather booth benches, white tables with chrome trim that now sport a weathered, well-used look. On top of every table, jukeboxes and bottles of ketchup and mustard sit alongside sugar packets and napkins in old-school metal holders. The black and white checkers on the floor continue up the side of the counter that separates the dining room from the kitchen. The countertop itself is white with cherry red trim.

"Viv, there's a gentleman in the corner that just came in. Would you mind?" Laura says as soon as I clear the swinging door. I'm pretty sure Laura makes a point of giving me as many tables as she can because she knows I need the money. It's either that or laziness. Either way works fine for me; I'll take what I can get.

"Sure." I reach for a menu and head over toward the far side of the diner.

As I approach table twelve, I realize that its sole occupant is wearing a rather expensive-looking suit and tie. Having come from trailer parks in the middle of Podunk Nowhere, Everywhere, my idea of an expensive suit is something you'd find at JCPenney. But this...this looks to be more than that.

"Good afternoon," I say, my southern accent echoing through the diner. You usually can't hear the accent, but it seems to come out when I'm trying to be friendly. I set the menu down in front of him.

"Thank you." His voice is deep, raspy. A bit of an accent rolling off his tongue. He grabs the menu and opens it. I cringe internally when I notice something stuck to the front cover. Ugh, that's so disgusting.

I shake off my mortification at the dirty menu and tell him, "Today's special is roasted turkey, mashed 'tatoes, gravy, with a side of veg'table medley."

I see him shake his head. "Would you eat that?" His question throws me off guard and I scowl at him. Right now I'm so hungry I'd eat a cow. Raw.

"Of course," I say softly. He is quick to catch the reverence in my voice about the mention of food. His head snaps up, hard, and he looks straight at me. His eyes are a deep blue-green. Ocean-like. Piercing straight into me. His gaze has me feeling like all my secrets are pouring from my body. It's unnerving and I try to tear my eyes away, but it's like he's got me under a spell. After a few heartbeats he releases me from his stare.

"So the special is not your favorite thing on the menu. What would you eat?" he asks, his voice rasping again. I still can't place the accent, but it's definitely not American. Irish maybe.

"The barbecue bacon burger is really good. With fries." I lean in a little and whisper slightly, so I'm not overheard by Radar-Ears Laura. "Avoid the slaw," I advise him. Having lived in Georgia a good portion of my life, I can say with authority that this slop Bartie calls coleslaw is a travesty. He nods in response and I find it hard to pull away. His scent has registered on me and I'm immediately drawn to him even more. It's warm, clean. He smells of leather and a delicious cologne. Committing the scent to memory, I back away. "You want a few minutes?" I ask.

"No," he says, sharply, and with a strong sense of authority. "I'll have the barbecue bacon burger, no slaw." I smile. "Fries, a Coke, and a side of mayonnaise."

I write down his order, though I don't need to. It's committed to memory, but my ass-hat of a boss has this thing about proof. He seems to think everyone is stealing from him. "Anything else?"

"No." That authority is back in his voice. It's strange: His tone isn't threatening or demanding, it just projects a sense of confidence and maybe even a little cockiness. Nonetheless, something tells me that this man knows what he wants and is not to be messed with.

"Okay, darlin', I'll be back with your Coke," I say and turn toward the counter. As I walk back, I can feel his piercing eyes on me. I'm tempted to turn around just to show him I'm not one to be intimidated by a stare-down, but I don't give him the satisfaction. Besides, he might get the wrong impression and think I'm flirting with him. Friendly maybe, but nothing more than that; I'm in no position to be flirting with someone intentionally.

"You were over there a long time," Laura says to me as I reach for a glass.

"He was having a hard time deciding what he wanted to eat," I say back, trying really hard to not be rude.

"Oh reeeaaallyyy..." she says, dragging out the last word.

I look up at her, shocked by her reaction. "What?" I say.

"You mean to tell me you weren't checking him out while you were over there?" I just shake my head and go back to filling the glass with ice and Coke. "Well he was sure checking you out."

"What's your point, Laura?" I say, and she glares at my tone.

"My point, Vivienne, is that he was checking you out and you flat-out ignored him. He's gorgeous. What is your problem?"

My eyes prickle with tears. My problem is that I'm broken and damaged and I don't need some deranged man to lust after right now. "I have a lot on my mind," I say out loud. Laura is insanely nice and sweet and — lest we forget — motherly. She doesn't need to know all the gory details.

"You always have a lot on your mind. You're twenty-two years old, what more can be on your mind than going out with friends and having a good time?"

Oh, if you only knew. "You know that's not who I am," I say as I turn back toward Mr. Suit. I look up in his direction. He most certainly is watching me, his eyes a bright light in his otherwise dark features.

I finally take a moment to really look at him. He looks to be not much older than me, actually. Maybe twenty-five or twenty-six? His hair is black, slicked back except for a stray strand falling into his eyes. His jaw is hard and sharp, leading into a very strong, square chin. His lips are a soft pink, full, and he has deep-set, bright blue eyes. There's an intensity to his gaze that has me so transfixed I nearly trip over my own feet as I make my way back to his table.

Damn it, Vivienne, get your head out of your ass, I scold myself as I approach his table. Tripping over my own feet and spilling Coke all down this guy's front is just the kind of thing that would get me fired, and I can't afford to lose this job.

"Can I get you anything else right now?"

"No, I'm good, thanks," he says, his eyes still boring into me with that intense stare.

Luckily for me we get busy, and aside from bringing him his food and his check I manage to pretty much ignore him for the rest of his meal. Which is why it surprises me when I go to clear the table and find a thirty percent tip.

TWO

No sooner do I set foot in the diner the next day for another shift than Mr. Suit from the night before shows up again. Our food is not that good. I can't imagine what on earth is bringing him back here again.

Laura takes to seating him, and I, of course, get left with the table. Tonight he asks me how I am, and we converse a little bit. Nothing too exciting. He orders the same thing as last night, and again I don't get to spend much time with him because we get busy.

He pays his tab, gives me another thirty percent tip and leaves.

Finally Thursday rolls around and I'm beyond exhausted. I've worked every day since Sunday. But I do what I need to in order to survive. I make squat for an hourly wage, and I lose a lot of money when it comes to tips paid with credit or debit cards because they're taxed through my meager paycheck. But luckily most of our customers pay cash, and I usually manage to walk out with about fifty dollars a week.

I find myself slightly disappointed when I'm in the diner for more than an hour and Mr. Suit from the last two nights hasn't shown up yet. Then I beat myself up for actually hoping he would come by again.

I head off to the back to grab some more silverware for the wrapping Laura and I are working on, and when I come back, I nearly drop the tub all over the floor.

Sitting at table twelve is none other than Mr. Suit himself. Looking as dashing as ever tonight in another suit and tie. If this man can afford to dress like that, why on earth does he eat here?

I look to Laura, who nods encouragingly, and I head on over to the table. Ironically enough, he has the same menu from the other night, the one I'd forgotten to clean. Obviously no one else has cleaned it, either.

"Hi there. How are you tonight?"

"Great, thanks. I'll have the same - if you remember." He smiles.

"Barbecue bacon burger, fries and a Coke?"

He smiles again. "You got it."

"I'll be right back."

After what seems like an eternity, I finally make it back to his table. The dirty menu is staring me in the face once again. "Here you go," I say, setting down his glass and pulling a straw from my apron. I reach for the menu, determined to go and clean it off. I realize as I reach out that my hand is shaking. This fact does not go unnoticed by Mr. Suit. He tries to reach for my hand. I pull it back quickly, clutching the menu.

"Do I make you nervous?" he asks in his usual stern voice. I shake my head. "You're shaking like a leaf." I look quickly at his face. His jaw is set into a hard line, his lips pursed. "When was the last time you ate anything?"

"This morning," I say quickly. It's true: I ate a hot dog for breakfast this morning. Cold, straight from the refrigerator.

"You should eat something," he says, attempting to soften his tone.

"Thank you, sir." I watch his nostrils flare. "However, I assure you, I'm fine."

"It's not you I'm worried about," he says, staring coldly at me.

"Excuse me?" There's no way. How could he possibly know?

"Forget it. I shouldn't have intruded."

I try to gather my thoughts. "Can I get you anything else?"

"Yes," he says. His eyes rake up and down my body from head to toe. Rest assured, he's not seeing anything worth looking at twice. I wait patiently for him to go on, but nothing comes.

"What would that be?"

"A duplicate of what I just ordered. For yourself."

I shake my head. "It's not allowed."

"And you need to eat," he all but growls at me.

"I appreciate your concern, but I can*not* afford to lose my job. So, thank you for your offer, however, I respectfully decline. Now if there is nothing else I can get *you*," I say, adding emphasis, "I will be back in just a few minutes with your food."

I turn quickly before he can trap me again with his stare. The look on his face is hard, unyielding. Something tells me that he's going to find a way for me to lose this argument.

When I return to the counter, Laura starts in with the Spanish Inquisition about my conversation with Mr. Suit.

"He saw my hand shake when I picked up his menu. Then tried to order a burger for me to eat."

"When was the last time you ate?" she asks.

"Jeez, stop. This morning, alright?"

"No, Viv, it's not alright. You need to eat, you're nothing but skin and bones."

I roll my eyes at her and turn to grab the washrag so that I can clean this stupid menu. "One meal won't solve that problem," I mutter bitterly.

"So let him buy you a meal," she says. I shake my head stubbornly. "I won't tell Bart."

"No, Laura. You know damn well he will find out, and when he does he will think I conned a nice customer into buying me food. It's not worth losing my job over."

"You say that as though your life means nothing," she says dryly.

I shrug. Lately I'm not sure how much I care about myself or my life.

"Damn it, Vivienne, what the heck is wrong with you?"

I just shake my head. "Stop. Please, Laura. I get it. I'll try and eat."

She just shakes her head and goes about her business. Antonio hits the bell on the pass-through, telling me that Mr. Suit's food is ready. I go grab a tray, wipe it off with the rag and put the plates on it, hoping and praying I don't get caught in his stare, trip and fall on my face and make an ass of myself on the way back to his table.

I make my way there, feeling a little more confident because I haven't actually looked at him. I quickly place his burger and fries on the table, followed by the bowl of mayonnaise. "Anything else?" I ask, not looking at him.

"Will you join me?"

"I..." I shake my head. "I can't."

Suddenly I feel a hand at my back, causing me to jump slightly, and Laura comes into my peripheral vision. "Is everything alright?" she says quietly and quickly.

"I asked her to join me," Mr. Suit says to Laura. Fantastic.

"Oh, what a fabulous idea. Vivienne, why don't you take a break," she says, more as an order than as a request.

"I just started. I don't–"

She cuts me off. "You're fine. Have a seat. No one else in here anyway," she says and walks away.

I look toward the man in the booth. He has a smirk of satisfaction on his face. "Now you have no excuse. Take a seat."

I huff loudly. I want to protest and throw a fit, but I have to admit, I'm curious. And, I realize with a sigh, I really am hungry. I concede to his demand and slide in across from him. As soon as I sit down, he pushes his food in my direction. I push it back and shake my head.

He pushes it at me again. I look at Laura, who nods and mouths, "Go ahead."

"What about you?" I say quietly.

"What about me?" he retorts.

"This is your food," I say. I'm trying to be tough, but the food in front of me smells so good. My mouth begins to water and I swallow back the saliva.

"I've eaten since this morning, for one. And for two, I think your co-worker over there has already placed an order for me." He nods at me. "So, now you have no excuses. Eat." His tone is gentle, but it still feels like an order.

With the smell of food in my nostrils, I'm too hungry to argue anymore. I reach for the ketchup, squirt it all over the fries and dive in.

THREE

Somewhere around the last of my French fries, Laura shows up with another plate for Mr. Suit, whose name I have yet to learn. She nods with approval at the fact that only half of the burger is left. "Do you want anything else?" she says.

I roll my eyes.

He scowls.

I shake my head.

"Water. And two more Cokes," he says as he hands his now-empty glass to Laura.

"I'll be right back." And she's off toward the counter.

I stare at the last half of my burger and debate whether or not to finish it, but then my stomach rumbles and I pick it up. Just as I lean in to take a bite, I see him staring at me again. "What?" I say around my burger, and he smirks at me.

"I'm not sure I've ever seen anyone eat with such purpose before. Like you're eating your last meal. Why don't you eat?"

Really? Bottom line, I can barely afford the hot dogs I do have. But there's no way I'm going to tell him that. "I'm just not hungry."

"That, Vivienne, is bullshit," he says with such an edge to his voice and such a straight face that I nearly drop my burger.

"What the hell do you care?" I snap. "I'm a waitress in some random diner, and you feel sorry for me, so you buy me a meal." Roughly setting the burger back on the plate, I slide to the end of the booth and stand up. "Don't worry about my food, I'll find a way to pay for it," I say and attempt to storm off, but suddenly the room is spinning. I feel my body start to sway, and the floor rises fast. I close my eyes — bracing for impact — and black out.

"We need to call an ambulance," I hear a male voice say. A voice that seems familiar, but...

"She'll put up a huge fight." That voice I know. It's Laura.

I feel arms tighten around me. "Vivienne." A hand strokes along my arm. "Vivienne." It's the male, Mr. Suit. My eyes flutter. "Vivienne, are you alright?"

I nod, I think. Or at least I intend to, but I can't quite tell if I have actually moved. "Ye—yes," I croak.

"Thank God," he groans, and my eyes open. Our gazes meet. His expression is soft, concerned. His eyes are warm, liquid. I feel his hand slide along my arm again. The sensation sends shivers across my skin and I squirm.

"Wh—" I breathe. "What happened?"

"You tried to storm off in a big bad huff, and I caught you on your way down." He's smiling at me. "Not my usual effect on women." I try to smile but instead I end up rolling my eyes. He laughs. "Yeah, you'll be alright."

I squirm, attempting to get up. He helps me sit upright, and Laura is quick to hand me a Coke. "You need the sugar," she says as she puts the straw to my mouth.

"I got it," Mr. Suit says as he takes it from Laura.

Laura smiles at me, then stands and heads back toward the counter.

I take another sip and I feel myself slowly coming back to normal. "Thank you."

His hand moves toward my face. I flinch and his expression changes, becomes instantly harder and more concerned. I shake my head and tuck the strand of loose hair behind my ear. I look up at him again. His eyes are warming, concern still etched in his features, and I shake my head again. "Sorry," I say.

He cocks his head to the side. "For?"

"Passing out. Flinching." *Existing*, I add in my head. His hand slowly strokes my arm. His touch is warm, soft. A tender gesture. Tears prick my eyes again. I turn my head away from him, instead looking down at the floor.

"What's your name?" I ask.

"Mikah."

"Well, Mikah, thank you for the meal. I truly appreciate it." I move to stand up. The flood of embarrassment I feel right now is overwhelming, and I just want to get away from him as quickly and gracefully as I can manage.

"Let me help you." He stands up quickly and then bends back down to help me come slowly to my feet. Once I'm upright, he steadies me so that I don't fall over again.

"I'm fine. Really." I still can't meet his gaze. "I'm going to go clean up. Why don't you sit back down and eat your burger." I start to walk away, gingerly, making sure that my head is not going to start spinning again. I catch a glimpse at the clock as I pass through the swinging door. Seven-thirty. Jeez, tonight is going fast. How long was I passed out?

Heading into the bathroom, I take care of business, then take a look in the mirror. "Jesus." I look like hell. There are deep hollows around my eyes, my cheekbones are way more pronounced and my cheeks look bruised. My bright red curly hair is pulled back into a tight bun, except for the strand Mikah was trying to move when I flinched. God, I can't believe I thought he was going to hit me.

Damn it, Riley really did a number on me. I hadn't realized that his actions would have such long-term effects. I've managed to stay away from him — from men in general — since he put me in the hospital, and I haven't really had to face any of it.

Riley was good at nothing except using me as a punching bag. A habit that nearly killed me two months ago. After Riley put me in the hospital, a social worker got involved and set me up with a place to live and a job. Which is how I ended up working here at the diner.

Pulling myself back together, I straighten my uniform, wash my hands and run cool water over my face before heading back out through the swinging door and into the dining room. My eyes scan the room. With the exception of Laura behind the counter, it's empty. I feel hope rush out of me as I realize that Mikah is no longer in the diner. Turning to Laura, I ask her, "Did he leave?" I can hear the disappointment in my voice and hope Laura doesn't catch it.

She just nods, so I grab the tub and head toward the table to clear off our plates. His is untouched; he never ate his food. Come to think of it, I never gave him his bill. Damn it all to hell, how am I going to pay for all of this? Irritation courses through me, and I turn back to Laura. "You let him leave without his bill?"

She shrugs. "He said he left the money on the table. I figured he would leave enough to cover it. Lord knows he can afford it." She goes back to wiping down the counter.

I turn back to the table. Man, he really didn't touch his food at all. I place the back of my fingers on top of the fries. They're ice cold. Jeez, how long was I out? I start gathering up the dishes and putting them in the tub. When I go to grab the plate I'd been eating off of, I see that something is sticking out from under it. I go to place the plate in the tub and nearly drop it.

FOUR

Sitting under the plate is a hundred dollar bill with a business card paperclipped to it. But when I pick it up, I realize there's more here than a hundred dollar bill. I pull the paperclip off to find four additional bills folded together — five hundred dollars in all — and a piece of paper. I slide into the booth, my hand covering my mouth and tears streaming down my face.

I suppose I should feel joy or relief about being given this much money, but all I can feel is indignation at the fact that he feels I'm some charity case. I unfold the small piece of paper that was tucked in with the bills. It's a note.

Vivienne,
I'm sure you're angry at this money, but please, don't be. Consider it a tip for a job well done and please, call me. I've attached my card.
-Mikah

I look at his business card. Its elegant silver lettering practically jumps off of the sleek black card.

Mikah Blake – CEO, MSB Enterprises

There is a phone number — maybe an office number — a website, an address downtown and an email address. I flip the card over. On the back, in the same handwriting as the note, are two phone numbers. A cell phone? Home phone?

I shrug and wipe the dampness from my cheeks. I'm not going to call him. I'm going to pay for the meal, take twenty percent for tip and find a way to give him back the rest. Despite the fact that this is enough to cover all of my rent this month, I cannot and will not accept a four hundred and seventy dollar tip from a man that sees fit to feed and take care of me.

The rest of the night passes by slowly, which is normal for a Thursday. We close at midnight and are out the door by five after because we spent the last hour of the shift cleaning everything up. I head out the front door with Laura, and she locks up.

"See you tomorrow," Laura says as I head toward the bus stop at the corner. "You want a ride?" Laura's typical nightly question.

"No, I got it. Thanks," I say and keep walking. It's early enough I can still catch the twelve ten west toward my apartment.

As I wait for the bus, my eyes droop, exhaustion registering. Luckily I only have to wait a few minutes. Al, the driver, opens the door and I climb up.

"Good evening, Ms. Vivienne."

"Hi, Al," I say sleepily as I put my money in the machine.

"How was business?"

I shrug. "Slow, as usual." I turn toward the back of the bus and let out a sigh of relief. It's empty. "Seems pretty slow for you, too, tonight."

"It sure is."

I grab a seat right behind him. Al is getting on in years, but he obviously loves his job. I asked him once why he drives the late night routes, and he said it was so he could see me. But I think it has more to do with protecting us girls that ride at this time of the night. Usually there are several of us on the bus: some traveling home from work, others looking for their next fix. Going anywhere at this hour can be scary. Fortunately for me, my bus stop is just around the corner from my shitty studio apartment in South Minneapolis.

I fight to keep my eyelids open as the bus rumbles along. Almost home. Almost to my mattress.

"Vivienne, honey, you're home," I hear Al say, and my eyes fly open.

"Thanks, Al." I gather up my things and step off the bus.

"Have a good night, Vivienne."

"You too, Al," I say as he closes the door. I watch as he pulls away, and I quickly make my way around the corner without drawing attention to myself. The street is dirty and it smells like trash and rotting food. Graffiti covers the walls around me.

I see my shadow lengthen as a car comes up from behind me, and I pick up the pace a little. Cars on the street this time of night, in this neighborhood, usually mean someone is up to no good. The car passes me as I reach my door. I glance up and see that it is a sleek black Mercedes. I scowl at it. What's a fancy car like that doing in this neighborhood? I push past the blue door and into the entryway and unlock the inner door.

The hallways are an uneven brownish yellow, almost like they're stained with nicotine. Judging from the smell, that's probably exactly what it is. The garbage that lines the baseboards of the entrance and the stairs is disgusting, but tonight I don't have the energy to care.

I shuffle up the stairs to the third floor. When I reach my door, I unlock the two deadbolts, turn the handle and slip into my apartment. I shut the door with my butt and lean back against it.

There is always a sigh of relief when I get home, knowing that I made it safely yet again. I've been harassed more than a few times on the streets and the bus, even in the less than twenty-five feet between the bus stop and the door.

I lock the two deadbolts and the knob and slide the chain. To be honest the door is so flimsy that someone could easily just kick it in, but the locks help me feel a little bit better.

My apartment is one room, a closet, and a bathroom. The kitchen consists of a small oven with a two-burner cook top, a half-size refrigerator, a small counter and sink. A few cupboards lie as empty and as useless as the fridge.

I head to the sink, grab a glass and fill it with water. I swallow it down quickly and refill it. As I drink half of the new glass, I unbutton my uniform with my other hand. When I reach the apron I put the glass down.

My hands slip into the apron pockets, and I feel the wad of cash from Mikah. My heart sinks. I can't keep this. It's not mine, and I'm nobody's responsibility. I walk the two steps over to my bed and fish around for my notebook between the mattress and the pallets that raise my bed off of the floor. I tear a blank piece of paper from the notebook and throw the money, the paper, and a pen from my apron onto the counter.

Then I take off my apron, smock and shoes. Looking down at my semi-naked form, I can see that small bump rising between my hips. It looks bigger tonight, no doubt because I've actually eaten a meal. Trying hard not to dwell on my swelling abdomen and the reasons for my current state of affairs, I shed my bra and panties and stumble into the bathroom. When I release the bun atop my head, the thick, curly red waves fall down my back and tickle my hips.

I turn the water on to the hottest setting possible, hoping like hell that there is some hot water left in the tanks downstairs. After a couple of minutes the water is lukewarm at best. I climb in, praying that it lasts for at least a few minutes before turning ice cold.

It doesn't. I don't waste time and I'm in and out quickly. Shivering, I towel off, turn up the heat a bit and grab my cotton pajama bottoms and a t-shirt full of tiny holes. I pull on the clothes and wrap my hair in the towel. A few more minutes of chattering teeth before I hear the heater kick on. At least that works in this damn place.

I need to write Mr. Blake a note, but it can wait until morning. The shower and shivering have drained me, and I can't stay awake any longer. I don't have to be to work until four tomorrow, so I'll have plenty of time to write the note before heading out.

I climb into bed and shiver again as the cool sheets touch my skin. Pulling the blankets up to my chin, I try and settle into the lumpy, uneven mattress as best I can.

As I close my eyes, the last image my brain conjures up is an image of Mikah bent over me as I woke up from my fainting incident.

FIVE

"No! Stop!"

"I could kill you, bitch! What the fuck? You're such a whore." Smack across the face. He grabs my arms and shakes me. "You little fucking whore. I knew you would do this. I knew you were a no-good bitch." He pushes me away, hard, and I slam into the wall. As I fall to the floor all I can feel is the crack against my skull and...

My eyes fly open. I'm covered in sweat and the blankets are all twisted around my legs. I stare up at the dingy ceiling. Light streams in through the small window by the kitchen. Blinking back tears, I attempt to calm myself down by rubbing absently at my tummy with one hand.

"You asshole," I mutter.

I spent three days in the hospital after that night with a skull fracture, a concussion, severely bruised ribs and a sprained wrist. I was purple and black from head to toe. On the second day I found out that Riley had been arrested and charged with domestic abuse. He was later charged with endangerment when the hospital revealed to the police that I was pregnant.

They had said there was a chance that I could lose the baby, but they took good care of me.

Yolanda, a state social worker, asked me if I had anywhere to go. I told her no, and she did what she could to give me a safe place for me to recover after leaving the hospital. Once I was in Amber's Place, Yolanda helped me find this apartment and set me up to meet grouchy Bartie at the diner. Given that I had no experience, he was reluctant to give me a job as a waitress, but he said I had a great smile and gave me a chance, and it all worked out okay in the end. I suppose Laura had something to do with it; she took to me quickly and was very attentive when it came to training me.

My stomach starts doing flips. I pull myself free of the blankets and stumble into the bathroom. At least I make it to the toilet this time.

After I'm done retching, I brush my teeth and run my fingers through my hair. As curly as ever. Looking myself over in the mirror, I notice that a little color has returned to my cheeks and my eyes don't seem as hollow. It must be the burger I ate yesterday, but it'll only last for a day or two and I'll go right back to the way I was.

I head into the kitchen but stop before I get to the fridge, shaking my head. I'm choosing to skip the morning hot dog. Despite having just emptied my stomach, I don't feel hungry. I settle for a glass of water.

I grab the pen and paper and sit on my bed. Pulling the journal out to use as a hard surface on which to write, I start composing my note to Mr. Suit.

Mikah,

Or should I call you Mr. Blake?

While I truly appreciate your gesture yesterday, I cannot accept your outrageous tip. Please accept your change from your meal at the diner last night — you know, the one you didn't eat, and the one you forced on me.

I've always found ways to survive just the way that I am. I don't need your money to make it through.

Thank you,
Vivienne

A little while later, I leave my apartment. I'm dressed as nicely as I can manage in the skirt and blouse I wore to my interview with Bartie and the Mary Jane shoes that were given to me during my stay in the shelter. The outfit is hidden beneath my worn, oversized hoodie. It's colder today than it has been.

My hair is down. I'm hoping that it will make me harder to recognize when I arrive at Mr. Suit's office. I really have no desire to see him again.

But before I can go there, I need to make a stop along the way. I cross the street to wait at the eastbound bus stop. It's still early – about seven thirty – and the street is mostly quiet. The daily commuters are mostly already at work, and the neighborhood crowd hasn't emerged from their houses. There are a few passing cars, but the neighborhood just looks rundown and abandoned compared to other parts of the city.

I'm used to living like this, though. It's the kind of life I've always known. I grew up the only child of a single mom who worked three and four jobs. But she did it more to support her drug habits than to support me. It's amazing that I managed to stay away from drugs.

The bus arrives and I climb up, put my money in the machine and grab a seat about halfway back. First stop, the diner. It's Friday — payday. Then I can run across the street to cash my meager check and head off to my next destination.

After cashing my check, I get back on the bus and head further east to my next destination: Moore's Family Home. I don't usually go to see my mother on Fridays, but I figure that since I'm running downtown today it makes sense to go, and I can just stay in my neighborhood tomorrow.

When I walk in, the lady at the counter greets me by name. Then she tells me, "She's in the game room."

"How is she today?" I ask.

"She seems to be having a good day today. Enjoy your time." This is the typical response when I ask about my mother. I nod, and the buzzer sounds.

I walk quickly through the drab, white-on-white, hospital-style hallway until I reach the game room. When I turn the corner, I see her sitting in a wheelchair facing the window. Her nightgown is light blue, very old and thin at the shoulders. Her gray hair is about shoulder length. She looks years older than the forty-eight that she is. Years of drugs and alcohol have completely destroyed her body. And her mind. Until she moved in here about five years ago, she had never sobered up. Now they have her on all manner of medication for paranoia, bipolar disorder and schizophrenia. Most of the time she's pretty out of it.

"Hi, Momma," I say as I sit in the chair next to her.

She doesn't respond, just keeps staring out the window. This is typically how our visits go. It's better than a bad day; it's not pretty when she's jumpy or freaking out. She can get very violent.

Knowing that I'm taking the money back to Mikah today has me on edge. To top it off, a lot of things from my past that I've worked very hard at suppressing keep floating through my brain. Like the way we moved around from city to city, state to state.

It seemed like every time my mother got a wild hair up her ass we were off. Sometimes in the middle of the night. Which of course was never a problem: She never let me keep toys, and I only had enough clothes to fill up half of a garbage bag. A few pairs of pants, a couple of t-shirts and a pair of sneakers were usually about it. Even to this day my list of material possessions is so small that I can probably pack everything inside of one box and a trash bag.

Hell, I moved into my apartment with about three days' worth of clothes, two pairs of shoes, my journal — compliments of the psychotherapist at Amber's Place — and my bag. Or purse. Or whatever you want to call it. Since then I've also acquired a small pitcher and a cooking pot. Not that they get much use; I've got nothing to cook.

My tummy rumbles. Maybe I should have had that hot dog before I left.

Momma still isn't saying anything, just staring out the window. Lord knows what she's looking at. Or if she's even looking at anything. Sometimes I think she's just lost inside of her own mind, trying in vain to pull herself out. But then again, that's probably just me hoping. Hoping she will come around. It's wishful thinking, I know, but it is one of the few things that keeps me coming back here time after time.

It's been about five years now that she had her stroke. We had just gotten into Minneapolis from somewhere in Chicago. We didn't stay there long, so I don't remember too much about it. Before Chicago we had been in Ohio, Michigan, New York, Maryland, Georgia - which is where we spent the majority of my younger years – Florida, Alabama and Texas. She told me that we had been in Arizona, California and Nevada when I was really young, but I don't remember it. I don't remember everything about Georgia either, but that is where some of the few brighter highlights of my life happened.

I never went to the same school for a whole year, but I was always enrolled. She found me easier to deal with when I was gone in school for eight hours a day. It meant she was free to do whatever she wanted without me around to bother her.

I was able to graduate from a vocational school shortly after coming to Minneapolis. I managed to test out of all the required classes and then some. I actually scored a seventeen hundred on my SATs — which I was told was beyond awesome — and that I could pretty much attend any school I wanted to. I even had a couple of colleges come after me, but the catch was, I was broke and couldn't afford their tuition. Besides, school wasn't anywhere I needed to be.

It wasn't long after that SAT test that my mom suffered a severe stroke that left the right side of her body useless and put her in the mental state that she is in right now. The stroke was a blessing in disguise. It forced her to detox and sober up, but the flip side is that she can't do much on her own and she's forced to live in this home. But when you break it down, it's better this way.

Better for me, or better for her? That is the question I always find myself trying to answer. The selfish side of me wants to say it's better for me that she's here. Hell, even the non-selfish side of me says it is better for me. Having her here means she's sober and not on the streets. Despite all the times I've been asked why I don't just walk away, I still come here, thinking that maybe my presence brings her some sense of joy. Maybe one day I will find the strength to move on. But today is not that day.

I say my goodbyes, kiss her on the cheek and leave the facility. I need to get downtown and then be back at the diner by four.

The bus drops me off right across the street from Capella Tower. It's a beautiful building, sleek and modern with glass walls and a rounded rooftop. I cross at the crosswalk and head into the building. The entrance is huge, with stone floors and glass-domed ceiling. There is a large directory toward the back, and I head over to it.

I've seen this building a hundred thousand times in the Minneapolis skyline, but this is the first time I've been inside. The elaborate decor makes me feel even poorer than usual, even more out of place.

I finally find MSB Enterprises. It's on floors forty-two through fifty-two. There's an asterisk next to level fifty and a note: *All Visitors Please Report To Level 50.* Well, level fifty it is.

When I get to the bank of elevators, I see signs over several of them indicating which floors they go to. I push the up arrow next to the elevator labeled *42-52*.

Jeez, they even have their own elevator?

I shift nervously from foot to foot while I wait for the elevator to arrive, again conscious of being completely out of my element. When it comes, I can hear voices — male voices — on the inside.

"Oh, no," I breathe, and I slink away toward the back of the hallway, hoping the men will just exit and turn toward the entrance, away from me.

The doors open and six men file out. Five of them head toward the entryway. The sixth gentleman quickly slides past me toward the door at the end of the hallway. Thankfully, I don't recognize any of them as Mr. Suit.

I duck into the elevator and look at the control panel. Above the buttons there's a little sign that reads, *Entry to floors 42-49 prohibited without a key card. Floors 51-52 only accessible from floor 50.* Well, I guess I have no choice but to go to the fiftieth floor. I push the button and lean into the wall, wrapping my arms around my ribcage. After a few moments the elevator starts to chime as we pass every third floor past the twentieth. I watch the numbers rise by threes, wrapping my arms tighter around my chest, nerves taking over.

I regret coming here. I hadn't thought this far ahead, and I don't have a clue how to go about leaving this for him. Maybe there will be a receptionist I can leave the note with.

I suddenly have the urge to see him again, something I hadn't expected. The image of Mikah looking down at me when I woke up from fainting yesterday pops back into my mind, and the urge to see him grows stronger. I look up to see what floor we're on. Forty-one. Almost there.

Ugh. It's stupid of me to want to see him again. He's everything I'm not, and I have no business thinking about him that way.

"When was the last time you ate?" a male voice says from behind me.

SIX

I jump, stop breathing and then try to sink further into the wall.

Without turning to look at him I mumble, "Uh, last night, with you."

Suddenly an arm reaches out for the panel in front of me. He presses stop and then presses the button with a phone on it.

A disembodied voice comes on the line. "Yes, sir?"

"Redirect us to the skyway level, please."

I huff.

"Yes, sir."

There are a couple of clicks, and the elevator starts to descend again. I'm still not looking at him.

"Why? What is so damn important about feeding me?" I try to growl and sound irritated, but the mention of food has made me hungry. Then again, I'm almost always hungry. But there's no way I'm accepting more charity from him. In fact, this is the perfect opportunity to give him his money back. Then I can leave via the skyway system and grab a bus back toward my apartment. It'll give me time to eat a hot dog, since it's still hours before I have to be at work.

"It's important to me because eating is healthy, and I don't like the way you look."

"Gah!" I exclaim. "Are you kidding me? What difference does it make to you what I look like? You're some random customer who's come into my diner for the last couple of nights. So what if I'm a little thin. That's my business and none of yours."

I look up, trying to see how long until we reach skyway level. I'm eager to get out of this conversation. We are still only in the upper twenties, and the skyway is on level two or three. Damn it.

I hear him sigh in frustration. "Because people, especially you, should not go without food."

Me? "What is so damn special about me?" I ask aloud. "For all you know I'm some random drug addict—"

"I know that's not the case," he says, cutting me off.

I finally look at him. His hair is slicked back in the same way it's been the other times I've seen him. His eyes are blue and warm, and there is a half smile playing at his lips. He's looking down at me, making me feel small at five feet, two inches. He has to be at least six feet tall. Broad shoulders. His suit today is gunmetal gray with blue or black pinstripes — I can't tell which. His shirt is a beautiful lavender color with a darker purple tie.

"How do you know I'm not an addict?" I ask softly.

He smiles at me, warm, genuine. "Because you've come to return the tip money I left you last night."

My jaw falls open. "How" — I swallow hard — "did you know?"

His smile fades a little. "Why else would you come down here?"

I close my mouth and look down at the floor. He says it almost as if my being here is unwelcome, but he has a point and his ability to read me is really scary.

"Since you haven't eaten since last night, I'm going to take you to lunch."

I feel my face flush bright red, both in anger and complete irritation. "That is not why I'm here. I've survived my entire life fending for myself, I don't need some rich, hot-shot businessman buying me food."

I reach into the pocket of my bag and pull the folded-up paper from it. I thrust it toward him. He refuses to take it. Tears of frustration trickle down my cheeks. "Damn it, Mikah, take it." I push it at him again, and again he refuses. "I'm not a damn charity case. I don't need your money or your food."

The bell chimes. We've finally reached the skyway. As soon as the doors open, I drop the folded-up paper with his money in it, bolt from the elevator and turn left, hoping and praying I can get away.

"Vivienne, stop," I hear him say behind me. I keep going, walking quickly but not running. Yet. I'm trying hard to not make a scene.

But he doesn't seem to care about that. He catches me quickly. Spins me around. I grab hold of his arm so I don't go sprawling onto the floor.

My stomach, on the other hand, has its own agenda. I cover my mouth quickly as my eyes dart around, looking for a restroom or at the very least a trashcan. I spot a trashcan about ten feet away.

I try in vain to free myself from his grip. "Damn it!" I bark at him. "I'm goin—" I swallow back the bile that's rising up my throat. "Throw up," I whisper. His grip immediately loosens on my arms and I dart to the trashcan.

He's there in an instant, pulling back my hair so that I don't vomit on it. Due to the empty state of my stomach, it doesn't last long, and I slink to the floor against the wall, drained and exhausted. Resting my head against the wall, I close my eyes. I feel a cool hand against my cheek and I flinch. A completely involuntary reaction.

"You should really go to the hospital," he says quietly as he pulls his hand back.

"For what? Ain't nothing they can do."

"In less that twenty-four hours, I've watched you faint and now vomit into a trashcan. You need to go to the hospital."

Oh for fuck's sake. "Damn it, Mikah, no. I don't need to go to the hospital. I'm pregnant, not diseased."

A harsh growl comes from between his lips. Thank God. Nothing scares a man away like the words *I'm pregnant*. I stand up, ready to try to leave again, knowing full well that he won't follow me this time.

I catch one last glimpse of his beautiful face. "Goodbye, Mikah," I say and take a step away from him.

SEVEN

I'm finally able to make it to the skyway and cross over to the next building. I follow the signs to an elevator and push the down button. A few other people join me in waiting.

I hear Mikah's voice talking to someone. "She went this way. You can't miss her – she has bright red hair, long, down to the small of her back."

I sink down into the crowd a little bit. The people around me are very pointedly staring at me. It's obvious that they know he's talking about me.

"Damn it, Vivienne," I hear him say, farther away this time.

Finally the elevator arrives. I'm quick to jump in. The rest of the little crowd follows behind me and I push *G* for ground level. Please, let me get out of here and on the bus before he catches up to me.

It takes but a few moments before the doors are opening on the first floor. As soon as they do, I see Mikah across the lobby, frantically looking for me. I draw my hood up over my head, hoping it'll hide my red hair. But it's a pretty day outside, and the hood may draw more attention. Damn it. I look to my left and spy an exit. Phew – I can slide that way and avoid him.

I put my head down and start moving along swiftly. All of a sudden I hear a man shout, "Blake!" followed by a whistle and the snapping of fingers far too close to me. I speed up.

I'm almost to the exit when a hand wraps around my upper arm. The grip is hard, painful. As he spins me around my hand comes up reflexively, hard and fast, and connects with his cheek.

"Shit!" he spats as his head snaps to the left with the impact of my hand. "Damn it, Viv, don't fight me."

"Jesus, Mikah, I'm—I didn—" I can feel the tears welling up in my eyes as I watch him rub his cheek. Regret fires through my heart as I realize that coming here was a really bad mistake. The tears spill over and I try to pull away from him.

"Hey, it's alright. I took you by surprise." He pulls me back toward him and wraps his arms around me.

I come completely unglued. Tears begin streaming, hot and heavy, down my cheeks as he cups me against his chest. Embarrassed by my lack of self-control, I push against him, trying to pull myself out of his arms.

"Vivienne, please, it's alright. Don't run."

The tears come even harder, stealing what little strength I had to begin with, and my legs begin to shake.

I give in to his embrace. It's strangely comforting being in his arms. I feel safe and protected, like nothing I've ever felt before.

With his hand over my left ear and my right pressed tight against him, I can't make out what he's saying, but I can feel the vibrations of his voice. He lifts his hand and says very gently, "I'm going to pick you up."

"No...no, no, no," I whine, but my protest is weak, and he ignores me. Sweeping me up off my feet, he walks through the doors I had been trying to get out of and onto the street. "Please, put me down."

"Not a chance, sweetheart. Not a chance." He shakes his head. "Not until we're in the car."

"Car? What car? No. Mikah, stop. I have to go to work." My protest falls upon deaf ears. I hear a car door open, and Mikah gracefully slides in. It's not until I'm inside that I realize that we're in a limousine. I want to protest more, but I know full well I'm going to lose the argument.

Then panic sets in. I don't like being locked into such a tight space. My body starts to shake again, harder than before, as my panic level rises.

"Hey." He pulls back to look at me. "Vivienne, what's the matter?"

I slip out of his grasp and crawl down onto the floor of the car. My teeth chatter, I'm shaking so bad. "T-t-tight...s-space.   Claustro...ph-ph-phobic. Too...dark," I finally manage to say as images of the hot dark closet I'd spent several days in swirl inside my mind.

"Red, hit the lights and windows."

"Yes, sir."

Suddenly light floods into the limo and I can feel a cool breeze flowing in from outside. The shakes reduce to a slight tremor.

Mikah leans forward on the bench seat, almost as if he is going to join me on the floor. He reaches out for my arm and I flinch away at the contact. He hesitates momentarily then tries again. This time I don't flinch, and he begins to gently rub my arm. I find myself soothed by the caress.

"Why are we in a car? Where are we going?" I finally manage to ask.

"We're in the car because I want some privacy with you. We'll stay here until you're ready to go. Then I'm taking you to H.C.M.C."

I stiffen and pull away from his hand. I slide back against the bench opposite him and pull my knees to my chin, steeling myself.

"No. I told you, no hospital."

He reaches out toward me, but I shy away and he stops. "I just need to know that you're alright. Okay?" He looks down at me. His eyes are comforting, warm. "Please, Vivienne?" His voice is pleading, but not insistent. A hint of desperation.

My heart starts to pound and my skin tingles. I look away from his face, not wanting to see his reaction to what I'm about to tell him. I know what I will see and I can't stand the sight of pity in someone's eyes when they look at me. But he has to know why taking me to the hospital wouldn't help me.

"If I go to the hospital, I will lose my job because Bartie is an ass-hat and he won't care where I am. I'm malnourished. My blood sugar is low, and I have high levels of anxiety. There, sir, is your diagnosis. And you know what they will do? They will run a battery of tests on me that I can't afford just to tell me everything I've just told you. Then they'll tell me that I'm not taking proper care of myself. That I should eat regularly and get plenty of rest, which are completely unreasonable expectations given my circumstances. They will make me feel shitty and useless. Then they will send me home to a closet-sized apartment with no food, a half-ass thing the landlord calls a mattress, and no way to pay my rent or buy what little food I have been able to afford because I will be without a job. So what's the point?"

I don't need to look at him to be able to gage his reaction. "Mikah, I work shit hours at a shit job for shit pay. I live in an overly shitty apartment and have no means of changing that fact anytime soon. So this is me, who I am. You're just going to have to deal with the fact that you can't save me." I start crying again, completely out of control.

"Jesus, Vivienne, why won't you let me help you?" His voice is soft, sincere and - more than anything - sad.

"Because! You have more important things to do than worry about some poor, pathetic, pregnant chick who works at a diner you stumbled into the other night. I've already told you — I've made it on my own, I will continue to make it on my own. Just like I always have. Please, Mikah.... Please respect that," I plead with him.

"I...Vivienne, I can't. I respect you for everything you've done, but you need more than you can provide for yourself. It's not just you that you need to worry about. I want to help you. And your baby." He takes a long, deep breath.

Guilt floods through me as I take in his words. "If I go to the hospital, get checked out, will that be enough for you? Will you walk away when I'm done?" I plead.

"I can't promise that."

"Damn it, why not? Mikah, you don't even know me."

"Vivienne Alison Callahan. Born September second, nineteen ninety, Boston Hospital. Born to mother Rebecca Callahan, father unknown."

I lift myself up onto the leather seat of the bench I've been leaning against to put as much distance between us as I can manage.

"Do you want me to continue?"

I shake my head. "Just because you know those facts does not mean you know me or who I am." Good God, he went digging for my history. Why would he do something like that? "You've known me less than three days. How on earth were you able to find that out?"

"I'm not sure you really want me to answer that." I glare at him. "When you flinched away from me after you fainted, I took off because...because..." He looks away from me. "Because I was afraid we would end up in this situation. In a car, heading to the hospital, with you feeling as though I'd trapped you in here."

My heart clenches tight.

"Please, Vivienne. Do this for me? There are reasons that I can't explain. It's not pity or charity. It's..." He pauses and looks back toward me. His eyes are warm, sincere. "It's a need that I don't understand. So please, let me help you."

"I..." I take a long, ragged breath.

"I understand your pride, your determination. Hell, I even admire it. But don't you think it's time you deserve a break? You deserve a chance to step back and take a break. Please, Vivienne, let me help you."

"Alright. I'll go," I say. I feel exhausted, emotionally drained. I barely register the fact that the car is in motion, but we're moving.

I realize deep down that he's right. I need to get checked out — at least for the baby's sake, if not my own — and honestly this might be the only way.

EIGHT

I'm brought out of my reverie when I hear Mikah shift in his seat. I look out the window and see the hospital as we pull into the parking lot. He leans forward and grabs my hand. This time I don't flinch away from him; I let his fingers slide in between mine.

"Come on. Let's go have you checked out." He smiles at me as the car comes to a stop. Tiny crinkles appear at the corners of his eyes, and I can tell that the smile is genuine.

"So can I say now that hospitals terrify me?"

His door opens and he starts to climb out. "Yes, you can tell me. But one of the biggest differences between your other trips here and this one is that you're not alone."

I can't believe I've agreed to let him take care of me. I'm not entirely sure what this is all going to imply, and it scares the hell out of me. I've taken care of myself since I was about six and my mother could no longer care for me.

When we enter, Mikah walks straight up to the nurse at the emergency care registration desk. "Mr. Blake. What can we do for you today?"

My heart sinks. They know him? How many other girls has he brought here?

"It's not me. Ms. Callahan is in need of some medical attention. She fainted last night." I roll my eyes. "Can we have her checked out?"

"Certainly. Ms. Callahan, why don't you follow me?" I look at Mikah, who is smiling reassuringly at me. I glare at him.

"What?" he mouths.

"Have you done this before?" I hiss.

"Done what? Come to this hospital?"

"Brought some lonely, practically homeless chick here?"

The shock that crosses his face tells me that I've said something offensive to him. "No, Vivienne, I don't go around preying on fainting, helpless women. I am the majority shareholder of this hospital."

My jaw clenches. Oh. But my pride won't let my anger fade so easily. "I'm sorry," I say, looking stonily into his eyes.

"You know, for being as small as you are, you put up one hell of a fight." He laughs a little. "Come on." He tugs at my hand, pulling me toward the nurse.

Twenty minutes later, I'm tucked into a room and getting into an open-back hospital gown. The cold material touching me makes me realize that I'm super sensitive, a live-wire. It reminds me of getting sick, when my skin is achy from catching a cold.

I lie back against the cold mattress and pull the blankets up to my armpits as Mikah enters. Suddenly I'm exhausted. My eyes feel like sandbags. Mikah takes a seat in the chair next to the bed, and I slowly close my eyes.

I wake up a few minutes later to the sound of Mikah's voice. He's talking to someone. "She fainted last night after eating a meal. Something I'm guessing she hasn't done in some time."

"Why not?" A female voice. "On purpose?"

"No, no. Nothing like that."

"Okay. Well, we will do some blood work. And I recommend an ultrasound. You know this isn't the first time she's been in here, right?"

Oh, no. I stir in the bed and open my eyes.

"Hi, Vivienne. I'm Dr. Alston." She extends her hand to me.

I try to sit up, but I'm weak with exhaustion. Suddenly there's a whirring noise and the top half of the bed starts to rise.

"Thanks," I mutter in Mikah's direction.

Then I notice a tugging underneath my gown. I look down at the wires coming out at the neckline. My eyes follow them towards the vitals monitor to my left. Turning my head back towards the doctor I notice the clip on my finger.

I extend my hand to Dr. Alston. "We've met before," I say, hoping Mikah doesn't ask too many questions.

"Pleasure to see you again. Mikah tells me you fainted yesterday after eating?" I nod. "Can you describe for me how you felt right before?"

"I was irritated," I said, darting a glance at Mikah. "Then I stood, the room spun and I realized that I was falling. The next thing I remember was waking up on the floor."

"Any headache after you fainted?" I shake my head. "Have you been dizzy since then?" I shake my head. "What about vomiting?"

"Twice."

"When?" She's looking from me to Mikah and I don't understand why.

"Once this morning, as soon as I woke up. Then again about an hour ago." I don't feel the need to add that a nightmare about that abusive asshole of an ex-boyfriend was the reason for my vomiting.

"I spun her around this morning, before I found out she was pregnant, and she vomited into a trashcan in the skyway downtown."

The doctor just nods and writes something else in her notepad.

"I throw up nearly every morning," I add.

"Do you remember about how far along you are?" I shake my head. I've tried to forget everything related to the last time I was here. "Okay, here's what we're going to do. I want to draw some blood and start an IV." My stomach churns at the thought of not one but two needles. "We need to get some fluids and some vitamins in you. Okay?"

I shake my head. "I don't like needles."

"I understand, but it is the fastest, best way to get you rehydrated. I can tell from the bluish veins in your arm that you're very dehydrated. You're also very malnourished. We need to check your blood sugar and run a few other tests. I also want to have an ultrasound done. This way we can take a good look at what stage in the pregnancy you are." She gestures to my stomach. "Can I take a look first?"

"Does he have to stay?" I ask, nodding in Mikah's direction. Some things are better done in private.

Zoey Derrick

"I just want to do an external examination, but if you want him to leave..." She looks pointedly at Mikah.

"Vivienne, if it's okay, I'd like to stay." His hand lightly strokes the back of mine. I flinch at the unexpected contact. I look at Dr. Alston.

"Mikah, why don't you give us a few moments alone," she says. "When I'm done you can come right back in here. Okay?" Mikah shoots a glance at me, then looks back to the doctor.

"It's okay," I tell him. "I'll let you back in."

He nods, his face somber as he stands and exits the room.

Dr. Alston closes the door behind him. Turning to me, she says, "Are you okay?"

I try to nod, but it's slow and small. The look on Mikah's face as I asked him to leave has me wondering what he's thinking, why he is so upset.

"I saw you flinch. Is Mikah the reason you were here two months ago?"

I'm shocked by the suggestion that Mikah could do that to me, but then I realize that she really has no way of knowing who put me here the last time. "No. I only met him a couple days ago. At the diner I work at. He bought me dinner last night, then tried to leave me a five hundred dollar tip and his business card. I went to his office today to give it back to him. I threw up, and he dragged me here."

"You don't want to be here?"

I shake my head.

"Why not?"

"I hate hospitals. The last time I was here, I spent three days here. I can't afford that kind of time, let alone the cost. I'm supposed to be to work at four."

"Mr. Blake has already informed billing that he is paying for everything today. In fact, for all your future visits here."

"What?" When the hell did he manage that? Irritation races through me and the machine beeps frantically as my heart rate increases.

"Calm down, Vivienne. He's a good person with a good heart. Maybe you should ask him why this is so important to him. You might better understand."

"I've tried." I look down at the sheet. I can hear the monitor slow as my heart rate calms.

"Give him some time. He'll come around. It is my duty as a doctor to make sure that Mikah is not the reason you flinched and that no harm has come to you by his hand, but my guess is that it has more to do with why you were here the last time." I nod, unable to look at her. "I don't want to pry, but we can set you up with someone to talk to."

I shake my head. "I appreciate that, but I'm alright." Sitting down and talking to a shrink creeps me out. When I was here the last time, they made one of the shrinks on staff come talk to me. He was a jerk and didn't seem to really care. He kept looking at his phone each time it buzzed. They let me go the next day, so obviously my silence didn't make him think I was nuts.

She shrugs her shoulders. No doubt she doesn't believe that I'm okay. She is probably right.

"How about you let me take a look?" She gestures again to my belly.

"Can Mikah come back in?" I ask before I can stop myself. If he's in here, she won't ask me any more questions about Riley.

"Of course," she says as she goes to the door to open it.

Mikah is right there.

"Come on in, Mikah."

His eyes dart from her to me and back again. I don't understand why he's so nervous.

"She said you can come back in," Dr. Alston tells him. "I was just about to start the examination."

His eyes widen.

"It's alright, come in," I say to him.

He nods and comes back into the room, taking the same seat as before.

I reach my hand out toward him, and he smiles a little. Something about his touch calms me.

The second our hands make a connection, my heart beats three times really fast. Okay, maybe *calms* is the wrong word.

We lock gazes. He lifts one eyebrow, then, as if to experiment, he pulls his hand away. My heart rate slows way down for a couple of beats before resuming a normal rhythm.

"What in the world?" I hear Dr. Alston say.

I look at Mikah. He's smiling like a Cheshire cat.

"Watch," he says.

Once the doctor's attention is fixed on us, he reaches for my hand again. Again my heart beats three times in rapid succession. Then he pulls his hand away, and my heart misses a beat, speeds up for a few seconds and then goes back to normal. Next to me, Mikah chuckles, causing me to smile.

"That is the strangest, most bizarre thing I've ever seen," Dr. Alston says, looking at me. "Well then, shall we?" She pulls on a pair of examination gloves.

I nod, but my heart rate increases again. I want her to turn it off so my emotions aren't so obvious, but at the same time I find strange comfort in being able to hear the reaction my heart has to him. I suddenly wish Mikah was attached to it, too. I'm curious whether I have the same effect on him.

"I'm going to keep you covered, but I need to lift your gown." I nod as Mikah lays the bed back down. "That's good," Dr. Alston says, and the bed comes to a stop.

I can still see everything she is doing. She pulls the blanket down and then gently slides it under my gown to cover my pubic area. Once the blanket is in place, she lifts the gown, bringing it to rest just under my breasts. Next to me, Mikah gasps.

"When was your last period, Vivienne?" the doctor asks, completely calm.

"Um, I don't know. Late June or early July. I discovered in August I was pregnant. The morning before I was here last."

Mikah's hand tightens against mine and his body goes rigid. He is no doubt contemplating the significance of that last statement.

"Okay, and if I remember correctly, you were four or five weeks along then. So that will put you between eleven and thirteen weeks." Her hands on my belly are cold; my stomach flinches at her touch. "Sorry," she says quickly.

I look down my body at my stomach. There are three very visible, well-defined points: Each of my hipbones are sharp against my skin, and the ominous bump from yesterday looks bigger from this angle. No wonder that skirt felt tight this morning. I hadn't worn it since my interview at the diner almost two months ago.

She pokes and pushes, doing what doctors do, and I flinch when some of the pressure points cause me pain.

"You're very skinny. Have you always been this way?"

I hesitate to answer her. The answer is no, I haven't. In fact, I used to be about a size ten or twelve, but I'm not sure I really want to highlight the fact that I've lost a lot of weight in the last six or seven months. The direct result of being told by Riley that I was fat — just one of the ways he had of bringing me down — and then of not being able to afford to buy food. After I left the hospital, it became increasingly difficult to take care of myself.

I shake my head. "No, not always." I have no doubt that Dr. Alston is pissed off at me for not taking better care of myself. Believe me, if I could afford more food, I'd eat it. It's not like I'm not trying.

She gently pulls the gown back down. "Aside from your weight — which is a big issue — everything looks okay. I'll have the nurse come in and get your IV and blood work going. I'll put in for an ultrasound, and I will be back in a little while." She pulls off the gloves and starts washing her hands in the sink. "Can I get you anything?" she asks, reaching for the paper towels.

"Another blanket would be good." I'm freezing again.

"I'll send one in. There is a button on the side of your bed if you need anything else."

"What about some food?" Mikah asks her.

Dr. Alston nods. "Keep it light, though. Soup or pudding would be good."

"Thanks, doctor." He looks at me. "Are you hungry?"

I start to shake my head and he scowls at me. It's actually pretty cute.

"Fine, yes, I'll eat." I smile at him and his eyes light up. His answering smile is blinding. "Why does that make you so happy?" I ask.

"Because you deserve far better than you're giving yourself, and I'm happy to give it. Whenever and however I can." I feel his hand tighten around mine. "Thank you."

He's thanking *me*? "What for?"

"For coming in, talking to the doctor. Being so calm about this and..." He pauses, looking deep into my eyes.

Something happens between us in this moment, a shift of some sort that I don't understand, and the heart monitor broadcasts my fluttering heartbeat. Geez, that is so embarrassing.

He smiles again. "And for letting me be here with you. Speaking of which, why did she make me leave only to have me come back in?" I look down from his penetrating blue-green eyes. "Tell me," he pleads.

"She saw me flinch when you touched my hand. She was concerned that you were the reason I was here the last time."

His face grows pale, and I feel his whole body go cold as he realizes why I was here a couple of months ago.

"I told him I was pregnant and he didn't like that very much. He took it out on me," I whisper.

"Fuck!" he spats, and I can feel his body start to tremble.

I can't look at him. I'm so ashamed. Ashamed of the fact that I was beaten, that Riley beat me whenever he felt like it. Ashamed that I let it happen more than once. I start to cry.

"I'm going to touch your head," Mikah says, finally getting why I flinch every time he touches me unexpectedly. "I want to..."

But I don't want his comforting. I feel the anger radiating from him, and though I know it's not directed at me, my broken spirit is already trying to push him away, to undo the intimacy between us. "It's okay. I'm okay," I sob.

"Like hell you are. I'm not going to hurt you or hit you. I would never – *will* never do anything to harm you. Ever." His voice is full of conviction.

I squeeze my eyes tight against the tears, willing them to stop, but I can't seem to control them. Then I feel his hand resting lightly against the top of my head. So light that I almost can't feel it. Then slowly, steadily, he starts to caress my head, stroking my hair. The movement is methodical, but it doesn't feel empty. My scalp tingles as goose bumps rise across it, then my neck, down my back and across my arms. My heart beats faster, keeping the machine busy with each pump and flutter.

He shifts closer to me. Keeping our hands entwined, he puts his head down on the pillow next to mine. "Please don't cry," he says quietly. His breath warms my cheek.

My heart continues to flutter, and a warm tingling sensation runs through my body, wrapping me in a feeling of comfort, safety, and an inexplicable need for his touch.

"Please, don't stop," I say softly.

"Never."

NINE

I wake up to a nurse coming in with a whole lot of stuff. Something that looks like a T.V. and a tray filled with vials.

"Hi, Vivienne. I'm Amanda. I'll be your nurse. I'm here to take your blood and get you set up with an IV. Once that's done, we will get you ready for your ultrasound. How are you feeling?"

"Tired," I groan. When I cry, it drains me completely and I just want to sleep. I think it is more of an escape-from-reality kind of thing than a physical need for sleep.

Mikah laughs. "She was sleeping when you came in," he says from much closer to my head than I expected. He's still stroking my hair, and his other thumb is rubbing along the back of my hand.

"Good. Sorry I woke you."

"It's okay."

I watch as she sets her tray of vials down on the table and starts going in for what she needs. As soon as she pulls out a tourniquet I roll toward Mikah, not wanting to see what she's about to do.

"I understand you're not a fan of needles. I'm going to do my best to not hurt you. I've been told I'm pretty good at being gentle." I nod. "Left arm, I take it?"

I nod again and she lifts my left arm, pulling it back slightly so it's out of my line of sight.

"Look at me," Mikah says.

I lift my chin upwards and find his piercing green eyes on me. That's strange; earlier they were more of a blue-green, but now they're almost completely green. Emerald. Almost like he put contacts in while I was sleeping.

The monitor sputters again. He smiles wide, and Nurse Fang — as I'm calling her in my head — has the tourniquet around my arm. I flinch as the needle pierces my skin.

"Long. Deep. Breath." I do as Mikah says and inhale slowly.

While it doesn't hurt, I can feel her shifting the needle around for nearly a whole minute before she hits pay dirt and releases the tourniquet from my arm.

She fills four vials with my blood; I feel a slight tug as each vial is replaced with the next one. Then the needle moves around again as she gets the IV set up. The tape comes next, and before I know it she's done. I let out the breath I was holding and Mikah smiles at me.

"Wow. Very well done, Vivienne," Nurse Fang — *Amanda*, I remind myself — says approvingly.

"Thanks. You're not so bad yourself."

She laughs. "I do try as best as I can. Can you roll back onto your back for me?" I shake my head in protest. "Please?" she pleads. She sounds almost like a whiny teenager and I roll my eyes.

"I'm comfortable."

"I know, but I'm going to get you set up for your ultrasound and the tech will be in here very shortly."

I sigh and reluctantly roll over. I realize I'm putting up a bigger fight than what I really feel.

Amanda repeats the procedure of pulling the blanket up to cover my pubis and raising the gown to reveal the little round mound between my hips. I hear Mikah's sharp intake of breath as my belly is exposed again. I can't tell if he's in awe or if it's a tortured sound. For my part, I'm starting to see that the mound and what it represents is unavoidable. Surprisingly, it's also growing more adorable each time I see it.

Amanda finishes up and leaves.

I look at Mikah. "Are you okay?" I ask him. He nods. "Is it hard for you to look at me like this?"

"Yes." He hears my heart skip a beat. "Not in the way you're thinking," he adds quickly. I give him a puzzled look, but he just shakes his head. "I will explain it to you later. Okay?" he asks, his voice soft.

I nod, still confused but trusting he will tell me later. I look up at the clock and panic sets in. It's three thirty and I'm supposed to be at work in half an hour. Stupid heart monitor goes nuts, and Mikah stands and leans into my line of sight.

"What's the matter?" he says, worried.

"I'm supposed to be at the diner in thirty minutes. I can't lose this job." Panic creeps into my voice.

"It's already been arranged. I spoke with Laura while you were sleeping, and she said that she would deal with Bartie and to keep her posted. If you were going to be gone longer than Sunday's shift we might have a problem, but right now, one day is okay. She said that she was going to tell him that you and Nyssa switched places because of Tuesday night?" The question in his voice tells me he's relaying a message he doesn't quite understand.

I take a deep breath and let it out slowly. "Thank you," I say quietly. "I do hope you're right. I can't afford to lose that job."

"Yes, you can." Or at least I think that's what he said. He was mumbling incoherently.

"What?" I scowl at him.

"Later."

"Why all this 'later' crap with you?" I huff.

"Because the doctor is coming in." And sure enough there is a knock on the door. How the hell did he know that? I leave the question for later and instead roll my eyes.

"How're you feeling?" Dr. Alston asks.

"Okay, just sleepy." She nods and walks over to the machine Amanda brought in, clicks a few buttons, and the screen flickers to life.

"I'm going to go ahead and handle your ultrasound," she says gently. Then she presses a couple of keys on a keyboard that came with the monitor and grabs a white bottle that looks a lot like the ketchup bottles at the diner, but with a shorter nozzle. I can't tell what's actually in the bottle.

"This might feel a little cold," she says right before the substance hits my belly. I watch as my belly flinches at the clear gel being squirted on it. "Now I'm going to use this." She holds a wand type thing that is wide and flat at the top. "I'm going to place it against your stomach and see what we can see. Okay?"

I nod. My heart starts pounding; it sounds super loud on the machine. Dr. Alston reaches over and presses a couple of buttons on the heart monitor. The beep gets quieter.

Mikah, who has been very quiet in the corner, gently squeezes my hand. I look over at him. His eyes are not on the doctor or the monitor; they are on me, on my face. I smile at him nervously and he squeezes my hand again as Dr. Alston presses the wand against my abdomen.

TEN

"Well, well. Hello there, little one," Dr. Alston croons.

I pull my eyes from Mikah's to look at the doctor, who is very intently looking at the monitor. The angle I'm at makes the monitor look black, and I can't see anything. The wand moves around on my stomach while Dr. Alston presses various buttons on the machine.

"Can we see?" I ask quietly.

As soon as the words leave my mouth, I have a sudden rush of fear. I want to see, but I'm scared. I'm scared that seeing the baby will make it real for me.

Mikah squeezes my hand again as Dr. Alston presses a couple more buttons.

"Just a...moment. I'm taking measurements. This will help us determine the age of the fetus, along with your blood work."

I bite my lip nervously and Mikah's hand resumes stroking my hair. This time, although I wasn't expecting his touch, I don't flinch, and I'm suddenly very grateful that she's turned down the heart monitor. His touch sends invisible shivers across my body, and I feel the knot in my stomach loosening.

75

That's when I realize that the knot has been in my stomach for months, not just minutes.

With a couple more clicks of the keys, she grabs the side of the monitor to turn it. Panic sets in and my heart rate skyrockets.

"Calm down, Vivienne. It's okay. I can give you some pictures instead, so you can look at them when you're ready."

I pull in a few long breaths, trying to imagine what this is going to be like, how I'm going to react. I remind myself that I chose this, that this is what I want.

"No." I take another long, deep breath. "I'm ready," I say, and once again, Mikah's silent reassurance is there as he squeezes my hand.

Dr. Alston slowly turns the monitor until the image comes into view.

It's grainy, black and white, narrow at the top and wider at the bottom. Smack in the middle of the screen is a black, odd-shaped oval, and inside that oval is...

Tears, hot and heavy, flow down my cheeks. There are no words for the beautiful image I see on the screen. Two arms, two legs, a head all visible. Suddenly the image zooms in, and I can see the baby's profile: faintest outline of eyes, nose, a faint shadow of lips.

"My God," Mikah says, so softly I almost miss it. Reverence in his voice. Part of me wants to see the expression on his face, but I can't pull my eyes away from the monitor.

To the right of a wedge shape on the monitor, something is pulsing. I point toward it with my free hand. "What. Is. That?"

"A strong heartbeat. Want to hear it?" Dr. Alston asks. I nod and she reaches for something on the keyboard. A second pulse enters the room.

"It's so fast," I say as I watch the pulsing match up with the noise. It almost sounds like a bad radio signal, full of static, but it is the sweetest sound I've ever heard. I start to cry again.

"That's very normal at this stage of pregnancy. In fact, up until well after delivery. Babies' heart rates run faster than ours for a while.

"As I suspected, you're about eleven to twelve weeks along. The baby is measuring at about three inches in length. In another five or six weeks, we should be able to fully determine the sex."

"When you say 'fully determine'...?" Mikah asks her.

"I mean that I can take a guess right now, based off of what I saw, but it would be a guess of experience and not expertise. Do you want to know what I think it is, Vivienne?"

I shake my head, wiping tears from my eyes. "I would rather wait until you're sure." My voice comes out hardly above a whisper.

She smiles at me and says, "That sounds like a plan to me. Do you want to take some pictures with you?" I nod and lay my head back against the pillow. I'm still tired but feeling a little bit stronger. I'm guessing it's the fluids being pumped into me.

Dr. Alston has frozen the monitor and pulled the wand away. On the screen is a still image of my baby's profile. It has to be the most beautiful thing I've ever seen. She pushes a few buttons again and I can hear a machine start up below me. Then she leans down and hands me a stack of several pictures, all black and white. Fuzzy, but still beautiful.

I feel the bed start to rise and I look at Mikah. His eyes are slightly red. Tears? That would explain why he was so quiet...but why? Why would he be crying over my baby? Then again, I can't imagine how Dr. Alston does this without crying. It really is a beauty of life.

"Okay," Dr. Alston interrupts my thoughts. "I'm going to go and see if your blood work is back, check on a couple of things and then we can decide on a plan of action." She releases the brake on the ultrasound cart with her foot and begins to pull it out the door.

I turn toward Mikah, and he beats me to my question. "How are you doing?" he asks. His raspy voice sends goose bumps across my skin.

"I'm scared."

"Of?" he asks.

"Everything. I don't know. But seeing that...just..." I pause, blinking back the tears again. "It just brings it all into reality."

He doesn't say anything for a long time. I rest my head back against the bed and close my eyes, but all I can see is that little baby. My baby. Until a few minutes ago, the life growing inside me didn't have much impact on my everyday life, but now, reality is setting in and I can't even begin to imagine how I'm going to do this. I'm an only child. I had friends growing up, but never really a baby around to take care of. I started to babysit when I was twelve or so, but those were usually kids just a couple years younger than I was.

Wanting to see the baby again, I open my eyes and look down at the pictures in my hand. In the upper left-hand corner it has my name, and in the upper right-hand corner it says *Baby Callahan.*

A sense of relief washes over me, seeing that and not Riley's last name. Then I feel the disappointment as I realize that, just like me, there will be no father's name on my baby's birth certificate.

"Vivienne?"

"Hmm?" I say, looking up from the picture and into Mikah's eyes. They are soft, warm, and a beautiful green.

"I'm wondering now if you will let me help you?"

"You already are. You're paying for this hospital visit and any other visits I need to make here."

"You know?"

I nod. "And...I appreciate it. Thank you, Mikah."

His lips curl at the corners slightly, like he's fighting a smile. "That's not what I'm referring to," he says.

"No, Mikah. While I appreciate your willingness to pay for my medical expenses, I have to do the rest on my own." I'm only accepting his help with the hospital bills because I can now see it's a necessity, but I draw the line at letting him help me with other things. What would he expect in return? Nothing I'd want to give, surely.

"How, Vivienne? How on earth do you plan to do this on your own? You can't even afford to feed yourself, let alone that beautiful baby."

My heart flutters at his words, which make me feel weak and unable to take care of myself. So many things start flying through my head about my past. Mom's boyfriends calling her useless, then Riley making me feel as though I couldn't make it without him. I'm trying so hard to leave those ideas behind.

"I will get a second job. I'll go back to the shelter. I don't know, Mikah, but this is not your responsibility. It is mine."

"Damn it, Vivienne, please don't be so stubborn. I just want to help you."

"Mikah, we've had this conversation already. I will find a way on my own. I'm capable of it, I've done it for years."

"Don't give me that bullshit, Vivienne, you are skin and bones."

All the years of not fighting back pour into what comes out of my mouth. "Stop it, please, just stop. You make me feel like a complete imbecile when you say shit like that. I'm not stupid, despite what you think about my job, and I'm smarter than I look. Just because I don't have some Ivy League education doesn't mean I'm not capable of taking care of myself. I will not be treated like this by you or anyone else." Fury races through my body. "Forcing me to take your help – demanding that I bow down like some servant at your feet while I gulp up all the help you can offer – will get you nowhere with me. If you want to help me, Mikah, forget about me. Go back to the life you had twenty-four hours ago. I'm not worth it."

The tears flow harder, faster, and I break out into full-on sobs. I pull my hand from his and rub at my eyes, burying my face in my hands. He reaches up to take my hand, but I pull it away from him and turn to face the opposite direction.

"Vivienne?"

I don't answer him. I'm afraid my answer will just piss him off, and I don't want to know what the outcome of that will be.

"Vivienne. Please? I'm sorry," he pleads.

"Just get out," I say.

"No, I want to stay."

"Damn it, Mikah, get out of here! Go home, go back to work, go...wherever it is you feel you need to be."

"I need to be here, with you."

"No, you don't! Now get out before I call the nurse!"

I feel the air around him go cold. My body starts to shake as panic sets in. I've upset him, made him mad.

The bed jerks slightly as he pulls back from it. I hear him stand and walk to the door. The knob turns, the door clicks. A couple more steps and I hear the door swing closed behind him.

The sobs start immediately. What have I done?

Riley's voice comes back to me, blasting through my ears and my brain. *You're a no-good whore. You're good for nothing, you will always be nothing, and you deserve nothing.*

My whole body convulses with sobs. I can't stop. I can't breathe. I pull in quick breaths, on the verge of hyperventilation.

I can't. I can't do this. What was I thinking? I can't possibly do this on my own. All he wanted to do was help, and I pushed him away. For God's sake, he was red eyed after the ultrasound. He was here, holding my hand, stroking my hair, supporting me, being here for me, and I just threw him out of my room.

I really am hyperventilating now. I'm not getting enough air, and I can't seem to calm myself down. I manage to press the call button. A glance up at the monitor confirms that my heart rate is climbing. I hit the button again and again. Then suddenly I hear feet running in the hall, shouts coming from outside the door. I'm desperate for air. Just as the door flies open I vomit all over the bed and black out.

ELEVEN

I come to slowly, my eyes fluttering before opening, and the first thing that hits me is that I'm in a different room. This one's decorated in a soft pink, and the lights are dimmed. I hear paper shuffling to my left and I close my eyes again, tight, hoping it's not him.

"He's not here," a female voice says. Dr. Alston? "He left just before you lost consciousness. Said that you asked him to leave. Why?" I just shake my head. "He was quite upset when he left here."

"I asked him to leave because he sees me as a charity case."

"Sometimes our pride gets in the way of seeing the truth," she says softly. I open my eyes and look at her. She is sitting in a small recliner, a binder on her lap. She's wearing dark-framed glasses, and her platinum blond hair is no longer pulled back. Instead of scrubs, she's in a full-length black skirt and sequined blouse that shimmers in the soft light.

She notices me staring. "Sorry. I have a benefit event to go to in just a little while," she explains. "But I wanted to stay up here as long as I could. I was hoping you'd wake up. I wanted to talk to you about your blood work."

"Is everything alright?"

She nods. "Everything is okay under the circumstances. You're pregnant and undernourished. Your white blood cell count is low, and that means you're more susceptible to infections. But the good news is, you don't have any of the more serious conditions that usually cause white blood cell counts to be low, so I'm guessing that a healthier diet will boost that right back up. In the meantime, I've given you some vitamins through your IV that should help start the process. You need to finish it by eating and getting more sleep."

I try to nod, not sure how I'm going to manage what she is asking me to do.

"I've made a couple of phone calls for you. Have you ever heard of food stamps or W.I.C.?"

"No."

"Well, food stamps are part of a state-funded program that allows people and families with limited income to obtain food, and W.I.C. is a program available for children and pregnant woman. It provides food vouchers for additional things that you need."

"I never knew." How could I have not known all this time there was help available? Why was I not told about this at the shelter? Or why didn't Yvonne, my social worker, tell me?

"Well, now you do. There are also other programs out there that can help you. I've made an appointment for you for Monday morning with W.I.C. The details are in the pile of papers on the tray next to you, along with some more information about food stamps and

W.I.C. In the meantime, H.C.M.C. is a county hospital, and we have a couple of programs that provide emergency assistance to patients. I've taken the liberty of arranging for some emergency food stamps and emergency cash. This will help get you home as well as get you some much-needed food. I can only lead you to it, though. You have to do the rest."

I nod. "Thank you."

"You need to take care of you. And that beautiful baby you're carrying." She closes the binder and stands up. "Believe me when I tell you, pride can be a royal pain in the ass. Sometimes you have to let it go."

"I'm trying, but it's hard."

"I know, and I understand. But think about this: If you can take what I've arranged for you, maybe you can consider whatever it is that Mikah's trying to offer you. I can almost guarantee there are no strings attached. He's not that kind of man."

I take a deep breath, trying to wash away all the thoughts of strings attached. "I will try," I say, quiet as a mouse. I'm tempted to explain to her my hesitation at accepting his help, but the wounds are deep and it would take more than one friendly conversation to want to share them.

She comes to sit at the foot of the bed, looking at me. "I've arranged for you to be discharged as soon as you're ready to go. On one condition?"

Oh great. "What condition?"

"That you stay at least until tomorrow morning. I'd like you to stay, get some dinner and eat some more in the morning. It's getting late and I know how difficult it would be to get something to eat where you live. So please, stay tonight. Have dinner, then breakfast, and whatever else you want in between now and then. Then go home. The nurse on duty in the morning can arrange a cab to come and pick you up. Or she can call Mr. Blake for you. Either way, get yourself to a store and buy some groceries. I've included a diet to help with the malnutrition and bring you back up to normal."

I try to remind myself that she is helping and not patronizing me or my abilities to take care of myself. "Thank you. For everything."

"It's my job," she states without any hint of irritation.

"Helping a girl like me medically is a part of your job, but not like this. So thank you."

"My pleasure, Vivienne." She turns to leave. "Oh" — spinning back around to look at me — "I almost forgot. As I am now your doctor, I've made an appointment for two weeks from today – Friday at nine forty-five – here at the hospital. I have a private practice space on the 3rd floor. I want to meet with you to see how things are going. After that, we will meet about every four weeks for regular ultrasounds. If you can't make an appointment, you need to call the number on my card. If anything happens and you can't get to me, call that card and I will come to you. Day or night."

Knowing that this is no doubt Mikah's doing actually pisses me off, and my face starts to turn red.

She reads my mind. "This is not his doing," she says. "It's mine, and on my dime. You need someone to help look after you, and there are so many programs out there to help pregnant girls just like you that most people don't know about. So please, if you come across a girl that needs help, send them here and have them ask for me by name. I will help them in any way I can."

I'm blown away by her generosity. Are there really people that good in the world?

And then I think that maybe Mikah, too, was just being generous. Maybe, just maybe, he really was trying to help without further motivation.

Tears prick. "Th-thank you," I stutter.

"You're most welcome. I mean it — anything, you call. Got it?"

"Yes, ma'am."

"Oh, and one last thing. If you don't call and don't show up to an appointment we have scheduled, I will call him. I have utter faith in his ability to track you down."

Oh, no! I'm pretty sure I make a face at her, but I get her point so I nod.

"Alright. Try and get some sleep tonight. You're safe here. And if I don't make it in before you're discharged, I will see you in two weeks."

"I will be here. Or I'll call."

"Good. See you then." And just like that, she's gone.

TWELVE

After Dr. Alston leaves, I start to go through the paperwork she left on the tray for me.

In the pile are several pamphlets about the various programs for women in my situation and a book, *What to Expect When You're Expecting*. There are also a few brochures on support groups for people processing past abuse, which I find strangely comforting. I'll have to try it out.

There is also an envelope that contains two hundred dollars in cash in various denominations. After what she told me earlier, I wouldn't have thought twice about it, except that the food stamp vouchers are in an official-looking envelope, and this isn't. Is this money out of her own pocket?

I'm trying very hard to accept the money without throwing a fit, regardless of its source.
I have enough money in my— "Oh, No!" I exclaim, looking around frantically.

"'Oh no' what?" a female voice says from the door.

My head snaps up and I see Nurse Fang from the blood draw earlier.

"My stuff?"

"In here," she says, pointing to the closet door. "Did you need something?"

"My purse, please?"

"Sure." She opens the door and looks around. I can see my skirt and top hanging on the back of the door. After a moment she bends down and retrieves my purse. The panic I hadn't realized was building in me rushes away in a flash as she hands me my purse.

"Thanks."

"Of course. How are you feeling?"

"Much better." I suddenly realize that my bladder's uncomfortably full. "I need to go to the bathroom, actually."

"No problem. I'll show you how to unlock the IV pole so it will move with you. Then you can move around freely. After you eat, I want you to take a nice long walk around this wing. If you can handle that okay, I'll remove your IV. Sound like a plan?"

I nod, and she shows me the button on the IV pole that unlocks the wheels.

I climb gingerly out of bed, testing my feet to make sure I'm stable before I take a step.

Upon entering the bathroom I'm grateful to see that the mirror isn't staring me in the face. I'm not sure I want to know what kind of messy state I'm in.

After only about a minute and a half, Amanda knocks. "You okay?"

I roll my eyes. "Yep."

When I come back out — still avoiding the mirror because I'm sure I'm hollowed out again — I climb back into bed and tell Amanda, "I'm ready to eat." It's been more than twenty-four hours since I ate last.

"I thought so. I ordered some soup, crackers and fresh fruit for you. You can have more whenever you want, but first I want to make sure it doesn't come right back up. Deal?"

I nod, slipping the white envelope with the money into my purse. Between this, what's left of my paycheck and the money Mikah foisted on me, I'll actually have some left after paying rent. Maybe with the little extra, I can find myself a new book at the used book store near the laundromat. A little something small for me?

"So are you babysitting me all night?" I ask as she's documenting my chart.

She laughs. "No, I'm just here until you eat, take a walk, and get settled in for the night. Is that okay?"

I snort. "Do I get a choice?"

She laughs again. "Nope, not really."

I chuckle. "At least that's settled." I smile. "Can I use this phone?" I ask, pointing to the phone beside the bed.

She nods. "The T.V., too."

"I don't watch T.V., but thank you." She gives me a puzzled look. "A luxury I can't afford," I explain. She nods and I dig into my bag for the little notebook I keep important information in, such as phone numbers.

As soon as I open it, Mikah's card falls out. I feel my chest tighten, and I quickly tuck it back out of sight. So far I've done a good job of holding myself in check and not thinking about him.

I find the number I'm looking for and dial. The phone rings three times, and then I'm met with a lot of noise. "Hello?"

"Hi, Laura, it's Vivienne."

"Oh my goodness. Hi, sweetheart. Are you okay?"

"Yeah, I'm fine. I'm staying in the hospital tonight."

"Oh dear."

"Don't worry, I will fill you in later. Was Bartie pissed?"

"Oh, sweetheart, no. I had Nyssa covering your shift before I told him. She said that she would cover Sunday for you as well."

"No need, but thank you. I'll be back in Sunday. Tell Nyssa I can cover her Tuesday shift, if she needs."

"I'll tell her, but she seemed pretty concerned when I called her today, so don't count on it. Okay?"

"Alright. I'll see you Sunday?" I say before she can start questioning me again.

"Okay, sweetheart."

"Thanks, Laura."

"Anytime. Bye, Viv."

"Bye." I hang up the phone.

I look to Amanda, who is smiling at me. "Is everything okay?"

I nod. "I work for a jerk of a boss that tends to be a bit on the harsh side if you don't work a scheduled shift. He's fired two girls since I've been there because they didn't show up, whether they called or not. So I wanted to make sure I still had a job."

"And?" she prompts.

"For now." I smile. "One of the girls covered my shift and offered to cover Sunday's as well."

"That might not be a bad idea. Get some extra rest."

"I wish I could, but I can't afford to go without the pay. Today will be hard enough to make up in tips. Which is why I offered to cover her Tuesday shift."

"I'm sure it will all work out," she says. She is trying to be nice, but I'm sure she has a hard time relating to being without money. The rock on her right ring finger is a dead giveaway.

There is a knock on the door. My heart stops. Before Amanda turns to open the door, she pauses to look at me reassuringly. She opens the door and I let out a rushed breath when I see it's a hospital staff member carrying a tray.

"Hi, Harold," Amanda says, opening the door wider so he can come in.

"Hi, Amanda. Ms. Callahan." He nods in my direction and I breathe in deeply through my nose. "Here you are, sweetheart. Have a nurse call if you'd like anything else," he says as he sets the tray down on the table and slides it in front of me. He pulls the dome off of the top, and the smell of chicken noodle soup fills my nose. It smells good.

"Thank you, Harold."

"Anytime." He smiles at me and quietly leaves the room.

"I'll let you eat. I'll be back in a little bit."

"Okay," I say. She follows Harold out the door, shutting it behind her.

Now that I'm alone with my thoughts and my dinner, I have a hard time moving past what happened with Mikah earlier today. He was only trying to be there for me, and I was being a bitch – something that he most certainly does not deserve. Slurping a spoonful of soup, I contemplate calling him and decide that all I would do is torture myself because I can't be the all-accepting person he wants me to be.

But there is also the fact that I reacted so quickly to his insistence on helping me that I don't even know what his offer to help entails. This doesn't help me feel any better about my reaction to him. Is he really trying to help, no stings attached? Just being generous? Would he have done this with anyone else, or is it just me? Is his help a long-term thing, or only until the baby is born?

For the first time since I told Riley I was pregnant, I consciously touch the pouch between my hips. Chills of delight dance across my skin. I switch hands, placing my right across my belly, and pick up my spoon to take another sip of broth.

Considering it's hospital food, it's really not half bad. But then again, cardboard would probably taste good to me right now. I meant to eat something earlier, when Mikah was here, but I kept falling asleep. I plow through the soup, bread roll, fruit and crackers in what feels like less than five minutes. I still feel hungry, but I don't want to overdo it.

I sit back and pick up the book that Dr. Alston left for me, *What to Expect When You're Expecting*. The cover has a picture of a pregnant woman standing against a blue background, and the back jacket promises that the book will help me understand my body and my baby throughout the various stages of pregnancy. It looks very...clinical.

I open it and start to read. I was right — it is quite clinical — but there are some really cool things in here. Now I understand why my breasts hurt so much. I also learn that the vomiting and exhaustion should start to ease soon. The prospect of this is exciting on so many levels.

Eventually Amanda returns to my room. Once she's satisfied that I ate everything, she pulls me from my bed to walk around the hallway. I'd rather not walk — I'm feeling sleepy again — but she lures me out with the prospect of removing my IV, and I can't resist.

It turns out that I am in the maternity ward. A couple of other women walk the halls, too. Every so often they stop and groan. They must be in labor. I shudder. I'm still trying to come to grips with the fact that I'm pregnant, never mind the prospect of labor or — I shudder again — delivery.

Once we are back in my room, Amanda removes my IV. Another nurse, Jackie, comes in and introduces herself as the nurse on duty tonight. I'm told to push the button if I need anything. She will be back in a few hours to check on me, but for the most part, she'll leave me to sleep.

I say thank you and goodnight to Amanda, who reassures me she'll be back in the morning even if Dr. Alston can't make it.

Once they're gone, I roll onto my side, gently placing my hand upon the small mound. Lying in this position again reminds me of when Mikah was here, his eyes bright green with wonder. I can no longer ignore the fact that I feel horrible for kicking him out. The more I think about it, the more I am convinced he was just trying to help.

I've never had someone willingly want to take care of me the way that Mikah does, and it makes it hard for me to accept without suspecting there is more to it than meets the eye. Riley always paid for everything and I never worked, but I was expected to do things to him and for him in return. But somehow I can't believe can't believe Mikah operates that way. But if I'm going to consider accepting his help, Mikah needs to back off from pushing me to do things.

What's more, since that ultrasound and reading some of the stuff Dr. Alston left me, I'm finally beginning to see that this is far bigger than I've allowed myself to realize.

I slowly rub my hand across my tummy. "You give me reason," I whisper, and then I fall asleep.

THIRTEEN

Around ten the next morning, I'm in a cab driven by Chuck - a nice man who's old enough to be my grandfather and who says he's a native of Minneapolis – ready to head back to my apartment. As we're leaving the hospital campus, a really nice, sleek black Mercedes drives into the lot next to us. I can't be certain, but I think it's the same one I saw in my neighborhood on Thursday night. And I'm pretty sure it's Mikah driving.

I toss the thought aside. I don't want to hope that maybe he was coming back to see me. Or that it was even really him to start with.

Fifteen minutes later, we are pulling up in front of my apartment. I reach into my bag to pay Chuck, but he stops me. "The hospital takes care of it," he says, smiling warmly. I try to tip him and he refuses that, too. Instead he helps me from the car and stays standing near the rear passenger door until I'm inside my building.

Once inside my apartment, I start to feel tired again and consider resting for a bit. But as much as I want to lie around all day, I have laundry – and now grocery shopping – to do. Better to stick to my routine.

I gather up my laundry bag and empty the contents of my hospital bag into it. I'm wearing a pretty cool pair of light purple scrubs Amanda found for me. The top is huge, but the pants are really comfortable. I leave the pants on and swap the shirt for a white t-shirt that used to say *meh* across the chest but has since faded. After taking a good look at my tummy during the ultrasound yesterday, I've realized that I'm going to start needing clothes here really soon. Most of the bottoms I own are pajamas or sweatpants with an elastic waistband, so those I know can wait to be replaced, but shirts are going to become a problem.

Once my laundry bag is packed, I grab a small envelope off of the fridge. It is addressed to my landlord and already has a stamp on it. I place the four money orders of a hundred dollars each inside — I got them when I cashed my check at the bank, like I do every payday — seal it, and throw it into my bag.

I pull out the wad of cash from my wallet. All in all, there are about two hundred and thirty dollars here, but I don't need to be walking around these streets with this much cash. I pull out forty dollars, place the rest between the pages of my journal and put it back under my bed. I also grab the food stamps and the list of approved foods to look over while doing laundry and head out the door.

As I step outside, I throw my laundry bag sling-style across my back, over my purse. I look like Rambo with bag straps instead of belts full of bullets.

It's a little cloudy out today, and there is a fall chill in the air. I pull my hood up over my head and start walking the two blocks to the Laundromat. This time of day is nice. Sometimes people even say hi. No one says hi today, but I get some nods and smiles —

which I return — from some of the people sitting or standing around outside their homes or shops.

I get to the Laundromat and head over to load my card with enough for wash and dry, plus detergent. Find a washer, load it, start it and sit back to wait.

My stomach grumbles. I pat my tummy. Having eaten so much in the last day or so is going to make it hard to not eat. It's only eleven in the morning and I just ate breakfast three hours ago, but I'm hungry again. I let out a sigh and decide that I can afford something from the coffee shop next door, so I get up and head over there.

"Hi, Ms. Wilson," I say to the elderly woman coming in the door. She is here this time every Saturday. Most mornings we talk - about nothing really, but the company is nice in a boring old Laundromat. Ironically enough, she reminds me of Mrs. Wilson from those Dennis The Menace cartoons.

"Hello, Vivienne. How are you today?" she asks.

"Better, thanks. I was going to go next door for a bagel. Would you like something?"

"Oh, no, dear. I have toast. Go have fun. Are you using your usual machine?" I nod. "I'll keep an eye on it."

I smile because I can't even begin to imagine the things she would do if someone was trying to steal my clothes. "Thanks, Ms. Wilson."

The coffee shop is decorated like a junkyard. There are tons of eclectic metal objects, from sculptures to wheels and old hubcaps. The furniture and tables are all mismatched, too, but in some strange way, it all works. There are a couple of computers lined up along the wall with a sign overhead that says, *Up to 1 hour free.*

The girl behind the counter is wearing a spiked dog collar, short jean shorts with pink-and-black striped leggings underneath, and a black fishnet shirt over a thin white t-shirt. The fishnet on her arms is ripped, and her black bra is visible beneath the t-shirt. It's a look that I thought had died about ten years ago, but she manages to pull it off spectacularly. It compliments the massive, six-inch-long Mohawk she's sporting.

"Hi, there, what can I get for you?" she asks in an overly friendly tone. The black lipstick she's wearing cracks when she smiles.

"Hi. Just a bagel, plain."

"Sure thing. Anything else?"

"A large glass of ice water."

She rings it up and grabs my order.

"Can anyone use those computers?" I ask as she hands me my change. I don't want to be told to get up if I sit down.

"Absolutely. You have one hour, but unless we get really busy, take as long as you like."

"Thanks."

I grab my water and bagel and head toward the computer on the end. I'm not super familiar with computers, but I know how to search the internet, and that's all I need to know today.

I sit down and jiggle the mouse, and the screen flickers to life. Clicking on the browser icon opens up to Google. I type in two words: Mikah Blake.

Thousands of results pop up in a matter of seconds. There's everything from his company to random news articles. I munch absently on the bagel as I start with the homepage for MSB Enterprises. Sure enough, there is a picture of Mikah. It's a formal picture, and he's not smiling. He's barely recognizable this way. I read his bio.

Born Mikah Shannon Blake, 1987, Dublin, Ireland. He's a little younger than I thought. Well at least I was right about the subtle Irish accent. *Mr. Blake moved to the Boston area in 1990*— My jaw drops. He was in Boston the year I was born. *—with his father and mother, who later had three additional children, two boys and one girl.*

I continue scanning the rest of the bio. I was right about the Ivy League education: *Mr. Blake graduated from the MIT Sloan School of Management in 2009 with a Master of Finance (MFin).* Holy crap, he was only twenty-one when he received his Master's degree. My age. Wow!

The last sentence captures my attention. *Mr. Blake is the youngest entrepreneur to make it into Forbes 500.* This explains a lot. Mikah is a very driven individual; I have no doubt that he will stop at nothing when it comes to something he wants. I smile slightly at the events that led up to yesterday's hospital visit.

I hit the back button and move on to some more articles. I finally find one that captures my attention, dated April 16, 2011. *CEO of MSB Enterprises, Mikah Blake, buries father, two brothers in Boston.*

"What in the world?" I click the link.

Mikah Blake attended funeral services at St. Ambrose in Boston this afternoon for his father, Shannon, age 48, brother Shane, age 20, and brother Ronin, age 17. All three were killed when their vehicle was hit by a semi-truck going the wrong way down Highway 95 Tuesday last week....

I can't read anymore; my eyes are swollen and tears are falling down my cheeks. I click the button to go back to the search results. The next two or three pages are filled with more articles about his father and two brothers. I finally come across one that says something about his sister, Victoria.

Victoria Blake, younger sister to CEO Mikah Blake, was admitted to Boston Medical Center early yesterday morning after an apparent suicide attempt.

I don't need to read any further. I click the back button again, but not before I catch the date on the article: April 11, 2011. Just before the funeral for his father and brothers.

Bottom line in my research today: Holy crap. I never, ever expected to find that. My heart aches.

I close the browser window, grab my water, pop what's left of my bagel into my mouth and place the plate on top of the garbage can.

"Thanks for coming," the girl behind the counter says.

"Thank you, have a good day."

"You, too."

After finishing up with my laundry, I decide to head back to my apartment to drop off my clean laundry so I don't have to haul it around the grocery store, which is in the opposite direction from my apartment as the Laundromat.

As I stomp up the stairs, I notice a piece of paper stuck in my doorjamb. I grab the note and go into my apartment, locking the door behind me. The handwriting is sloppy. So different from Mikah's tidy penmanship.

Vivienne,
I stopped by just to make sure you made it home okay. Looking forward to seeing you in two weeks.
Dr. Anne Alston

Okay, this is getting a little bit creepy.

Something on the floor catches my eye: another envelope. No address, and this one is thicker. Weird.

I pop the seal. Inside are the ultrasound pictures that Dr. Alston took yesterday. The first one has a Post-it note attached to it: *These were left in the emergency care ward by accident when we moved you.*

Odd that I hadn't even thought about them. Pulling them out, I look at them again. It is still so hard to believe that this little guy — or girl — is growing inside me. Flipping through the pictures, I notice that there are only seven of them.

"What the hell?"

I check the envelope again, but there is nothing else inside. One picture is missing.

"Who would want someone's ultrasound picture?"

But even as I ask myself that question, the image of one beautiful face comes to mind. Mikah Blake.

FOURTEEN

On Monday morning I meet with a really nice lady named Jessica at the W.I.C. office. She tells me that it usually takes weeks to get into their office, but because Dr. Alston had called, saying that it was an emergency, they were able to see me right away.

She explains the program to me and I sit through an orientation class about the W.I.C. process. Every four weeks I can come back to pick up new vouchers for various foods. It seems like way too much food for one person. I know it's not true, but I feel like I'm taking the food away from someone else who really needs it.

On Tuesday I swing by the nursing home to see my mom. She's the same as ever: She just sits there staring out the window, seeing nothing. I ask myself why I go out of my way to visit her, and the only answer I can give myself is that she's my mom.

We didn't have the best relationship — if you can even call it that — while I was growing up. She never saw fit to take care of me, and more often than not, I found myself taking care of her. I got up every day in time for school, went to school, came home, studied, made dinner, cleaned the house, studied some more,

103

Zoey Derrick

and went to bed, only to repeat the process the next day.

Weekends often found me alone in whatever apartment we were staying in while Mom was off with God only knows who, doing God only knows what. Usually she'd stumble home late Sunday night or sometime during the day on Monday and pass out for a couple of days. Then she'd be right back at it again.

I learned to steer clear of her when she ran out of money. She had a venomous temper and would storm around the house yelling and throwing things. Sometimes she would hit me just because I asked a question. At the time, I didn't understand what I'd done to deserve it. I understand better now that she was unable to control her own anger, and her means of coping were always drugs or alcohol.

On my way home from visiting my mother, I stop at the grocery store again, picking up some repeat things, and some new. I discovered very quickly after cooking up some chicken Saturday night that chicken does not sit well with me — I threw it up — so chicken's out. I look at the store's selection of red meat, and my stomach turns. Hm. Evidently all meat is out for now. I'll talk to Dr. Alston next week about some alternative options.

For the moment, macaroni and cheese, peanut butter and jelly sandwiches, and scrambled eggs seem to be my foods of choice, and I'm okay with that.

Wednesday and Thursday pass quickly without incident; all I do is work, eat and sleep.

But Friday night at the diner is strange. It's extremely busy — which is nice because it passes the time quickly — but only a few of our regulars are

104

here. The rest are classier, well-dressed and well-behaved people who look like they'd be more comfortable in a swank hotel bar than in Bertie's shitty little diner. Laura chalks it up to something happening downtown. It still seems odd to me, but I can't complain. I leave work at around twelve thirty with over three hundred dollars in tips — something that is completely out of the ordinary. Happy with the fact that I've managed to make more than half of my rent in one night, I head home.

Once again, Al is behind the wheel. We have our typical conversation and I notice that I don't feel anywhere near as tired as I was just a week ago.

"You're looking well," Al says when we're almost to my stop.

"Um, thanks," I say, confused.

"No, I mean it. Have you gained some weight?"

I think back to putting on my uniform before work and realize he must be right. "I'm trying," I say.

"Keep it up."

He drops me at my stop and lingers until I round the corner. As soon as the bus moves on, headlights appear behind me, casting my shadow across the pavement and illuminating my path. The vehicle isn't moving. I quicken my pace, my heart pounding.

I push on the door to my building, and as I slip inside, the car drives by. A black Mercedes.

Inside my apartment, I drop my mail on the counter, strip off my uniform and head toward the shower. I stop to check myself in the mirror – something I haven't really done since before the trip to the hospital – and I suddenly see what Al was talking about.

Zoey Derrick

My eyes are a lighter, brighter blue. My cheeks are still a little hollow, but they seem to be filling out a bit. And I don't look quite so pale. Though my collarbones are still visible beneath my skin, they're a little less pronounced. The biggest shocker are my breasts, which seem a lot fuller. Not bigger, just fuller. And my nipples are a few shades darker than they used to be.

I look down my body to the bump between my hips. It too is more rounded and softer looking, though my hipbones are still well defined. I gently caress the bump with one hand as I remove the hair tie from my bun with the other, letting my hair cascade down my back.

I turn on the shower, all the way to the hottest setting, and pray. It's warmer than usual, so I jump in, but I barely get my hair washed before the water starts to run cold. I move quickly and hop out. For once in my life I'd love to take a shower that is hot and stays hot for as long as I want.

As I towel off, I notice that I'm moving more gingerly than I used too. I'm a little more cautious in my movements. After I get into my pajamas, I make myself a pb&j with grape jelly and grab the book Dr. Alston gave me. Flipping to the section on week twelve, I start to read by the tiny lamp near my bed.

While reading, I realize that Dr. Alston seems to be spot-on with her assessment of how far along I am. Over the last couple of days my breasts have switched from being painful to feeling heavy, my tiredness seems to be waning slightly, and I'm beginning to feel my energy level rising. I'm also hardly ever hungry. But then again, these days, if I feel hungry, I eat —

something I've never done in my life. I'm beginning to wonder how I survived this long.

FIFTEEN

I'm running through our apartment. He's right on my heel, chasing me.

"Abigail, get her!" he says.

"You want her, you get her," my mother shouts from another room.

Suddenly I'm flying backwards. The pain in my scalp surges through my body and I go limp. I'm being dragged backwards by my hair into a room along the hallway. Only it's not a room, it's a closet. He pulls my hair harder and suddenly I'm spinning around. A hard, heavy hand comes across my face.

My head snaps back, knocking into the jamb of the closet door. I see stars. He grips my arm so hard it burns. I start to cry. He grabs my other arm just as hard. I can feel the veins popping and burning.

"Get your sorry ass in that closet and stay there."

I can't move because of the grip he has on my arms. Suddenly one of the hands is gone and I can feel him shift his weight. I try to flinch away but his grip tightens further as his hand comes down hard across the same cheek, snapping my head back into the jamb again.

He shoves me roughly into the closet and I stumble, falling to the floor. The door slams shut. Something heavy scrapes along the wall and bumps to rest against the door.

"Now you can't get out."

Panic sets in. I try in vain to open the door. My arms are weak, throbbing from his grip, useless.

"Alright, bitch, you have work to do." His voice comes from down the hall. Then I hear the smack. "Damn it, bitch, get to work."

I start beating on the door, panicked in the dark. I'm hot, I'm alone, and I'm hurt...

My eyes fly open. My heart races, my breathing coming fast and hard. I try to shake the memory, but the adrenaline is still pumping through my veins. It hadn't been the first time I'd been locked in the closet by one of my mother's drug dealers or pimps while they beat and fucked her, but on that occasion I'd spent at least three days in that closet before the paramedics finally showed up.

It never made sense to me that she kept going back to those types of men. Did she enjoy the beatings? Get off on them? The thought makes me queasy. Maybe she just didn't know how to do things any different. Maybe she didn't know they *could* be different.

Thank goodness I got away from Riley. Even if I was a little late in realizing the importance of pulling away, I did it. Despite the consequences.

Still trembling, I climb out of bed and head into the bathroom.

When I come out I feel calmer. The clock next to my bed reads nearly eleven in the morning. I yawn and stretch, ignoring the little flutter of panic at exposing my belly, and try to decide what to do first.

It's Saturday, laundry day. I consider skipping it — I still feel unsafe after that dream and laundry means going out in public — but one look around my apartment at the dirty clothes strewn about tells me I don't have much of a choice. I bend down and start stuffing clothes into my laundry bag.

The intercom buzzes. My heart jolts. "Who on earth?"

I push the intercom button. "Who is it?" My voice comes out a little harsher than I intend. I take a deep breath and let it out slowly while a male voice crackles through the intercom.

"My name is Alex. I have a delivery for Vivienne?"

"What is it you're delivering?"

"Groceries," he says back.

What the hell? Do I go downstairs and meet him or stay here and let him up? Not wanting him near my apartment, I tell him, "I'll be right down."

"I was told to bring them up to apartment nine."

Damn it.

Okay, I can let him up and stay behind the door and the chain. It's not much, but at least if he tries to break down my door, other people might hear.

I buzz him into the building.

After a moment, I can hear someone climbing the stairs. He sounds heavy. My heart starts pounding. He gets closer. Then I hear him take the two steps across the landing to my door.

Knock, knock. "Vivienne, it's Alex."

About now I really wish I had a peephole. I unlock the deadbolts and the knob but leave the chain. I open the door a crack. On the other side is a boy, really, not much taller or bigger than I am, wearing a Cub Foods shirt and carrying a paper bag with the Cub logo on it.

The panic settles a little, but I'm still cautious. "Who sent the groceries?" I ask him.

"A gentleman by the name of Mikah Blake."

I curse under my breath. "Send them back. I don't need them."

"He said you'd say that."

"Well, take them back, then tell him if he insists on my having them, he can deliver them himself."

He chuckles. "He said you'd say something like that too, so he told me to give you this." He slips me a piece of folded paper.

I take it from him, keeping my leg pressed against the door, and open it up. Sure enough, it's Mikah's handwriting.

Dearest Vivienne,

If you're reading this I know you're protesting my groceries. I send them with Alex here because I am trying hard to not force myself on you. But I want you to have some of these goodies that I know you won't buy yourself. Please accept this gift as an apology for the way things happened at the hospital.

I hope you're well.

-M

The bottom of the letter has his phone number on it, the same one that's on the back of his card.

"Alright, Alex, you can put the bag down."

"I'm supposed to bring it in and put it away."

"Nope. I'll spare you your job by accepting the bag. You can do me the favor of putting it on the floor and going down to the landing."

He nods skeptically and places the bag on the floor. He slowly backs away to the stairs. When he's on the landing, I close the door and unlatch the chain. Then I open it again just wide enough to drag the bag inside. Alex is watching me from the landing.

"Thank you, Alex."

"You're welcome."

I watch for a moment as he heads down the stairs, then I shut my door and look into the bag.

On top is a bag of goldfish crackers. I shakily remove the crackers and my heart flutters a bit. Below them, a bag of Oreo cookies. My tummy rumbles. Moving the cookies aside reveals a square package, wrapped in silver paper, and the top of what looks like a champagne bottle. As I pull out the bottle, I see it is actually sparkling cider. My heart warms to Mikah just a little more. Then I grab the package. I look in the bag to make sure there is nothing else in it, but there is: a container of beautiful, bright red strawberries. As I lift the container, something on the bottom of the bag catches my eye.

It's a card in a light blue envelope. It says, *Open Me 2nd*.

"Huh?" I huff.

I look back at the package and decide to save it and the card for later, after laundry, when I'm ready to...

I look at the package again. What on earth did he do? My curiosity gets the better of me.

I pick up the package and shake it, hoping that its rattle will tell me what it is. Silence.

I turn it over and slide my finger underneath the seam. Rip off the paper. I'm looking at a plain black box. I raise an eyebrow at it, like it's going to tell me its secrets if I look at it in just the right way. It just sits there.

Well, only one way to find out, I guess.

SIXTEEN

Underneath the lid is purple tissue paper, and underneath the paper is a silver frame holding a picture. My picture. The missing ultrasound picture. The one where the baby looks like it's waving at me.

Tears fill my eyes, making it hard to read the inscription.

Baby Callahan's First Picture
Friday, October 12, 2012

I raise the picture from its resting place in the box. Beneath the frame is another note.

I'm sorry I took this image from you. I know it was your favorite. I wanted to give you something special. -M

My heart clenches as I realize that Mikah is quickly becoming more than I realized. Although I'm a little upset that he took the picture without asking, I'm also flattered.

"You're forgiven," I say aloud, and I wipe the tears from my cheeks. I grab the card and rip it open.

On the cover is a single yellow rose on a white background. Next to the rose in an elegant font it says, *Thinking of you.*

"Why, Mikah? Why me?"

The inside of the card contains a longish note in Mikah's penmanship.

Vivienne,

For reasons I can't explain, I need to be close to you. At least to know you're okay.

I saw something in you that first night that made me think of happier times, times that have long been forgotten.

Seeing your beautiful baby last week made me think about all the things that truly matter in life, and for that I'm grateful.

You give me reason, you give me hope and you give me life. No amount of time will allow me to repay that debt to you, but I'd like the chance to try.
-M

P.S. I know it's not champagne, but I hope you enjoy your cider and strawberries.

P.P.S. Thank you for accepting my gift and for reading my card.

I grab the picture and curl up on my bed, hugging it and sobbing. The picture in the frame is larger than the original. Which makes me wonder where the original is.

As much as I want to accept Mikah into my life, I can't seem to allow it to happen and I don't understand why. I had a panic attack after I kicked him out of my hospital room for crying out loud, but I'm scared.

Despite the fact that he keeps pushing me to accept his help, I'm extremely comfortable around Mikah. Up until now, I've only known Riley and the men my mother kept around, so my instinct is to be afraid. But Mikah brings me such comfort. It's the oddest thing. Somewhere deep down I'm starting to think that not all men can be lumped into the Riley category. Riley stole my innocence and tore up my heart. But Mikah - Mikah seems bound and determined to repair the damage Riley did.

When I smacked him across the cheek, he did nothing more than embrace me, comfort me. He knew instantly what he had done to scare me, and he apologized. Apologized! When I'm the one that hit him!

And in that hospital room, he was nothing but kind and generous. He supported me like no man ever has. He stayed with me and comforted me. He was awed by my baby. And I threw him out. God, I'm such an idiot.

I'm drawn to him, but I can't seem to let myself get close to him. I'm terrified because he gives me so much hope, and I know that if I let my feet float off the ground, I will come crashing back down so hard that I won't recover this time. I'm damaged, I'm broken, and I have permanent scars that not even someone like Mikah can erase.

Maybe Mikah is pure-hearted and has fabulous intentions. He's just picked the one girl on the planet that can't be saved.

SEVENTEEN

On Tuesday I go spend some time with my mom. She's a little more animated, and it's kind of nice to see. On my way out I ask the nurse if she's usually like that - animated.

"No, she pretty much just sits quiet and doesn't say much."

It makes me feel a little bit better knowing that her level of sedation or animation has nothing to do with me.

I've often wondered if she holds me responsible for how her life turned out. I know that it's stupid to think that way, but sometimes, remembering how she let her men treat me, I wonder if she resented me.

On Wednesday I get to work with about twenty-five minutes to spare. When I step off of the bus, I do a double take, my heart seizing in panic. Across the street, moving away from me, is a skinny man with dirty blond hair who looks a hell of a lot like Riley. I know he's in jail so it's stupid to think it could be him, but I scurry quickly into the diner anyway.

Once inside, I see Bartie sitting near the register, his usual spot.

"Hi, Bart," I say. He gets really annoyed if you call him Bartie to his face. He's about five feet eleven inches and two hundred fifty to three hundred pounds. Garrison's Diner has been owned by his family since the early 1900s and is practically a historic landmark in Minneapolis. It's unfortunate that the neighborhood around the diner has gone to pits, but he still stays in business.

I haven't seen Bartie since before the hospital visit, so I'm a bit disappointed that he's here tonight. It also makes me anxious. He's not normally here when I come in, so I instantly start to think he's going to fire me.

"Vivienne?"

"Yes, sir?"

"How are you feeling?"

I suppress the shock I feel at his question. "Great, thanks. How are you?" I begin walking toward him, but stop about five feet away. Though he's never really done anything to make me mistrust him, there's this invisible danger zone around him that sets off my warning bells. Maybe it's my inexplicable desire to please him. Or maybe it's the fact that he's quite the grease monkey when it comes to his clothes and hygiene.

"I'm good. You're looking well. You've gained some weight?"

"I think so. I don't own a scale, so I can't say for sure."

He laughs his awful, too-many-cigarettes laugh. "Well, I can see it. Can you come here, please?"

I'm momentarily dumbstruck, and then I manage to make myself move another couple feet toward him.

"What's up, Bart?" I ask, trying to sound nonchalant.

He lowers his voice. "I just wanted to let you know that Laura and I talked yesterday. You know, about last week." Oh no. "I just wanted you to know that you've done a great job working here. As long as you don't make a habit out of it and we can cover your shift, I will never fire you because of being sick."

Release breath. "I don't plan to make it a habit. More than anything, I really like and need this job."

"I know, and I like having you here." He smiles. His front tooth is severely crooked and he is missing two teeth on the bottom.

"I will remember that. Thank you, Bart."

"Good deal. Now, there is a woman in booth fourteen who asked for you by name. Go change your shoes and help her out, okay?"

I nod and head off, wondering who could've asked for me. The only women I know that would be in this restaurant claiming to know me are Amanda and Dr. Alston. I turn to look, but I can't see over the top of the high-backed booth.

I change my shoes quickly, shed my hoodie and tie up my apron. The top of the apron quickly slips below my belly. Initially I think it makes me look huge, but when I look at myself in the mirror, it's not all that noticeable. Which is good, because despite Bartie's claim, I have no doubt that he would be quick to harass me about it. I've heard stories - even from his own son - about some of the things he's done because someone made him mad. I know I can't hide my pregnancy from him forever.

I can't stop myself from looking at table twelve - Mikah's table - on my way over to the booth next to it. My heart aches at the sight of that empty table, and I suddenly have this need to see him. To thank him and—

My heart stops and my steps falter. Sitting in the booth I'm heading toward is a black-haired girl I had hoped never to see again - Rebecca!

Fear grips my throat as I consider the possibility that it really was Riley outside after all.

Rebecca is Riley's wannabe girlfriend. She thinks he's the greatest thing since sliced bread, and I have no doubt Riley cheated on me with her. He was always saying I was lousy in bed and even made a point a few times of telling me that he'd slept with other women. Rebecca, I'm certain, was one of them.

"What the hell are you doing here?" I snap as I approach the table.

"Well, hello to you, too, Vivienne."

"Answer my question," I say through gritted teeth.

"Is that any way to treat a customer?"

"No, but you are no customer."

She turns her head to look at me. I gasp. Her right eye is purple and swollen shut.

"No, I'm not. I came to warn you."

"Warn me. How the hell did you know I was here in the first place?"

"Word gets around."

"That's funny, because there isn't anybody that knows I'm here."

"Guess again."

This is just damn fantastic. I feel my anxiety level rise dramatically, and I'm suddenly desperate to get her out of here.

"What's your warning?"

It's taking all the self-control I have to keep from giving her another black eye. Another part of me is debating on whether to run out the back door.

"Do I have to explain it to you? Isn't it obvious?" She looks at me full-on, showing off her bruises.

"You have a black eye. What does that have to do with me?"

"Riley gave it to me. To show me what he planned to do to me if I didn't find you and report back to him. When I told him I found nothing, he did it again. And again." She wants sympathy from me. Is she serious?

"Well, he put me in the hospital."

Her jaw drops. "I didn't know that."

"I'm sure you didn't. What I want to know is how and when he got out of jail."

"You know his father. Drug charges are enough to motivate him to act. He bailed him out."

Fucking fabulous. Drug charges. Is she kidding me? "I need to get back to work."

She stands up and I catch the first glimpse of her body. "Dear God, please tell me that's not Riley's," I say pointing to her easily six-month-pregnant belly. She flushes and looks down coquettishly at the floor. "Whatever you do, don't tell him that. I'm surprised you've managed to get away with it this long without him figuring it out," I whisper, remembering his reaction. I gently place my hand on my little mound. "That's how I ended up in the hospital."

In an instant, she starts crying. "I'm sorry, I didn't know."

"Get out of here, Becca, and get away from him," I say in a tight voice.

"I can't."

I feel a surge of pity as understanding washes through me. Becca's situation is not much different than mine was. Walking away isn't easy.

Neither of us says anything, and after a moment she leaves. Once she's gone I go over to Bartie. "Can I have a minute?"

"Sure, but stay close."

"Thanks." I turn to head off toward the bathroom.

Jesus. Becca looks like hell. I'm not sure if I should feel sorry for her or what. I am surprised that he lets her around him; she's easily three months further along than I am. Which confirms that he was cheating on me. Becca, no doubt, is one of dozens of women out there with a Riley stamp on them, knocked up or otherwise. The thought brings chills, and I make a mental note to try and discuss some things with Dr. Alston on Friday.

I suddenly feel very dirty. I wash my face and arms, trying to shake the feeling.

It's a slow night, and around eleven, the cook, Bart Jr., or BJ, who also happens to be Bartie's nephew, tells me to take off early. I look at Nyssa for reassurance and she nods.

I step outside just in time to catch the next bus. As I'm climbing on board, I catch a glimpse of a man with slick, black hair and nice threads walking into the diner. He looks a lot like Mikah. But the bus takes off before I can ask the driver to let me out. I consider getting off at the next stop and walking back, but the next stop is a ways down the road; by the time I get back to the diner, he'll have left.

About forty minutes later we get to my stop. This driver isn't Al, so he doesn't linger. Right before I turn the corner, headlights come on across Lake Street, shining on me from behind. By the time I get to the door the headlights have moved on, just like the other times. And just like the other times, I look over my shoulder to see a sleek black Mercedes.

I'm exhausted tonight, so I forgo my shower and climb into bed, bringing the bag of goldfish crackers with me.

I smile at the thought that Mikah just might be trying to disobey my order to leave me alone, and then find myself comforted by the idea that it's him in the Mercedes making sure I get home okay. Though I'm wondering how he beat me to my apartment tonight, considering I got home an hour early and he had just been going into the diner when I left. Assuming that was him.

I realize after a few minutes that I've been absentmindedly rubbing my belly and the little bump there. "Maybe one day soon we'll get our timing right," I whisper.

Holy crap, I'm talking to my stomach again. I smile and roll over, reaching for the light. Right before it goes out, I catch a glimpse of my baby waving at me.

EIGHTEEN

Knock, knock, knock.
I groan. I don't want to wake up.
Knock, knock, knock.
"Who is it?" I say groggily.
"Vivienne, it's Mr. Crowley from downstairs."
"Yes?"
"I have a Detective Stevens with me to see you."
My eyes snap open.

In my mind's eye: an image of Detective Stevens sitting in a chair toward the foot of my hospital bed while he asked me questions about Riley. I'd expected him to make me feel like an idiot, to tell me that if I'd been smarter and left sooner, I would never have ended up where I was. But he didn't. Instead he helped me see that I was really a victim, not some dumb girl that didn't know any better.

He is the first cop I've ever come to respect. He's the one who caught and arrested Riley, and I trust him completely.

Come to think of it, he's the first *man* I've ever respected or completely trusted.

But what on earth is he doing here?

"Just a minute," I bark as I scramble out of bed. I really have to pee, but I doubt the detective is going to wait much longer.

I unlock the knob and two deadbolts, leaving the chain in place, and crack open the door. Sure enough, it's the same detective from the hospital.

"Thanks, Mr. Crowley," Detective Stevens says.

"No problem. You okay, Vivienne?" I nod. "Okay, I'll be downstairs if you need me," he says, then heads downstairs.

"What can I do for you, Detective?"

"Can I come inside?"

I hesitate. I don't let anyone in here, ever.

He is quick to sense my hesitation and adds, "I need to talk to you about Riley Bennett and I'd prefer to talk to you in private, if that's okay?"

I feel an emotional waterfall wash over me: hope that maybe he's been picked up again, downright freaked out that I have to once again talk to a cop about Riley, and, finally, fear that something bad is happening.

I shut the door slightly and unhook the chain, then open it back up. A sweet smile spreads across his lips - tender, appreciative. His eyes are looking downward, and panic rises from my toes.

I look down. Sure enough, my tank top is up, exposing a good portion of my bump. "Sorry," I say as I pull my tank top down, and he smiles wider.

"It's a pleasant sight to see, Vivienne. I was worried for you and that little one after we met the last time."

I nod shyly and back up so he can come in. "Listen, I just woke up, can I use the restroom real quick?"

"Of course."

I shut the front door and leave it unlocked. I don't feel threatened by Detective Stevens, and if anyone is going to come in here they can deal with him.

I shuffle off to the bathroom. When I come back out, he is leaning casually against the wall opposite the apartment door, between my bed and the kitchen window.

"What can I do for you, Detective?" I ask again.

"Are you aware that Riley was released last Friday on bail?" he asks, taking a small notebook out of his coat pocket and flipping it open.

I take a deep breath. I expected this when he brought up Riley's name. Hopefully that's all he's here to tell me.

"Sort of. A somewhat mutual friend of Riley's and mine showed up at the diner I work at last night to warn me that Riley was looking for me."

He makes a note. "Which diner?"

"Garrison's."

"Was this friend Rebecca Black?"

I look at him, puzzled. "I think so?"

"About five foot seven, black hair?"

I nod. "That's her."

"What time was she at the diner last night?"

"She was there when I got there at about three forty. She left at about four-oh-five, four ten-ish. Not sure."

"What else did you talk about? Besides Riley's release?" He's fishing for something, but I can't see what, and I'm confused as to why Becca is being brought up in this conversation.

"She had a nasty black eye and told me that Riley had beaten her up, both as an example and because she hadn't given him what he was after."

"What was he after?"

"My whereabouts."

"Why would he want to know that?" There's nothing in his tone besides curiosity.

I shrug, but my stomach is doing flips. "I'm assuming it's to see if he did what he set out to do."

"Which is?"

"I'm sure if you think about why he attacked me that night, you can answer your own question, Detective?"

He nods. "You're right, I could. But what do *you* think?"

"Well, he was after one of two things that night - to kill me, or to kill the baby."

I take a deep breath and shudder as the thought occurs through me that if he'd succeeded in killing the baby, he might have succeeded in coaxing me back to him. I might not have ever gotten away from him. I push the thought away.

"Couple that with the fact that he was thrown in jail, his father is probably pissed that he had to bail him out. Probably threatened to cut him off. Who knows what's driving Riley this time. It doesn't take much to set him off. Most men would have walked away from a pregnant girl, not beat the shit out of them."

He nods and writes something down.

"Believe me, if I'd known that was the reaction I was going to get, I would have never told him. I expected him to be angry, or demand an abortion, but never did I imagine that he would beat me to the extent that he did. I warned Rebecca of that last night."

The detective's eyes widen and his nostrils flare.

"What aren't you telling me, Detective?"

"I'm not at liberty—"

"Don't give me that bullshit. Riley got to Becca too, didn't he?"

He hesitates, then nods.

"So why aren't you questioning her?" I stop. Cold shivers rake through my body. "She told him..." Can't breathe. "He killed her?"

I put my hands on my knees. I hear a strange noise, and it takes me a moment to realize that it's me, gasping for air.

"Relax, Vivienne. Calm..." He has moved to stand next to me. His hand is gently stroking my back.

I'm hyperventilating again, too panicked. I fall to my knees. The jolt of pain causes me to gasp, and suddenly I can breathe again. I begin to calm.

"That's it," he says as I take long, deep breaths and pull myself up onto the bed. "Sorry," he says. "I'm sorry. I didn't mean to frighten you."

I nod, focusing on my breathing. "It's okay," I say between deep breaths. "I'm okay."

Before he leaves, Detective Stevens assures me that there will be officers watching me go to and from work while they try to track Riley down. He says at this point they can't do much except talk to him; when they found Becca, she had high levels of methamphetamines in her system. I never knew Rebecca very well, but Riley certainly wasn't the drug-doing type. Selling, yes; doing, no. Even if she did do drugs, would she do meth while pregnant? She didn't seem high last night when I saw her, but there were more than eight hours between her diner visit and her death.

When I head out for work, I look around and spy a cop car parked down the street, facing my direction. And when I get to work, there's another one coming down the street just behind the bus. I don't linger on the street, just hop into the diner.

NINETEEN

"Hi, guys," I say to Laura and Nyssa as I head back to the lockers. Their answering hellos follow me through the door.

When I come out of the back room, Laura is quick to start asking questions. "There was a Detective Stevens looking for you here today. About gave the old grouch hound a heart attack. Care to tell us what that was all about?"

"Not particularly."

"Are you in trouble with the law?" she is quick to ask.

I laugh nervously. "Seriously, Laura. You think I'm in trouble with the cops?" I am in trouble, of course, just not with the cops. But I'm not sure my co-workers need to know that.

She purses her lips. "No, of course not. But usually when someone doesn't want to talk about why a cop was looking for them, it means they're the one in trouble."

Nyssa laughs a little. "I can't imagine Vivienne hurting a fly, let alone committing some random crime." Nyssa is about the same age as I am, maybe a couple of years older. I know that she works here

130

because she enjoys the job. She is sweet - overly so sometimes, but we get along well. I don't get the motherly vibe from her, but she definitely seems protective.

"Thank you, Nyssa."

"It has to do with the girl that was in here yesterday, doesn't it?" Nyssa says.

My eyes widen as she puts two and two together. "What makes you say that?"

"It was in the *Trib* today. There was a picture of a girl that looked a lot like her. It said something about her being found dead this morning near a dumpster by that old motel down the street."

Oh God. I know my face starts to turn green because the idea makes me want to vomit. "She and I have an old mutual friend. A friend known for beating women," I say quietly.

Laura's shock is almost palpable. "Is this mutual friend why you were in the hospital last week?"

I shake my head, not sure how much I want to tell them. I work with these ladies. Their need to know about my personal life is severely limited, and it already bothers me that Dr. Alston and Mikah know so much. My past is my past and not something that everyone needs to know.

"You know, Vivienne, you can trust us," Nyssa says with sincerity.

I toy with the idea of telling Laura and Nyssa about my pregnancy. I don't want to be sympathized upon, and these two are exactly the two that would do it. Laura in particular will take it upon herself to mother me or find some way to try to take care of me, which would be no different than what Mikah is trying to do. If I knew that their concern would only extend to asking how I was doing, I might feel a little different about telling them more about me. But I realize quickly that explanations might be necessary in order for them to better understand, and the head off future questions.

"Laura, do you remember when I first started working here, and you noticed the bruise on my shoulder while I was changing in back?" She nods. "That was the remnants of an argument between me and the man I mentioned earlier."

They both gasp. This is exactly the kind of reaction I didn't want.

But now that I've started, I find that the words just keep pouring out of my mouth. I tell them about Amber's Place and the social worker who hooked me up with this job. I tell them about Detective Stevens and Rebecca. When I'm finished, I add, "Rebecca's death tells me she made the same mistake I did."

"Which was what, exactly?" Nyssa asks.

"Rather than getting away from him, like I told her to, she went back. I made that mistake too many times, and it put me in the hospital. Nearly killed me."

Both Nyssa and Laura gasp again.

"Stop, both of you. I don't need sympathy or pity. At least that got me out of his grasp and finally on my way to moving on. It's helped me become a stronger person than I was before." I wish I could say the same for Rebecca.

"If you need anything - anything at all - you tell me. Okay?" There is the mother in Laura again.

"Thanks, Laura, but I'm alright."

"So then why were you in the hospital last week?" Nyssa asks.

I sigh. I don't want to go into all the details regarding Mikah and his money, so I just say, "Because the day after I fainted here, I turned around and vomited in a public place. Someone there was worried enough about me to take me to the hospital."

Nyssa was the first to say anything. "I'm glad you went. You were wasting away in front of us. No matter what we did, you wouldn't let us help you."

I blush, sheepish. "You're right. I realize now that I was doing a pretty poor job of taking care of myself, but I've been able to get some more permanent help that's making a difference, and that's what I need right now. But I can't in all honesty say I'd let you help if I needed it. I don't like to be taken care of."

She nods, but I can tell it upsets her. "Nyssa, please know, I've done this my whole life. I've struggled and survived. It's all I know. It's very hard for me to take a handout."

She nods again. "I understand, and I will try hard to remember that." She gives me a hug.

I smile, then frown. "I have a follow-up appointment with Dr. Alston tomorrow morning. She's the one who set me up with food stamps. I've been eating like a pig." I laugh.

"That explains why you've gained so much weight," Laura says.

"Ha! Not that much weight," I retort. Again the idea of telling them about the pregnancy comes to mind, but right now, I'm just not ready to do so. When it's necessary, I will tell them.

"Enough to fill in all of your beautiful features," she says as she squeezes my arm.

"Thanks. Now can we get back to work?" I ask.

Zoey Derrick

And then I realize that Nyssa's shift has been over for a while; she should've been gone when I got here. "Nyssa, are you staying tonight?"

"I stuck around just in case you didn't show up. You know, after the cop was here and all, I wasn't sure what was going on. I'm more than happy to stay if you want to go home."

"No, I'm good. I feel safer here than at my own apartment right now." I shudder slightly. Talking with Nyssa and Laura has been a good distraction from the Riley situation, but now it's at the forefront of my mind again.

Suddenly the bells on the door clink against the glass. We all turn.

TWENTY

When I see Detective Stevens, followed by two cops in uniform, I let out a breath I didn't know I'd been holding.

"Hello, Detective. Who's your friends?"

"Hello, Vivienne. Ladies." He nods his head in their direction, almost like he's tipping his hat to them. "This is Officer Ruiz and Officer Hoffman," he says, pointing to the man and the woman in turn. "We were in the area and thought we would pop in for a bite to eat."

"Wonderful," Laura says, grabbing three menus from the stack. "Follow me."

They dutifully follow her to the one of the tables in the center of the diner. I head behind the counter to wash my hands.

Nyssa follows me over and asks again, quietly, "Are you sure you don't want to go home?"

"No, Nyssa, I'm good. I'll be fine. And besides, you've already been working all day."

She sighs. "I know, but I really want to help you out. Any way I can. I like you a lot, Vivienne, and I..." She trails off. "I just wanted you to know that."

I dry my hands off. "Thanks, Nyssa. I appreciate your concern and your willingness to help me out when it comes to work," I say, remembering that Nyssa saved my skin two weeks ago when Mikah took me to the hospital. I have no doubt that she would do the same again, if needed.

"Vivienne," Laura says, coming behind the counter and reaching for a tray. "I'll grab their drinks, but it's your table."

"That's not necessary," I say back. I'm more and more certain that Laura's been giving me the tables to be nice. Now that the financial burden is not as great as it was even a week ago, I feel self-conscious about continuing to accept all the tables.

"I know dear, but...you know," she says as she scurries off with their drinks.

After the cops are done eating, I take the bill over. "Can I get you anything else?" I say as the door chimes again.

All heads turn in that direction except for mine. The presence of the three cops in front of me is a comfort. If Riley were stupid enough to walk in here right now, these three would protect me.

I look over in Laura's direction. She's smiling toward the door. I look up then, my heart fluttering at the prospect that Mikah might've walked in the door. But it's not Mikah - it's another regular that Laura is friendly with – and my heart sinks.

"No, I think just the check will do," Detective Stevens says.

"Did you guys want it split or all on the same?"

"It's my turn to pay, so just one, thanks," Officer Ruiz says. I hand him the bill. The scowls on the other two's faces are almost comical. Officer Ruiz looks it over quickly, then hands me a fifty dollar bill. "Keep the change."

"Oh no, that's way too much," I say before I can stop myself. I purse my lips, feeling like I've been rude.

"You did a fabulous job, and you had to put up with us. It's not too much." He is smiling warmly at me.

"Thank you." I nod in his direction. "Would you guys like some more coffee?"

They all shake their heads and stand.

"We're good," Detective Stevens says. "Need to get back at it. That was good. Thank you, Vivienne."

"Anytime, Detective. And thank you."

After a short while, we start to get busy. Several tables fill up with customers, and once again we're met with some of the better-dressed, don't-belong-in-this-neighborhood type.

Once the crowd dies down, I tell Laura, "I'm going to go help BJ with the dishes. Holler if you need me."

She scowls at me. I don't normally do the dishes in the back, but I kind of need a break from running around. My feet are a little sore tonight. Plus, washing dishes means that I can stay out of sight for a bit. Each time the bells chime on the door, I jump slightly. I've been getting edgier since Detective Stevens and the officers left, and going to the back will - with any luck - help me relax just a little bit.

After about fifteen minutes, Laura calls back for me and I dry off and head out front. When I come through the door there are five more tables with new people at them. I look at Laura and shrug. Back at it we go.

Around eleven thirty, the diner is finally empty and BJ is out mopping the floor while Laura and I clean up the counter. Filling bottles and sugar containers is boring work, but somebody has to do it.

"Sit," Laura demands.

"I told you, I'm not made of glass and I'm the same person I was yesterday."

"I know, but there is no reason to stand up while you're filling up containers."

"Alright." I take a seat on one of the stools and she slides all the containers my way. I start to marry the ketchup bottles together, then work on the mustard bottles, topping them off and putting them back in the wire baskets that go on the tables.

At some point I realize I'm inadvertently working a little slower than I normally would. Going home is not a high priority tonight like it normally is; the prospect of being at home alone makes my flesh crawl.

TWENTY-ONE

It's a quarter to midnight when Laura says, "Screw it, let's lock up."

I shrug at BJ and head to the door to turn the deadbolt.

I look out the door. No one seems to be anywhere in sight. Not even the cops. As I turn the deadbolt, my eyes spot something across the street in the small space between two shops. It looks white, almost like a t-shirt. It's unmoving. Goose bumps crawl up my arms. I try to shake it off; it's probably just my eyes playing tricks on me.

After we pull down the chairs and BJ shuts down the kitchen, we grab our stuff and head out as a group.

"How long until the next bus, Viv?" BJ asks.

I look at my watch. "About three minutes," I say, heading in that direction. He follows right behind me. On instinct I know that Laura has told him about the detective today. I'm not going to argue.

When I get to the bus stop and turn to BJ, I see that Laura has followed, too. I want to roll my eyes, but I can't deny that I feel safer knowing they're here with me.

I look back to the crevice between the buildings, and the white shirt I thought I saw earlier is gone.

I hear the bus approach from my left. It stops, and the doors swing open. It's Al.

"Hi, darlin'," he says as I climb up. I place my money in the box. "How you doing, sweetheart?"

I smile at him. "Good. Tired, but good."

I look over my shoulder. "Thanks, guys," I say to Laura and BJ. They smile and turn to leave.

I scan the bus, terrified that Riley might be on it. When I realize he isn't, the tension in my shoulders eases by a fraction. Then I noticed a gentleman sitting toward the back. Buzz-cut, dark blond hair, black t-shirt, good looking. Not the type to normally be on this bus this time of night.

I grab the sideways seat behind Al instead of the forward-facing one opposite him. If I need to, I want to be able to make a quick escape.

I look back to the gentleman and he smiles at me. Warm, friendly. Then his hand slides out from behind the seat.

My heart pounds.

I see what's in his hand.

A shield. He's a cop. I start breathing again. He smiles again and nods in my direction slightly. I give him a half-smile in return as my heart rate returns to normal.

A few minutes later, the bus stops to pick up another passenger. I hold my breath again, but it's only a female cop in uniform. "Hi, Al," she says as she climbs up. "How we doing tonight?"

"Great, thanks. Don't usually see you guys this time of night," he says as she slides past the box.

"I'm just taking a ride down the street, back to my car. Had some vandalism at one of the stops, so I've been checking some other ones. No biggy."

She acknowledges me with a nod as she takes the seat I usually sit in, but it's not clear that she knows who I am. Whether she's been assigned to me or not, I feel safer with two cops on board to protect me.

But she gets off two stops later, and then, at the stop just before mine, the male cop pulls the chain. He stands up as Al brings the bus to a halt, looks at me, smiles.

"Have a good night," he says as he hops down the back door of the bus. I'm not sure why he's decided to get off now.

We rumble up to my stop. "You okay, darlin'?" Al asks as we slow. Maybe he can sense my nervousness.

I nod. "Yup, just tired."

"Have a good night. Be safe out there."

"You do the same," I say as I climb down the front steps. Al lingers until I reach the corner.

Headlights fire up behind me. I'd almost completely forgotten about the Mercedes. The headlights break up as Al passes in front of the car.

I quicken my pace.

The street looks different. It takes a minute to realize why. The light over the door to my complex is out. Great.

As soon as I hit the door to my building, the headlights pass, just like always. I wish I'd thought to find a way to wave down the Mercedes. It's starting to bother me that he's so close yet so far away. I visualize seeing him sitting in the driver's seat, watching me, his beautiful blue-green eyes. Maybe tomorrow I'll call him.

I turn to smile at the car and notice a police car parked in the same spot as this morning. In the dark I can just make out a silhouette in the driver's seat. I give a little wave; it's too dark to see if they wave back.

Stepping inside, I unlock the inner door. Tonight I skip the mailbox and head straight up the stairs. I won't rest easy until I'm locked safe in my apartment.

As I pass Mr. Crowley's door, I notice it's slightly ajar. It's dark inside. He's probably just answering a call from a tenant and forgot to shut his door all the way, but the thought of calling out or going in to investigate makes me scared enough to want to scream. I climb the stairs faster. My scalp prickles as I climb the last flight of steps, and I rub at it.

I reach my door. Do a quick glance around. Nothing jumps out at me or seems out of the ordinary. My heart is pounding, pumping blood through my ears as I place my key in the top lock and turn it. Then the next lock, and finally the knob. I push open the door, letting my breath out in a whoosh.

I'm about to step inside when a hand covers my mouth and nose.

TWENTY-TWO

"Well, well, well...what do we have here. The little whore is all alone."

Riley!

His hand is tight over my nose and mouth, blocking my air. I start to fight back, but he wraps an arm around my chest, squeezing hard.

He pushes me inside my apartment, slamming the door behind us.

I can't breathe.

I claw at his hand over my mouth but my grip is weak and my strength is failing the longer I go without oxygen. I scratch at his arm with my nails.

"Bitch, please. That shit don't hurt. But I have more than a few things that will. At least before I kill you." Panic washes over me as his determination registers.

The next thing I know, he releases me and his hand comes away from my mouth.

I gasp for air.

He pushes me hard.

I bounce off the bed, and then I'm falling toward the floor. I put my hands out, hoping to catch myself before I hit the ground. There is a loud popping sound, and blinding pain races through my body from my right wrist. I cry out and roll onto my side.

Blinking through the pain, I look up and see him looming over me. His dirty blond hair is mussed in short spikes. He's wearing a white t-shirt and black jeans. His eyes are dark, drawn and detached. A look I've seen more times than I care to remember.

"And here I thought this was going to be hard, though I had to deal with your nosey neighbor first."

Mr. Crowley. No. That's why his— No, no, no!

"But yet here you are, just like I like you."

He reaches for my leg. I pull it back and swing hard, narrowly missing his face as he flinches away. The momentum of my kick has sent me rolling back onto my stomach and onto my broken wrist. I scream as pain stabs across my body.

"Bitch!" he says as he reaches once again for my legs.

Before I can react and swing again, he comes down hard with his knee on the back of my leg. "You're mine, bitch! You're going to pay for what you've done to me."

In a flash all of Riley's narcissistic words come rushing back to me. It doesn't occur to him that his own actions put him in jail; it's that I put him there.

"I've done nothing to you." As soon as the words leave my mouth, I brace myself for his retaliation.

Something comes down hard and heavy across the back of my skull. All I can see is brilliant white light.

CHAPTER TWO

Give Me Hope

One

"Let them in," I tell Red. The familiar hum in my back dulls out, and I take it to mean that there's no immediate danger. "I haven't a clue on earth why they're here, but let them in."

He turns for the door and opens it to reveal two men dressed in police uniforms. The man in front is about my height, stocky, and a little pudgy around the midsection. I estimate that he's well into his forties, with graying, short, military-style hair. He has a very intense look about him, like he's unsure of me, but he's confident in getting what he's after. The combination is strange, but he has a rather stoic, typically neutral expression.

There is another officer behind him and to his left who is much shorter but well-built and rather young.

Both men are very confident in their uniforms, and they both radiate authority. The intention is clear on their faces: They're out for information. But what?

"Mr. Blake?" The older one asks.

"Yeah, that's me. What can I do for you?"

"May we come in?"

I nod. They stalk into the room like giants, their boots echoing off the tile and entryway walls.

"I'm Detective Stevens, and this is Officer Ruiz. We are with the Minneapolis Police Department. We'd like to ask you a few questions, if you don't mind."

"Of course I mind, but I'm not going to stop you from asking."

Stevens's face remains impassive, and he is quick to continue with what he came here to do. "Would you please tell us what your car was doing on the corner of Lake and Chicago about thirty minutes ago?"

Vivienne's apartment. A sharp warning stab zings across my back, and I'm not sure I should trust these men. "Excuse me?"

"Doesn't seem like the type of neighborhood you'd usually be caught hanging out in," Stevens says, gesturing to the marble floor and the leather couches before turning his attention to his notepad.

I bristle at the word caught. "That really doesn't seem any of your business. Have I done something wrong? Broken any laws?"

Stevens looks up from his notepad. "We never said you did, we just want to know why you were there."

Thinking about Vivienne's apartment sends another sharp zing across my skin. Something is off. "I was... checking up on a friend."

Stevens's eyes widen slightly, and then a scowl forms. "Do you know Riley Bennett?" he asks sternly. Zing.

Riley Bennett. Why does that name ring bells? Something about that name... "No, I can't say that I do. Does he work for me?" I ask back.

"What about Rebecca Black?"

I shake my head.

"And lastly, Vivienne Callahan?"

All the breath in my lungs rushes out of my body. I feel my knees shake violently and I try to steady myself. The hum surges like a shock of electricity across my entire body, pulsing with each frantic beat of my heart. "Vivienne? What about Vivienne?" Then it dawns on me like a bolt of lightning. "Riley! Riley is Vivienne's ex-boyfriend. The bastard that put her in the hospital."

The cops look at each other, and Stevens turns back to me. He shifts his feet as he does, taking a rather defensive stance. "You know about that?"

I nod. "I..." I try to relax a little just so I can talk. "Can you tell me first if she's alright? Vivienne?"

Two

Officer Ruiz nods. "She's fine. Got home about half an hour ago." I feel a harder jolt across my back. Something is *definitely* off. "We're watching her apartment. Which is how we ended up here. Your black Mercedes was seen parked across Lake Street from her apartment. Then you left the area once she got off the bus and to her door."

I let the sense of relief flood over me, and I take a deep breath. I hadn't realized that my breathing was so slow and shallow. Emotions I don't understand wrack my body, mind and soul. I can't take it if I lose another--

I stop the thought short. I've had enough tragedy in my life. I can't even begin to think about losing Vivienne too.

I nod. It is difficult to form words with my throat still so tight. "I met Vivienne about two weeks ago at the diner. I was in that area attending a reception. I was hungry, so I stopped in. I met her then." No need to tell them that it wasn't my stomach that led me to the diner.

"I'd seen what kind of condition she was in, and I wanted to try and find a way to help her. A few days later I tried to help her by taking her to H.C.M.C., where she was seen by a Dr. Alston."

"Go on," Detective Stevens says, scribbling in his notebook.

I nod. "It turned out it wasn't the first time Vivienne had been Dr. Alston's patient. I eventually put two and two together. At some point that afternoon, I did or said something that upset Viv, and she threw me out of her room." That was probably one of the worst experiences of my life. I pushed her too hard, and she snapped. It is not an experience I want to have repeated anytime soon.

Detective Stevens smiles in a good-for-her way. "She seems the type."

I shake my head at the expression on his face and snort at his words. "You can say that again. Anyway, I made sure she was taken care of. Due to my being a major shareholder in the hospital, Dr. Alston agreed to keep in touch with me about her progress, and she was released the next morning. She wouldn't take money from me, but Dr. Alston was able to collect some cash from the hospital to help her out. I've stayed away from her since then. But I need to know she is safe, and I feel a sense of responsibility toward her to make sure it stays that way. Every night, I wait near her apartment until she gets home, and then I leave. Nothing more."

"A bit stalker-ish dontcha think?" The younger officer asks.

"Maybe, but she is a tiny little thing. She is about thirteen weeks pregnant, with no money, living in one of the roughest neighborhoods in Minneapolis. I worry about her safety." I sigh. "Is there a point to all of this, Detective?"

There is no immediate reply, but the less stoic expression on Stevens's face is telling me that he's deciding something. Whether or not he trusts me? I'm not sure I care, but it is rather obvious in his defensiveness regarding Vivienne that he too cares about her in some strange way. I take some comfort in that fact, all the while realizing that Vivienne is very easy to care about.

"Riley Bennett was released on bail last week." *Zing.* "We have reason to believe that he is looking for her." The sharp stab returns, and I know my face scrunches up. "We came here to find out whether there's a connection between you and Riley Bennett." He scowls slightly, scrutinizing my reaction. Reading me.

"I'll admit, my actions are probably a little over the top when it comes to Vivienne, but I'm not doing anything illegal." Technically. "And I'm certainly not in league with Riley."

He nods, accepting that I'm telling him the truth, and continues, "I spoke with her earlier today, let her know the situation, and she was willing to cooperate with the police presence. Officer Ruiz, Officer Hoffman and myself made our presence known at the diner by having dinner there tonight."

"That was nice of you." I try to smile, but something is off. I can't see it yet, but something.

"One of our detectives rode home on the bus with her tonight. He said that at first she seemed wary of him, but once he showed her his badge she relaxed a little bit."

Rage washes over me. "Why on earth are you trying to scare her half to death with shit like that?"

"We're doing our job, Mr. Blake. She needs to know we are there to protect her."

A sharp zing of pain stabs hard and fierce across my back. Jesus, what the hell is this all about? I don't understand it.

"She's had it hard enough as it is. You need to stop scaring her. She does not need to be worked up like this right now." Both the detectives look at each other, as if questioning my words. This makes my desire to be at the hospital tomorrow burn hotter. I need to know that she's safe, and I will do whatever it takes to make her see that. Is it possible that maybe, with all this going on, she will willingly let me help her? Let me protect her from Riley? That's assuming she needs protection from Riley. I have a distinct feeling that Riley might not be all she needs protection from.

I'm suddenly very curious as to what has led the police to this point. "What makes you think that he is after Vivienne?" I ask. They both look at each other, deciding. "Well?"

"Wednesday afternoon, Vivienne had a visit from an old mutual friend of hers and Riley's. When I spoke to Vivienne yesterday, she told me about that conversation. But we're still working on what transpired after this friend left the diner. Vivienne was under the impression that Riley was using her to get to Vivienne."

"Why the hell would she think that?"

"Because she told Vivienne that she was there to warn her about Riley." *Zing.*

Shit. I really don't like the sound of this. I have a sudden urge to drive over there and knock on her door.

But when the detectives leave a few moments later, the urge to drive to Vivienne's apartment subsides. I don't want another run-in with Stevens; plus, if she is safe in her apartment, then I do not want to scare her further by showing up in the middle of the night.

Three

I turn to Red. "Did she make it into her apartment tonight?"

"She did," he says back.

"Good." I'd only been home for all of five seconds when the cops showed up. I had a business meeting that ran over, so Red had gone to Vivienne's tonight in my place. "Anything unusual?"

"Not a thing, except the light over her front door was out. She didn't seem too bothered by it, and the bus driver hung around just a little longer than normal. I almost missed the drive-by timing." He smiles. "She was smirking at the car as I drove past."

"Even better. Maybe now she will be ready to talk to me."

He raises his eyebrows in a you've-lost-your-damn-mind kind of way. He's probably right.

There's something undeniably special about Vivienne, but I can't quite put my finger on it. Not yet. But eventually I will. I will find a way to do just that.

"I'll be in my office for a bit if you need me."

"Certainly, sir. Anything else?"

"No, not tonight. Thanks, Red."

"Anytime, sir."

I turn and head toward my office.

The police showing up here because of my car makes me question their motives altogether. What on earth is the connection between Vivienne, Riley and myself that they're seeing and I'm not?

Sitting down at my desk, I flick the mouse on my iMac, and the screen comes to life. The background comes up and I smile. It is a scanned copy of Baby Callahan's ultrasound image.

That baby is so unbelievably special, and Vivienne hasn't even begun to grasp that yet. Well, maybe she does a little now that she's had her ultrasound.

I can only imagine the emotional strain she's under, knowing that she's doing this alone. I'd really hoped to help her, maybe even be with her, if she'd have me. Be everything she needed me to be.

Until I met Vivienne I had no idea what love at first sight meant, but now I do. In more ways than one. I'd known when I was standing across the street from the diner with all those images flashing through my mind that there was something different about her, but I wasn't able to put my finger on it. When she was shaking from hunger and I told her that it wasn't just her I was worried about, I didn't realize what had come out of my mouth until after it had left. I had the fleeting thought that maybe she was pregnant, but it came and went so quickly that her telling me she was pregnant surprised me.

It was not what I'd expected to hear out of her mouth -- I was initially concerned that it was drug- or disease-related, and a pregnancy was the furthest thing from my mind -- but when she told me, it felt somehow familiar, like I'd already known.

I fell in love a second time when Dr. Alston raised her hospital gown, and there on her right hip was a heart-shaped birthmark. A mark that had become a legend in my family.

When I was a boy in our small town outside of Dublin, there was a crazy old lady who would walk past our house at the same time every day, muttering nonsense. My father said that she was just talking to herself, but each thing she said had something to do with one of us. It wasn't until we moved to Boston and my brother Shane was born that my parents started to believe there was something more to the old woman's mutterings.

"Light and darkness all at once," she used to say. Shane was born on the same day that my great-grandfather died.

Then my little brother, Ronin, came along. He was born with bright red hair and a pattern of freckles that formed a star under his right eye. This, too, the old woman had foretold.

Victoria's prophecy was the spookiest. The old woman had told my mother that they would have "a daughter of four," meaning fourth, and that she would be "frail and sickly, too", or something like that. When Victoria was born, she didn't leave the hospital until she was nearly six months old. I suppose some part of me expected that she'd die young, but of my whole family, Victoria and I are the only ones still living.

Though in Victoria's case, *alive* might be a better term. She resides in a state hospital in upstate New York -- one of the best. I wouldn't have it any other way. But I'm not sure she's really living in the sense of having a life of her own.

My prophecy went something like: "Alone he'll be, a wealth of three, a wife she'll be." There was a poem, too, but that's all that I really remember.

The prophecy, if it can be called that, alluded to a heart shape on her. It wasn't until we were in the hospital and Dr. Alston was getting ready to do the ultrasound that I saw it. There, over her right hip is that heart-shaped mark.

I only wish there was someone that I could talk to about all of this as it seems to slowly becoming reality.

Four

Thoughts of Vivienne bring me back to the reason I came in here in the first place.

Shaking my head of those thoughts, I turn to the computer; pull up Safari and type in *Rebecca Black*. There are a lot of women with that name, but none of the entries are recent.

I search instead for local crime reports from the last two days and find a *Star Tribune Online* article about a girl who was brutally murdered in South Minneapolis. Victim still unidentified.

My stomach turns, and the shivering sensations on my back intensify briefly. I peruse the rest of the article. The information it contains is weak and provides me with no real concrete proof that it has to do with the Rebecca Black the cops asked about. Though the location suggests it could be.

I go back to Google and search for Riley Bennett. These results seem more promising, and within a matter of minutes I discover a connection I no longer like -- a business relationship that will soon be severed. Riley Bennett is the son of Elton Bennett, CEO of Bennett and Lisbon Enterprises, a company that I do business with on a regular basis.

No longer. I will not stand side by side with a man that bails his kid out of jail after that kid viciously beats a girl for being pregnant with his child.

I grab my BlackBerry, pull up a contact and press send.

"Good evening, Mr. Blake. To what do I owe this pleasure?"

"Hi, Jack. I need you to put your research skills to work. Are you ready?"

"Absolutely. Fire away."

Not only will I sever my ties to Bennett and Lisbon, but I will bring Elton down in a fiery inferno. I'm not generally this vindictive, but damn it, this is Viv we're talking about.

When I'm done talking to Jack, I head for the bedroom and a shower. My back is starting to itch. That's odd. I try to scratch it, but its right in the middle of my back where I can't reach.

As my feet hit the bedroom carpet, I start shedding clothes, first unbuttoning the shirt and letting it slip from my shoulders onto the floor. Then off come the belt, pants and socks. Finally my boxer briefs hit the bathroom floor.

As I reach into the shower to turn the knob, something catches the corner of my eye.

I turn quickly but see nothing. It must be the stress. Maybe I'm even a little freaked out by the fact that Riley has been freed, and he's wormed his way into my unconscious mind.

I turn again and it's back. This time I turn slowly, hoping to catch sight of whatever it is. For a moment I see it in the mirror, faint before it disappears again. I turn my body so that my back is facing the mirror. I'm looking over my shoulder, and in an instant the old lady's words come flooding back to me.

An angel is he
Alone in this world
With the wealth of three
He'll meet his true love
Answering her song
His wings he will grow
His heart will respond
Him she will follow
His wife she will be
Two joined making three.

Jesus, I'm losing it, I swear to God. I'm seeing things, and now, all of sudden after twenty years that old lady's words come back to me.

Is it even possible that I am an angel? I thought angels were born of those that die and earn their right as angels. How is it that I'm walking this earth and can be an angel? 'Cause that makes a lot of sense, doesn't it?

Vivienne. How on earth does she fit into all of this? The heart on her hip, the birthmark. The need I feel of being around her.

What if all this is really coming true?

Five

My body is burning. The hum I've been experiencing of late has begun to burn across my entire body.

Opening my eyes, I look at the clock. Eight. I get up quickly, hoping that moving around will soothe the burning feeling, but it doesn't.

Last night's realization that something is changing in my body comes flooding back to me.

I'd never taken my family's story as anything more than gibberish until now. The story tells, in some mixed-up way, that I'm supposed to become an angel.

An angel is he...

I shake my head. Jesus, I'm losing it.

"I'm hardly pure enough to be an angel," I mutter as I shed the t-shirt I slept in and exchange it for a light gray undershirt and a gray button up dress shirt. I pull on my favorite pair of faded Wrangler jeans and slip on black socks and my black boots.

Every time I've seen Vivienne so far, I've been dressed in a suit. Not my usual attire unless I'm at the office, and I'm hoping that my normal, everyday clothes will be a little more appealing and less intimidating to her.

In case I make it to the office, I grab the hanger with a black dress shirt, black slacks and my silver tie.

As I leave my walk-in closet I sigh. "If only I had some answers," I say out loud to no one, and my skin vibrates, hard and hot. I stumble. "Ow." But just as quickly as it came on, it's gone. "This is getting ridiculous."

I march out of my room, irritated that I don't understand what is going on with me. I doubt it's something a doctor could help me with; I'm left to my own resources to try and figure this out.

I step into the kitchen to find Celeste, my housekeeper, is there. I hired Celeste about a year ago. She's a plump little thing, standing at about five feet tall. She has stark blonde hair – no doubt from a box – and baby blue eyes and is not at all unattractive. She's in her mid to late thirties and insists she loves her job. Despite my offer to let her live in one of my condos in this building, she doesn't. She'd rather live at her boyfriend's place.

"Good morning, Celeste."

"Good morning, sir. Breakfast?"

"Please. The usual."

"Coming right up," she says as she gets to work.

"I'll be in my office."

She nods and goes about my breakfast.

As I walk toward my office, I take a look around my condo, wondering idly if it is something Vivienne would enjoy or feel comfortable in.

The shades are open, and light is flooding into the dining and living rooms. The floor is a beautiful walnut hardwood with a dark, glossy finish. My walls are painted a neutral tan, and the furniture is an eclectic mix of modern sofas and high-backed chairs.

It's quite stuffy and formal, if you want the truth of it. But I don't spend mountains of time in the living and dining rooms.

When I'm home, I'm usually in my office, working, my bedroom, sleeping, or my entertainment room, which from here is behind the kitchen.

I reach my office door at the far end of the long, rectangular living room, I turn back towards the kitchen again and there is a sudden image shift of a little girl making a figure eight on a big wheel. I smile at the thought and open the door.

The flooring changes from wood to black slate, an after-market modification to accompany the bleached white walls. My desk, to the right of the door, is contemporary: black with silver accents and white drawers. The drawers are out to the sides and the top of the desk only sits on the corner of the cabinets. The front is held up by a single leg, and the overall appearance is that it's floating.

When I wake up the computer, I find two emails from Jack. The first one lets me know they've tapped into some information and that he wants to meet with me later today once they have something a little more concrete. The next contains a single image. A photo taken by one of the Capella Towers security cameras last night at about two in the morning. In the image I can see Elton and a younger gentleman. "Hello, Riley."

I pick up the card Detective Stevens left when he was here last night and forward the image to his email address with the note, *Taken Friday morning around 2 a.m. outside of Capella Towers.*

"Here you are, sir." Celeste comes into my office carrying a tray.

"Thanks, Celeste."

She sets it down on the desk and departs.

I plow through my food and grab my jacket on the way out. I'm hoping to catch Vivienne leaving her apartment this morning on her way to the hospital for her appointment. My intention for being there is so that she can see me and know that I knew about her appointment. It will either irritate the crap out of her or warm her up to talking to me at the hospital. The only reason I'm going is to see her, and I don't care if she knows that or not.

Six

By the time I arrive at the corner of Lake Street and Chicago, my back is on fire once again. There is a cab parked right outside the entrance to her apartment. Good – maybe she called a cab to take her to the hospital. If not, she has about five minutes to catch the bus if she's going to make it to the hospital on time.

I park in my usual spot and watch. I look for the police cruiser Red told me about and see it parked less than a block away.

The bus that she should have been on comes and goes, and the cab remains. It's chilly out this morning; a plume of exhaust smoke billows out of the cab's tailpipe.

My phone rings. It's Jack.

"Blake."

"Hi, Mikah. Listen, I have something I need you to see."

"Like?"

"Well you dropped a couple of names on me last night. Rebecca Black for one. She was found dead Thursday morning by the dumpster of a motel near Vivienne's that's well-known for prostitution and drug use."

"Was she a drug addict?"

"We don't know that yet, but that's not what's important."

"What is?"

"The gentleman in the picture I sent you is Riley Bennett."

"I figured. I forwarded it to Detective Stevens this morning." I'm getting a little annoyed that he's not getting to the point. And why the hell hasn't Vivienne come out yet?

"We have video evidence that we need to submit to the police. We have a video of Riley Bennett dumping Rebecca Black's body. Then he appears to inject something into her arm. After he leaves the scene, she moves and twitches a bit, then falls still."

"Fuck!" I spat out. "Can we send it to Detective Stevens?"

"We're working on that. The source of the video is unclear. We're not sure if it's a legal recording. I have a couple of guys on their way over there to find out. If it is a legal recording, we will turn it over anonymously."

"Find out, and fast. I want this fucker to fry."

"On it, boss."

"Thanks. Anything else?" I ask.

"Not that can't wait until this afternoon. I will let you know if anything else comes up."

"Perfect, thanks."

"No problem." He hangs up.

I pull the detective's card from my pocket, dial the number and wait.

"Hhhello?"

The voice is tentative, groggy from sleep. Not like the confident officer I met last night. "Detective Stevens?" I ask.

He clears his throat. "Yes."

Much better. "This is Mikah Blake. We met last night."

"Oh, of course. What can I do for you?"

"I sent you an email this morning that shows your boy Riley meeting his dad outside my building around two this morning. I have a security detail working on the full video exchange."

"Are these cameras yours? The ones used to capture these images?"

"Yes, I had the security system installed a couple years ago, the previous one was shit." I can hear my own irritation coming through. "If we find something you can use, you call your evidence boys and have them come get it."

"Uh...that's great. Thank you." I can hear it in his voice: He's not used to being told how to do his job.

"Don't thank me yet. I want a report on Vivienne's building from last night."

"It doesn't work like that, Blake. This isn't *quid pro quo* here. What is your need to know?" The skepticism can be heard in his voice and the pain in my back spikes.

"Because when I arrived here this morning, there was a cab parked outside. Still is. I'd like to know when it arrived."

"I can't do that, Mr. Blake."

"Don't give me that bullshit. Why don't you call your guy parked down the block from her apartment and ask him. Then we can move on from there."

"Alright, hang on." There is a series of clicks. Then he comes back on the line. *Ring.* "Blake?"

"Yup." *Ring.* "Thanks, Detective." I know he's violating company policy. *Ring.* And, I know it's killing him to give in to my demands.

"Yeah." Irritation fills his voice. *Ring.* "Just don't say anything when he answers." *Ring.*

Click. "You've reached the voicemail of Officer Anders. Please leave—" *Click.*

"What the hell?" Stevens says. "It's ringing, so it's on. But why not answer?"

"Let's find out, shall we?"

Seven

I turn off the car, climb out and start walking across the street. I don't like the tingles radiating through my body. "When was he due to check in?"

"Once every two hours or so. Less if we're in an unmarked stakeout. So he would be checking—"

"Alright." I cross Lake Street and approach the cab. The driver is there, reading the paper. He jumps when I knock on the back window as I keep walking along the car. "What are you doing here?" I ask him.

He cracks the window a bit. "Waiting for a fare."

"Who?" I demand.

"What the fuck do you care?" he spats back.

"Just tell me who you're here for."

"It's none of your damn business." He rolls the window back up.

"Who is that?" Stevens asks in my ear.

"The cab driver of the cab outside the apartment. I'm almost to the squad car."

As I approach the squad car, I slow my pace. Nothing moves inside the car. "If this asshole is asleep, I'm going to have your department for lunch," I say into the phone.

I reach the car and rap loudly on the window. Nothing. Bending down, I look inside the car. Red. Bright, red fading to brown blood...

"Stevens, you have an officer down." I don't wait for his reply. I drop the phone and take off full tilt toward Vivienne's apartment.

Jesus, please, dear God, no. Not her. My back is ablaze, my body trembling with the buzzing I've been feeling for the last couple of weeks.

I beat on the cab's hood. "Call nine-one-one! NOW!" He nods.

I can hear sirens in the distance.

I grab the outer door, swinging it open so hard that the glass shatters. The next door is locked. I shoulder-check the glass — once, twice. Finally, on the third try, it gives way, and I go stumbling inside.

As I climb the stairs three and four at a time, I feel like I'm in a nightmare with never-ending hallways.

I reach the third floor and apartment nine. I pound on the door. "Vivienne!" Harder I pound and turn the knob, but it's locked. "Vivienne!" I ram my shoulder into the door, harder each time, and the door flies open. I storm into her apartment.

"Jesus! God! NO!" I shout.

I rush to the bed. Reaching up to her face, I pull the tape away from her mouth with one hand while I check for a pulse with the other. I can't feel one.

"No, damn it!" *Do not do this to me!*

There is blood everywhere, all over the sheets. It's still wet, but wherever she was hurt is no longer bleeding.

There is so much blood.

When I place one hand on top of the other and press into her chest to give her CPR, her sternum gives way more than it should, and I pull back immediately, afraid of causing more damage.

I lean down and place my cheek by her mouth, hoping and praying I will feel her breath against my skin.

Nothing.

Nothing...

Tears, tears – hot, molten tears stream down my cheeks – and the buzz, the buzz is gone.

Eight

Click...
Squeak...
Click...
Squeak...
Click, squeak. Click, squeak.
Click, squeak. Click, squeak.
White floors, white walls, white doors. No windows. Long, white hallway after long, white hallway.

Must...*buzz*...find...*buzz*... The zing is back, a mellow humming.

Finally I see the sign over the door at the end of the hall. The sign I've been seeking for at least the last ten minutes: *Chapel.*

I push hard on the doors, but they don't budge.
Breathe.
Breathe.
Damn it.
Reach for the handle.
Push handle downward.
Pull on handle.
The door opens.

All mechanical actions – no matter how seemingly simple, like breathing – have eluded me. *Breathe*, I tell myself over and over again.

I walk straight forward and collapse hard onto a rail that runs along the altar and I grip the upper part for support. My eyes drift upward, seeking the crucifix above the altar.

"Why? Why her?" Is all I can manage to sob.

Breathe.

I can't close my eyes. When I do, all I can see is her lifeless body strewn at awkward angles across her bed. Blood-soaked, pale, lifeless.

Breathe.

I know nothing about her. I do not know her from a woman I pass on the street. But my heart. My heart has been ripped from my chest.

Click. Steps. Heels. *Clang.*

"Mikah?" A woman's voice from behind me. A familiar voice. "Mikah. Mikah, look at me," she says.

I can't. I shake my head.

"Mikah, she's alive."

My head jerks up. I look her straight in the eye, unable to believe that I heard her correctly. Dr. Alston nods her head, as in answer to my unasked question.

Long, slow exhale. My head wobbles back, facing forward. *Thank you, God.* I feel a small sense of relief wash over me, quickly replaced by anxiety.

"She is in very bad shape, but she is alive. Mikah, look at me."

I slowly turn my head in her direction. My body is not my own. I feel disconnected. Seeing the expression on my face, she falters.

"Keep—" *Breathe.* "—talking," I finally manage to let out.

"She's in bad shape, Mikah. She lost a lot of blood. We've given her more than four pints."

Breathe.

"She has a skull fracture."

My breath hitches, and I stop breathing again.

"A serious concussion, swelling on her brain, a broken wrist, a dislocated shoulder..."

Start breathing, slowly.

"Six broken ribs and her right lung is partially collapsed. It's not going to be an easy road, Mikah."

"Bab—" I can't even finish the word. My breath has been stolen from my body.

She nods and takes a seat in a nearby pew behind me. I fall backwards off of the altar rail, landing awkwardly on my ass.

"Jesus, Mikah."

"Can— Bre—" I point at my mouth.

She gets up and rushes over to my side. "The baby is fine."

Sharp, loud inhale. "Fine?" What the fuck is going on with me? I can't wrap my head around why I'm having these reactions.

"For now, yes. We are far from out of the woods yet." She helps me to sit up. "I've set her arm and shoulder. I have to surgically repair one of her ribs and her lung. She is being prepped right now. I also have a neurosurgeon coming in to see if we can help reduce some of the pressure on her brain. All of this will be very taxing to her body, and I cannot make any promises. Do you understand me?"

I just nod.

"When you're ready, head up to surgery - the waiting room. I'll find you there when we're done. We will do everything we can to save both of them,

Mikah. I promise you." She grips my shoulder as she stands. "I'll see you soon," she says as she leaves.

From farther back in the chapel she turns to me. "She's gained more than fifteen pounds since I've seen her last. Her weight gain may have just saved her life."

I want to smile, but I can't. "Thank you," I say very slowly.

"You're welcome."

She turns and leaves. I'm no longer having to force myself to breathe. She is alive. She's survived.

"Jesus, God, thank you."

I pull myself up off the floor and take a seat in the front pew, leaning my elbows into my knees.

I feel a vibration along my thigh. My phone. That is about the fifteenth time in the last half hour it's gone off, but frankly, I could care less right now.

Resting my head in my hands, I let the tears flow. They pool into my palms. Breathing deep, ragged breaths, I try to pull myself back together.

I need to go upstairs, but I can't go in the state I'm in. I don't understand why I'm having such a strong reaction to the news about Vivienne. Something I can't explain is happening to me. I need to see her.

"You will see her soon enough."

My head snaps up at the elegant, soft female voice. Nothing. I see no one.

"You've been chosen to protect her, Mikah. Chosen to see to it that she is safe."

I stand quickly, spinning around. Sharp, blinding pain bounces around my body, and I crumple to my knees.

"What— What is happening to me?" I say aloud.

No response. I ball my fists in frustration, and the pain stops as quickly as it started.

I climb back up into the pew, shaking now because it's not just the pain that's gone but the hum, too. My connection to Vivienne, and it's gone. Panic seeps in.

"Relax."

Relief washes through me in instant response to the command. I have no control over it.

"Why can't you tell me what is going on?"

"Your answers will come in time, when you're meant to hear them."

I feel like I'm losing my mind. I'm hearing voices, talking to myself. Yet I can feel someone with me.

"I am not for you to look upon, young angel. I am here to guide you, to help you into your new life. She is ours to protect, and we will. Without fail, we will protect her in the way she is meant to be protected. But we can only initiate the healing; she must do the rest on her own. When the time comes, you will be told what to do next."

"She doesn't want me around," I whisper.

"You do not need to speak aloud, young angel. I know what you think, and I feel what you feel. I believe that her life has taken the turn you need to keep her within reach. Do not fret."

I sigh. With the heels of my hands, I press against my temples, trying to dispel the idea that someone is talking to me inside my head. I'm not crazy, am I?

A sweet female giggle radiates through my whole body. The tingling is back, but this time it feels different; it tickles. I squirm. Then suddenly the sensation becomes a spreading warmth that comforts me.

I realize that, for the first time, I can interpret the sensations. The tickling is something happy. Or laughter? The warmth feels like love or adoration.

The sensation stops.

Hello?

There is no answer, but a warm calm spreads across my skin. I decide that staying down here in the chapel is only going to drive me nuts, so I head for the door.

I pull my phone from my pocket. Thirty-seven missed calls. I'm not at all interested in any of them. Most of them are from Jack. But one...

I open up the visual voicemail app.

Elton Bennett
09:57 32 seconds
"What kind of game are you playing at, Blake? How dare you pull of out of our arrangement. You will not get away with this. She's just a white trash tramp who needed to be dealt with. Don't go getting too hasty, you will burn for it. I'll see to it."

I click into my voicemail, find the message from Bennett and forward it to Stevens.

"A little tramp, huh? What are *you* playing at, Bennett?" I say as I reach the door to the chapel.

It doesn't surprise me that he's found a connection; he's a crooked-ass, wannabe politician. It's clear to me that his attempts to cover his own ass are backfiring already.

Nine

I leave the chapel and head down the hall towards toward the bank of elevators that will take me up to the surgery floor. I'd rather wait up there then down here.

Jesus, what the hell was all that about? I shake my head but can't dispel the image of an angel – the painting my mom had above the hutch – from my mind. Could all that talk, all those years ago, really be true? Am I really an angel? But if I'm an angel, doesn't that mean that I died?

"Not necessarily."

"Jesus!" I sputter, stumbling in my surprise. Falling against the wall, I look behind me, but there's no one there. There's not a person to be seen in either direction.

"No, not Jesus, angel. I am Seraphina – your guardian, your teacher."

Rather than look like an idiot talking to myself in the middle of a deserted hallway, I try speaking to her in my thoughts. *Then show yourself.*

Good God, I really am loosing it.

"I cannot show myself to you. Not until you're ready."

But don't you think it will help me better understand what is going on?

"Not hardly, young angel. You have a lot to learn. When you're ready, you will see."

The more she talks, the more convinced I am that she's not the same voice that spoke to me in the chapel. Ugh! I don't know how much of this I'm supposed to handle before I break.

Does this have anything to do with the tattoo on my back?

"Everything. Although, young one, it is not a tattoo."

I nod my head. *I'm growing well aware of that. I swear I saw it shimmering last night. What on earth is it?*

"Why, what else would an angel have upon his back?"

My knees buckle as reality strikes. *Wings?*

The answer to my question comes in the form of a tingling sensation radiating across my back. The reinforcement of my conclusion leaves me shaking my head. This is all just way too much. *Are you going to keep blindsiding me when you start talking?*

"Yes, and no. Now, young angel, know that I will be ever-present and will do my best not to frighten you."

I push away from the wall and begin moving back down the hall. Finally I reach the elevator and press the up arrow.

There are so many unanswered questions, I feel like my head is going to explode. But something that the other voice told me comes flooding back.

The voice before, she said something about helping Vivienne. What did she mean?

179

"She meant that we can only help her start the process. The rest is up to her. You are here to protect her, to keep her safe and to help her heal."

How on earth am I supposed to do that?

"Be here."

Well that won't be hard., I have no intention of leaving. Not until she does.

The elevator finally arrives and I step in. As the elevator rises, all the angst and anguish I felt earlier returns. I get this strange sense of emptiness, and I wonder if the voice has gone.

When I get no answering reply, I'm assured that she is. At least for now. With each passing floor, my anxiety rises, and the buzz strengthens across my skin. But for the first time in all of this, I feel a sense of hope.

Ten

I've never been a fan of hospitals, let alone waiting rooms. The last time I spent any amount of time in one was after the accident. My youngest brother, Ronin, had survived the initial accident, then surgery, only to pass away about six hours later. We waited, Victoria and I, for nearly four hours while he was in surgery. We had already found out about Dad and my other brother, Shane.

I spent hours pacing the room while Victoria slowly lost her mind. She was far closer to Dad and Ronin than I ever was. I had always been closer to Mom.

All things considered, I will take this waiting room over that one, only because I feel completely confident in Dr. Alston's abilities as well as my newfound sense of hope.

Though that doesn't stop me from pacing the room, thankful that I'm the only one in here.

My phone starts to vibrate. Hoping that it will offer some distraction, I pull it from my pocket. My eyebrows knit together.

"Blake."

"Mikah, it's Detective Stevens."

"Have you caught Riley yet?"

"No." So not the distraction I was looking for. "I called because I received your recording. How in the hell did you obtain this?"

"It's a simple voicemail recording. Leaving a voicemail is public record."

I can hear a heavy sigh on the other end of the phone. "I see your point. How is she?"

My eyes water almost instantly at his seemingly innocent question, but his sense of guilt is palpable even through the phone. "She's in surgery, so I don't know."

"Alright. I'll try back later."

"Detective?"

Another sigh. "Yeah," he says, clipped.

"How are you holding up?" I ask. Doubtless, his dead officer weighs heavy on his mind.

"Officer Anders was a good friend of mine. I'm..." Pause.

"No need, Detective. I understand."

"Thanks, Blake."

"Yup. When my people get in touch with you, let me know if you need anything from them. Or from me."

"Will do. Thanks."

"Anytime." I hear the disconnecting click.

I pull the phone from my ear and hit end. I take a step back when I see more of the missed calls. My leg bumps into a chair, so I sit down and begin scrolling through them.

Most of them are from Jack, and looking at the time on my watch and the call log tells me that the majority of them were from before Elton left his message. It's good to know that, had I been coherent and not hearing voices in my head, I would've had a heads-up about what he knew before calling me.

I go flipping through the emails. I quickly see why Elton knows about my severing ties to Bennett and Lisbon, which means pulling out of the condo project we broke ground on a couple weeks ago. Elton knows that he cannot continue without MSBE's involvement. Ninety percent of the investors on that project only joined in because I was fronting the majority of it. The project was a major risk, given its location.

Jack has also forwarded some more information regarding Riley and his involvement in Rebecca's death.

I can't look at this now. I don't need to have what could've happened to Vivienne shoved in my face.

Jesus. Vivienne. She was done, gone, out of Riley's life, and by the sounds of it, never to return. She could've had anything she wanted out of Elton. Or Riley, for that matter. She could've used them, blackmailed them, anything. But she didn't. Why?

I know why. She's not that type of person. Her determination to be independent through all of this is my answer. Whether it is to prove it to herself or not, she's determined to make it on her own.

Eleven

A hum radiates quickly through my body as the sound of footsteps registers in my ears. This time it's light, but doesn't tickle. Someone that I know is coming?

After four more steps, a man steps into the doorway. My heart races for that brief second before recognition, and then the humming stops.

"Red. What are you doing here?"

"I came by to check on you."

"How'd you know I was—..."

"You would think, after the last three years, you would know the answer to that question."

I nod my head. "She's in surgery."

"I feel awful about this."

I look to him, puzzled. "For?"

"I was there. Last night. Waiting for her to return home from work. If I'd gotten there sooner I—..."

"Stop. There was a cop who was killed in Riley's quest to get to her. Do not think that it would have been any different with you had you arrived earlier." I lean forward, resting my elbows on my knees, and look down at the floor. "The truth is that I don't know when the cop was killed. Riley could have been in that building for hours before she got home. Or he could have managed to sneak his way in, leaving the cop for later. Something that surprised me most was the fact that her door was locked, but only the knob." I wonder idly if Riley had left, met with his father outside of my building and then went back.

The buzz comes back, same as a moment ago, as I hear Red's shoes hit the carpet.

He sits down next to me. "I know, but still, it makes me wonder." He stops talking and I can sense his mood change to distress. "Good Lord, Mikah, you're bleeding."

I give Red a sideways glance as I try and recall how I could have started bleeding. He's looking at my back. Shit! "Where?" I ask, a little bit of panic in my voice. I can't feel any pain anywhere.

"There, on your shoulder and your back. Let me look at it."

"No, it's fine it's probably not my blood,." I say, as my body runs cold and as the vision of Vivienne splayed out on that bed, blood everywhere, goes flashing through my mind.

"Jesus, Mikah, you're white as a ghost." I try - and fail - to dispel the image from my mind, so I open my eyes, attempting to give myself something else to look at.

Red is quick to distract me. "You alright *mo chara*?"

My lips turn up slightly at his use of Irish and English together. "I think so." Is all I can manage to say at this point.

"I have some jeans and a t-shirt for you in the car if you'd like?" Red asks. I just nod. "Alright, I'll be right back. Anything else?"

"Coffee would be great. Thanks." I look up at him. There is pity on his face, and though the look doesn't bother me, I can understand now why Vivienne would see that look and hate it.

"Sure thing." He turns and walks out of the room.

Looking through the glass at the nurse's station reveals that nothing has changed. Though I can't see everything, I can see that line number four, Vivienne's line, still says she's in surgery with Dr. Alston.

Despair washes over me in a rush. Come on, damn it. Something. Anything.

Twelve

A few minutes later, Red returns with a bag containing a pair of jeans, a gray t-shirt and my sneakers.

"Will you stay here? Wait until I get back?"

"Of course, sir," he says with a smile.

I give him a half-hearted lift of the corner of my mouth and head toward the desk.

"We haven't heard anything yet, Mr. Blake," says the young blond nurse behind the desk.

"I figured as much. But I need to change my clothes. Is there a restroom I can change in?"

"Not really, but room three—" she points to her left and down the hall "—is empty. Feel free to use it to change and freshen up."

"Thanks," I say.

As I pass the whiteboard, I glance just to make sure that nothing has changed. Nope. Still says *Callahan, OR 4, general/personal, Alston, 2 hrs.*

So much for two hours; it's been nearly three.

I pick up my pace, wanting to be back in the waiting room when Dr. Alston comes out.

Room three is obviously a recovery room: There's no bed, but there are several machines that appear to be turned off. I can't help but notice the ultrasound machine in the corner opposite everything else. The room smells like bleach and sanitizer. Fresh. I silently hope this is not where she will go when she's out of surgery. She deserves better than this room.

I shake my head and get to work unbuttoning my shirt and pants and kicking off my shoes. Opening the bag reveals a stash of toiletries – shampoo, conditioner, shave gel, a razor, two combs, cologne and deodorant – and I smile a little at Red's foresight.

Once I'm down to my undershirt, boxer briefs and socks I head for the bathroom.

I take stock in the mirror. There are dark red to brown spots of varying sizes on the shoulder of my undershirt. It is also ripped in several places. My other shirt wasn't like this, was it? No doubt Red would have thrown a bigger fit about my being looked at had my shirt been ripped.

I turn around to pick it up to check, but before I can complete my turn, something on my back catches my eye. I turn my back to the mirror and look over my shoulder, and the emptiness I felt earlier disappears completely, replaced by the sense that someone is with me.

"Do not fret. You have done well, young angel. You knew I was here." It's the same voice as in the hallway.

"What is all over my back?" I stare blankly at the silver-gray tint to the back of my already gray shirt.

"Ah, young angel, it has begun."

"What, damn it? What is going on?" I nearly shout, and then quickly silence myself, hoping no one heard my outburst.

"Calm, Mikah. Remove your shirt and you shall see."

I reach for the hem and turn my head back toward the room before pulling my shirt over my head. I take a deep breath as the voice starts to sing.

Is the singing really necessary?

She laughs. "No, young one, it is not, but I am bored."

"Seriously?" I say out loud. "I'm on the verge of a damn freak-out and you're bored. Brilliant."

She laughs again. "Mikah, you will quickly see that I am bored constantly. You, young angel, are alive. Blood courses through your veins, your heart beats. But I, I am left here in whiteness for eternity. Yes, I get bored – very easily, mind you – and the only time I get to have any amount of fun at all is when I am in your head."

I shiver at the thought of this voice having a good time in my head. "How long have you been in my head without me knowing?" She laughs again. "This really isn't funny, Seraphina."

"You are right, Mikah. Getting your wings is serious business."

"My what?" I'm thrown. Wings? Real wings? "How am I supposed to go walking around with wings on my back?"

"Now we're getting somewhere." I feel an attitude shift in my head, almost like excitement. "Go ahead, take a look in the mirror. You will see."

I begin to turn my head and the excitement bubbles. But it's not my excitement.

Seriously?

"Oh, come on. This is fun," she says, and now I can hear the excitement in her voice.

I try to shake her excitement off and turn my head a little bit more. I don't know what to expect, and I'm freaking out about what I'm going to see. *Good grief, stop being such a baby.*

"I agree."

"Would you stop that?"

She giggles. Out of all the angels in...wherever she is...I get stuck with the damn comedian.

"Hmph," she huffs.

Finally, I continue turning my head until I'm able to see my back.

Thirteen

There on my back, in vivid detail, are two beautiful wings with white, gray, and silver feathers. They are nothing but a flat, two-dimensional image, yet they seem to be alive.

My knees give out and I tumble to the floor, breathing heavily.

She is quiet for a few moments while this all soaks in. "The legend is true, an angel are you," she finally says.

I'm unable to speak aloud. *You can say that again. But me? Why me?*

"Because, young angel, it is who you are. It is who your mother was and is to this day; though she never grew wings while she was alive, she is one of us now."

Can I see her?

"Perhaps in time. She is one of our *máithreacha*, who are very busy."

Máithreacha? *Mothers?*

"Yes. They are second in command to our *máthair go léir*. Your mother was the one who spoke to you first and, as you no doubt guessed, she can be a bit testy."

How did I not recognize her voice? It's a voice that plays in my head constantly whenever I do something profoundly stupid.

"If you think about that long enough, I'm sure you can figure that out."

Suddenly I understand: She didn't want me to know it was her.

"Or perhaps you didn't recognize her because you were not thinking of her that way."

I think back to the voice in the chapel. I still can't hear it as my mother's, but I take Seraphina's word for it.

Anxiety washes over me as I contemplate the responsibilities that might come with these wings. *What happens now?*

"We wait until the right time and place for you to take control of them. Then you can learn to use them to your advantage."

I let out a rushed breath, thanking the stars that I can deal with this later. Given that there was blood on my shirt but no pain, I'm not quite convinced that I'm not dreaming.

In the instant that thought crosses my mind, sharp, white-hot pain races around my body, and I fall flat on my back.

Alright I get it; I'm not dreaming!

The pain stops, and I regain control of my own body and senses. I stand up and look into the mirror, this time facing forward. Where the blood had soaked into my t-shirt on my shoulder and chest, there is...nothing. Absolutely nothing there.

"You're a fast healer, young angel."

"The door at her apartment. The one I shattered with my shoulder. It caused all that blood, but where...where are the cuts?" I whisper.

"As I said, you are a fast healer."

"I... What? Jesus. Is there anything else you want to tell me about before I discover it for myself and go ballistic?"

"You've already had enough for today. Get dressed and go back to the waiting room. I will do what I can to leave you alone for the rest of the day."

I nod, and once again the emptiness returns. The hum in my back disappears. I flex my shoulder, testing its strength, but it feels fine. Completely normal. Which ranks up there with talking to angels in my head in my list of strange things that have happened to me today.

Fourteen

As I walk past the nurse's station, I glance at the board and it's changed: Vivienne's name is no longer listed on the forth line. I jog back to the waiting room.

Stepping into the room, I notice Red in the corner, reading a magazine, and a family sitting opposite him. I walk straight up to him. He puts down his magazine.

"Has Dr. Alston been here yet?"

"No, but the nurse came in and said that she was out of surgery and the doctor would be in as soon as she could."

I let out a rush of breath as a weight lifts from my shoulders. She's out of surgery. "Oh, thank stars."

He chuckles a bit at my expression, something he does all the time. I explained to him once why I have a hard time thanking God or some other higher power for the things that happen to people. After you've lost your mother, your father and your two brothers and you have a sister that is lost inside her own head, it's hard to be thankful for the things that God does.

I take a seat, though I know it's going to be pointless; I'm beyond keyed up, and I feel like pacing again. But I don't want to freak out the family sitting across from us.

What a damn mess today has turned into. First Vivienne, and then angels start talking to me in my head. Now my back. How in the hell does this stuff happen to me? Why me? I cannot seem to find a reason for it. I grew up believing that to become an angel you had to die first, be pure of self, and follow a spiritual path. All of these things I'm not.

Wings? Really? How on earth am I supposed to hide these things? What in the world is going to happen to me – physically and mentally?

I've only been sitting here for a few minutes when the skin on my back starts to crawl. I shiver and grab the back of my neck, massaging it, hoping that the contact will lessen the sensation. But instead, a strong sense of unease comes over me. I feel restless. I need to move, be doing something – anything but sitting here idle and waiting. But I can't make myself move.

"Err, you alright, lad?"

I turn to look at Red. His eyes flare momentarily and there is an instance of unease that bounces off of him. Jesus.

"What's wrong?"

"Your eyes, they're..." he pauses, and instinctively I shut them tight. "They're almost black." Shit.

Seraphina, damn it, where are you?

"I don't know," I answer him.

In the next instant, my body tenses and I feel a warmth radiate through my body and dissipate instantly. "I'll be right back." I get up and start for the door and the hallway. I walk past the nurse's station, back to the room I just came from, and quickly lock the door behind me. I head straight to the bathroom mirror.

I shudder at the sight of nearly black eyes.

"Oh dear." I hear Seraphina's voice.

"What in the world is going on?" I say out loud.

"You're in the hospital."

"Yeesss..." I say, trying hard not to be sarcastic with her.

"Is your skin crawling?"

I just nod, not able to answer because I can't stop staring at the solid black of my eyes.

"Someone near you, not known to you, has died."

My heart sinks momentarily. "So why am I reacting this way?"

"Because the person who has died has been taken by evil."

I feel a tightness in my shoulders that pushes outward.

"Oh, no, you don't. Not here. You'll rip your shirt."

"What?" I say sharply and turn quickly. In the mirror I can see two rather sharp, knobby points beneath my shirt, up near the tops of my shoulders. Right...where...

Fifteen

I feel my head start to spin. Seraphina begins to chant in a tongue I do not recognize. An ache spreads across my back, and I can feel my shirt shift as it settles back against my skin.

I brace myself against the sink, my stomach rolling. I feel like retching.

"Eventually, young angel, you will be able to control this yourself. I've put your angel soul to rest. It won't last forever, but it will be enough to allow you to calm down."

Thank you.

I'm so confused. All of this is just...it's too much. The wings, the changes – it's all so overwhelming. I haven't even begun to process it all, and I feel like my life is no longer my own.

"I understand that this is difficult for you."

Gah! Stop that. It's hard to think when you're in there listening to everything I think.

She laughs. "Yes, it can be a bit obnoxious, but it is also something to take comfort in. I am here to guide and teach you."

I know, but it's hard. I know the story and I know the poem, but I feel like I'm missing something. I feel like I need my head examined.

"Believe me, young one, when the time is right, you will know. When you accept your destiny, you will be taught all you need to know."

How will I know when I'm ready?

"When your mind is free. Now go. Your young lady needs you."

The emptiness returns, and I shiver. How am I supposed to accept this?

I slowly turn around to face the mirror, hoping that what she has said is right. I slowly open my eyes. Back to blue and green. I let out a rushed breath.

Now how on earth do I explain this to Red?

I walk slowly back down the hall toward the waiting room. Anxiety knots my stomach, but – I suddenly realize – the buzz in my back is gone. I flex my shoulders. My back is no longer tight, but loose and normal. Weird.

In the waiting room, Red is still in his same chair, reading the same magazine. I take my seat next to him.

"Feel better?" he asks as he puts down the magazine.

"Much," I say back.

He doesn't press for more information. I gather that he has been around me long enough to not ask questions.

"You can take off," I tell him.

"I'd like to stay. Make sure you're alright."

I shrug my shoulders. "Alright."

I notice that we are alone once again in the waiting room and outside the door there are several nurses gathered around the desk. Looking beyond them to the board, I see that the majority of the rooms are now empty.

"What is taking so long?" I ask aloud, not expecting an answer.

"The nurse came in about three minutes ago, said Dr. Alston was on her way."

"Finally."

I sit back and pull my ankle up onto my knee. I put my head back against the wall behind me and close my eyes.

And instead of seeing the black of my eyelids, my vision shifts…

Sixteen

The image is white but three-dimensional, almost like a room. Yes, now I can make out a couch and table in front of me, but they too are as white as the walls and the floor. I can see something in the distance – not white, but dressed in white – coming closer to me. My heart rate speeds up, not in fear but in anticipation. Whatever is coming toward me is something I want, something I need. But what?

I watch as the figure draws closer. I feel myself growing restless with excitement. It seems to be taking forever, and I want to walk toward the figure, but I can't. I'm frozen in place.

The figure draws nearer still, and finally I'm beginning to make out who is walking toward me. The bright red, curly, flowing hair belongs to Vivienne.

"Mikah." It's not the voice I was expecting, not Vivienne's voice. "Mikah." It's Red. I feel his arm nudge mine. My eyes fly open. "Dr. Alston's coming."

"What?" Shit. I rub my eyes, hoping to dispel the image, but as soon as my eyes close again, I see her. She hasn't moved.

I open my eyes again to the drab carpet of the waiting room, blink a few times and stand up. "How long was I out?" I ask Red.

"About three minutes."

"Well shit. I feel like I was out for hours." That is an understatement. Red just laughs.

"Nah, you're alright," he says.

I turn my head to look out the door. Dr. Alston is standing at the nurse's desk. It looks as though she's signing something. I start walking toward the door, but she holds her palm up toward me, gesturing for me to stop, then quickly puts up one finger.

Gah! Doesn't she know this is killing me?

Seventeen

I start to pace: toward Red, back toward the door, and back toward Red again. Come on, damn it. This is killing—

"Mikah."

My head snaps up and I turn around to face the tall, leggy blond. Dr. Alston. Under different circumstances I might have found her attractive. In fact, at some point I probably did. But that was before I met Vivienne.

"What's taken so long?" I ask her sharply. Too sharply. "Sorry."

"It's alright, I know you're anxious." I nod. "It's taken so long because we needed to do a post-op CAT scan. I wanted to have those results before I came to talk to you."

"And those are what, exactly?"

"I'll get there. First, she is out of surgery. The next twenty-four hours are critical, so we have her in a medically induced coma."

I feel my eyes flare. I'm instantly worried about what happened earlier. I take quick stock of my body, but nothing has changed.

202

"We were able to repair her shattered rib and her lung, but she has some significant swelling in her brain and we weren't able to do anything to relieve the pressure. However, the post-op CAT scan showed some improvement since the first one we did. Which is a good sign. Keeping her sedated will mean better chances for a faster recovery. We will do another scan tomorrow morning to see how the swelling is doing. If it has gone down some more, we may be able to gauge how much longer we'll need to keep her in a coma until the swelling is gone completely."

I'm forcing each breath in and out of my body as she is telling me this, trying desperately to soak it all in. "Can I see her?" I ask shakily.

"Yes."

I start to move toward the door.

"I'm not done."

I stop and turn back to her.

"She is being moved to a private room upstairs. A cot is being brought in. I'm assuming you will refuse to leave her until she's awake?" I nod. "Okay, so let them get her moved and settled."

"What about the baby?" I say, breathless.

"Relax, Mikah. As I said, the next twenty-four hours are critical. We won't know anything definite for a couple of days, but I can tell you that there is a very strong heartbeat and we are monitoring for any distress."

It just became a little easier to breathe. I've yet to figure out why I have such an attachment to this baby, but I do.

"Anything else?" I ask.

"Medically, no, not right now. Other than she has a broken wrist and her shoulder has been set. It is in a sling and strapped across her body to prevent any movement. It is also acting as double duty for her ribs."

I remember her telling me this before, but it still strikes me dumb at the brutality. I haven't even wanted to imagine what he did besides cut and beat her, but I guess my face betrays the unasked question.

"She wasn't raped." I fall into the nearest chair. "Judging by the severe bruising on her ankles and wrists, and by those around her neck, I imagine that was the intention, but we've checked her for any internal damage and there are no recent signs."

My head falls into my hands. "Jesus Christ, what has she been through?"

"As a medical professional, I can't tell you that. The only reason I'm telling you this much is because I know that her next of kin is her mother, who isn't of sound mind, and..." She pauses. I look at her to continue. "When she was here last time, when you brought her in." I nod. "She listed you as her emergency contact on the paperwork I left for her. Amanda, my nurse, found it in her room after she was discharged."

My heart skips a few beats, and I know I stop breathing. I have no clue why something as inconsequential as leaving my name as a point of contact has such a profound effect on me. Hell, I don't know much of anything anymore.

"She's broken, Mikah, and as much as I know you want to fix her, you need to talk to her first. Get to know her. Her physical history is telling. I have no doubt that if approached in the right fashion, she will open up and start talking to you. But don't push her," she says with a glare. I nod my understanding. "She's upstairs, top floor."

Immediately I stand and hold out my hand. She takes it. "Thank you," I say sincerely as I fight back the tears that threaten to spill over.

"My pleasure. Go. See her, be with her. I warn you though – she has a tube in her mouth, a machine is breathing for her, and she is very badly bruised up. And that is only what is starting to show now. So be ginger with her."

I nod solemnly and head for the door and the elevator to my right. As I push the up button, I sense Red approaching.

"Go home, *cara*. No need for you to be here," I say at the same time that he pushes the down button.

"I know."

"Thank you. I really appreciate you being here."

"I know. I'll be back around six with food. Here, take this." He hands me the duffle bag with my stuff in it. I take it from him. "Your chargers are in there, plus your laptop. Need anything else from home?"

I hear the ding of the elevator to my right and head toward it. "Right now, no. I will call if I think of something."

He nods as the doors slide open and I step in.

"Oh, call Detective Stevens for me. Tell him what Dr. Alston said and that if he needs me, he knows where to find me."

"Got it," he says as the doors close.

Eighteen

As I come around the corner from the elevator, I see two cops standing outside of a room. Neither is talking to the other, which I find strangely comforting. At least I know they're paying attention. The one closest to me turns in my direction as I approach.

"How can we help you?" he says.

"I'm Mikah Blake. I'm here to see Vivienne Callahan."

He nods in recognition of my name but turns to face me, feet apart, at the ready.

"I need to see some identification, please."

I'm not sure whether to be irritated or impressed by his question. I reach for my wallet, but it's not there. Damn it.

"It's in my bag," I say, letting him know that I need to reach into someplace he can't see.

"Mind if I check?" he asks.

I hold out the bag to him.

"Set it down, please, and take three steps back."

I seriously want to roll my eyes. I'm the last person they need to worry about. But I take a comfort in knowing that if I have to go through this much trouble, so will everyone else.

I take the three steps back plus one for good measure, trying not to seem as impatient as I feel. "It should be right on top," I say. "If it's not there, then it's in the long side pocket."

He begins opening up the zipper on the top. I can see when he opens it that my wallet is not there. My heart skips a beat. Crap, I could have sworn I put it in the main compartment.

He doesn't hesitate but goes straight into the side pocket. I can't see what he's seeing, but he puts his hand in and moves a few things around. "Is this it?" He looks up at me as he pulls out my black leather wallet.

"Yes, sir."

He stands back up, looking inside the wallet, glancing from me to the driver's license. "I need to search your bag, Mr. Blake."

"Whatever you need."

He bends back down and starts glancing through my bag. Nothing but a few articles of clothing and my shaving kit are inside. Laptop and cell phone chargers are also in there, but he seems satisfied at a cursory glance.

"Can you put your hands on the wall next to you?"

Oh for crying out loud. I turn toward the wall, put my hands up and spread my legs slightly. He comes up behind me and quickly pats down my under my arms and hips and runs his hands down the outside of my legs to my ankles and stands.

"Here's your wallet. As long as were here, we won't bother you again. Our shift changes at midnight. After that, make sure you have at least your wallet when you leave the room," he states matter-of-factly.

"How long will officers be posted here?" I ask.

"Until she is discharged or the suspect is caught, whichever comes first."

"Detective Stevens?"

He nods curtly. "He's pretty adamant about keeping her well-protected. From what I understand of the situation, I don't blame him for that."

I nod at him. "May I go in now?"

"Absolutely." He steps aside, and the other officer moves away from the door to allow me to pass.

I can't help but feel slightly grateful for their presence here. "Thank you, gentlemen," I say.

After all my eagerness to see her, I suddenly feel anxious.

As if in slow motion, I watch my hand reach for the door handle. Turn it. I hear and feel the click as it unlatches. I push, moving forward with the door. It feels like minutes before I clear the jamb and step into the room.

A curtain separates me from the rest of the room. I shut the door behind me. Soft lamp light comes through the curtain.

It takes a moment before I can make myself step past the curtain; after everything Dr. Alston told me about her condition, I'm afraid of what I'm going to see on the other side. Then the image of her walking toward me in the dream surfaces – Vivienne in a white gown, her vibrant red hair flowing over her shoulders. Beautiful.

I take a deep breath, reach for the curtain with my free hand and gingerly slide it back. I let out the breath I've been holding when I realize that I can't really see anything yet. There is a small hallway and the room opens up to the left.

I set my bag down along the wall opposite the bathroom and take a few steps forward. The room is decorated in pale blues with a flower wallpaper boarder at the top of the walls. The only furniture is a cherry wood cabinet, a roll-away bed with blankets and pillows on top, and Vivienne's bed.

As I take another step into the room, I hear the faint, rhythmic wheezing of pressurized air being forced through a tube, then sucked out again. In and out.

Suck it up, buttercup, I tell myself and take that last step to bring me around the corner of the short hallway so I can get a full view of the bed and Vivienne.

Nineteen

The bed is laid out flat, but she is turned slightly away from me. It only takes me a moment to realize it's because there's a pillow underneath her shoulder and arm, which allows her arm to rest on the pillow rather than being held by a sling.

Her gorgeous red hair is splayed out across the top of the bed, and I can see the tube going into her mouth. Her eyes are closed. Her face looks peaceful, relaxed.

She actually looks quite comfortable.

On closer inspection, I see the bruising around her neck that Dr. Alston was talking about, and my heart stutters. I see where they put the IV into her left arm, and further down, the deep purple bruising around her wrist. I just want to cry, an urge further aggravated by the constant pushing and pulling of air through the machine.

A small movement next to the bed catches my eye. Coming from a machine, below a monitor, is a long, narrow strip of paper that has piled up and curled around on itself. It looks like calculator tape. My eyes pop up to the machine it's coming from. A heart monitor line bounces quickly across the screen with the number one hundred fifty above it. To the right of the one hundred fifty is the name *Baby Callahan*.

The baby's heart rate is so fast. Is that normal? I have no idea. I remember it was fast before, but I didn't realize it would be that fast.

My eyes follow four thick black wires that disappear under the covers. On the other side of the bed from the fetal monitor are the IV machine, monitors for Vivienne, and a brown leather chair.

I walk around the bed and sit down. It's only about four thirty, but I'm exhausted. All the adrenaline of the day is more than my body can handle. Looking at Vivienne makes me ashamed of my own tiredness; she's been through far more today than I have.

God she looks so pale, fragile. She always looked fragile, but right now she looks so vulnerable to everything. But she has survived all this; I can never think of her as weak and vulnerable ever again. She is strong, and this woman has an amazing determination to survive. Compared to all I imagine she's been through, living through the deaths of my family members is nothing.

I lean forward and place my forehead on the bed railing. "Vivienne, I'm so sorry," I say. "I wish I'd gotten there faster. Or that I'd never let you go back to that apartment in the first place."

Beep, beep, beep.

The sound is coming from my right. I look up at the heart monitor, which shows a flat line sliding to the left of the screen followed by the up and downs of her heartbeat. Above the normal monitor line is an image. It is the same as what is scrolling along the bottom, except in the place of where there should have been two of her regular heartbeats, there is nothing but a flat line.

"Vivienne?"

A slow beat, then silence.

"Vivienne, can you hear me?"

Another slow beat.

"Vivienne, I'm here. I'm so, so sorry."

Silence.

My heart races, then the machine blips again and the heartbeat comes back strong. I can't help but smile. She knows I'm here. Whether it is a conscious thought or not, she knows.

I blink back the tears. I want to touch her, but I'm afraid to. It looks like everywhere hurts. I decide against it for now. But I do lower the bed rail so that it's not separating us, pull the chair closer to the bed, and put my head gently on the mattress near her shoulder. "I'm here, I won't leave." And I let my eyes slowly close.

Twenty

It doesn't take but a moment for the vision to return. A different white room this time; this one has two windows. But the scenery beyond them is little more than a white blur. Taking a moment to look around, I see that some other things have changed. There is a white vase on the white coffee table, filled with white flowers.

The only color is Vivienne's red, flowing hair as she continues to walk toward me. This time she is moving faster, but she's still so far away. I try once again to walk toward her but I can't; I'm rooted to the floor by some invisible force.

I watch as she comes closer and becomes clearer, more defined. I can make out some of the silver accents on her dress. Intricate designs on the white material. The dress is a plunging v-neck with a silver belt below her breasts. It flows out behind her as she walks. She looks beautiful with a white flower over her left ear. She smiles at me and my heart melts. I want to hold her so bad.

I put out my arms and notice that they are bare and more muscular than in real life. And there's an intricate tribal tattoo running along my right arm.

Where the hell did that come from? I look down at my body and see first that I'm shirtless and then that the tattoo continues onto my chest. I am wearing pants, thank God. White ones that almost look like pajamas.

I look back up at Vivienne. She's gotten a lot closer, but she is still a ways off. I flex my shoulders in impatience, and that's when I hear and feel it at the same time: a shifting on my back. I flex again, and Vivienne giggles.

My heads snaps up in her direction. She is covering her mouth with her hand in an attempt to stifle her laugh. I want to ask her what she is laughing at when I feel the movement again.

My stomach sinks. I'm not sure I'm ready for this, but I turn my head slowly to the right. I'm met with a wall of white feathers.

Instinctively I turn to better see it, but as I move, so does the wall of feathers. Damn it.

She laughs again.

"This is not funny," I say out loud.

She laughs again anyway.

I turn again, and still it moves with me. With my left hand I reach out, trying to grab it, to touch it. The moment my hand makes contact with the feathers, pure, undiluted pleasure courses through my body and I feel my knees buckle. I quickly pull my hand away and look back toward Vivienne.

She is pointing to my left so I turn in that direction. A mirror. How did I miss this before?

I look back at Vivienne. She points again, with more urgency, so I take a step toward the mirror. And another.

Shapes and colors begin to coalesce in the mirror with each passing step. I close my eyes, afraid of what I might see, and take three more steps.

"Mr. Blake."

I can't open my eyes.

"Mr. Blake." The voice comes again. Damn it, no.

Twenty-One

"Mikah." Again the voice comes. I slowly open my eyes. I'm back in the hospital room and a nurse wearing pale pink scrubs is standing over me.

"Huh?" I ask.

"Hi, Mr. Blake. Remember me?"

I look up into the soft round face of Vivienne's nurse from before. "Hi, Amanda."

"Hi there. I'm sorry to wake you, but we need to run some tests on Vivienne and shift her a little bit."

"Uh, sure." I stand up and push the chair back. "Can I stay?"

"Of course. Just step back, okay?"

I nod and step toward the foot of the bed. I notice that there is another nurse in the room with us. I rub my eyes to dispel the fog of sleep.

The moment I close my eyes, the dreaming sensation returns. I open them quickly, not wanting to slip back into that dream. Not just yet. I look at my right arm for the tattoo from the dream, but there is nothing there. I let out a long exhale.

Amanda and the other nurse go about their business. I watch as they check a couple of things on the monitors, but when they turn her onto her left side, my heart starts to race. Amanda holds her while the other nurse puts the stethoscope to Vivienne's back. She moves it around a couple of times and nods to Amanda, and they lay her back down.

The other nurse, whose name I can't see, continues to go about checking things as Amanda comes over to me.

"She's doing alright. Her vitals look good. You seem to have a profound effect on her heart when you're around." She smiles at me and I return a quizzical look. "Dr. Alston told me, and I can see the snap shot on the monitor." She smiles again. "Her lungs are clearing up, which is a good thing, and she doesn't seem to be in any pain right now." I nod. "Have you had dinner?"

I look at my watch. It's nearly six. "No, but Red should be bringing some food shortly. Thank you."

"Of course."

She turns to go back to the bed to finish up.

"Oh, I almost forgot," I say. "The number over on that monitor. Is that the baby's heart rate?"

She looks over to the monitor and back at me. "It sure is."

"Is that...normal?"

She smiles. "That is a great number to have up there. Babies' hearts beat far faster than ours do. The monitor will go off here and at the nurse's station if the rate drops below one thirty five. Which is still in the normal range, but we want to keep a very close eye on it."

I nod. I'm not normally this speechless when it comes to things, but all this medical stuff is so foreign to me.

"If the heart rate drops, it may also be a sign that Vivienne is in distress."

"Okay. This is all so out of my area of expertise." I feel helpless right now, and asking these questions is the only thing I can think of that might help me feel more in control of a situation I clearly have no control over.

"That's why we're here, Mr. Blake," the nurse behind Amanda says.

"Thank you," I say. They both gather up their equipment and head for the door.

"Do you need anything, Mr. Blake?"

"Mikah. And no, I'm fine. Thank you."

"Of course, Mikah. If that changes, go ahead and press the button on the remote on the bed and we'll do what we can."

"Thanks again."

She nods and ducks out the door.

I look back at Vivienne. This is going to be a very long road, and I am not a very patient person. It nearly killed me to give Vivienne the space she wanted after the last time we were here, and the only reason I did it was because I knew that I'd pushed her beyond her limits. After leaving her room that day, I researched post-traumatic stress disorder and, while I'm no expert, I see now what I did wrong. Given the chance again, I won't make the same mistake twice.

Although I'm still tired, and on top of that have a burning need to see what will happen next in the vision, I decide that it's best not to shut my eyes yet. I'm pretty sure Red will be here before long, and I'd much rather have some uninterrupted time to see where this is going.

I make a quick trip to the bathroom and then grab my laptop and head back to the chair, placing my computer between me and the armrest, facing Vivienne. She looks the same: peaceful.

When I gently touch the back of her hand, I'm momentarily taken aback by how warm her skin feels, but that is more than likely a good thing. Once the shock wears off, I notice that there is an unfamiliar pulse that runs through my body. But this time it's not from my back; it's from my heart.

A couple of weeks ago, this beautiful woman waltzed into my life. A life I'm not sure I'm familiar with anymore. Nothing is as it seemed. I'm not sure how I feel about all this angel nonsense, but I have the distinct feeling that I don't have a say in the matter.

The unwelcome realization hits me: If I want to be with Vivienne, I'll have to tell her about this angel business. What if she thinks I'm crazy? What if she doesn't want anything to do with me?

I sink back into the chair, staring hard at her beautiful, bright red, curly hair. Her face. What I wouldn't give to see those beautiful, ice-blue eyes, warm and full of wonder.

What am I bringing her into? What if what I'm facing is too dangerous for her? What if I'm leading her down a path that she isn't meant to go?

I can't stay away from her – that much is obvious – and more than that, I've been charged with protecting her. How on earth am I supposed to do that?

Twenty-Two

A sudden knock on the door causes me to jump clean out of my chair. I'm on my feet, fists clenched at my side, but the absence of the buzz in my back does not go unnoticed as the door clicks open.

"Mikah," says a male voice – one that is familiar, but in my moment of panic, I can't place it.

"Yeah!" I say, clipped.

"It's Detective Stevens. Can I come in? I'm off duty. I came by to check on you and to see Vivienne." His voice is calm, casual, almost friendly.

"Come in."

I look down at Vivienne and become conscious once again of the sucking and pulling of the ventilator. She hasn't changed; she's still sitting there, empty.

"My God." I hear him exhale, and I look to my left. Detective Stevens is wearing blue jeans and a navy blue MPD t-shirt, tucked in. I notice he is without his gun. I turn back to Vivienne and take my seat again.

"Have you captured Riley?" I ask. I'm pretty sure I know the answer to that question, but I have to ask it anyway.

"Not that I should be telling you this, but no. We have not."

I bristle at this. "I can be a very valuable asset in your search for him. It's to both our benefit for you to share information with me."

"I'm not here to argue or pick a fight, Blake. I came to see Vivienne. Whether you believe it or not, I care about her," he says. I can hear the sadness in his voice.

"You care, but yet you let this happen?" I ask, still looking at Vivienne. It's unfair and I know it, but seeing her like this....

"Blake, we both know how this happened, and I can't turn back time, I can't bring my officer back any more than I can make Vivienne's injuries go away." The more he talks, the more sadness filters into his voice.

"I know," I say. I lean forward, putting my elbows on my knees and my head in my hands.

Neither one of us says anything else for a few minutes. Finally I stand and gesture for him to sit: my peace offering. I go to the opposite side of the bed and sit by her feet, careful not to jostle her. I gently rub along her leg and fight the urge to smile as the heart monitor goes nuts.

"She's like a daughter to me," Stevens says. "After seeing her in the hospital the last time, I did my best to keep tabs on her. I spoke with Al."

"Who's Al?"

"The gentleman who drives the bus that she normally takes home after work. I told him to keep a good eye on her because I wasn't always able to do so."

"How did Rebecca Black get to her?"

I'm genuinely curious, not accusing, but his head shoots up and he looks hard into my eyes. "We weren't looking for her. Didn't know we needed to be looking for her. It wasn't until one of our drug task force guys noticed Riley coming and going from a well-known drug neighborhood that we started to get suspicious that he was up to no good. At the time that Rebecca was in Vivienne's diner, Riley was in North Minneapolis. We had no reason to suspect that he would send someone else to talk to her." He takes a deep breath and rubs his face.

"The task force was working on trying to catch him on drug-related charges. They had intel on Riley that pointed to him wheeling and dealing. They tried a couple of times to pull him over or pick him up, but each time they had nothing to go on, and the worst we could charge him with was speeding." He rubs at the stubble on his chin. "We lost track of him the night of Rebecca's murder and haven't been able to pinpoint him since."

Twenty-Three

The Detective finally leaves when Red arrives with food. Red hands me a large, surprisingly heavy picnic basket. "Celeste insisted that you would prefer this to something from a restaurant, which is why I'm so late, but I can go get you something else. I don't mind at all."

Puzzled, I open the basket to find French bread, a large bag of potato chips, two containers of fresh fruit, and a container of her amazing chicken salad. I smile.

"I guess maybe I was wrong," Red adds when he sees my smile.

"This," I say, pointing to the basket, "is beyond comparison. No restaurant food could come close."

Further exploration of the basket uncovers a thermos of coffee - no doubt the way I like it - and two cans of Mountain Dew. I shake my head at the latter: my one not-so-healthy vice in this world. There are also napkins, plates, and utensils.

"She's thorough," I mutter as I close up the basket.

"That she is. You really should eat something," Red says, eying the basket as I put it on the floor.

I nod absently and take my seat back on the bed at Vivienne's feet. "I will."

Zoey Derrick

"Yes, sir. I don't mean to meddle."

I roll my eyes and shake my head at him. As annoying as it can be sometimes, his so-called meddling is what gets me places, allows me to do things, and makes sure that everything runs smoothly. "I enjoy your meddling, Red. It's alright."

"Has there been any change?" he asks, looking at Vivienne.

Shaking my head, I say, "No, but Amanda - one of her nurses - was here again about twenty minutes ago. Said that Dr. Alston will be up shortly. I'll try and eat after she leaves."

"Fair enough." Red smiles, but I can tell he is watching me carefully. Looking for something, or making sure I'm really as okay as I say I am. "Do you need anything else?"

I quickly run through a list of possibilities. "Besides her better, I'm not sure."

"Understandable, though I cannot help with that. As much as I would like to."

"I know. I'm alright for now."

"Very well. I'm only a phone call away. I'll come back in the morning."

I look at my watch and realize that it is after eight. "Alright, we'll see you in the morning then." I nod at him.

He nods back, takes a look a Vivienne, then turns and silently slips from the room.

I stay sitting on the bed with my hand gently rubbing along her leg and watch the monitor. The longer I keep my hand on her leg, the less crazy the monitor gets. Which is probably a good thing because I don't need anyone telling me that I can't touch her.

The thought sends a shiver through my body, and suddenly my back has come alive once again.

This time, it's different. My emotions are heightened by a desire that I haven't felt in a long time. I try in vain to shake it off, but I can't. My heart aches with a need to be near her, to hold her, to touch her, to—

Oh, no, you don't.

I stand and make a beeline for the bathroom, quickly shutting the door behind me. I grip the sides of the sink hard, hoping that the pain in my hands will drive away the unexpected, unwelcome erection.

"Damn it," I curse under my breath, gritting my teeth and squeezing my eyes shut. But my back vibrates with excitement as I grow harder and the need grows stronger. If this desire doesn't die down soon on its own, I'm going to have to make it go away.

When I finally open my eyes and look into the mirror in front of me, they are electric blue, intense with arousal.

I feel the back of my shirt push outwards, away from my body. I reach for the hem and pull it up over my head.

Placing my hands back on the counter, I lean forward, eyes closed, trying to think about anything nonsexual. But everything I think of turns sexual in some form or another. Planes, cars and trains? Excellent places to have.... I drop that thought quickly, as it's only egging me on. The stock market? Up and.... Nope. Work? Nope. Vivienne? Hell, no.

Little by little, I can feel my body calming. Without Seraphina around, I don't know how else to do this. I quickly shift the image in my head to that of Rebecca

Black and the video I watched this morning, but before it gets too involved, that sense of fullness associated with Seraphina comes over me and I hear her voice, singing the same gentle melody as before.

Thank stars. It took you long enough.

"Now, now, young angel. I was giving you a chance to rectify the situation yourself, which you had obviously started to do so well. Not the images I would have chosen to use to calm myself, but it worked nonetheless. Now to settle those wings of yours."

My head flies up and my eyes open. After I removed my shirt, I became more interested in calming my erection than the possibility that my wings were coming out. I lean forward slightly so that I can see over my shoulders, and I can instantly see what she's talking about. Coming from my back are the white tips of feathered wings. My eyes widen in shock as I watch them slowly retreat. Once my back becomes flat again, I feel a light clicking within my body. A lockdown on my back.

Thank you again.

"In due time you will learn to manage this yourself. I'm rather impressed that you were able to stop the full spread from happening. Though I would imagine the time is coming where we need to work on letting them out and locking them down, provided you want to stay where you are."

"What is that supposed to mean?"

"You will need to learn to control your emotions, not allow your inner angel to get the best of you. If you don't, you will expose yourself to the world and to the demonic ones who surround you. One thing to remember is that instances of heightened emotion –

whether it is happiness, sadness, or carnal desire –
will cause your body to react differently." I watch in
the mirror as my eyes flash to black and back to their
normal greenish-blue again.

"Relax, young angel. They cannot harm you unless
you expose yourself to them."

Knowing that certain highly emotional situations
could bring about this kind of reaction will help me
better understand what can trigger an unexpected
response. Knowing this will help me be more
conscious of my reactions.

The thrum in my back flares and settles just as fast.

"Your doctor friend is coming," Seraphina adds,
and she quickly retreats.

I take a big, long breath and reach for my shirt.

Twenty-Four

I step out of the bathroom to find Dr. Alston and Amanda looking over Vivienne.

"Hi," I say and try to smile as Dr. Alston looks up.

"Hey, Mikah. We're just checking her vitals and making some notes. Amanda tells me that Vivienne is responding to your touch?"

I blush. "My voice too, I think."

Amanda lets out a snort. My head turns in her direction and then follows her line of sight to the monitor.

"I'll say." Amanda retorts. "That is by far the strangest thing I've ever seen. What makes it even stranger is that you hardly know this girl and vice versa, and she has this completely subconscious reaction to your presence. But it also means that things are not as damaged up there as we first thought."

"What does that mean?" I ask.

"It means that we could probably bring her out of the coma right now and yield a pretty positive result." Dr. Alston says very matter of fact.

"So why don't you?"

She smiles back at me. "Well, two reasons. One, the coma is keeping her in one place and allowing her shoulder, lung, ribs and wrist to heal better. And two, I think we should wait at least another twelve hours, run a CT and make sure that we're not jumping the gun on the swelling."

"Alright," I say. I heard what she said, but I'm not sure it is registering properly. I want Vivienne to wake up sooner rather than later, but it really needs to be on her terms. But I also feel a little relieved that, with any luck, she will be awake sometime tomorrow. "What else can I do for her?"

"Well, nothing really. Sit here and talk to her. Or go home and get some rest." Seeing me scowl at that second option, Dr. Alston adds, "Or eat something, take a walk, or find something to read or talk to her about. Regardless, if she is having that kind of subconscious reaction to your presence, I wouldn't recommend leaving. It's obvious that it is helping her."

"I feel so helpless though."

"That makes two of us. All we can do right now is wait. It sucks, I know, but all her vitals are good, and the baby is doing great, all things considered. Some more time to heal is all she needs right now, and that is something we can all give her."

I nod in agreement, though I'm not sure this conversation has made me feel any better.

After a couple more minutes, they finish up. Dr. Alston and Amanda are leaving the hospital for the night, but the nighttime nurses have specific instructions to call immediately if anything changes. I'd honestly be surprised if Dr. Alston is really leaving the hospital instead of taking up residence in her office.

Once I make up my cot, I look dubiously at the basket Red brought in and decide that I can't really eat anything right now. The idea of having a meal, here in Vivienne's room without her, is unsettling.

I sit back down in the chair next to her bed. Resting my head next to hers, I start to play with a strand of her hair. I start thinking about the last time we were here. And how we got here.

I don't know what came over me that day, but something kept nagging at me to get her to a hospital, have her checked out, make sure she was okay. I try not to smile at the memory. She is like a kitten that thinks she's a tiger, and it is one of the many things that attracted me to her.

I never expected her to kick me out that day. Again, my need to protect her overcame any other rational emotion, and I pushed too hard.

The minutes that followed killed me. I paced around the emergency room, hoping that maybe she would ask me to come back. Then I saw Alston and a couple other nurses running toward her room. When I got back to the door, a nurse stopped me from going in. I paced. I hadn't a clue what was going on.

Eventually Dr. Alston emerged and explained what happened and what they were going to do at that point. I felt better knowing she was doing better, but guilt quickly set in because I realized that I was the cause of that. I don't know what set her off – whether it was a trigger or me leaving.

"I'm here. I'm not going anywhere," I say as I lift my head and gently kiss her forehead. "I miss your baby-blue eyes. Come back to me. Please."

Twenty-Five

I stay by her side for another minute or so, kiss her forehead once more, then grab my phone from the bedside table and go sit on the cot.

Turning my phone back on – I'd turned it off when I came into Viv's room – I silence the ringer and check my email. There are several emails from Jack, ranging in subject from video footage to other, non-Riley related information. There's one from my assistant, letting me know she's cleared my calendar for the next three weeks, and an email from Sydney – who is not only one of my business partners but also a very good friend – letting me know she's got things covered in my absence.

A second email from Sydney captures my attention. The subject line reads *Elton Bennett.*

Mikah,

Elton is on a warpath – he's attempting to destroy MSBE. We're choosing, at this time, to maintain a low profile and let him run his mouth in hopes that he digs his own grave. I have John and Phil working on maintaining our relationships with our top clients. The remaining managers are working on the rest. The general consensus among our top companies is that Elton is an idiot. However, we've prepared our own team to defend at a moment's notice, and legal's working on a defamation suit against him.

Will keep you updated as more develops.

Regards,
Sydney A. Harper
Sr. Vice President
M.S. Blake Enterprises
Minneapolis, MN

I shake my head. Elton is a ruthless businessman who will stop at nothing to get what he wants. Right now, what he wants is to save his own ass. Without MSBE, the bulk of the funding for three very large, very expensive condo projects in Minneapolis is gone.

His phone call earlier today proves that he's pissed and will do whatever it takes. But does that include murder? Is it really possible that he is behind his son in all this mess?

I shake my head. I don't want to think about all that right now.

I put down the phone and look over toward Vivienne lying in the bed, seeming peaceful. I wish I knew whether or not she is resting comfortably.

I've been tuning out her ventilator, but now it catches my attention once again. I look over towards it. It's an innocent machine, but I have an image of something that looks a little like a cloth accordion lengthening and contracting as it presses air in and pulls it out. The sound is mesmerizing, and before I know it I'm lulled into a trance-like state, dreaming once again.

233

Twenty-Six

The air is shifting around me, light and gentle across my overly sensitive skin. I open my eyes to find myself back in the white room, looking through a tall, narrow window at a man with tanned skin, black hair and electric blue eyes.

On his back are a massive pair of pure-white, feathered wings in full extension. The wingspan alone has to be eight feet, if not more. The right-hand side of his chest and his right shoulder and arm are covered in an intricate black tribal tattoo, similar to the one I saw previously.

I stumble backwards as I realize it's not a window. It's a full-length mirror, and the winged, tattooed man is me. I watch my reflection try to regain its balance. The weight of the wings on my back finally registers, and I'm briefly knocked around as I try to stabilize.

"Easy there, angel. You're alright." This beautiful voice coming from behind me can only belong to one person. I feel my knees buckle again. This time, I'm a little more prepared for it and I don't lose my balance.

"What's happening to me?" I ask, but she doesn't answer.

I flex my shoulders and the wings shift. I try, for curiosity's sake, to pinpoint the muscles in my back where the wings are. I find them, push them downward, and instantly the wings follow suit. They've gone down enough that I can see Vivienne standing behind me. Instinctively I shrug, and the wings come back up, taking her out of my line of sight. She giggles behind me and I smile. Repeating the same motions as before, I lower them again and pull inward, and the wings fold in. Vivienne is looking at me appraisingly for the work I've managed to accomplish. I smile at her.

Her face lights up and I start to turn toward her, but she stops me by saying, "No, no. Keep facing the mirror. Keep practicing."

My heart sinks. I want to hold her, to touch her, but instead I do as she's asked and turn back toward the mirror. I push the wings back out, marveling at the fluid motion and at the force of air that comes from them.

"Can I fly?" I ask her.

"Yes, in time." Her voice is soft, approving, and much closer than before.

Then it happens – so fast that I'm not entirely sure what's happened – but my wings shiver, sending a rapid pulse of pleasure through my body. "Ahh!" I moan. And the sensation comes again. My wings go limp, and through hooded eyes, I see Vivienne standing behind me. She is smiling, happy.

She strokes my wing again. I don't know how much I can hold back and I moan again. She moves away - I feel the air shift in her wake - and I'm lost and empty without her touch. I close my eyes.

A warm, soft finger trails along my jaw. I lift my chin. Her touch has left a searing desire in its path.

"Keep them closed," she says softly.

"But I need to see you," I say, hoping the need in my voice conveys the feelings running through me. Each emotion, every sensation, is heightened beyond anything I've ever felt before.

I feel a whoosh of air go past me. My wings? But they're in the same position, still unmoving.

"Open your eyes, Mikah." Her voice is sweet and warm. I attempt to obey, but I can't seem to bring my eyes to open.

"Mikah." I feel a nudge at my shoulder. "Come on, Mikah, wake up."

Still I can't open my eyes. "Mikah." A deeper tone.

Twenty-Seven

My eyes fly open to see Red standing over me, and I jump and slide away from him. Sweat rolls off my forehead.

"It's alright, lad, it's just me."

I plop back down onto my pillow. "You really need to stop waking me up," I grumble.

He laughs. "Interrupting a good dream?"

"Yes." I groan.

I want to shout at him, but it seems that this dream is going to continue until it draws to its conclusion, so eventually, when I close my eyes again, with any luck it will come back.

"Sorry. Dr. Alston will be here in a couple of minutes. You've been sleeping like the dead, it's nearly ten in the morning." Holy shit. I can't believe I've been asleep for nearly twelve hours. "They've already taken Vivienne for a CT and some additional tests and brought her back again. The doctor will be here soon to talk to you."

"Shit." I climb out of bed quickly, looking in Vivienne's direction as I stumble to the bathroom.

When I come out a few minutes later after having freshened up as best I could with cold water from the sink, Red has made up the cot, so I take a seat on the end of Vivienne's bed.

Red hands me a travel mug and I take a sip.

"Thanks for the coffee."

"Any change?" Red asks, gesturing toward Vivienne.

"Not that I'm aware of. They didn't wake me, so I'm assuming no." I take another sip of coffee. "What time did you get here?"

"Around seven. I figured you wouldn't have slept much last night and that you would be awake. It was a few minutes after that they came for Vivienne and took her for tests. I stayed because I figured if you woke up you'd likely panic, and I didn't want you freaking out the staff. They only brought her back about thirty minutes ago."

I let out a soundless chuckle and bob my head. "You do know me well, don't you."

My back buzzes quickly and calms just as fast, just like it did yesterday when Dr. Alston was coming. Let's see if it is the same as before.

After a few heartbeats the door clicks open, followed by the clacking of heels on the linoleum floor.

"Good morning, Mikah. Red." She is wearing a black dress, black nylons and black heels.

I cock an eyebrow at her.

"I had a private appointment this morning and haven't changed." She laughs a bit.

I smirk at her and she smiles a little wider.

"So what's the verdict, Doc?"

"Well, the swelling in her brain has completely diminished, which is beyond what we thought would happen. Also, her lung and her shoulder look great. I'm a little perplexed about her wrist, though."

I raise my eyebrows at her. "How so?"

"Well, there seems to be very little sign of swelling underneath the brace she's in. It's not normal." She shrugs like it's no big deal.

"Maybe she's a fast healer."

She snorts. "Maybe, but this is beyond fast healing." She just shrugs again, and I make a mental note to ask Seraphina about Dr. Alston.

"Ask me what?" It's not Dr. Alston speaking now.

Where'd you come from?

"I've been here the whole time. I came in sometime around the time Red showed up."

How'd you not hear my question then?

She sighs. "Because I wasn't paying attention."

Alright then, give me a minute.

"So what now, Doctor?"

"Well, we are going to pull back on her sedation and bring her out of the coma slowly. We will keep her on the ventilator until all the sedation medicine has stopped, which will take a couple of hours."

"Why so long?"

"We want to make sure that she doesn't come out of it too fast, it can cause undue harm or stress to her and her body. Doing it slowly allows her a better chance to come out of it on her own. When she's ready."

I nod slowly at her, trying to process all of this. "So now what do we do?"

"I'm going to go push a few buttons, and we wait," she says with some hope in her voice.

"What are the risks of bringing her out now instead of waiting a little longer?" I'm not sure I want to know the answer to this, but I have to ask.

"Minimal. But there is still a chance she might not come out of the coma for a couple of days, and...there is still a very small chance that she may never come out of it at all."

Twenty-Eight

My heart starts racing and my palms start sweating.

"Relax, Mikah." Dr. Alston and Seraphina say in unison. It's rather obnoxious and I have the sudden urge to yell jinx.

Seraphina laughs.

"I'm trying." I take a few deep breaths as Dr. Alston goes to work pushing buttons.

"I'm going to have Amanda come in with some new fluids and take some vitals in about twenty minutes, then about every thirty minutes or so after that. We will also be monitoring for signs of discomfort. If she is in pain we may see her heart rate spike, and as she becomes more conscious, we'll see little things like finger twitches or a furrowing of her brow. If you see this, press the call button and we'll come in. Okay?"

"Okay," I say breathily.

"I have complete faith that she'll be alright. If I didn't, I would not be doing this now."

"Alright."

She grabs my shoulder as she passes and squeezes.

"You alright, sir?" Red chimes in. Jeez, I forgot he was here.

I turn to look at him. "Yeah, I think so. Listen. The other apartment downstairs, the one Celeste isn't using?"

"Yeah, the one across from me?"

"Right. Look, get in touch with Rusty and get them in that apartment. Make sure that everything is working properly, get the water turned on...you know the drill. She'll need a place to stay when she leaves the hospital and I'm no longer giving her a choice. Once we have a better idea of when she'll be released, we'll get it stocked up. Oh, and one last thing. Send Celeste on a shopping spree. Vivienne is going to need some new clothes, towels, linens, etcetera."

He nods. "Alright, we can handle that."

"Perfect. Thank you, Red. For everything."

"My pleasure, lad, you know that."

I nod and he leaves the room.

Are you still there?

I feel the fullness return once again. How does she do that?

"I'm here. I do that by becoming one with your angel self. Something you too will learn how to do eventually. I was here the whole time, just distantly communicating with you."

"See, and here I thought my head was my own when you weren't around."

She laughs. "Nope, I'm always connected. It's just a matter of whether or not I want to listen to you."

"Hardy-har. Alright. Dr. Alston. Is she familiar with all this angel, otherworldly stuff?"

"Not that I'm aware of. I can check. There are only a few common people that know – or at least think they know – that we exist. So it's unlikely that she does, but I will ask."

"No, it's alright. She was just a little too cool about fast healing. Did you have anything to do with Vivienne's healing?"

"Nuh-uh. Nope. That's all you."

"How me?"

"Your presence is enough. Your kindness, warm nature, your nurturing...and the fact that you're an angel of course helps, too."

"Huh?" I guess it is something else to add to my list of learning.

"Not really. I'm not entirely sure there is anything to learn. Her healing is a combination of just you being here supporting her and the natural aura of healing you possess as an angel." She sounds almost chipper. It's rather odd, given the circumstances.

Not wanting to discuss this any further because I'm not sure how much more of this I can handle right now, I slide off of the bed and head toward my bag.

I'm going to shower. Any chance you can scram?

She laughs and vacates. Her absence sends a chill through me. I look back to Vivienne, who is still unconscious.

Please let her wake up okay, I pray, and then add, *But not before I get back into her room.*

Twenty-Nine

After my shower, I start to pace, impatiently waiting for Vivienne to wake up. Around noon, Red brings me lunch from a restaurant near the house that I enjoy, but my nervous energy makes it hard for me to want to eat anything.

Finally I decide to distract myself with work. Not long after I've picked up my laptop and replied to a couple of emails, Sydney jumps on my case about working. I let out a nervous chuckle at her response and move onto the emails Jack has been sending me over the last twenty-four hours.

Information about Riley's background, Elton's background, some Riley sightings and a new batch of evidence on where he's possibly hiding. Jack is a real genius at tracking people. I have no doubt that at least half of the information he obtains is illegal, which is why we have to be careful about what we send on to Detective Stevens.

One of the emails catches my attention.

It's encrypted - for my eyes only. Unfortunately, I'm not equipped at the moment to open it, as I'm not sure of the level of security I have on the hospital's network. If he is sending this to me, it means he's found something important in relation to Riley or Elton. Which is good, but it could be pretty bad too.

After the voicemail from Elton yesterday, combined with Sydney's email, I begin to wonder, idly, what Elton is up to and how he plans to go about 'destroying me', as he so eloquently put it. Huh? I wonder if that's what Jack's email is about?

I try to push it from my mind entirely, and in doing so, it registers once again that all the humming is gone. Okay, maybe it's not gone, because I can still feel it slightly as I flex my back and shoulders. For now I'm going to take this as a positive sign that there is little to be concerned about right now.

Just as I think this, a prickling spreads across my skin. It's not painful, but rather it's pleasurable. Instinctively my eyes drift to Vivienne lying on the bed, and in the instant that I look at her, I see the corner of her mouth twitch slightly.

My heart swells to see some life in her face. Though her eyes are still closed, that twitch is more than I've seen from her in the last day, and I become hopeful that she is going to be alright.

I quickly close the laptop, set it aside and lean forward toward the bed.

"Vivienne." I gently place one hand on her upper arm and my other hand on her gorgeous red hair, stroking lightly. "Vivienne. Vivienne, can you open your eyes?" I pause a moment, waiting for a reaction.

There isn't one.

"Vivienne," I whisper.

Still no response.

I stay where I am, playing with her hair, until Dr. Alston comes in to check on her again.

Before I can tell her about the mouth twitch, Dr. Alston pulls up the blankets at the foot of the bed.

"What are you doing?" I ask a little defensively.

She doesn't flinch at my tone. "I'm looking for reflexes. To see if she has any reaction."

She takes a pen from her jacket and runs the top of the pen from heel to toe on one of Vivienne's feet.

We both watch intently.

After a heartbeat, Vivienne's toes curl in slightly.

I can't help the smile that spreads across my face.

Dr. Alston checks the other foot, and the end result is the same.

"What does this mean?"

She tries the first foot again and then the other before answering. "Right now it means that her brain is registering sensations."

"Is the delay in the reaction normal?"

"For now, yes. It really doesn't mean anything, only that she is still under the medication. Which is okay. As it wears off, that reaction should get a little faster."

I nod.

"Have you seen any movement?" she asks.

"A little while ago, I thought I saw her mouth twitch."

"It's not impossible. About another hour and the sedative should stop working altogether. Once we reach that point, I will be sending Amanda in here to keep a close watch on her vitals."

She moves around the bed, pulls the tape out from the fetal monitor and begins to look over it.

The action sends a shiver of excitement through me, and I'm not really sure why.

"What kind of plans have you made for her once she is released?" Dr. Alston peers at me out of the corner of her eye. "You know she can't go back to that apartment," she states matter-of-factly.

"I'm aware, but her will and determination are going to make it quite the battle."

She smiles at me. "But you're just the right person to argue with her."

I let out a breathy laugh. "You're right, I am. I have an additional condo in my building that's not being used. If I can't convince her to stay with me, she can live there until either she is back on her feet again or this whole mess is taken care of." As I say this, a sharp warning zing lights up my back, and I get the sudden impression that getting to the bottom of this mess is not going to be an easy task.

"Well, once she is fully recovered, I don't see any reason that she can't find a way to take care of herself. Whatever you do, don't stifle her. You might be able to get her to stay with you or to take that apartment, but whatever you do, make sure that she has the freedom to do things on her own. I could be wrong, of course, but she is very independent, and I don't see her changing that. So if you can help her while letting her make her own choices, she will be much better off." She puts down the tape and looks at me. "She needs help, counseling - especially that. I can take care of her physical medical needs, but you need to make sure that she sees a psychiatrist."

I nod, contemplating. "I wish I could just take it all away from her. All the memories, all the hardship she's endured. She deserves so much better than that."

"You're absolutely right, but we cannot change the things that have happened to her, we can only help her move forward."

She unwraps the stethoscope from her neck and holds it to Vivienne's chest.

I wonder idly if, when she's ready, I can convince Vivienne to work for MSBE.

I watch Dr. Alston move the stethoscope around, listening. When she is done, she pulls up the blanket to look at the incision on Vivienne's ribs. She pulls back the gauze.

"What the hell?" she says.

Thirty

"What's the matter?" A pulsing radiates throughout my entire body. It's the same sensation that came yesterday when I got really excited. Oh, no.

"Her incision."

I panic slightly. Fighting the sensations across my back, I stand up. "What's wrong with it?"

"Nothing."

I scowl at her.

"I mean, well, nothing is wrong except for the fact that it's..." She pauses and I lean over to look. "Come around, you can see better."

I sidestep the chair and the bed, walking around to come up on Dr. Alston's right.

"Look." She holds out her hand. A couple of thick staples rest on her palm.

I look at the area under the bandage. "What on earth? It's practically gone." In place of what was probably an angry red incision just yesterday is a faint, nearly perfectly healed line about an inch and a half long.

"I've heard of - and even seen - some fast healers, but I'll be damned if I've ever seen anything this fast."

She slowly pulls the rest of the gauze aside and rolls Vivienne forward just a bit.

SERAPHINA! SERAPHINA! DAMN IT, WHERE ARE YOU?

My skin is on fire as I take in what is across her back. Suddenly it all clicks into place.

"Has that always been there?" I ask Dr. Alston.

"Has what?"

SERAPHINA!

Damn it. No wonder. "Nothing. Thought I saw something."

No Goddamn wonder why my parents could never get anyone to do anything about my back when I was a kid.

SERAPHINA!

They couldn't see it. I could see it. And Mom could see it, for reasons I now know. But Dad...did Dad ever see it? That would explain why he never asked to see my back after Mom died.

SERAPHINA! Now is not the time to disappear on me. I'm gonna wring her damn neck. *SERAPHINA!* Damn it, where is she?

"I'm going to order an x-ray of her arm and shoulder. See what is going on in there." I just nod and move out her way. "Hey, you okay?"

The excited pulsing has not calmed down one bit since I stood up a moment ago. "Yeah, why?"

"You look very distracted."

"I'm a little jolted by the whole healing thing."

"So am I. But I doubt that there is a test in the world that can tell me how or why. All I know is that it has and..." She just shrugs.

"You completely baffle me with your nonchalance. Most doctors would be thinking of a way to exploit a miracle like that."

She laughs. "Mikah, let me tell you something about that."

I sit gingerly on the side of the bed, giving her my full attention.

"I didn't go to medical school to be a doctor so that I could become rich and famous. I became a doctor because it gives me a great opportunity help those in need. I specialized in obstetrics because I love babies and I'm thoroughly fascinated by the way we grow and develop in the womb, but I don't think that the little miracles we see everyday are cause for exploitation. I will just be amazed by it. And maybe do a little research about it," she admits, "because eventually the curiosity will take over. But in the end, I will do nothing to take advantage of it. I've seen a lot in my time that I can't explain, and I'd rather spend my time on something that I can explain or fix than something that is solving itself." She smiles at me, warm and genuine.

"I wish there were more doctors like you."

She chuckles a bit. "I love my job. And her. I fell in love with her when she was here a couple of months ago. She is an intelligent, gorgeous young lady who deserves to have her past wiped away and a future that is bright and full of prosperity, hope and love. Never forget that, Mikah."

She places her hand on my shoulder, squeezes briefly. "She's an angel. She deserves to be treated like one," she says as she leaves the room.

"Oh, you have no idea how right you are," I mumble.

Then, in my loudest silent mental shout: *SERAPHINA!*

Thirty-One

Instantly my back is ablaze and the feeling of fullness has returned.

What the hell took you so long?

"What?"

I've been screaming for you for at least the last five minutes. What took you so long?

I can't shake the image of Vivienne's back from my mind.

Seraphina catches on to what I'm thinking about. "Vivienne?" she asks.

I turn back to the bed and pull back the covers, gently pushing her hip to move her forward.

Peeking out between the gaps of the hospital gown are clear markings of wings that resemble my own.

"Explain this to me?" I say aloud. "What on earth is going on with her?" *How is this even possible?*

"Sit down, young one, and I will show you."

I'd rather stand up.

"No, sit down and I will show you."

Reluctantly, I step back from the bed, walk back around to my chair and take a seat.

"Get comfortable. Relax."

Instinct has me on edge because I don't know what to expect. But I lean forward to rest my head on the bed. My right hand plays with a strand of Vivienne's hair while the other one is rests along her arm.

"Close your eyes."

I do as she tells me, but I can feel the anxiety rising.

"Relax, young angel. I will not harm you. You've already seen most of this."

The dreams? I relax almost instantly; this is something I've wanted to see since Red woke me up this morning. I take a deep breath, filling my lungs, and then slowly exhale.

Suddenly I'm back in the white room on my knees – I can feel the hard floor digging into them. I open my eyes.

Standing behind me is a beautiful, pale-faced Vivienne, her red hair curling down her back, bright against all this white. Atop her head is a tiara, resting right along her hairline. In the center of the circlet is a shiny white opal surrounded by a beautiful silver Celtic design that extends into her hair.

My heart melts. She is simply stunning.

Her dress is white, with silver accents along the bodice. The design is flowery, with a beaded band directly below her breasts. Two thin straps, accented with the same style of beadwork, go up and over her shoulders. Coming off the straps is sheer chiffon that extends down beyond my line of sight.

Looking a little closer, I see that she looks healthier, filled out in her face, and her arms look well toned.

"You look beautiful, *A chuid den tsaol*." My voice is not what I expect to hear; it has an echoing quality.

She smiles back at me in the mirror. "Close your eyes."

I close my eyes and can feel her moving around me. Her hand trails feather-light along my wing; the pleasure it brings is breathtaking. She caresses my wing from where it comes out of my back all the way to the tip, and by the time she reaches the tip, I'm on the verge of losing control. But yet I feel rooted in my spot.

I feel the air shift as she comes to stand on my right. "Turn toward me."

With the sensation of her touch still pulsing through my body, it is hard to coordinate my movements and turn. I let my shoulders drop slightly, and I feel a rush of air as my wings fold inward. I lift my face but keep my eyes closed as I feel a finger trace lightly along the bridge of my nose down to the tip. Then her finger presses against my lip and I kiss the pad.

She gently lays her palm against my cheek. I lean into her touch, desperate to open my eyes, but I keep them closed, relishing the sensation of her warm touch against my skin. I raise my right hand and hold hers against my face, weaving my fingers in between hers.

"Keep your eyes closed and give me your hand," she says, the sound of bells in her voice.

I lift my hand slowly, remembering the way she's flinched before, but my caution proves unnecessary. I can feel her other hand shift, and then her knees rub along mine as she kneels.

She gently takes my other hand in hers and says, "Open your hand flat."

I do as she asks and she tugs on my arm. I feel her warmth beneath my fingers, and at my fingertips I can feel the cool metal of her circlet and her cheek pressing into my palm.

She leans into my touch.

My heart soars and warm tears stream down my cheeks as I take in the magnitude of the gesture: She's just allowed me to touch her face. I feel her fingers along the back of mine as she press my hand to her.

"Do not cry." I can hear the emotion in her voice, and a moment later I feel her own tears.

I release her hand against my cheek and bring it up to meet her other cheek. Eyes still shut, cupping her face in my hands, I rise up onto my knees.

I feel a soft nudge against my stomach and then feel her press into me. My body becomes a live wire as our bodies draw closer to each other.

She lifts her chin.

I slowly lower my mouth, seeking hers.

When we connect, a surge of pleasure and hope courses through my body; it is almost uncontrollable.

She presses her hands against mine for a moment, holding them against her cheeks, and her fingers weave in between my own. I can feel her tug slightly as I kiss her again, lingering longer this time. Then she pulls my arms past her shoulders until they bump into something behind her. She slowly lowers my hands onto an object. The surge of desire flies through me once again as I come in contact with something hard surrounded by soft velvet.

My eyes fly open and I gasp. "Vivienne."

"Don't stop," she says breathily, and I gently slide my hands along the pure white feathers of her wings.

Looking down at her, reality becomes clear. This is the future. Our future.

"She will be our *banphrionsa*." The voice that comes now is not Vivienne's but a different female voice that comes with some sense of recognition, but yet not familiar.

"Princess?" How is this even...

I let the thought trail away and close my eyes. When I open them again, Vivienne has vanished. I turn quickly, looking for her, and realize that my wings have also gone.

I spin back around. In the spot where Vivienne stood just a moment ago is another woman. A familiar woman.

I stumble backwards.

"Mom?"

"Yes, baby." Her voice radiates with emotion.

I can't speak as I steady myself, looking again at the beautiful woman standing before me. She looks amazing. Her gorgeous blonde hair, bright blue eyes, and soft features are warm and inviting. She looks years younger than the pictures I have, almost like a teenager.

"How?" I finally manage to breathe.

In answer, she spreads her wings. "I am like you, my son. I too am an angel. Which is how you have become one."

"But..." I have no words, and I crumple to the floor on my knees and sit back on my feet, my hands balling into fists against my thighs.

"There is much to learn, *A leanbh*, but your love is in danger, and you are the only one who can save her. The child she caries is the key to restoring the natural order bestowed upon us as *aingeal*. There is an imbalance among our kind, made worse by the *foinse olc,* the source of evil, as Satan too will breed with one that will stand by his side no matter what.

"Your need for her is strong, your hope for her burns bright and hot. She needs you to help her, to guide her. She is pure. Despite the life she's led, she is pure of heart. Never doubt that."

The breath moving in and out of my lungs is thick. "She gives me hope."

"As she should, my son. She should give you reason to be whole and pure yourself. You, too, know hardship. Your father did all he could for you and our family, but raising children was not his strength in life. You were forced to do it alone. Without me."

I snort a laugh. This is all too much to handle.

"There is much more to learn, but know that we are here, we will help you, and when you return home, I will see to it that you have our histories at your disposal. It will help you understand your purpose. And ours..."

Her voice trails off at the end and I look up.

She's gone once again.

Thirty-Two

I put my head in my hands. This is too much. All this angel stuff is too much to understand all at once. I don't know how I'm going to handle all of this without going crazy. It's surreal.

Cool fingers on my cheek bring a zing of pleasure. Once again I put my hand over hers, only this time it's not the soft, warm touch of before. Her fingers are almost cold, and there is something hard and rough pressing into my cheek.

I let out a rushed breath and pull back, my eyes flying open. Bright, ice-blue eyes and a mess of beautiful red hair.

I stand up, stumble and fall back into the chair.

Her lips turn upwards in a smile behind the ventilator hose.

"Is that funny to you?" I laugh and smile at her.

She nods. Then tries to pull on the hose.

"Don't." I reach for her hands to pull them back. She doesn't flinch at my quick movements, and my heart swells once again. I take her hands in one of mine and pull the chair up close to her bed.

A hum of hope and life and undeniable pleasure radiates through me. "I missed you." The words are out before I can stop them.

A faint trace of a blush kisses her cheeks.

I notice that the natural light in the room has faded significantly. It's later than I would have thought possible.

"Are you in pain?"

She shakes her head slightly.

"I'm going to push the button for Amanda to come, okay?"

Her eyes widen in recognition.

"Yes, Dr. Alston and Amanda have been taking care of you."

She nods again, and I reach for the call button. As soon as I touch the button, there's a commotion outside the room and the door clicks open.

Dr. Alston comes in first, followed by Amanda.

"Hello, Vivienne. Pleasure to see you again. Are you in any pain?"

I watch Vivienne shake her head. I can't take my eyes off of her. An overwhelming sense of joy is taking control of my body at the fact that she's awake.

She is looking at me, too.

Dr. Alston has gone to the fetal monitor again, looking over the last foot or so of tape. "How long has she been up?"

"I don't know, I was sleeping against her bed. She woke me up."

Vivienne pulls her hand from mine and holds up five fingers.

"Five minutes?" Dr. Alston asks. Vivienne nods, and Dr. Alston goes back to reviewing the tape.

I look up at the baby's monitor; the heart rate is around one-fifty. Curious, I look at Vivienne's monitor. Sure enough, captured about five minutes ago, there is the now-familiar pattern of Vivienne's heartbeat when I'm around. I can't help but smile.

Vivienne's head moves in the same direction. I look at her and watch her roll her eyes. I laugh and she squeezes my hand. Her other hand goes back to the tube in her mouth.

"Not just yet," Dr. Alston says. "How do your ribs feel? Do they hurt?"

She wiggles in the bed just a little bit, then she shakes her head.

"What about your wrist, does it hurt?"

She flexes her fingers, rotates her wrist and shakes her head again.

"Is it really possible that she is healed already?"

"Yes." This time the voice is in my head. Seraphina again.

You know, you could make yourself known before answering my questions.

She laughs. "I was here when you went to sleep, remember? Not my fault if you forgot."

Fair enough.

"Viv, how does your neck feel? Does it hurt?"

She scowls at the question then she shakes her head. I'd forgotten all about the bruises around her neck. Had I remembered those, then I'd have seen, like I do now, that the marks are much fainter than they were yesterday.

"Is she still on pain meds?" I ask, and Vivienne's eyes meet mine again.

"She's on a light dose of pain meds. But I'd be able to tell if she was giving me the runaround so I'd take out the tubes. She didn't even flinch." She turns to Vivienne. "Alright, Vivienne, we will take out the tubes. On one condition?"

She nods at Dr. Alston but is still looking in my direction.

"You don't go running a marathon at least for a few days."

I laugh out loud and see Vivienne's eyes scrunch up and her shoulders shake with laughter, though she doesn't make a sound.

"Mikah, I need you to move so Amanda can get in over there."

I watch Vivienne scowl at Dr. Alston, and I laugh again at her expression.

Dr. Alston laughs in return. "He's not going anywhere. We just need the room, okay?"

She nods reluctantly.

I stand up and sidestep Amanda's approach, taking a seat at the end of the bed near Vivienne's calves.

Amanda has gone to work pulling back some of the tape holding the tubes in place.

"Alright, Vivienne. Go ahead and breathe through your nose."

Amanda reaches over and turns off the machine.

"Now I need you to take a big, deep breath through your nose and hold it, and then on the count of three, I want you to exhale as hard and fast as you can. Are you ready?"

Vivienne nods.

"Okay, breathe in."

With the machine off the room is silent, and I hear the air enter though her nose, past the pipe. She scowls a little at the fullness of her lungs.

"One, two, three."

Thirty-Three

On three I hear Vivienne's rushed exhale. At the same time, Amanda holds down Viv's shoulders and Dr. Alston pulls on the tube.

Then Vivienne starts coughing and wincing slightly. The coughing lasts for a few moments.

"Water?" Vivienne says in a raspy voice when she's recovered.

Amanda is quick to grab the cup she brought in a few moments ago.

"Ice chips," she says as I take the cup from her, and then she presses the button on the side of the bed to raise Vivienne to a sitting position.

"Hi, there," I say, handing Vivienne the ice chips.

"Hi," she says, still raspy.

"How you doing?"

She nods and puts a couple of pieces of ice into her mouth. "I'm okay."

"Vivienne, how are you feeling? Any pain?"

She shakes her head. "No, but I'm really hungry."

I smile.

So does Dr. Alston. "We can work on that."

"How long...?" She trails off, clears her throat.

"It's Saturday." Dr. Alston pauses to look at her watch. "Seven twenty in the evening. You've been out since you came in yesterday morning."

Both Dr. Alston and I are watching for any reaction from Vivienne, who lets out a long breath.

"Is everything..." Her free hand reaches for her stomach, and relief washes over her face.

I can feel the emotion wrap around me, engulfing me.

"Everything looks good. You both are doing good."

Vivienne nods slowly, and then her eyes glass up.

"Can you guys leave us for a little while?" I ask Dr. Alston.

"Of course. Hit the button if you need anything, and we will get some dinner up here."

"No need. I'll take care of it. She deserves something better than hospital food."

Dr. Alston laughs. "This is true. Okay, but keep it light, like soup or broth." I nod. "I'll be back in shortly."

When the door clicks shut behind the doctor and nurse, I turn back to Vivienne, and she mouths, "Thank you."

"Of course."

I don't say anything more. I'm not going to force her to talk. I get up to get my phone.

"Where are you going?" she asks.

I turn back to her and smile. "Getting you some dinner."

"Oh."

I smile a little wider and call Red.

"Hello, sir."

"Hi. She's awake and she's hungry. Can you bring us both something, but keep it light and soft, like soup?"

"Of course. Celeste's already got some stuff going, in anticipation of her waking up. I'll be there shortly."

"Thanks, Red. If you could, leave it with the staff and have them bring it in."

"Absolutely. Call if you need anything else."

"Actually, can you bring me one of my t-shirts and a pair of sweatpants?"

"For you, sir?"

"No, for Vivienne. I think she'd be more comfortable." I look to her and she nods.

"We have clothes for her here if you'd like."

I hadn't realized they'd gotten that far already. "Pants. But bring one of my t-shirts."

"On it. See you soon."

"Yup." I hit the end button.

I turn back to Vivienne. "Red will be here soon with some food."

"Thanks."

"Anything, anytime." I pause. "How are you doing?"

She just shakes her head.

"I won't pry, but if you need to talk about something, I'm here. I'll listen."

"It's not that, really. It's more that...I'm trying to figure out how I ended up here," she says softly.

"Are you sure you want to talk about that?"

"No, but I know it's something I will need to know eventually." As she speaks, her eyes begin to droop.

"You're tired?" I ask.

She nods. "I am, but I'm confused."

"Is my being here making you uncomfortable?" Please, no. I don't want to leave.

She shakes her head. "I'm glad you're here." I walk toward the chair, but before I can sit down, she says, "I really need to go to the bathroom."

"You have a catheter." I try to not look at her, but I see the blush of embarrassment that spreads across her cheeks regardless. "I can call for Amanda."

"Nurse Fang," she says, and I laugh. "Go ahead." She smiles a little bit.

I reach for the button and a beep sounds over our heads.

"Yes, Vivienne?" Dr. Alston's voice.

"I need to go to the bathroom," she says, looking up toward the ceiling.

"I'll send Amanda in."

"Thanks."

A few moments later, Amanda comes into the room.

"How we doing, Viv?" she asks.

"Okay. I need to go to the bathroom and I don't want to use the catheter."

"Is it because he's in here?" She hitches her thumb in my direction and I nearly blush, embarrassed myself.

"I can step out," I say to Vivienne.

"No, I just want to go to the bathroom. Can't I just go?"

"Alright, but you can't get mad at me if we have to put it back in. Fair enough?" Vivienne just shrugs. "Mikah, can you give us some privacy?"

"Uh, sure." I turn on my heel and head toward the door.

"Don't go far," I hear Vivienne say.

"Right outside the door."

Thirty-Four

I wander aimlessly into the empty waiting room a couple of doors down from Vivienne's room.

A warm tingling sensation spreads and then quickly subsides before giving way to the tingling I'm most familiar with: icy stabbing sensations. I try in vain to not arch my back and curl in on the feeling, but it's hard; it hurts like hell.

I hear the chime of the elevator followed by footsteps. I reach into my pocket and press a button on my phone.

Scuff. Thud. Scuff, click. The door closes.

Someone is walking across the floor behind me. The icy stabbing continues as I realize the person behind me is a threat. The hairs on the back of my neck stand on end.

I spin around, preparing to defend against whatever is coming after me.

"Well, well, well. Look at what we have here."

My heart pumps faster and bright red rage fills my vision as I take in the man before me. The icy stabbing flares momentarily then settles. My veins almost feel frozen, but the feeling brings about an unusual sense of strength and I flex involuntarily as I grit my teeth.

"What the hell are you doing here, Elton?" I spat at him.

"I heard your girlfriend was in the hospital and that you were hiding out here."

"Why are you looking for me?" I ask him. I know from his voicemail that he knew about Vivienne, in some fashion. Though I'm not sure if he knew, at the time, that she was alive. Has he put two and two together? Does he know that his son is responsible for the state of my 'girlfriend' as he puts it?

"We have something in common." He straightens his stance and his tie, a gesture that strikes me as ridiculous here in this context.

"And that is what, exactly?"

"Your little girlfriend is causing quite a problem for my family."

Rage flares hotter, brighter. "How do you suppose that is?"

"Well she broke up with my son. They were supposed to be married soon."

"Ha!" I bark at him. "That is the biggest line of bullshit I've ever heard. Though I'm curious, is your coming here your idea, or is it Riley's?" He doesn't respond. But I'm going to see where this goes. Elton could be the key to finding out where Riley is. "Your son seems to think he can control you too. So let me put it to you this way. My 'girlfriend,' as you call her, almost died because of the damage your son inflicted on her."

His eyes widen marginally. "How dare you accuse my son of beating a woman! That's preposterous!" His face begins to turn red. "He was in the process of getting her back, bringing her back to him."

"Wow Elton, you really are dense on so many levels. Did you not just bail your son out of jail for domestic violence?"

"It was a misunderstanding."

"Jesus, you make me sick. First, you post bail for your son who was arrested following the brutal beating of the woman you say he was trying to get back. The woman he beat to near death again Thursday night that fought for her life, and the life of your unborn grandchild."

"That's preposterous! She was never in the hospital. It was a misunderstanding."

"Jesus H-Christ Elton, wake the fuck up. Here's a thought for you. Why don't you go grab your son and walk into the downtown office of the MPD. See how they react to your son's arrival on their territory. If you're so inclined to find out the truth, that just might be the quickest, most efficient way to know for sure."

His face turns redder by the second. A career businessman hoping for a career in politics doesn't want to have this kind of negative publicity looming over his head.

"Did you know that your son is wanted for questioning in the murder of a twenty-three year old girl named Rebecca Black?" Deeper red. "Not to mention the brutal beating of a twenty-two year old woman who went through hell and back to save her life."

Purple to blue, then back to red. He shakes his head. "I don't believe you," he spats at me.

"I don't care if you believe me or not, Elton. The point is, it always comes out in the end. So you can decide here and now what side you're going to take in this matter. If you choose Riley's, then I suggest you get the hell out of here and get to work. You have one hell of a conspiracy to try and cover up." I turn my back on him.

"She is a Goddamn liability," I hear him say.

Bright red rage twists me around and launches me back in his direction. He doesn't flinch or back away. As my fist connects with his jaw and nose, I hear the crunch of breaking bones. See the blood spray across the floor as he grabs his face.

"You son of bitch!" I rage. "How dare you speak of any human being that way! We do not live in a world where you eliminate people just because they don't fit into your business plan, Elton Bennett. I will see your son fry for what he's done, and I will gladly stand by to watch you take the fall with him."

Glaring at me, he spits blood and mucus onto the floor. "You're not old enough to understand the true meaning of business. Do not ever talk to me like that again. In business you do what needs to be done to survive." His face contorts and he bends over and dry heaves, no doubt from the pain. "You have a choice to make Blake. Either reinstate your investment or so help me God I'll have you arrested for assault and destroy MSBE."

"Bullshit! That does not include murder and my stance with your investments will never change." I peer through the window towards Vivienne's room and fight a grin from spreading across my face. The cops outside of her room are making show of looking at the ceiling and rocking on their heels. I stalk past him, push the crash bar on the door and step out into the hallway.

As the door clicks shut behind me, I reach into my pocket, remove my BlackBerry and press pause. At the touch of a couple more buttons, the recorded conversation is on its way to Detective Stevens's email.

Thirty-Five

As I approach Vivienne's door, Amanda comes back out of the room.

"She alright?"

"She's great. Stubborn as all hell, but she's doing good. She wants the sling to come off. Said her shoulder doesn't hurt. I told her that it was up to the doctor and that I would discuss it with her. I know that Alston wanted to take some x-rays, but when we went in to get her you were sound asleep on her bed, so we decided to wait. Once she's done that, she'll decide what to do next."

"Thanks, Amanda."

"Of course. Call if you need anything."

I go back into the room. The bed has been lowered again, and Vivienne's eyes are closed. What a difference watching her sleep now compared to before. Color has returned to her cheeks and the absence of the hoses makes her look human again.

Her cheeks are flushed. No doubt the trip to and from the bathroom was exhausting.

I quietly walk over to the chair and sit down.

"Don't pry with her."

Hello, Seraphina. I hadn't planned on it.

273

"I know, but she seems to be doing a pretty good job of suppressing what's happened. She does remember, but, no doubt due to the years of abuse she's faced, she's learned how to suppress much."

I'd already assumed that and it's the reason I'm not pressing. I know she will need to talk to the cops at some point, and I'd rather she save her energy for that conversation. I will make arrangements for her to meet with someone she can trust to discuss all this bottled-up trauma.

"Don't be surprised if she won't do it. She will when she is ready, and not before. But it will only come at a time and place she knows with absolute certainty she is safe. All I ask is that you give her some time to get there."

I roll my eyes. *I know, Seraphina, this is not my first rodeo. Are we forgetting my sister?*

I change the subject to avoid more lecturing I don't need. *So, that dream. What on earth was that all about?*

"Well, first of all, you weren't on earth." She laughs and I shake my head. "You were in Elysium."

Elysium Fields? As in Greek mythology, where you go when you die?

"The same, only we no longer call it *Fields*. The mythological definition of Elysium is ideal happiness, though that's not entirely accurate. It's a place where angels live. A place where you yourself can go anytime you wish. The souls of the dead do pass through Elysium, but they do not stay unless they have a predestined purpose for being there. Like your mother, for example. She passed into Elysium upon her death because it was where she was supposed to go."

What about my father?

"That is something you will need to discuss with your mother. It is not my story to tell. But your mother is free to pass between heaven – as you call it – and Elysium. You will likely be able to do the same, should you wish."

As I call it? What do you call heaven, if not heaven?

"It used to be known as *Aether*, though not many of us call it that anymore. If you know some of your Greek mythology, then you would know that *Aether* was the first of the elementals to be born and represents the purest life and happiness. In all honesty, heaven and *Aether* is really all the same. But where the angels gather is separate. Those in *Aether* do not pass into Elysium, and vice versa. Unless, of course, you are one of the Chosen, which I believe you are."

What makes you so certain about that?

"You will find out soon. It is not something I can tell you."

Bull— I stop myself.

She laughs. "No, really, I can't. I'm bound by restraints that prevent me from disclosing certain secrets, and that is one of them. Just like you are unable to tell anyone other than those of your own species that you're an angel. Try it sometime." She laughs again. "Okay, I'm going to go. Red will be here shortly, and I'm neglecting my chores."

She doesn't stick around long enough for me to argue. I feel the rush of her leaving my mind and body.

Thirty-Six

About thirty minutes later, Red arrives with dinner for Vivienne and me, and Amanda brings it in.

"How long has she been sleeping?"

"About half an hour. She was sleeping when I came back in after her trip to the bathroom."

"Oh, okay. I'd try and wake her so she can eat. Plus, Alston will be back in shortly. She was going to be on her way up after seeing a patient with a smashed in nose downstairs in the E.R.." She smirks at me in a I-know-what-you-did kind of way.

"Alright." I say quickly before I start laughing hysterically at the fact that Alston is more than likely treating Bennett's busted nose. I'm not sure what to make of his whole ordeal, but it proves my earlier theory about doing anything to get what he wants.

Amanda goes about checking the monitors and IV fluids.

Elton came here to try and 'convince' me to reinstate my investments, as if I would see things his way.

Amanda interrupts my thoughts. "She can start drinking water, too. The ice chips were a way for her to slow down her intake. Her throat is probably pretty sore and will be for a day or two."

I nod. "I'll keep an eye on her."

She smiles and leaves.

I gently stroke Vivienne's arm. "Vivienne," I say softly, and her eyes flutter. "Dinner is here."

Her eyes flutter again, but they don't open.

"Come on, sweetie." I rub her arm a little more and she finally, slowly begins blinking, waking up. "Hi, there."

She smiles. "Hi," she breathes.

"I have soup. Are you hungry?"

She nods and I go about unpacking the dinner Celeste sent over. She's included her creamy chicken noodle soup, minus the big noodles and hunks of chicken. Instead it is more of a broth. And she used little tiny ring noodles. There are also bread rolls and some crackers.

"Smells good," she whispers.

"Is your throat bothering you?"

She nods.

"The soup should help."

She nods again.

I pour soup from the thermos into one of the two bowls Celeste put in the basket. The soup is steamy and smells wonderful. I reach for the button to raise Vivienne up, and I notice as she tracks my hand's movement. I mentally shrug it off and raise her up. She starts to pull her arm out of the sling and I scowl at her.

"It doesn't hurt," she says a little more vehemently.

"I know, I just—"

"Mikah, please, it's alright."

"I know, I'm sorry. I just..." I pause. "I just really need you to get better. I don't want to see you do unnecessary harm to yourself."

"Honestly, all things considered, I feel pretty good. Just very tired."

I smile at her. "I will try and remember that. Now eat. Before it gets cold."

Maybe she really is mending that fast. Maybe those markings on her back play a great deal into her quick recovery, and maybe they're the reason the bleeding had stopped by the time I found her. Maybe they're even the reason she's still alive. Chances are good that Riley wouldn't have left her apartment until he thought she was dead.

I grab my BlackBerry and text Jack with one question: *Has there been any announcement regarding Vivienne from the police?*

I know that Elton was here, but he wouldn't know what kind of condition Vivienne is in. The only way he could know anything is if it has been leaked to the press.

I grab a bottle of water from the basket and open it for Vivienne, then grab one for myself and sit back down.

"Aren't you going to eat?" she asks.

"When you're done, I'll take from what's left. I want to make sure you get enough to eat."

"This will be enough."

"We'll see."

My phone chimes and I glance at it. It's a reply from Jack:

No. All they've said is that they are investigating the deaths of a police officer and a young woman.

They've said that there is some information that suggests both are related, but that is about all at this point. Why?

"Is everything okay?" she asks me.

As I look up I realize that my brow is furrowed. I relax it quickly. "Yeah, just checking on a few things." I take a sip of my water.

"You don't have to stay." I can hear an underlying sadness in her voice.

"I have no place else to be other than right here. Unless of course you want me to leave."

She shakes her head quickly. "No, I want you to stay, I just don't want to keep you from anything."

I smile at her. "You're not. I'm trying to get some information on what has been sent to the media regarding you."

"Why?"

"Curious, aren't we." I smile.

"A little." She smiles back at me and takes another spoonful of soup into her mouth. "This is really good."

"Celeste is a great cook."

A scowl comes across her face and she looks up at me, confusion in her eyes. I can feel the tension and concern coming off of her.

"Oh. No, Celeste is my housekeeper. She's the one who put all this together for you."

As soon as the word *housekeeper* leaves my mouth, the crease on her brow disappears and her eyes almost glow. "Oh. I thought..." She turns away, back to her food, and takes another bite.

"That she was someone else?"

She nods.

I smile again. "No, Vivienne, there is no one else." *Only you,* I say, but only in my head because that is just too much right now.

She takes a few more bites in silence, then asks a question that catches me off guard. "Did you find me?"

Thirty-Seven

"What?" is all I can think to say.

"In my apartment. Did you find me?"

"Are you sure you want to discuss this?"

She nods slowly, hesitant.

"We can discuss this another time, Vivienne. We don't need to do it now."

"I need to know."

I take a deep breath, trying to decide if this is the time to do this. I'm not entirely convinced that it is, but if it helps her feel more at ease...

"Yes, it was me."

"How did you know?"

"That's complicated. I can't say for certain how, but I knew. I..." I pause and take a drink. Standing up, I walk toward the foot of her bed. "I'd planned to be here at the hospital when you got here for your appointment. I really needed to talk to you." I walk back to the chair and then back toward the end of the bed. The pacing helps me think about the best way to explain all this.

"So I didn't show up?"

"No, I...um, was running a little earlier than I planned, so rather than go to the hospital, I went to your apartment. There was a cab waiting out front."

"I don't remember calling for a cab," she says.

As I turn back toward the chair she is looking at me. "I think Dr. Alston had called for one for you."

"Oh. So what did the cab sitting outside have to do with anything?"

"Well, I assumed that you were still inside your apartment. Then, as time passed, I grew more and more concerned about why you weren't coming out." Back and forth I continue to pace, slowly. "So I called Detective Stevens."

Her head pops up at the name and a look of frustration and anger crosses her features.

I'm confused by her reaction. "What's wrong?"

"He was supposed to protect me." Her voice is small, but a hint of the tiger is in it. She's angry.

Anger surges through my body at her words. She's right – he was supposed to protect her, and he failed. "I don't want to defend Stevens, because I don't think he deserves it, but there were some unforeseen circumstances that got in the way of that."

Her eyes flare wider for a moment, as if she's remembering something.

"Do you know...?" She stops there.

"The cop that was stationed outside of your apartment was killed."

I watch as her eyes glass over. "Mr. Crowley, my neighbor. I remember Riley saying something..." She stops.

"I don't know anything about him," I say.

She takes a deep breath, steeling herself. "Why did you call Stevens?"

I can see in her eyes that she doesn't want to further discuss Mr. Crowley. I vow to ask Stevens or Jack about it.

"They came by my place Thursday night because of my car being near your apartment. That was when I learned about Rebecca's murder and the association between her and Riley. Stevens told me that you were under MPD protection. And then I knew that I needed – for my own peace of mind if nothing else – to be at your apartment to see you leave to meet Dr. Alston."

I continue pacing and I notice that she's stopped eating. "You have to finish your soup if you want me to keep talking."

She nods and goes back to it.

"The next few minutes in the story are a bit of a blur. I had Stevens call the officer that was stationed outside your apartment for a status update. When the officer didn't answer, I ran across Lake Street to the cop's car, only to discover that he'd been killed. That's when I went into your building. The rest, I imagine, you can figure out for yourself."

She finishes off her bowl of soup, takes a hunk of bread from the roll, and takes a bite, wincing as she swallows. She dips the bread into the bowl and soaks up the last of the liquid. She takes a smaller, soaked bite and then puts the rest down again. "I'm full."

"Are you sure? There is more soup."

"No, I'm sure."

"Alright." As I start to clean up, I finish my story. "I've been here at the hospital since they brought you in, and I've been in contact with Stevens, who will be anxious to talk to you."

"What's there to talk about?" she says sulkily.

283

I smile at her attitude. "Well, they're going to want to know what happened."

"There's not much to tell. I only remember little details." She is staring off at the far end of the room. "He came up behind me just as I was about to open the door. After he pushed me inside and shut the door, he threw me down onto the floor." She takes a deep breath. "That's when my arm broke. I was trying to protect the baby by stopping myself from falling on my stomach."

My heart lurches in my chest. What she went through is just unbelievable, but I know I need to let her get it out.

"I passed out from the pain after he kicked me in the ribs." She squeezes the blanket in her hand so tight her knuckles turn white. "When I woke up next, I was strapped down on the bed, something over my eyes and mouth. My shoulder was in so much pain that I couldn't even feel my arm until I tried to free myself. My wrist was bound and broken."

I reach for her hand. She doesn't flinch or look at me, but she allows me to pull her hand away from the blanket and interlace our fingers.

"I don't remember much after that, other than something cool and sharp running along my chest. I think I passed out again. The next thing I remember is waking up here." She finally looks at me, and there are tears in her eyes.

I use my free hand to wipe them away. "You're alive, you're safe, and I will let nothing harm you."

"Have they captured him?"

I shake my head, and Vivienne begins to shake.

"Hey, hey, hey. Breathe, Vivienne. In. Out."

She takes a deep, shuddering breath in and lets it out.

"Slowly," I say. "I'm not going to let anyone hurt you."

I gently squeeze the hand I'm holding. The monitor beside me starts beeping. My head snaps up to see what is going on. Her heartbeat is erratic.

Then I hear the blood pressure cuff on her arm go off. She squeezes my hand harder.

"Vivienne, look at me." She turns to look at me. I smile at her. "Hi, darlin'. Take a deep breath with me. Ready?" She nods but I can see that she is turning pale. "In." I watch as her chest expands with mine. "Out." I watch as she slowly exhales and count to eight in my head. "Good, again."

We repeat the process again.

Then another machine starts going off. I look and see that her blood pressure has spiked.

Thirty-Eight

At the same time the blood pressure alarm goes off, I can hear commotion outside. A couple seconds later, the door clicks, and in walks Amanda.

"What's going on?" She looks to me.

"Keep breathing, Viv." I turn to Amanda and the door clicks again. Dr. Alston is standing in the doorway. "We were talking and she started to freak out. First the heart monitor went off, then after the pressure cuff was done, the next one went off."

"Vivienne, how we doing, sweetheart?" Dr. Alston asks from the foot of Vivienne's bed.

Vivienne seems to be on the verge of hyperventilating. "I—" Breath. "Don't—" Breath. "Know." Breath.

"Amanda, let's get her on oxygen. Vivienne, we're going to put a mask on you for oxygen and I need you to take some big, deep breaths, okay?"

Vivienne nods as Amanda brings the mask to her face.

"Deep breath in for eight counts. Deep breath out for eight counts. Okay?"

Vivienne nods again. I watch the monitor as she breathes in and out. Her oxygen level starts to climb, and I hear the pressure cuff go off again. Slowly her heart rate returns to normal.

"Good job," I say quietly so only she can hear me.

"Vivienne?" Dr. Alston says and we both look at her. "Good job. Do you feel better now?"

"Yes." Her voice sounds muffled coming through the mask.

"Okay, good. We can swap the mask out for a nose piece, but I want to keep you on oxygen for tonight, okay?"

She pulls the mask away from her face. "When can I go home?"

"In the morning we'll run a few tests and do an ultrasound. Once those are done and the results are in, I'll make that decision, but don't count on anything earlier than tomorrow afternoon. Once you leave here, though, you will be on bed rest until I see you again in two weeks."

"I can't do that," she says vehemently.

"You can and you will. I will see to it that you're able to manage things while you're off of work. Alright?"

"I'll lose my job," she says.

"Don't worry about that." As I say this she scowls and looks at me. The angry kitten is back, and I can't help but laugh. Always so feisty. A feeling of warm satisfaction ripples across my body. I sober quickly and add, "We'll take care of it, okay?"

Her scowl grows deeper, and this time Dr. Alston lets out a chuckle.

"Remember what I told you last time?"

She nods, and I'm curious what she told Vivienne the last time.

"Alright, Vivienne, everything looks good. I'm going to let you get some sleep tonight. I'll take off the fetal monitors so you can move around if you'd like. Push the button if you need anything." Vivienne nods and Dr. Alston goes about removing the monitors and tucking them away with the machine.

"Is the IV still necessary?" Viv asks.

"After you finish the fluids that are in the bag now, Carol, your night nurse, can remove it. Okay?"

Vivienne's eyes shoot up to the two bags attached to the IV pole and scowls again. They only just changed them out the last time they were in here, and the bags are still about half full.

"Alright," she concedes.

"Good night," Dr. Alston says as she and Amanda leave.

"Good night," I say back. Turning back to Vivienne, I ask, "Do you need to go to the bathroom?"

She nods. I stand up, go to the cabinet near the TV and pull a blanket from the cupboard. Then I walk back to the bed, unfolding it as I go. "Lean forward, please."

She gives me a funny look but complies. I wrap the blanket around her shoulders and let it fall down to cover her exposed backside.

"Do you want to change while you're in there?"

"Uh huh."

"Okay, let's get you in there first. Then I'll bring your clothes. Put your arm around my neck."

She doesn't protest as I help her from the bed. But instead of letting her feet touch the ground, I pick her up. "Grab your IV pole."

She weighs next to nothing and I don't even have to adjust my balance as she shifts in my arms to grab the pole.

"Got it," she says.

"Okay." I turn toward the bathroom, savoring the feeling of having her in my arms.

She nuzzles her head onto my chest, settling in. "Thank you."

Without thinking, I kiss the top of her forehead. "You're welcome."

Thirty-Nine

After I get Vivienne settled back into bed, she falls asleep quickly - no doubt the day wore on her – and I take the opportunity to check my voicemail. It's full, and I quickly forward anything work-related, which eliminates about ninety percent of what I had in there. While clicking through the voicemails, I come across one from Stevens, left about an hour ago.

"Blake, it's Detective Stevens. Listen, I got a call from the hospital that said she was awake. How's she doing? Look I, um...I need to ask her a few questions and I will come by tomorrow sometime. We've gathered a pretty good mountain of evidence against Riley, including fingerprints from her apartment. Initial results on the blood found at the scene point to two different kinds. All we know so far is that they're different and one belongs to Vivienne. Once we know more, it may be enough to solidify the case against that idiot. We have a couple of leads on his whereabouts, too. I will let you know as soon as he's in custody. Please call me back at this number when you get a chance. I really need to speak with Vivienne."

Instead of calling Stevens back right away, I email Chrys, my attorney, requesting that he meet with me on Monday at my condo to discuss representing Vivienne should this case go to trial. Knowing Chrys, this will not be outside of his area of expertise, and I'm confident that he'll be able to represent Vivienne well. Once that is done, I call Stevens back.

As I'm hitting send, a sharp buzz rings across my back, the same one I get anytime there is something to do with Stevens. Odd.

After three rings and a series of clicks, he answers. "Stevens."

"You called."

"Ah, Blake. How is she?" he asks.

"Alive. Torn up emotionally, but she's here and well as can be, all things considered." My tone is clipped. Her hyperventilating earlier has me on edge when it comes to Stevens. She's right: He was supposed to protect her and he failed to do so. Riley running free in the streets isn't helping my mood.

"I don't doubt that at all, but I'm glad she's awake. I planned to stop by tomorrow to talk to her."

"Don't bother. She has a mountain of tests in the morning and she will, with any luck, be discharged in the afternoon. You can wait until Monday afternoon, my apartment."

"You know I can't wait until Monday."

"You can and you will. She needs a chance to recover and get settled. On top of that, she needs a chance to speak with her lawyer before you get your hands on her."

"What does she need a lawyer for? She hasn't done anything wrong."

"No, she hasn't, but I'll be damned if I let that fucker walk out of a jail cell on bail again. Vivienne will have her chance for justice this time." I can hear the resolution in my voice and Stevens picks up on it, too.

"Speaking of justice, I received your recording. How in the hell did you get it?"

"Elton came to the hospital looking for me."

"You know that I can't use this in court, right?"

I roll my eyes. "That depends, Detective, on how you want to use the information. It doesn't exactly implicate Riley in the crimes, but it certainly indicates that Elton is fully aware of what his son was going to do and the reason for which he bailed him out of jail, don't ya think, Detective? Regardless, use it how you want. Use it to build a separate case against Riley or Elton. There's no doubt in my mind that if his lips are that loose with me, he will most certainly talk to someone else."

I can hear a heavy sigh on the other end of the phone. "I see your point. But Blake, it's in her best interest to give me a statement as soon as possible. The longer we wait, the more time there is for her to forget what happened or – as Riley's defense will say – for someone to tamper with her memory."

"Wait until Monday, Stevens. She's not well when it comes to what's happened to her. She started freaking out when I told her that he was still on the run. We don't need another incident like that one. Give it a rest until Monday, alright?"

Another heavy sigh. "Alright, Blake. Monday afternoon at your place." He pauses, and I can almost hear him consider arguing with me more, but in the end all he says is, "Thanks for calling me back."

"Yup."

I hit end before he can protest further.

Forty

"I would have talked to him tomorrow." Vivienne's small voice comes from behind me.

"Shit, I'm sorry, I didn't mean to wake you."

"It's alright. Nothing new?" I shake my head. "I'm alright. I know I'm safe here, and I know these things take time. The only reason he was arrested so fast the last time was because he left the apartment when he was done and a neighbor heard me screaming and called nine-one-one and I was whisked away to the hospital. When he returned to the apartment he found it without me in it and full of cops. At least that's what they told me."

"Fine. But that's no excuse for why they can't find him now."

"Sure it is. Riley has a lot of connections in this city. A lot of people will hide him, stand up for him, or defend him if necessary. Not to mention a few cop friends, too, who are no doubt keeping him up-to-date. Whatever you do, don't underestimate him."

"Do you know who those cops might be?"

"No, I don't. I don't really know much about his circle of people. He rarely ever brought business home, it was always done somewhere else. Which really sucked because when they arrested him, they wouldn't have found any drugs around, nothing that could've kept him in jail longer." She takes a deep breath. "If they'd asked me about this before, I would have told them then, too, but I didn't have solid evidence that pointed to anything that would've helped my case against him, and I doubt even now I have any good information for them."

Wow, I think that is the longest speech I've ever heard her make, even when she was mad and yelling at me. "Well, I've put Stevens off until Monday. For right now at least."

"I heard. What's all this about your apartment and a lawyer?"

How can I put this so that she doesn't freak out again? "I, um, I emailed my lawyer asking him to meet with me Monday at my apartment to discuss your situation. I'd like you to be there."

"Do I need a lawyer?"

"I'd like to have one lined up for you in case this goes south and you either have to testify or press your own personal charges against Riley. Or both."

She's very stoic, no real reaction to what I've said. It's almost as if she's shut down. "I'll think about it."

I'm not sure I can take that as an answer, but I don't push her right now. I don't need her getting mad at me; I need her to know that I'm on her side so she'll agree to come stay in the condo I've had prepared for her.

She yawns.

"You're exhausted. Get some sleep. I'll be here in the morning and we can talk some more if you want."

She nods. "Thank you."

"For what?"

"For being here, for..." She pauses. "For rescuing me."

My heart swells nearly to the point of explosion at the tenderness in her voice. "I only wish I'd gotten to you sooner."

"Don't. I'm alive, my baby is alive, and you're here to protect me. That more than makes up for any mistakes you may feel you've made." Her voice is sincere and heartwarming.

I walk over toward her bed and lean down to kiss her forehead. Again she doesn't flinch, and I'm thankful for that.

"Thank you for your forgiveness." I lower the bed a little more. "Now, get some sleep. I'll stay off of the phone."

She laughs a little and closes her eyes.

Forty-One

I don't linger at going to bed myself, curious as to what the night will bring me. The dream I had earlier seemed to come to an end.

I settle into bed and, by the light of the bathroom I left on in case she needs it, I watch her sleep until I fall asleep.

This time it's different. I'm not in a white room. Or even a room that could be in Elysium for that matter. No, I'm...where am I? I know this room but I can't place it.

It's a bedroom with plush, light tan carpet and a king-size canopy bed made from a dark cherry wood with modern spindles made of what look like stacked blocks. The sheer white curtains flow down on all sides.

Someone is sleeping in the bed.

I walk toward it to see who it is. Sprawled out across the pillows is a mane of curly, bright red hair. It's the beautiful, pale, sleeping form of Vivienne.

I hungrily look her up and down and notice, under the blankets, the rounded baby bump propped up by something. Judging from the size of the bump, this is in the future, but not too far in the future. I come

297

around to the far side of the bed to see her bare back. And it is covered in the same silvery and black wings as mine. *She really is an angel.*

I hear a noise behind me and I turn toward it. It's me.

What?

I watch myself move around the bathroom with a towel around my waist. The wings on my back are vibrant silver and black. On my right shoulder and extending down my right arm is the tattoo from the first dream. I'm shaving and brushing my teeth, the two things I usually do just before crawling into bed. It won't be long now; I need to get out of here before he sees me. Before *I* see me.

I look back to Vivienne, sound asleep on the bed. I could watch her sleep for hours: so peaceful, so angelic.

The light in the bathroom goes out. Crap. I look around quickly for someplace to hide, but it's too late; I'm already walking toward myself, looking straight at me. *Can he see me here?*

The other me walks straight through me and around the bed.

Nope. I back away from the bed as I watch myself climb in behind her, moving her hair out of the way so as not to lie on it. It looks a lot longer than I'm used to seeing it.

The other me wraps his arm around her and snuggles into her neck.

She moves, rolling backwards into him and turning so he can kiss her.

"Hello, beautiful. I didn't mean to wake you."

She laughs at him. "It's alright. I was missing you anyway." She smiles and kisses him. I watch as she reaches around his back with her left arm. His eyes roll. *She's touching his wings.*

Her motions have forced the covers down and her chest is now exposed. I feel a surge of excitement.

Sensing movement elsewhere in the room, I look up. Standing on the opposite side of the bed is Vivienne, just as she was when she left me in the last dream: beautiful, wings extended, and her hand resting gently against the swell of her stomach.

I look back at the couple on the bed. I now feel as though I'm invading their privacy, but I'm captivated by them.

I watch as I push the covers down further, exposing more of Vivienne. She's glowing - a white, blue, and silver aura around her, similar to the one I saw that first night.

Vivienne rolls over and straddles me - or him - and I watch intently as my hands roam slowly and softly along her breasts and her extended belly. I can feel my own arousal watching the two of them.

What happens next surprises me. Slowly the wings on Vivienne's back come alive and extend outward. It is an amazing sight to witness. Her wings are beautiful - white, with the slightest hint of silver accenting many of the feathers, and they shimmer in the dim light of the room.

I look past the Vivienne on the bed to the Vivienne standing opposite me. Her clothes have changed. She is wearing the gray, too-big t-shirt and black sweatpants I helped her put on before going to bed. I cock my head at her, puzzled.

Forty-Two

Suddenly I feel a tug, like someone is pulling on my shirt. I open my eyes and look up into Vivienne's shadowed face. "Vivienne? What's wrong?"

"I-I'm sorry, I can't sleep, I—"

"Come here," I say, and I pull back the covers. She slides in carefully, lying on her left side with her head in the crook of my shoulder. The harsh velcro of the sling rubs against my chest through my shirt. "Are you in?"

"Yes."

I wrap the blankets around us. "Good?"

"Uh huh."

As I start to pull my hand back from covering her up I feel her wrist brace against my arm, stopping me from pulling it back to my side. It takes me only a moment to realize that my hand is resting, open-palmed, across her bump. I have no words for the flood of emotions that wash through me.

As I lie here with her cascade of hair spread across my body, I contemplate how we got to this point. I can't imagine what's changed since I last saw her that has made her so trusting to the point of coming to me for comfort.

I snuggle into her a bit more. The warmth of her body pressed against mine is the beginning of an addiction I know I will never break.

Snuggled next to Vivienne, I think back to the dream I just had and the centuries-old story my mother used to tell me about *A chuid den tsaol,* or soulmates: the belief that there is only one person for everyone and that finding that one perfect person is rare. When you find yours, you know instantly because there is a bright aura surrounding that person; you will see it when you first lay eyes on them.

I think back to the night I met Vivienne, the night my back led me to her. Up until then, I'd had some indication that something was going on with my back, but I chalked it up to the old stories of the markings on my back and didn't make much of it.

I think I see now that it was a sign of what was to come: an omen, like dreams can be. Not like the dreams I've had these last few nights – nothing so overt – but something more along the lines of subliminal messages telling me who I am or what I would become.

The day I met Vivienne, my markings had been bugging me ever since I'd arrived at the site of the groundbreaking. As the afternoon progressed, it got worse, until it was so annoying I had to leave.

Just before I got in the car to go home, it was like my back took on its own personality, driving me toward my destination. Then, I didn't know why. But I'm sure now. It was driving me toward my *A chuid den tsaol.*

And now that I've seen parts of our future, I know that it is not just for her sake that I fight for her. It is for me, too. I can't imagine my life without her. She is as essential to me as air.

Is it possible that she is seeing some of the same things that I'm seeing? Is that why she's changed toward me?

While I know this battle is far from over, Elton made that very clear earlier tonight, I now know a glimpse of what the future holds for me, for us. Is that future set? Or is it up to me to protect her so that we get to that future?

Forty-Three

I can feel Vivienne moving in my arms, and my eyes open lazily to see morning light streaming in through the window.

"I'm sorry, I just have to go to the bathroom."

"It's okay. Do you need some help?"

"No, I think I'm okay."

"Okay."

She gets her legs over the side of the cot, stands up and starts for the bathroom, IV pole in tow. I'll be dammed – someone changed the bag. She's gonna be pissed. But I also notice – and it didn't register last night – that she is without the oxygen. I just shake my head. When she climbed out of her bed and into mine, she removed it.

No sooner does the bathroom door close than the door to the hospital room opens and Amanda comes in.

"She went to the bathroom."

"Ahh. How's she doing?" she asks.

"Don't know. I haven't had a chance to ask. We just woke up," I tell her, and she smiles.

I can hear the toilet flush in the bathroom and then the water starts running. A few moments later, the door opens. I haven't moved from where I was in the cot, and she smiles slightly when she sees me. I jerk my head in Amanda's direction.

"How are you feeling?" I ask her.

"Good. Tired, but good."

"That's good. Are you ready for some tests?" Amanda asks her.

"Um, no." She scrunches up her face. "Can we finally ditch the IV though?"

Amanda laughs, "Yeah. You fell asleep so she just changed out the fluids."

"I noticed. Can we please take it out?"

"Yes. Climb back up in the bed." Amanda says, and I head toward the bathroom.

"Don't go far, please?" I hear Vivienne ask.

"Nope, not a chance, just going to the bathroom."

She nods, but I see sadness on her face. I smile at her reassuringly.

I begin to wonder whether she feels the need to be near me because she feels safe with me. I take great comfort in this thought.

When I come out, Vivienne is IV-free and Amanda's pulling up Vivienne's shirt. I stop dead in my tracks and start to turn around.

"It's okay," Vivienne says. "She's just checking on the baby."

I smile and ask, "Are you hungry?"

"Famished."

"Can you wait a little until the tests are done?" Amanda asks.

"If I have to," Vivienne says sulkily.

My smile widens. "I'll call Red and have him bring up some food."

Amanda has finished revealing Vivienne's stomach. The little mound stands out even further than it did a couple of weeks ago. The sight is actually really sweet. Amanda puts a microphone-shaped thing on the bump, and almost instantly there is a rapid whooshing sound. The image of Baby Callahan's heartbeat on the ultrasound monitor the last time we were here comes to mind.

Vivienne's face lights up at the sound. She smiles and looks right at me, then smiles a little more brightly at my returning smile.

I don't know why I feel such a connection to her baby, but I do. I have this strange sense of hope that this is only the beginning of what's to come with us.

The whooshing sound stops as Amanda removes the microphone from her tummy.

"Sounds great, and I got one hundred and forty-nine beats a minute." She puts the equipment away and turns back to Vivienne. "Are you ready to go for a ride?"

"Can I walk?"

"No, you can either ride in a wheelchair or we can push the bed."

"Wheelchair then," she huffs.

"So feisty," I say, and she scowls at me. I stick my tongue out at her and she bursts out laughing. "That's my girl."

When Amanda comes back with a wheelchair, Vivienne slides down from the bed and sits down in it.

"Are you coming?" she asks me.

I look to Amanda, who shrugs. "That's up to you," she says.

"If you want me to, I'll come," I say, looking at Vivienne.

"Yes, please."

"Alright." I slip into my sneakers and fall in behind Amanda. "Can I push her?"

"Sure," she says and steps aside for me to take the handles on the back. "Follow me."

Forty-Four

We return to the room about two hours later to find that Red's already been here. He's left sandwich fixings – more of a lunch-type food than breakfast, but that's good because it's nearly noon anyway.

Vivienne's ultrasound went well, and Dr. Alston seemed pleased with what she saw.

Once Vivienne and I are alone, I put together a sandwich for her and she digs in. Probably not the best food on a weak stomach, but she dives in with gusto and I'm not going to stop her.

After a few bites she asks me a question I never thought she'd ask. "Why is helping and feeding me so important to you?"

I wonder if this is something that she and Dr. Alston talked about last time. I take a sip of water and swallow the bite of sandwich I'd just taken.

"My dad was not my father," I begin.

She looks at me, puzzled.

"My dad, Shannon, met my mother when she was about six months pregnant with me. When he met her, she was nothing but skin and bones, living on the streets of Dublin. Her own father had kicked her out

307

of his house when she told him she was pregnant, so she did what she needed to in order to survive.

"When she met my dad, he fought to take care of her. And of me." Wow, this sounds very familiar. I'd never thought about it like this. "He wasn't a wealthy man - he worked seventy or eighty hours a week to bring home squat for money and food - but he endured and managed to save enough money to bring my mom and me to the States. That's when things finally started to look up for our family. There were times when we all still went hungry, but the Irish community in Boston I grew up in was very supportive, and we managed to turn things around.

"My dad taught me that persistence, perseverance and determination drive any man to do the things they're good at. Mom taught me never to give up and to always help those that have less than you."

I look carefully at her. "Because of that and my mom's history, I'm a strong supporter of the shelters in Minneapolis and a big contributor to Hope House, which is a home for women, and specifically for pregnant women and their families.

"While I didn't know you were pregnant when I met you, I did see a young woman who needed a good meal and a new lease on life, which is why I left you that tip and refused to take it back from you."

I reach into my back pocket and pull out the now extremely wrinkled piece of paper wrapped around the cash still inside. "I've never opened this, and I never will. I brought it with me Friday with every intention of making sure you got it back. Now that you know the why, maybe you will accept it?"

My heart breaks to see the shiny wet spots on her cheeks. "Oh, Vivienne, don't cry. Please."

"I feel so stupid. I feel like...I feel like if I'd accepted your help when you offered it, not kicked you out of my hospital room...or if I hadn't even shown up at your office that day-"

She sniffs and I reach for a Kleenex. "I feel like had all that not happened, I wouldn't be here. After I kicked you out, Dr. Alston said that you really were just trying to help me. That it was a no-strings-attached kind of help and that I might be overreacting to your generosity." She wipes her nose and the tears from her face with the tissue I hand her.

"But at the time, I was so determined to prove to myself - and only myself - that I could do all this on my own. I realized very quickly that you both were right, but I didn't know how to swallow my pride and call you."

I'm not entirely sure what to say to her speech. I'm completely blown away. "I understand what it means to swallow your pride. It's not easy, and I understand why you couldn't. I'd planned to be here on Friday for your appointment, hoping that I could convince you that all I was really trying to do was help."

"I understand that now," she says. "But you also need to understand where I'm coming from, too. I've spent so much of my life without a parental figure, struggling to survive everyday...but somehow someone was always there to pick up the pieces. It was never my mom, it was the little old neighbor lady. Or Riley." I watch as her face distorts on his name.

I cock my head at her and she takes a deep breath, as if having decided something. "After my mom had her stroke, I was homeless, with nowhere to go except school and a little cubby inside my old apartment until I met him and he basically took me in." She shudders. "I grew up in a house full of drugs, alcohol and abuse. It turned out Riley was no different, though instead of doing drugs, he dealt them. And that is something that I will have to deal with the rest of my life."

"What if I told you that I would never let that happen to you again?"

"Mikah." The sound of my name on her lips sends flutters through my body. "You can't take care of me forever. I'm not your burden to bear."

"You're not a burden, and please do not ever let me hear you speak of yourself like that again. I give my help freely, Vivienne, and without strings. You and I both know that you can never go back to that apartment. So where are you going to go?"

Forty-Five

She doesn't answer, and I know she is contemplating her options and how few they are. But I need her to answer me. Finally she says, "I can go back to the shelter until I can right myself again. I've done it before, Mikah, I'll do it again."

My heart breaks. "No, you won't. I will not let you struggle to make ends meet. I won't let you roam around the streets of Minneapolis, and I will not let you be alone. Viv, please. Understand that I cannot walk away from you. I care to much about you."

She is crying again, but she doesn't argue with me.

"Look, Viv, I won't force you to do anything you don't want to do, but I ask that you consider something for me."

She nods slightly through the tears.

"I have a condo by the river. In my building I own three units - mine, Red's, and one that was meant for Celeste, my housekeeper. Celeste refuses to live in the unit. I want you to take it."

"Mikah, I can't..."

"Please, just hear me out?" I ask, and she nods. "Alston said yesterday that you won't be able to return

311

to work for a couple of weeks. How are you going to make ends meet if you aren't working?"

"So this would only be for a couple of weeks?" she asks.

"If you wish, but let me finish. The apartment is yours, to do as you wish, decorate how you like. My crew is at your disposal. When the time comes and you can return to work, I want you to come work for me."

"Doing what, Mikah, I have no skills. That diner was the first job I've ever held longer than a couple of weeks."

I'm taken aback by her rebuttal - not because she is arguing, but because she is devaluing her abilities.

"I have an entry-level administrative assistant position for you. It will pretty much be answering phones, taking messages, making copies, things like that. It's easy, relatively stress-free work, and more importantly, it comes with a salary you can live off of. You won't have to be on your feet, and it would even offer medical benefits so that you can pay your own way for the things you need if that is what's important to you."

"What about the apartment? There is no way that I can afford it, even with a salary."

"We can work out a lease. You can pay me rent every month, if that's what you need to do to feel comfortable."

Her brows pull together. "How long do I have to think about this?"

"Until you're discharged, but know this: I will not allow you back into that apartment, period. And I will not allow you on the streets or anyplace where Riley can track you down. So until he's caught and this

312

matter is resolved, I need you to come and stay where I can be close to you, keep an eye on you."

She doesn't answer me but nods, acknowledging that she's heard me. I didn't expect an answer from her, at least not right away, and I don't get one.

Forty-Six

The room has been completely silent for a while, and the loud click of the door makes us both jump. Looking toward the door, we see Dr. Alston coming into the room.

"Am I interrupting?" she asks both of us.

"No," we say in unison, and Vivienne smiles, giving me hope that she's not upset with me.

Dr. Alston laughs. "Well, okay then. Vivienne, I have some good news."

"Yay! Do I get to get out of here?"

"I'll get to that. First of all, your shoulder and wrist look great. I will let you take off the sling, but I'd like you to wear the brace for at least another couple of days. You can take it off to shower, but put it back on when you're done. Okay?"

"Okay, is that all?"

"Eager, aren't we?" Dr. Alston smiles at Vivienne. "Your lung is still healing. While the outside is nearly completely healed, which is nothing like anything I've ever seen before, it's still a bit inflamed. But it's nothing that will keep you here in the hospital."

"What about the baby?" I ask, and Vivienne looks to me for reassurance.

I move closer to her, hoping to provide a little more comfort, and she surprises me by putting her hand on my back. I feel a rush of pleasure through my body that has to do with something more than the fact that she is touching me, and I realize that she is tracing her fingers absently along my right wing. When her fingers cross over to normal skin, the difference in the sensation is marked.

"The baby is doing fine. You're measuring a little bigger than fourteen weeks, but clearly that's due to the fact that you've been eating more food." She looks pointedly at the remains of Vivienne's sandwich on the tray. "What with the unnatural rate at which you're healing, I'm not going to be concerned right now about weight.

"Also...I didn't ask you during the ultrasound because I didn't want to get you worked up, but I was able to determine Baby Callahan's sex, and I've taken the liberty of putting the proof in here." She pulls out an envelope from her pocket. "I've never been wrong," she says a little smugly, "but it's not guaranteed. And I'd rather you look when you're ready to find out. If you choose not to look, well, it will be a surprise when you have the baby."

"Okay," Vivienne says, taking the envelope. "I'll let you know next time whether I've decided to look. Now can I leave?"

Dr. Alston rolls her eyes. "So impatient." Then she asks, "Where are you going to go?"

My ears perk up and my heart sinks, dreading the answer.

"I can't discharge you unless I know you're going somewhere safe," Dr. Alston continues. "Hospital policy. Do you have something set up?"

She nods.

I grow hopeful that she will take me up on my offer.

"Mikah has offered me a place to stay for a while, until I can get back to work and on my feet. I'm going to go home with him."

YES! I shout inside my head, and at the same time Vivienne gently pats my back, right between my shoulders. I have the sudden thought that Vivienne has been in my dreams with me.

"I think that is a great idea. I've scheduled an appointment for you for two weeks from tomorrow at ten. And no working at least until then, okay?"

"Yes, ma'am."

"Okay, here are your discharge papers." She hands Vivienne a stack of papers. "You cannot walk out of this hospital – it is a liability – but someone will come with a wheelchair to get you in a little bit. That'll give you a chance to get packed up, and then that's it, you're free to go."

"Thank you, Dr. Alston. For everything."

"You're welcome, Vivienne. It's what I'm here for. I rather look forward to seeing you under happier circumstances. I will be in touch in a couple of days to see how you're doing. I'll see you in a couple of weeks, but feel free to call me if you need anything before then."

As soon as the door closes behind Dr. Alston I turn to Vivienne. "Thank you. For not putting up a fight about my request."

She lets out a breathy laugh. "Yeah, 'cause you gave me so many options. But in the end, you're right, I really have no place else to go, and I'd much rather be closer to you."

I lean over and kiss her forehead. "Thank you, thank you, thank you."

"For what?"

"Giving me hope."

CHAPTER THREE

Give Me Desire

Prologue

"Do not toy with me." His anger radiates off him in waves and the temperature in the room rises.

"It is done, Master. I've completed the task you've assigned me." He does not look upon the other man's face as he speaks. He's kneeling some distance away, causing him to shout to be heard.

"Get up!" The evil voice fills the room, stunning everything inside.

The young man stands but does not raise his head.

The scene changes, and instead of a small, dark room, they are in a cavernous one, with strange pockets of steam rising through cracks in the rock floor. Somewhere nearby echoes of the hollow screams of tortured souls can be heard.

"Your job was simple, you were to kill her. Here you stand, not only her blood but the blood of at least two others on you. And yet I do not believe you have completed your task, minion. Why is this?"

"I don't know. I left her dead, she was dead when I left." He begins mumbling – low and incoherently - and twitches as though he can't stand his own skin.

"Ah, but she is not dead. If she were dead, I'd have all my powers back, and..." Suddenly the room is lit up by a bright white flash. The air is instantly charged, static making hair stand on end, and the young man crumples to the ground. "And I'd be able to kill you."

"No! Don't. Don't hurt him," a female voice says, and a girl runs from behind a rock to be at the young man's side.

"Who are you?" the dark, mysterious man shouts.

"What are you doing to him?" She looks down at the crumpled form on the floor and reaches out to touch his dirty blond hair. Looking up in the direction of the voice. "Who are you?"

A deep, throaty laugh comes from the man in the shadows, making the hairs on the back of her neck stand to attention. "I am your worst nightmare, child."

The echo of heavy footsteps across the rock floor fills the cave, each step getting closer. She cowers, trying to pull the young man with her, but she fails. She lets him slump to the ground as she scrambles backwards on her hands and feet.

"What are you going to do to me?" she whispers breathlessly. Her body shakes in fear.

There is no response as the shadowy figure keeps walking closer with slow, measured steps.

"It is not you I wish to harm, child. It is this boy who needs a lesson in obedience." There is an edge of reverence in his voice, as though he's longing for something.

"What are you going to do to him?" she asks, the fear dropping away from her voice.

"If he'd done what he was supposed to do, I'd do nothing to him. But he has failed me and he deserves to be punished, perhaps tortured." The voice is menacing and yet also strangely enticing to her.

"Take me instead," she says, and she rises to her feet.

The footsteps stop. "What would I want with you, girl?"

"Anything, everything. Let Riley go and take me instead."

"Tell me your name, child." It comes out a growl.

"Nyssa."

ONE

Vivienne

I feel amazing, but why?

I look around, but there is nothing to see, nothing to look at, but solid white. Am I dead?

"No, darling, you are very much alive."

I spin around, trying to find the source of the gentle female voice, but I see nothing more than the white walls surrounding me.

"Who are you?" My voice is calm, but inside anxiety spikes at the unfamiliar voice.

"I'm here to help guide you," the voice says. It is soft, gentle and reassuring, but I'm still confused. "Someone is waiting for you down that hallway behind you."

I turn around hastily and am momentarily thrown off balance. *Oh yeah, my wings,* I think, as though I've had them my entire life, and flex my shoulders. A part of my mind – the part that knows I've never had wings – finds it odd that I'm so unconcerned about it.

After a moment, I regain my balance and begin heading down the hallway, and my heart starts to pound at the idea of what's waiting for me at the end.

As I'm walking, I take a look down at my dress. It's soft and white, with silver beads along the bodice in an intricate design below my breasts. My chest looks bigger - a lot bigger - than I remember, but looking down beyond them I can see why.

Standing out in perfect roundness is my baby bump, no longer a bump but very much a pregnant belly. I stroke it absently and note the silver, cuff-like bracelet around my wrist, its beautiful Celtic design highlighted by a shiny white stone in the center. The cuff extends down the back of my hand almost to my knuckle with its very detailed design.

Then I realize that there is also something cool pressing against my forehead. I can't see it, and when I try to pull on it, it tugs at my hair, so I leave it alone. It feels like a tiara or some type of headpiece.

I keep walking further down the hall; it's long and narrow, with no end in sight. I can't imagine how big this place is with a hall this long. My feet make no sound against the floor and I realize that I'm barefoot.

After a few moments more, I see something up ahead. A figure. I can't make out the details, but a rapidly growing longing churns inside me, and I quicken my pace.

But no matter how far I go, I just can't quite get there. Frustration boils. I'm reminded of a never-ending nightmare and my heart rate increases with unease.

Finally the figure comes into better focus. It's a man, shirtless and sporting an intricate black tattoo along his right shoulder and down his right arm. His skin has a nice tan tone to it against all the white behind him and the white pants he's wearing. His black hair is tousled as though he's been sleeping.

Seeing the image as a whole sends a jolt of desire throughout my entire body. Every nerve is alive with an urgent need to be close to him.

And then an undercurrent of fear washes through me as the idea that I could need or want someone this much washes through me. I've never desired anyone before.

Mikah? I ask myself. Could it really be him? What is he doing here? How did he get here?

The wings, the fact that I don't know that I've ever felt this good in my life...this has to be heaven; there is no other explanation for it, despite what I was told earlier. But if I'm in heaven, what is Mikah doing here? And does this mean I'm dead?

That female voice from earlier returns in the same friendly tones as before. "You are not in heaven, my dear. You are in Elysium, a place where only a few chosen are allowed to travel. Your presence here has nothing to do with being dead. You are very much alive."

"Who are you?" I ask again.

"My name is Zirah, and I am your guide."

"Guide for what?"

"I am here to help you understand all the changes your body is going through. Mainly, I'm here to help you understand that you, my child, are a Chosen. You are an angel."

Suddenly the view in front of me shifts. The room is an ominous grayish-black. I blink a few times, adjusting to the dark after the stark white of a few moments ago.

There is a bright flash up ahead that lights up the room, and I hear a girl scream. Picking up my skirt, I run as quickly as I can manage on the rocky floor. A hot flame arcs across my back, and my wings twitch. I look over my shoulder, but there is nothing there. The flame grows hotter but is not yet painful as I approach the place where the flash of light came from.

"What would I want with you, little girl?"

"Anything, everything. Let Riley go and take me instead."

"What is your name, child?" The deep, menacing voice echoes through the cavern.

"Nyssa."

TWO

"Vivienne.... Vivienne, come on. Wake up."

That voice. I...I know him. I know that voice.

"Come on, sweetie. It's time to go home."

What?

My eyes begin to flutter open. I see his eyes – blue and green mixed to create the most beautiful effect that mimics the ocean – and they are warm, caring...and there is something else in them that I can't name.

"There you are," he whispers. "You were having a nightmare."

I can feel my mouth make that O shape, but nothing comes out.

"It's alright, you're safe."

I blink a couple of times, trying to shake the dream I was having and bring myself back into the present. Instinctively I know what I was hearing, but how? Why? Why me? Why was Nyssa in my dream? I couldn't see her, but is it possible that it really is the Nyssa I know? Instinct tells me that it is.

"Hi," I grumble sleepily to Mikah.

He smiles at me. "Hi. You ready to go?"

I nod my head. My neck, though I've played it off, is still a little sore. I've managed not to look in the mirror, but for as much pain as I was in when it happened, my arm doesn't hurt at all. I've finally ditched the sling, but Dr. Alston is making me keep the brace on my wrist. It seems utterly pointless, but I'm not going to argue anymore.

An orderly comes into the room pushing a wheelchair. At least this one doesn't have the stupid yellow flag on top of the pole like the one earlier did.

I let out a sigh. I get to leave the hospital, but I've capitulated to Mikah's demand to take me back to his apartment – or rather to a different one originally meant for his housekeeper, Celeste. A part of me wonders whether or not he'll actually let me stay in that apartment or whether he'll try to convince me to stay in his.

But the fact remains: The longer I thought about whether or not to go with Mikah, the more I realized that I couldn't come up with any rational reasons to not go. Riley is still on the loose, and no matter where I go, he can always search for me. The idea of Mikah getting hurt makes my heart constrict, but Red will be there, too.

Furthermore, Dr. Alston and Nurse Fang – Amanda – have told me that I can't work again until after I see Alston in a couple of weeks, which means I can't afford my apartment anymore.

My apartment. It suddenly dawns on me Mikah is right: I won't ever be able to go back there again. The memories are too horrible, and I know that I'd never feel safe there again. But I also know that there are things there that I want.

I turn to Mikah as he helps me get down off of the hospital bed and whisper, "I need to go back to my apartment first. My stuff," I say, not wanting to display the fear I'm feeling about going back there.

His eyes widen a fraction. "What's in your apartment that you need?" he asks.

"My journal, my clothes, and the picture you gave me." My breath hitches at the idea of my baby's ultrasound picture.

Mikah stiffens at the mention of the picture. His eyes take on a very distant, thoughtful look, almost as though he is trying to recall something. "Where are the picture and your journal?"

"The picture is next to my bed, and the journal is under the foot of the bed, wedged between the pallet and the mattress."

He doesn't respond but rather reaches for his phone as he helps me sit in the wheelchair. He presses a button and puts it to his ear.

"Are you ready to go, Ms. Callahan?" the orderly behind me asks.

"I just need my stuff."

I spot a rather expensive duffle bag sitting at the foot of the bed.

"Red, can you go to Vivienne's apartment and collect a picture and her journal?"

"What about my clothes?" I say as Mikah reaches for the bag. He holds up one finger.

Slinging the duffle over his shoulder, he looks to the man behind me. "Let's go." But he hasn't said anything to Red about my clothes. "When did you do that?" he says into the phone. "Oh, okay then. Wait, what about the picture?" My heart sinks as Mikah's face falls. "I'll tell her. Thanks, Red."

He pulls the phone from his ear, presses a button, then puts it back to his ear as he walks alongside me, not giving me a chance to say anything.

"Celeste, we're leaving the hospital now. Were you able to take-" He cuts off.

"Perfect, thank you. We'll be home shortly. I'm going to take her downstairs." He pauses. "Okay, thanks."

We stop in front of the elevators. As Mikah pulls the phone away from his ear, the orderly hits the down arrow and I turn toward Mikah. "What about my picture?" I say. My tone is clipped, irritated.

Mikah's eyes dart to mine; they're wary. "The picture was gone when Red went by your apartment last night."

My heart sinks. I loved that picture. But where could it have gone? Why is it gone? Did Riley take it?

"Celeste already ordered a new frame, same as the other one. It should be here by Tuesday. And I still have the original picture, so I can replace the image."

"Thank you," I say quietly, still contemplating where the photo could've gone in the first place.

"You're welcome." He smiles. "Red took care of your apartment. Cleaned it up and moved all your stuff to the condo."

I nod, relieved that I don't have to deal with it myself but still sorry to see the apartment and my independence go, at least for now.

We ride the elevator down in silence. As we approach the entrance of the hospital, through the glass doors I see a limo parked in front of the door. I can't tell, but I'm pretty sure that it is the same one from a couple weeks back. We come through the double doors and there are two men standing on either side of the car, both very tall with broad shoulders. One has bright red hair, similar in color to my own, but in a short military cut. The other has darker hair, also cut short, but not as short as the first one's.

My heart rate increases and anxiety flares as we come through the door. The one with red hair moves to the back door of the limo and opens it. Mikah hands him the bags, and he moves around to the trunk. My nerves settle a little as understanding registers: These are more of Mikah's men.

As Mikah extends his hand to me, I catch the orderly's movement in the corner of my eye. I flinch, panic washing through me, and I jerk away from him. He reaches for the wheel lock on the chair. On my other side, I can see Mikah's hand, but I'm frozen in place. Then I realize all the orderly is doing is securing the wheelchair.

"Vivienne," I hear Mikah say quietly, and I turn stiffly in his direction. He mouths, "It's okay." I feel the fear wash out of me and I place my hand in his.

Stepping out of the wheelchair, I'm steadied by Mikah, who says to the orderly, "Thank you."

"Have a safe trip home," the orderly replies and wheels the empty chair back into the hospital.

THREE

Mikah leads me to the door of the limo and urges me to climb in. My hesitation to do so doesn't go unnoticed by him.

"Andrew?"

"Sir?" the dark-haired one replies.

"Can you hit the interior lights and roll down the windows?" Mikah asks him.

I try but fail to smile at Mikah's quick thinking.

"Yes, sir," Andrew says, and I watch as the interior lights come on and the windows go down. I even catch motion in the top as the sunroof opens.

"Thanks," I say so only Mikah can hear me.

"Of course." He starts again to help me into the limo, and this time I go a little more freely, as I can see everything inside. "If you sit up toward the front, you won't be as cold."

I clamber up to the small bench seat, not at the front but on the driver's side, and I sit down.

Mikah follows behind me, taking the seat next to me, his back to the driver. I shiver slightly as the colder air registers, and he puts out his arm. I slide closer to him and rest my head on his shoulder. In a slow, calculated move he brings his hand down so

331

that his arm is along my back and his hand is on my hip. Holding me to him, he lightly kisses the top of my head.

We ride in silence, me fighting heavy eyes as exhaustion tries to consume me. I close my eyes but don't fall asleep.

I replay my dream - the one in the white hallway - trying hard to make sense of it.

I felt so alive, so free, and yet so well-protected, like nothing could hurt me, like I could feel no pain.

An angel? How is that even possible?

I don't get much time to linger on these thoughts before I feel Mikah squeeze a little tighter against my hip. "Wake up, sweetheart. We're here."

I blink my eyes a couple of times. I feel slightly energized. But I can still feel the worry and fear in my body, not because I'm afraid I'll be unwelcome or even that I'll overstay my welcome, but because of the emotions I feel for Mikah. I've given up everything I've earned for myself to come here.

He slowly pulls his arm away from me and I sit up. Feeling heavy and uncoordinated, like I'm just waking up, I rub my eyes and then look out the window. A man dressed in livery is coming through a revolving door and heading straight for the limo at a rather intense speed.

I freeze. I don't know who he is or why he's charging toward us.

Mikah notices my hesitation and is quick to explain. "That's Arthur. He's the building doorman."

I nod slowly as Arthur moves to the back of the limo where Andrew, I think, is opening the trunk for the bags.

Mikah slides past me to the door just as the red-haired gentleman opens it. Mikah climbs out. "Thank you, Connor." I smile a little at the name; it doesn't suit him at all.

As I start to get out of the limo, Mikah holds out his hand, almost automatically, and I use him to climb out. Standing next to Connor I feel like a child standing next to her dad. He has at least a foot and half on me, and he's taller even than Mikah.

Mikah leads me to the doors, but he bypasses the revolving door for the normal one. I can't help but smile at the idea that he's using it because of my claustrophobia. He really does pay attention. But I also notice that he doesn't let go of my hand as we walk through the door.

FOUR

Stepping inside the building, I see that the lobby décor is all tan and neutral tones with accents of black in the furniture. Opposite the door we've just come in is a security desk with a man sitting behind it.

"Good day, Mr. Blake."

"Hello, Charlie," Mikah replies to the man behind the counter. He's much older, heavyset with gray hair and glasses. He stands up in greeting as we pass toward the hallway to the right of the desk, and I find it comforting in some strange way to see a gun on his right hip.

We reach a bank of elevators but keep going, passing four different sets of doors until we come to the end of the hall. Directly in front of us is another set of elevator doors, and Mikah presses the up arrow. "This is the only elevator that will reach my apartment and where we're going."

As soon as he finishes, the bell chimes and I jump slightly. I know my fear is due to the fact that we're so exposed. Once we're in Mikah's apartment, I know I'll feel better.

As we step into the elevator, I see Connor and Arthur coming in through the front doors. Arthur has the duffle bag. "Shouldn't we wait for them?" I ask, pointing in their direction.

"Nope, we're good to go up."

Mikah places a key card in a slot below the two buttons, then pushes the button for the sixth floor. I'd expected him to push the button for the seventh, assuming Mikah's apartment would be on the top floor.

"I thought we were going to your apartment?" I say, puzzled, as the elevator starts to climb.

He shakes his head and looks at me out of the corner of his eye. I can see a touch of worry in his expression. I remember he'd said something about my own apartment, but for some reason I thought he would take me to his. He's been so protective of me these last couple of days; I can't imagine him letting me out of his sight.

Before I can question him further about it, the elevator comes to a halt. The bell chimes again and I notice that, in a completely subconscious move, I inch closer to Mikah so that I'm standing behind his right arm, shielding myself.

The doors open on a hallway that is only a couple feet wider than the elevator doors. I can see straight down to a window at the far end.

Mikah takes a step toward the door, tugging me by my hand, bringing me with him. I slowly follow behind him. The hallway is drab: nothing on the walls, and the carpet has some crazy red and gold pattern on it. It makes me dizzy looking at it, so I look straight ahead as I follow behind Mikah.

We approach two doors, one on either side of the hall. "Red and his wife, Maria, live there." He nods toward the door on the left. "These are the only two apartments on this floor, and you can only access it by key card or a security code." I feel a little more comfortable now, knowing it's secure. "Also, Connor will be manning the hallway until around midnight, then Andrew will take over until morning."

He places a key in the door on the right, turns the knob, pushes it open and ushers me in. I look around cautiously and he reassures me, "Red checked it after we left the hospital. There is no one in here."

I take a few steps inside. The floors are a beautiful, light-colored hardwood. There is a closed door immediately to the right. "The laundry room," Mikah says, opening the door. Inside are a washer and dryer and some shelves with detergent and dryer sheets on them.

He steps across the hall. "Here is one of the bathrooms. The other is off of the main bedroom." He turns on the light. The tile is a pretty royal blue, the cabinets and accents a light wood.

What catches my eye, though, is the big, deep tub that has a step up in order to get into it. There are two faucets to fill it up. The idea of a warm bath is very inviting.

He pulls back, clicking off the light, and we proceed further into the apartment. It opens up to the right into the kitchen, which is bigger than my entire apartment. It's been done in beautiful dark countertops and cabinets, not quite black, that make the silver appliances stand out. A breakfast bar that separates the hall from the kitchen has three bar-height chairs whose color matches the cabinets.

He moves on, opening a door directly across from the kitchen. "Here's the second bedroom."

I peek inside: deep blue carpet; a white dresser and some matching bedside tables; light blue walls; and pictures of beaches, beach houses and even one of a pretty lighthouse.

"This room can be used for anything you want. Add a bed...or a crib." I can't begin to imagine what the softness in his voice on the last word means, but it's comforting.

I pull back from the door. "It looks lovely."

He smiles in return and closes the door again. He leads me into the living room and I'm surprised by how comfortable the space looks. There is an oversized L-shaped couch with large pillows and deep seats, the kind you just want to curl up on all day. On the wall in front of the couch is a large TV, probably the largest I've ever seen. Below that is an entertainment center that houses two sleek black boxes that are probably for the cable and maybe a DVD player.

The coffee table between the couch and the TV is made of wood similar to that of the floor, and underneath the table is a pretty, deep purple rug that stands out against the light furniture.

On the other side of the couch, the curtains pulled back, is a large sliding glass door leading out to a patio, and beyond that, a view that has captured my attention. The balcony overlooks the river down below, and I can see a barge making its trek upriver. Even with the trees nearly bare from the cold, the view is still breathtaking.

I sense Mikah's eyes on me, but I don't pay him much attention as I walk around the couch, wanting to have a better look at the view.

The door slides open easily, and a rush of air sweeps into the apartment – not overly powerful, but strong enough to cause my body to shiver. I step out onto the balcony and just stand there, dazed by the beauty below.

After a few moments, I feel my heart skip a beat and the hairs on the back of my neck stand up, then Mikah's hand on the small of my back.

"It's beautiful out here," I say, not wanting to pull my eyes away from the scene to look at him.

"This apartment has the best view. Come, I've got something else to show you."

I scowl at him. My heart pounds in my chest for reasons I don't quite understand, but I let him lead me back inside, his hand still resting on my lower back.

He reaches around and closes the door behind us. "Over here," he says, pointing toward a door on the wall opposite the TV I take a tentative step in that direction, unsure of why I'm hesitant now.

He reaches for the handle and pushes the door open.

FIVE

Beyond the door, the lights are on, low and warm. The room is decorated in purples: a purple comforter on the king-size bed, pillows in dark purples and lavenders, pale purple walls emitting the faint scent of new paint. Sitting in the middle of the pillows is a small bunch of what look like purple lilacs.

There are only three things in the room that aren't purple: two lamps and the carpet. On either side of the bed, two chrome lamps with cream-colored shades help to give the room its warm ambiance. The carpet is a light, not-quite-white shag that looks very plush.

I want to feel it between my toes. I kick off my skimpy ballet flats, sensing Mikah's delight as I step over the threshold and onto the carpet.

Realization dawns. "This room, this apartment...it's mine?" I ask quietly.

"Technically, I own it. However, it is yours for as long as you like."

Tears pool in my eyes as I take in what he's done. He knows that being on my own is important, but then he also knows that my living conditions were not great for me. Shame and gratitude wash over me in

339

waves as I realize that Dr. Alston was right: no strings attached. If he wanted something in return, then I'd be in his apartment, but his giving me my own place proves even further that he really is only out to help me.

I feel him come up behind me. I turn quickly in his direction, throwing my arms around his waist.

"Whoa," he says, but I can hear his smile. "What's this for?"

I pull back slightly, unsure of what's come over me and afraid that I've overstepped some line, but his arms wrap around me, holding me to him, and I can no longer stop the silent tears from streaming down my cheeks.

"Thank you," I whisper.

His hand comes up to the back of my head. Gently, he strokes my hair, down my back, and for the first time, I feel a strong sense of comfort wash through me. I melt into his embrace.

The gravity of the last few days weighs heavily on my shoulders and my knees give out.

Mikah is quick to catch me as I let go. He reaches down and lifts me. I don't protest; the fight in me is gone. "Shhh, sweetheart, don't cry," he whispers, and I want to scream, to shout, to sob, to just break down. He reaches down for something I can't see, shifts slightly, and then he's pulling back the covers on the bed. He lays me down gently. I curl up into a ball, my back to him, and he slowly pulls the covers up to my chin.

He kisses the top of my head, then pulls back. I hear his jeans shift as he steps away, and his feet on the carpet, getting further away from me.

"Don't," I say through tears. "Don't leave."

I hear his sharp intake of breath. Then the door clicks closed. But the knob rattles as his hand comes away and he's walking toward me again.

I reach behind me and pull the covers back. He hesitates, and I turn my head to look at him. Worry and sadness mar his beautiful features. He's confused. I'm confused. I don't understand what is causing this need to have him close to me.

"Please," I say quietly, and his features thaw. Reaching down, he pulls the covers back a little further then climbs in, jeans and all. He turns so that he is closer to me, like last night. I roll back onto my side and his arm wraps around me. His other hand slides in under the soft feather pillow. He holds me close.

I tried to be strong. I tried to be everything I thought I needed to be for myself, and all that did was nearly get me killed. Again. Mikah was there to rescue me and nothing I can ever do in life will repay him for that. His generosity knows no bounds.

As he snuggles deeper into the bed, I realize that something is changing between us.

SIX

Walking. I'm still walking down the white hallway, though the opening seems to finally be getting closer. I'm suddenly reminded of what happened the last time, of the dark cave, the heat and screaming.

"Do not fear, you're safe."

Zirah?

"Yes?"

I don't understand.

"What don't you understand?"

Well, I'm here, in this hallway, walking toward something. Mikah, I believe.

"Yes, it is him. He's waiting for you."

But am I in the future?

"No, you are in the present day."

But how?

"You are in Elysium. You are in the land of your true self."

My hand slides along the baby bump - which is much larger than when I'm awake at home – letting the gesture silently ask my question of Zirah.

"It is because when you are in Elysium you are your true self. When you are on earth, you and your body conform to normal standards so you don't alert anyone to the existence of the supernatural."

I'm confused by the fact that this doesn't all seem stranger to me. It all seems so natural, like second nature.

"That's because you've been here before, while you slept," Zirah says, answering a question I haven't asked. "When you were attacked, you were essentially dead, and that brought you into Elysium. While you were here, you learned of your fate." Her voice is reassuring.

Why don't I remember?

"You were not meant to remember. But it is why this all comes so easily to you. Mikah was primed by his mother - he was told of his legend in his younger years. You, Princess, were not." She pauses as if pondering something. "You were not meant to come to Elysium a few days ago."

Realization stumbles its way into my mind. *I died? He - Riley - he killed me?*

"Yes, but Mikah found you in time. He accelerated your healing and brought you back to Earth, which is where you are supposed to be. Your time has not come."

I mentally shake my head, trying to process all of this information.

"Dreams are a form of Elysium, Princess."

Princess?

"Yes, you are a princess of Elysium, and Mikah is your protector, your guardian."

I let that thought sink in deep. Mikah's my guardian. I was right: He really was only trying to help, to protect me.

I stop walking. *So my feelings for him aren't real?*

"Your feelings for your guardian are real, Vivienne. Never doubt them."

My heart leaps and I quicken my pace, anxious to be closer to him.

Finally he comes into full view. I watch him standing there, dumbfounded by what's happening to him. His wings are spread: full and beautiful in all their glory, white and perfect. My heart melts. Desire grows. I feel like a magnet being pulled toward something to attach to. Something to cling to.

He's looking at his arm now. The black tattoo that covers half of his body is detailed and beautiful. He is shirtless; my gaze lingers on his deeply defined biceps and his abs, which are on glorious display. His hips arc into a beautiful V that disappears into the waistline of his pants.

His skin is darker, seeming even more tan against the stark white of the room. I watch as he brings his hand up over his shoulder and takes hold of his wing. Instantly his eyes roll upwards, showing the whites, and his knees give way.

I giggle at his reaction and his head snaps up to look straight at me. I point to the mirror behind him. He cocks his head at me, so I point again, more urgently.

He turns slowly toward the mirror. I can see him squint and close his eyes. He takes a few steps in its direction and, after a beat, he slowly opens his eyes.

His eyes are a beautiful blue, like the ocean, warm with excitement. His spreads his arms wide; his wings are longer than his arm span.

I approach him quietly from behind. He stumbles slightly.

"Easy there, angel. You're alright."

THE REASON SERIES - COMPLETE COLLECTION

He falters again but recovers quickly.

"What is happening to me?" His voice is strained, concerned, but there's a hint of wonder.

I watch as he slowly starts to move and flex his shoulders. His back is equally as toned as his front, and there is something extremely sexy about his wings. I giggle at how awkward he looks testing them for the first time, but his face lights up. He starts to turn toward me.

"No, no. Keep facing the mirror. Keep practicing," I say to distract him and watch as his expression changes to disappointment, but he continues to practice as I quietly sneak closer to him.

"Will I be able to fly?" I hear him ask as he watches the motions of his wings.

"Yes, in time." My answer surprises me – I didn't realize I knew that. Then I remember what Zirah told me. I try again in vain to recall being here before.

I'm within an arm's length of him. I reach out, tentatively, and lightly brush my fingertips along the feathers of his wings.

He moans – a sound born not of pain but of pleasure - and crumples to the floor. I touch him again, watching his eyes roll back and then close.

I smile at the idea that this is something he enjoys. I do it again and he moans once more.

I pull back slightly from him and begin to make my way around his now-collapsed wings.

"Keep your eyes closed," I breathe.

"But I need to see you." His voice confirms his need, but I have other plans before he opens his eyes.

I trail my finger along his nose to his lips, and he kisses the pad of my finger. My palm cups his cheek. He instantly leans into my touch. His skin is warm, slightly prickly from the stubble on his chin. My heart flutters at the excitement of touching Mikah.

"Give me your left hand," I say.

He slowly lifts his hand, and I recognize it as a calculated move, but it's unnecessary; I no longer feel threatened by Mikah.

As I take his hand, I kneel down in front of him. "Open your hand," I say.

He does so without hesitation, and I place it gently against my cheek.

A flood of emotion runs wild through my body. Tears form in my eyes and drip down my cheek. I can feel his tears, too. Something is shifting between us, a change in our relationship, a change that will bind us together.

SEVEN

There is a rather loud crashing sound behind me. I jolt and my eyes fly open. My heart is pounding, but I quickly realize that I'm back in the new apartment. I can hear some more shuffling behind me and I relax.

It's dark except for the light streaming through the slightly open door. Mikah is not in the bed with me.

I hear him curse.

I smile.

Then feel disappointed that I was pulled from the most bizarre and yet amazing dream I've ever had. If only it were true.

I sit up. There is a strange tingling sensation across my back and I scowl. It diminishes rapidly and I realize that I really need to pee.

I crawl out of bed, feeling slightly off balance as I stumble into the bathroom and close the door behind me.

I come out a couple minutes later, after running cool water over my face, realizing I would really like to take a bath, or at least a shower.

I quietly pad across the carpet to the slightly open door and peek through to see Mikah in the kitchen doing something near the stove. The air is filled with the smell of chicken and vegetables. Soup, perhaps?

"No, Seraphina," I hear him say, and my eyes scan the kitchen and the living room. There's no one that I can see.

Who's Seraphina? I wonder.

"She's his teacher," a familiar female voice says, and I spin around, stumbling into the chair next to the door in an ungraceful manner. Though the room is lit only by one soft light in the corner, I can clearly see that no one is in the room with me.

"Wha-?" I start to say.

"No need to talk aloud, Princess. I can hear you."

I shake my head. Princess? Wait, the dream.... I let the thought stop and I shiver.

"'Twas no dream. You are an angel, Vivienne, and a very special one at that."

How can this be happening?

"It is who you are, Vivienne, who you were always meant to be."

But if this is what I'm supposed to be, why then has all this... Words fail me as I let the reality of my dream sink in.

"Why have you had the life you've had? Well, your mother was once one of us, as well."

Once?

"She has fallen. She is one of our fallen angels. Though she has not sinned against the angels, she's chosen her own path."

She doesn't say any more, and I don't need any further explanation from her. My mother made her choice, her decision to be who she is. There is nothing I can do about that. She never showed any willingness to change her situation. She just kept on doing what she was doing. In a sense, I understand addiction and how it takes ahold of a person, but she never once expressed any need or desire to quit. Nor did she ever try on her own to quit.

Dread washes through me. I was never religious and have never gone to church, but I've read enough literature to know what heaven and hell are.

"Heaven and hell do not exist in that form, my child. When in your dreams you are in Elysium. Though very like heaven, it is far from it. Hell is a loose interpretation of what it is. Though Dante got it right."

Dante's Inferno*?*

"That's the one. Your mother, though fallen as she is, will not go to hell. She will still be among the souls in heaven, as you call it. Her choices and her actions were ruled by her substance abuse, and while she made all the wrong decisions in that life, she's never actually done anything to send her to hell."

But what about me? What about all the things she's done or let be done to me? Tears of frustration form. I understand what she's saying, truly I do, but what about the fact that she never so much as tried to protect me?

Realization dawns anew and I understand her words. I would never want to see my mother in hell. My mother is in a living, breathing hell of her own, lost inside her mind and trapped in a body that is riddled by her choices.

"Very well done, Vivienne. You're right - she suffers enough as it is right now. She does not need to suffer more. When she comes upon us, she will be free of her living prison, free of pain and suffering. Perhaps one day she will make amends with you."

Who are you? I ask inside my head, then fight the urge to go running and screaming from this room because I'm talking to someone or something inside my mind.

A soft laughter echoes around in my mind. "You are not crazy, dearest Vivienne. I am Zirah." The dream. "I am assigned to be your guide and your teacher, just like Seraphina is Mikah's."

Mikah's name brings me back to the present, to this room. *Does Mikah know about me?*

"He knows, more or less. The two of you have been having the same dreams; he is seeing the same as you are seeing in Elysium. However, he does not know that you're aware of being an angel when you're awake, and more than that, he does not yet see that the dream is shared and that you know he, too, is an angel."

I smile slightly at the idea that I know what he is, but he doesn't yet know that I know.

I smile wider as the memory of Mikah, asleep with his head on my bed when I woke up from the coma, comes to me. I knew instantly that his presence in the hospital was why I was alive. I knew that he'd saved me. The surge of devotion and gratitude I felt toward him in that moment was stronger than anything I've ever felt in my entire life.

Though I put up a fight about coming here to stay with him, I really didn't mean it. I knew the moment Riley came up behind me that Mikah was right all along: I'm no match for someone like Riley, someone who can easily overpower me. I needed help then, more than what Dr. Alston had been able to provide to me. I needed protection.

"He is your guardian, sweet Vivienne. What happens between the two of you now is up to the Fates. Go to him. Be with your angel," she says wistfully, and I feel a shimmer as she departs from my mind.

EIGHT

My stomach growls as the smell of warm chicken broth fills my nose. I get to my feet and turn toward the door. His back is to me still, but now he is at the breakfast bar with his laptop. I can't see what he's looking at, but the muscles in his neck are strained, tense.

I silently pull open the door and step onto the cool hardwood floor. As I pad quietly toward him, I see him stiffen, but he doesn't turn. The oddest of shimmers skates across his back, noticeable only because of the tight t-shirt he is wearing.

I say nothing as I come up to stand beside him, placing my hand on his back, right where I saw the shimmer. His breath rushes out of his lungs.

"Hi," I say as casually as I can manage, given that I know something he doesn't know.

"Hi," he says. His voice is raspy, slightly more so than normal, and the effect on my body is instantaneous. A shiver of anticipation zips across my back. "How did you sleep?"

I pull my hand away and place it on the of the bar stool.

"Wonderful, thank you. How about you?"

The corners of his lips turn up in a small smile. "Very well. Are you hungry?"

I nod, a little too enthusiastically, and he hastily closes the lid on his computer and stands.

"Good, the soup should be heated up. It's the same from the other day, is that okay?"

"Yes, that soup was delicious."

He busies himself in the kitchen, grabbing bowls, silverware and two placemats. As he puts them on the breakfast bar I take the seat in the middle.

"What would you like to drink?"

"Ice water is fine."

He scowls at me as he places the bowls and plates on the placemats.

"What?" I say. "I drink water all the time."

"How about some milk?"

I resist the urge to roll my eyes. "Fine," I say all breathy.

His lip twitches at my exasperated tone and he turns to the refrigerator.

When he opens it, I see that it is fully stocked with all manner of fruits and veggies, along with milk - which he takes out of the fridge - something that looks like iced tea, and a two-liter bottle of Mountain Dew. I smirk. He closes the door before I can inspect any further.

He grabs two glasses and pours us both some milk. I raise an eyebrow.

"What?" he says sheepishly.

I grin. "Never pictured you as a milk drinker."

He smiles. "I'm not, but if I'm forcing you to do it, I can do it, too."

I shake a little with silent laughter at his tone.

He reaches for three potholders sitting on the counter. Placing the biggest one between us, he takes the two smaller ones with him to the stove. He clicks it off, grabs both handles of the pot and brings the soup over to sit between us. Then he tosses the potholders aside and grabs a ladle as he comes around the bar.

In a very gentlemanly fashion he serves me first, then fills his own bowl.

When he's done, he takes the seat next to me. "How are you feeling?" he asks as I pick up my spoon.

I think about his question before answering. "I feel great, just really tired for some strange reason." I bring a spoonful of soup to my mouth, blow on it and take a sip. "Mmm," I moan, swallowing it down. "This is really good."

He too takes a bite and nods. We eat in silence for a little while. I drink down all of my milk and stand to get some more, but he stops me.

"I can get it," he says and stands quickly.

"I'm not broken, Mikah, I can do it." I try to sound sweet about it, but he scowls at me. I mentally shrug it off and go to the fridge for the milk.

"I never meant to imply you're broken."

My heart sinks a little bit as I realize it was more of an act of chivalry than waiting on me.

I return to my seat with the milk and begin eating some more. Before I know it, my bowl is empty and I still feel hungry. Just as I'm about to reach for the ladle, there is a knock on the door. I freeze.

"It's just Red," he says quietly as he takes in my frozen state. "He said he would be back with a change of clothes for me. I was hoping you wouldn't mind if I stayed on the couch tonight?" His gaze is warm, soft.

"Yes, please." I smile slightly. I hadn't thought about staying here alone, and Mikah's willingness to stay on the couch warms my heart, though I kind of wish he would sleep with me.

He walks toward the door. "I thought the couch would make you more comfortable," he says as he checks the peephole in the door. "Oh, it's Celeste." He reaches for the knob and then turns back to me, like he is seeking reassurance.

I nod hesitantly. I've at least met Red. Not sure if I trust him, but I've met him. Celeste is another story. I'd never realized I was so skittish about people before.

Then, as he opens the door, I'm reminded of the dream right before we left the hospital. Hearing Nyssa's name in that dream has given me the idea that people really aren't always as they seem. But I also don't yet know why she would be in my dream in the first place.

"Thank you," I hear Mikah say, pulling me from my thoughts.

"I'd love to meet her," a sweet, soft voice says from the doorway, and I watch as Mikah turns toward me.

I take a couple steps in his direction, and he opens the door a little wider.

"Come on in." He steps aside.

On the other side of the door is a very pretty yet average-looking woman with blond hair; big, blue eyes; and a warm, welcoming smile. She is taller than I am, though that's not hard to accomplish. I guess she's in her early thirties.

"Hi, Vivienne. I'm Celeste, Mr. Blake's housekeeper. It's a pleasure to finally meet you."

"Hi, Celeste. Your soup is fabulous," I say with a small smile.

"Thank you. I'm glad you like it. Can I get you guys anything else?" she asks, looking from me to Mikah and back again.

I shake my head.

"No, I think we're good for now," Mikah says to her, and she hands Mikah a bag.

"Vivienne, I'm not sure if you saw or not, but your closet has some clothing for you, mostly yoga pants and t-shirts. If something doesn't fit, let me know and I can exchange it for you."

I'm pretty sure my face shows the shock I'm feeling at the idea that there are clothes, not to mention that Mikah has spent money on me. "Th-thank you," I finally manage to mutter.

I see concern in Mikah's face as his brows knit together.

"You're welcome." She turns to Mikah. "Call if you need anything else. I'm going to take off for tonight, but I can come back if there's a need."

"Thanks, Celeste. See you tomorrow," Mikah says, and she waves at me. I wave back halfheartedly as she steps back out the door and Mikah closes it.

NINE

"Why did you buy me clothes?" I ask.

His back tenses and ripples at my words. The tension in his back is not anger; it's fear or worry.

"Mikah?"

I watch him come to a decision.

With his hands against the front door and his head down, he says quietly, "I wanted you to have a fresh start." He turns and leans against the door. His eyes are closed. "When you walked out of that hospital today, I wanted you to have a fresh start on everything. A new place to live, clothes on your back, proper food in the kitchen, and..." He pauses and opens his eyes. "I wanted to give you the tools you'd need to be able to take care of yourself." His voice is soft and his accent is thick.

I step back slowly toward the stool. I need to sit; my thoughts are swirling at a mile a minute. I can't speak. He's already given me so much. He saved my life. This just...it's too much.

"Vivienne, I needed to know that you'd be safe, that you'd stay safe, that I could give you the tools you needed to get back on your feet. Clothes, food, a job - whatever you need, it's yours."

Zoey Derrick

I can barely hear him by the end of his speech. Eventually I get my mouth working again. "Why?" I breathe.

He runs his hands through his hair and pulls away from the door, slowly walking toward me. "Because..." He pauses in his stride, clearly deciding something. "Because you deserve it. There is no reason for you to live a life of poverty if I can easily prevent it."

"That's not what I asked. Do you do this for every girl in my situation?"

He shakes his head. His eyes are wary, unsure of my reaction. He should be unsure. He knows how much I don't want to be taken care of. Yes, I've progressed some in allowing him to bring me here, to give me shelter, food.... Are clothes really that much worse? I mean, I don't have any, and whatever clothes I had in my apartment should be burned.

He's wanting and willing to help me, and I push him away at every turn. Is it so terrible to let someone help me? No, it's not. But it's hard; I've fought for so long on my own that I don't know how to do this.

He watches me as I take in his words. The reality of what he's said sets in. Maybe he's right: Maybe I've been fighting for so long to prove that what my mother has put me through hasn't broken me. But for whom? Who am I trying to prove this to? I get fighting for myself, but for what else?

Am I trying to show my mother, prove something to her? For what? She's never been there for me. By doing it all on my own, was I just trying to prove that I don't need her, that I didn't need her? Or is it more than that? Am I really just being stubborn? It's hard to let go of everything I've done for myself, but what

358

have I really accomplished? A shit job, a shit apartment, barely surviving.... How is that living?

I let out a deep sigh.

I wasn't living. I was alive, but not living.

I look at Mikah, whose face shows that he's worried about what I'm mulling over. The bottom line is this: I've obviously failed miserably at proving to myself that I can take care of myself. Maybe with a little help from him, I can get back on my feet, get back into a better place.

"Thank you," I finally manage to say, and his face and body instantly relax and a slow smile spreads across his lips.

"You're not mad?"

I shake my head slowly. "No, I'm not."

"Good. Okay." He's not sure what to say, as if I've taken away all his argument. "Are you still hungry?" I roll my eyes and he playfully scowls at me.

"Changing the subject much?" I tease him back.

He laughs. "Maybe a little." He looks at me expectantly.

"No, I'm alright for now."

"Good. I'll clean up the kitchen. What would you like to do?" His eyes follow mine toward the guest bedroom as I remember the huge, inviting bathtub in there. "Take a bath?" he asks.

I nod enthusiastically, and he turns on his heel.

"Why don't you go find some comfortable clothes, and I'll start your bath before I clean up."

I stand and head for the bedroom, hitting the light switch on my way in. I hesitate just a moment at the closet door, suddenly nervous about what I'm going to find in there. Then I realize that I've agreed to this, and I turn the handle at the same time I hit the light switch on the wall next to the door.

The closet is huge - about the size of the bathroom and equally as long - but thankfully it's not stocked full. Hanging up on the right-hand side are about ten different t-shirts, and below them are various pairs of pants, cotton ones by the looks of them. I also catch a glimpse of the dresser at the back of the closet, its top drawer slightly ajar.

I step up to it and pull open the drawer. Inside are several pairs of white and fun, colored socks and a stack of rather slinky looking underwear. I shiver at the idea of wearing what I'm looking at.

I pull open the next drawer: some bras and some other, not-so-slinky underwear. There are some really cute designer boy shorts and I start to feel excited; they look really comfortable.

I grab a bra and pair of underwear and turn back to the clothes. On the floor under the pants are two pairs of shoes: a pair of gray-and-white Converse and a pair of fuzzy slippers.

I smile and grab the house shoes, a pair of black pants and a t-shirt.

I leave the closet and head out into the living room to see Mikah in the kitchen cleaning up. "Did you find something?"

"I did, thank you."

He smiles at me and then nods in the direction of the guest room.

I scurry quickly through the bedroom toward the bathroom. The closer I get, the more pronounced the sound of the running water. I push back the door and I'm hit with a rush of steam that is warm and inviting.

TEN

Once inside the bathroom, I shed the purple scrubs - similar to the ones Amanda had given me last time - and drop Mikah's t-shirt to the floor with the pants.

For a moment I study my naked reflection in the mirror. It's almost as if nothing ever happened to me. Other than a faint, small line on the side of my neck and the brace on my wrist, there are no visible signs of my trauma.

I'm filled with satisfaction at the idea that I don't have to go through the nasty healing process. Was I really only out for a couple days?

Instantly, there is a shimmering sensation across my back, almost like a call to attention. I try to look over my shoulder but I can't see anything, so I turn so that my back is facing the mirror.

As my back becomes visible in the mirror, I do a double-take. A brilliant display of whites, blues, light purples and silvers form a beautiful wing-shaped tattoo across my back. My wings.

My head starts to swim as realization settles in, and I take a seat on the side of the tub.

The dream I could have written off as exactly that: a dream. The mental conversation with Zirah after I woke I could also have written off as some kind of momentary delusional episode. But this - these wings - solidify the reality of those dreams, the reality of my conversation, and the idea that my super-healing ability is a product of my true nature.

An angel? I muse as I fling my legs over the side of the ginormous tub. Reaching over to the faucet, I turn the water off.

The gentle swirl of jets under the water causes the surface to ripple slightly. There is a slight bubble film across the surface. I slowly sink down into the water, and my muscles begin to relax instantly as they're engulfed by the warmth.

I close my eyes and my mind drifts back to Elysium, but not like before. I'm not there; I'm just replaying the events from my dream this afternoon.

The emotions I felt about Mikah during that dream were heightened beyond anything I consciously feel for him now. The fact that my feelings for him in Elysium are so strong is intense and frightening, though I think a lot of that is due to my own self-preservation and holding back, to not wanting to admit to myself what Mikah really means to me.

He was genuinely concerned about my reaction to the clothes. He knew that I would be upset with him, and to be honest, I still am. But he's right: I can't work until at least after I see Dr. A. in a couple of weeks, and therefore I have no income and am incapable of taking care of myself. At least in the fashion that Mikah – and even maybe Dr. Alston - wants me to.

The bottom line in letting Mikah help me is that I have nowhere else to go. I'm essentially back to being homeless because I am unable to return to that apartment.

I also know, after Riley's attack, that I'm not able to protect myself.

Is Mikah capable of protecting me? I believe he is.

Suddenly my image of Elysium shifts to the image of the dark cave. I heard Nyssa's name. How does she fit into this? Where was I? In hell?

All these nasty unanswered questions. I can feel my anxiety growing quickly, but I'm brought out of my thoughts by a knock on the door.

"Viv, you alright?"

I smile. I'm in a tub for crying out loud. What could happen? "Yeah, I'm good."

"Holler if you need me."

"Okay." I can't help the smile that spreads wider. For some strange reason, I can still sense him on the other side of the door. I sink underwater, giggling as the idea of Mikah making sure that I'm okay and that I stay okay hits me. It's heady and mildly overwhelming, but at the same time it sends a ripple of happiness through me. Something similar to the way I felt in my dream.

ELEVEN

After what feels like forever, I finally climb out of the tub, warm and sleepy. After drying off, I put on the pants I pulled from the closet, noticing that they have a wide waistband that hugs my bump nicely. The pants are soft and comfortable. I forgo the bra, opting instead for just the t-shirt. Then I wrap my wet hair in a towel, grab my dirty clothes, and head out into the hallway.

I take a moment to really look around the apartment. Although it has rather expensive-looking electronics, it's also very common: no fancy artwork on the walls, no fancy leather furniture. It has a homey feel to it. Is this the way it's always been, or was it done this way just for me? I'm struck by a sudden curiosity to see Mikah's apartment.

Only then do I notice Mikah on the couch, his laptop on his knees and a look of intense concentration on his face. He doesn't notice me until I get closer. There are very few lights on in the condo, which is nice, and he's drawn the shades on the large glass patio doors.

The TV is on, but muted. I can't tell what's on, but it looks like news or sports.

Finally he looks up and smiles. "Feel better?" he asks.

I smile back. "I feel great. Just going to go put my clothes away, and then do you mind if I join you?"

"Not at all," he says as he closes his laptop and places it on the table in front of the couch.

I go dump my dirty clothes on the floor of the closet near the Converse, and as I come back out toward the living room, I see the TV flickering as he changes channels, looking for something to watch with me. His bare feet are stretched out on the coffee table.

I stand quietly in the doorway and just watch. So normal, so mundane. Not something I'd picture a big-time businessman doing on a Sunday night.

After a couple of minutes of watching him, I walk quietly around the couch to sit on the far corner opposite him.

"I don't bite," he says playfully.

I turn and smile at him. "I know."

"Then why are you sitting all the way over there?"

I shrug. "It seemed appropriate." All the other times we cuddled together have been on his initiative, and I don't feel comfortable pushing a boundary I'm not sure of.

He gestures with his outstretched arm for me to come closer to him.

A flash of excitement runs through me and I crawl across the couch toward him. I put my head on his shoulder and snuggle into him. It only takes a moment for him to bring his arm around me to rest his hand on my hip.

I let out a silent sigh of contentment.

"What would you like to watch?"

I shrug. "I don't care."

"Okay then."

He flips through a couple more channels and comes to settle on some show. My eyelids are very heavy so I'm not paying much attention. Before I know it, my eyes close and I'm asleep.

"Wake up, angel. Let's get you into bed." His voice is sweet. Wait, did he really just call me *angel*? "Come on, sleepyhead."

My eyes flutter just a little bit, but I don't want to move. I'm comfortable.

"Do you want me to carry you?"

I wiggle a little deeper into our cuddling. "No, just leave me here," I mumble.

He laughs. "Then where will I sleep?"

"Right here." I snuggle in a little deeper and hear his heart rate speed up. Unlike mine, it doesn't calm right away. But he continues to stroke my lower back, down near my hips, and I lean into his touch.

"See I knew you were awake. Come on, I'll carry you."

As he slides out from under my head and shoulder, I don't fight it but I don't help either, and I flop to the couch. I giggle a little bit and he reaches for my hand.

He pulls on my right arm and then is somehow lifting me. His other arm sweeps under my legs and just like that, he's carrying me. I don't put up a fuss, I just snuggle into his chest as he whisks me off to the bedroom.

TWELVE

The next morning I wake up rather early – five thirty, per the clock - and I fight hard for more than an hour to go back to sleep. When that fails, I climb out of bed.

I open the bedroom door quietly, remembering that Mikah's sleeping on the couch and hoping I won't wake him. But I find Celeste in the kitchen and Mikah sitting at the breakfast bar. He's working again on his laptop, papers spread out before him covering about half of the bar.

Celeste catches my movement and turns in my direction. She doesn't say anything, but she smiles at me and Mikah notices. He turns around on the stool so that he can see me.

"Good morning," I say quietly.

His smile lights up the room, prompting me to smile back at him.

"Good morning. Did you sleep well?" he asks as I start to walk toward him, running my hand through my hair as I do.

"I did, how about you?"

"I did. Didn't mean to wake you, though."

I shake my head. "You didn't. I've been awake off and on since about five thirty, but I wasn't ready to get up."

As I approach, he holds out his arms slightly in invitation. I take him up on it, and he wraps one arm around me, turning back toward the bar.

Movement on his computer screen catches my eye: I see a bunch of numbers ticking by across the top. I point. "What's that?"

He smirks. "That is the stock market."

"The what?"

Celeste lets out a chuckle as she goes back to whatever she was doing before. "Seriously, Mikah, don't bore her with the stock market. It's too early for that."

Mikah chuckles, and I can't help but smile at their exchange. "You're right," he says and closes the browser window.

I gasp. The background on his laptop is the same ultrasound picture that was in the frame he gave me.

"Sorry," he whispers. "I..." He doesn't continue.

"It's alright," I whisper back.

"I rather like that picture," he says as he looks at it again. "I hope it's okay?" His voice is quiet, shy.

I just nod, surprised. Not only did he take the picture in the first place, but he had it enlarged slightly for my frame and it's also on his laptop. I'm not sure how to process this new information.

Celeste interrupts my thoughts. "How about breakfast?"

Mikah looks to me. I look back at him, a little wary about the picture, but I'm rather hungry. I nod.

Mikah releases my waist and starts to gather up all of his papers. He reaches over to the middle stool and pulls it out. I walk around him and take a seat.

Within seconds of my sitting down, Celeste places a plate in front of me with an omelet that has diced-up ham and cheese sprinkled all over it. Next to it are hash browns. It smells amazing.

While I admire my food, she sets a plate of the same in front of Mikah.

"I'll be back a little later to clean up," she says as she leaves the apartment.

"Where is she going?" I ask, curious.

"To my apartment. She's not one to pry while others are eating," he says and smiles at me. "Eat up."

Picking up my fork, I dive in as my stomach begins to rumble.

Once we've finished eating, Mikah is quick to clear the bar of our dishes, placing them near the sink.

"Would you...would you like some hot chocolate?" he asks.

I give him an amused look. "You drink hot chocolate?"

He turns to me, smiling. "No, I drink coffee, but I wasn't sure if you'd like it."

"I'd love some hot chocolate."

He turns and reaches for a cupboard door. Inside are all manner of plates, bowls, glasses, wine glasses, and mugs. He grabs two mugs and then reaches for the kettle on the stove. Sliding to the left of the stove, he opens another cupboard; I can't actually make out its contents because he grabs something and closes it quickly.

He goes back to where he left the mugs. I can't see from this angle what he's doing, but watching him move about the kitchen, making me hot chocolate, has me thinking about how thoughtful and caring he is.

A couple moments later I hear the clinking of silverware against ceramic, then the noise stops and he turns around with a mug in each hand.

"Here you go." He sets them down on the bar.

I smile as I pick up the purple and blue mug. It's comfortably warm to the touch, and I can see little billows of steam rising.

He turns to put the stirring spoon in the sink. "Would you..." As I blow across the top of my hot chocolate, he takes a deep breath and starts again. "Would you like to see my apartment?" he asks with his back toward me. I see the tension in his back and shoulders and can feel it in the air.

"Of course," I say, and he relaxes. I'm not sure why he is so worried about me seeing his apartment. "I'd love to." I put the mug down without taking a sip, push back from the bar and stand up. I feel a little dizzy, but I recover quickly. "I'll go change," I say.

"No need, just grab your slippers. It's right upstairs," he says, finally turning to look at me. His eyes are bright and he's excited. So why the tension?

"Alright, I'll be right back."

I move quickly toward the bedroom, a little excited to see his apartment. Curious to see what Mr. Suit lives in. I have no doubt that this apartment was furnished with me in mind. All the furniture here is soft and comfortable, normal and everyday. Is his apartment like this too?

I grab my slippers from the closet and step into them, then turn off the bedside light before heading back into the living room.

As I come back out of the bedroom with my slippers, he hands me my mug. "You can bring that with us. Are you ready?"

I nod as I blow across the top of the mug and finally take a sip. It's really good.

"Come on, sweetheart," he says, and I follow him to the door.

I smile at the term *sweetheart*, something so simple yet so powerful at the same time. He's called me sweetheart before, but somehow, here in this apartment, it means more.

THIRTEEN

Connor is standing on the other side of the door when Mikah opens it. "Good morning, sir," he says quickly.

"Good morning, Connor. We're just going up to my apartment."

Connor nods quickly and steps aside.

Mikah and I head down the hall and Connor, thankfully, doesn't follow.

When we reach the elevator, Mikah slides a card in a reader over the arrows and presses up. "I'll give you this card. In order to come upstairs, you need to swipe it, then press the up arrow. You're welcome upstairs anytime you want," he says as the elevator chimes and the doors open.

Once again I notice that I'm standing slightly behind Mikah as we step inside the elevator.

Mikah pushes the button for the seventh floor and the doors close. He switches his mug from his right hand to his left, then slowly brings his arm down to his side. His fingers brush against the back of my hand. I turn it slightly, opening it to him, and he takes it into his. A charge develops between us and I can't stop myself from smiling.

The elevator chimes again and the doors open on a small entryway, about ten by ten feet. Andrew is standing in front of the only door.

"Good morning, sir," Andrew says. He directs a friendly smile at me. "Good morning, ma'am," he says sweetly, and I know I blush crimson.

"Good morning," I say back shyly as Mikah lets go of my hand and reaches for the door.

We step into a small hallway and Mikah releases my hand to close the door behind us.

"Does he always stand there?"

Mikah grins. "No. I'd mentioned to Celeste before you woke up that I might bring you up here. She obviously told them, and they made adjustments. Security on my floor is tighter than on yours. You really can only access this floor by keycard, the pass code does not work." He's looking at me with a reassuring look on his face. "There are cameras throughout this building. Anytime seven is pressed, it activates an alarm in Red's apartment, one on his phone, and a video feed showing who is in the elevator. He also has a control to stop the elevator if someone who should not be here managed to gain access."

Holy crap, it's like a fortress in here. Suddenly I feel safer than I've ever felt in my entire life. I know my eyes are wide and Mikah can sense my immediate mood change.

"I will let nothing happen to you," he says then smiles. "Come on, let's have a look, shall we?"

I nod and he takes my hand again.

The hallway is similar to mine, only shorter and with only one door on the left-hand side. We reach it, and Mikah opens it up.

We go through the door into a living room that has plush gray carpeting, a coffee table, an L-shaped couch similar to the one downstairs, and a massive TV surrounded by speakers. Shelves beneath the TV hold a ton of movies. The lone door on the opposite wall is closed. I turn around to find that the door we've just come through is flanked by two massive bookshelves stacked full of books.

"Do you like to read?" Mikah asks me softly.

"I love to read," I reply and walk toward the shelves. When you do anything you can to avoid being at home, sometimes the library is the only place you can go. The books are arranged in alphabetical order by author and range in type from thrillers to romance to classic literature. "You have good taste," I say as I pull out Louisa May Alcott's *Little Women*.

I hear him snicker. "I suppose. I have several books, including that one, that were my mother's."

I gently place the book back on the shelf.

"You're more than welcome to help yourself to anything you see here. If there is something you'd like to read that isn't here, let me or Celeste know and we will get it for you."

I look over my shoulder at him. "There are more books here than I could ever imagine in one private library. I'm sure I can keep myself entertained with this lot."

As I turn to face him, he heads toward the door on the opposite wall and opens it to reveal a hallway. I go through, and he follows close behind.

The floor here is hardwood, and this hallway is longer than the one on the other side. An open door directly in front of me reveals a toilet and sink. Then I notice a closed door to my left.

"That leads to the stairwell and is often what Red uses to come upstairs," Mikah says.

He leads me toward the right. We pass by a couple of closet doors along the left wall, and then the hallway opens up into a rather large space. The wall in front of me from here to the end of the room is made entirely of glass, and on the other side is a large patio with the same view of the river as I have from my patio downstairs. At various points all along the glass wall there are doors that lead out onto the patio.

The room itself is cavernous, with ceilings at least two floors high. The floor is a beautiful light hardwood that stands out against the dark furniture. Between us and the patio is a large dining room table set for eight, and at the far end of the room to the left is a sitting area, with tall chairs in a loose circle formation around a coffee table. To the right is the kitchen, done in the same cupboards and countertops as my apartment: dark wood cabinets and black countertops with stainless steel appliances. I put my mug on the counter.

Behind me I hear a door click open. I turn toward Mikah, who has been silent while I've been looking around his apartment.

"And this is my bedroom," he says, and again I see the tension in his features.

He flips on a light. I cross over to him and take a step into the room, and my heart stops.

FOURTEEN

I can't focus on anything besides the king size, four-poster bed that dominates the room. It's *the* bed, the one from the dream I had the other night at the hospital. The one where...

I let the thought end there as the image of Mikah and me, cuddled inside this very same bed with its tall canopy and stacked block posts, fills my mind.

I look to Mikah, who is still tense. Was he in that dream, too? Did he see us as I saw us?

"It's beautiful," I breathe, and he relaxes. I'm not sure whether he's tense because he is showing me his room or whether it has something to do with that dream.

"The closet and bathroom are to your left," he says, and something is different in his voice. It's almost husky.

I look in that direction and see a large opening into a closet area. His clothes are hung neatly, shirts across the top bar and pants and jackets along the bottom bar. But I don't stare too long; closets and bathrooms are personal space.

I look back to the bed once again and wonder: Will that be me? Us? Someday, one day soon? I remember from the dream that I was much larger than I am now, nearing the end of my pregnancy. But Mikah in the dream was just as sweet then as he is today. Tender in a very un-masculine way.

Mikah takes me through the rest of the house, leading the way back across the main room into a guest bedroom on the other side of the house and then his office.

As we come out of the office back into the main room, he comes to a sudden stop. "Hello, Red."

I peek around the doorjamb. Red is standing near the breakfast bar.

"Hello, sir. Vivienne," he says and nods in my direction.

"Hello," I say quietly.

He smiles and turns back toward Mikah. "Chrys is here. Shall I have Andrew bring him up?"

Mikah looks quickly to me then back to Red. I can feel my brow furrow.

"Give me about five minutes, then go ahead and bring him up," Mikah says to Red, but he is still looking at me.

"Yes, sir," Red says and walks toward the entryway.

"Who's Chrys?" I ask as soon as Red is out of sight.

Mikah takes a couple of steps into the sitting area in front of his office.

"Chrys is my lawyer. The one I'd like you to talk to about..."

"Do I have to?" I ask.

"No, you don't. But Stevens will be here around one. I'd like you to have some time to discuss things with Chrys before Stevens arrives. I'd like Chrys to be present while Stevens is here."

"I don't understand why all this is necessary." I lean into the jamb of the office door and take a long, deep breath.

"I'm not entirely sure it's necessary either. You've done nothing wrong, but I...I'd like Chrys to be here as a buffer from Stevens. He'll know if the questions are crossing the line or making you uncomfortable. And..." He pauses. "And he can help keep me in line from doing or saying something I shouldn't to Stevens." He runs a hand through his hair.

"I don't mind talking to Chrys as much as I mind talking to Stevens. The only thing that I have to tell him, he already knows." My voice is soft but I'm suddenly very nervous. "Or he should know. He would have access to my medical file as far as my injuries were concerned. If he suspects anyone other than that asshole, then he's barking up the wrong tree."

Mikah nods. "I know, sweetheart. I don't know what it is that he's after, what information he thinks you can provide that he doesn't already have. But unless there is some legal way out of you talking to him, I can't hold Stevens off forever, as much as I'd like to." I can see the concern in his eyes.

"I'll talk to both of them if it means that once it's done, it's done, and I don't have to do it again."

I have a gut feeling that it's a waste of time to talk to either one of them. If that cave dream is any indication, I have a feeling that whoever that dark voice belongs to is having his own way with Riley. I shudder.

After a few heartbeats of silence, I hear a door close and shoes clicking across the hardwood floor. I lean back, shrinking into his office as a rather tall, well-dressed man emerges from the hallway.

FIFTEEN

For being a lawyer, Chrys is surprisingly gentle when it comes to asking me questions. It's hard to talk about again, and I can tell Mikah is uncomfortable with my answers, but they're the same ones I gave him in the hospital on Saturday night. I'd hoped that Mikah could act as a buffer and handle most of the answers, but Chrys is adamant that the answers come from me and me alone.

When I'm finished telling Chrys everything I remember, I say, "I don't want to talk to Stevens."

"I don't see any reason for you to talk to him," Chrys replies matter-of-factly. "The evidence of what happened to you is in your medical file. You can identify Riley in a lineup if necessary."

I shudder at the idea of having to look at him again.

Chrys continues, "With the previous case, Riley presents with a history of violence toward you, the police shouldn't need anything more. I will try talking to Stevens first, see what it is that he's after, and then we can go from there." He doesn't look at Mikah when he talks, which is reassuring.

Chrys is rather handsome, with dirty blond hair that falls to just below his ears. Definitely doesn't seem like the lawyer type. Maybe that's why I can talk to him without issue. I've never had to deal with a lawyer before, and if I ever have to deal with one again, someone like Chrys would be great. He's not abrasive in any way, and I like that.

"I have a feeling he just wants to see her, talk to her, maybe even apologize to her," Mikah says, and I look at him, puzzled. "He's pretty messed up over what happened to you, and while I'd like to wring his neck for letting it happen, in the end he and his department were hurt far more than you were."

I nod slowly, taking in his words. I remember him telling me about the cop who was parked outside of my apartment and how he was killed. Guilt knots my stomach. If Stevens hadn't felt it necessary to protect me from Riley, his cop would still be alive. In a way, it's my fault that the officer died.

"I'll talk to Stevens," I blurt out. "Despite the fact that what happened to me happened, he deserves a chance to say his piece."

Mikah looks at me, awe etched on his features.

"Okay, would you like me to talk to him first?" Chrys pulls my attention away from Mikah.

I nod. "Sounds good to me."

I hear the door open and the squeak of tennis shoes across the floor. "Lunch is ready downstairs," Celeste says.

"Chrys, would you like to join us?" Mikah asks him.

"No, I'm going to make some notes. I'll take a sandwich, though, if you don't mind."

Mikah turns to Celeste. "Would you mind?"

381

"No, not at all," she replies and walks into the kitchen.

"Chrys, why don't you call me when Stevens is ready. I'll tell Red to bring him up here and you can chat with him first. We will come back up when it's time." Mikah stands and offers me his hand. I take it and stand too.

"Sounds good," Chrys replies, and Mikah and I head for the door.

SIXTEEN

We've barely finished our lunch of salad and chicken soup - I'm thankful this soup is so good, otherwise I might tire of it - when Mikah's phone rings.

"Blake," he answers. I see his face fall slightly.

We haven't talked too much over our meal. I get the impression that Mikah is waiting for me to talk. Though about what, I'm not sure. Or maybe he is just trying to make sure that I really am okay after what's happened to me.

"Alright, Chrys, we'll be up in a moment," I hear him say, then he shifts the phone and pushes a button.

"Chrys says that Stevens is satisfied with what he's told him regarding what happened," Mikah says rather stoically, as if he's thinking about something.

"I'm still mad at him," I say quietly. I look up at him and he smiles.

"That makes two of us." Mikah wraps his arm around my shoulder and pulls me close. He lightly kisses the top of my head. "It will be okay." He squeezes my shoulders. "How are you feeling?" he asks.

"Okay. Just tired."

"Alright, we'll make this quick and you can come down here and take a nap."

"Will you join me?"

He smiles a little wider. "Maybe." He grins.

I smile back and we head for the door and back upstairs.

As we walk into the apartment, I hear Chrys talking but I can't really make out what he's saying. We come around the corner to find Stevens, Chrys and another cop - one of the ones from Thursday night, whose name I can't remember - sitting at the dining room table.

Stevens stands and turns to face us. Mikah still has his arm around me protectively, but Stevens smiles when he sees me.

"Hi, Vivienne," Stevens says, then he points in the direction of the other cop, who's now standing as well. "This is Officer Ruiz."

"Hi," I quietly, not sure why I'm so shy.

Mikah leads me a little closer to the table and Stevens comes over. He's dressed in full uniform, though I notice that both his and Ruiz's gun holsters are empty. Red must have made them leave them downstairs.

"How are you feeling?" Stevens asks. There is a lot of emotion playing on his features.

"I'm okay, just very tired."

"I'm sorry, Vivienne. Very sorry," Stevens says. His voice breaks and I can see raw emotion in his eyes. The look makes my heart lurch.

"Stop. I'm alive, it's alright," I say, and as I do, I realize that it really is okay. I have no reason to be mad at Stevens or anyone else for what happened to me, except Riley. "Riley is a very driven individual. He will let nothing stand in the way to getting what he wants," I say, and Stevens relaxes a little bit. I step out of Mikah's arm and gently hug Stevens. I feel all eyes on me as I do this, but I understand the pain he is going through. If it helps him heal from what happened to me, I'll do it again and again.

"You're too kind to me, Vivienne." He wraps his arms gently around me and squeezes just a bit. I can tell he's being cautious.

I pull back. "Is that the only reason you're here?" I ask and step back.

Mikah is quick to wrap his arm around me, and exhaustion washes over me.

"No, I wanted to ask you a few questions, but Chrys has answered most of them for you."

Mikah leads me to the table and pulls out a chair for me.

"Thank you," I say as I take a seat.

Stevens, Chrys and Mikah all sit. Ruiz stays standing about ten feet away.

"I just wanted to ask you a couple of follow-up questions. I'll make this quick, promise," Stevens says. "First, Mr. Crowley, downstairs from your apartment. Do you know whether he would have let Riley into the building?"

The mention of Mr. Crowley brings a knot to my stomach. "I don't think so. He knew his tenants pretty well. Especially if Riley said my name, he wouldn't have let him in."

"That's something we've been trying to figure out, how he got into the building."

"Again, Riley's determination got him into that building. I vaguely remember Mr. Crowley's door being open when I got home. I didn't think much of it because he's done it in the past when he's run off to a tenant's apartment," I say, my voice still quiet and weak. But Stevens is listening intently.

"Detective, do you know why his door was open?" Mikah asks.

Stevens face scrunches up a bit. "Mr. Crowley was..." He pauses and looks at me. I nod slightly for him to continue. "He was killed. From what we can tell, it happened before he got to you."

I feel my eyes fill with tears. Mr. Crowley was a really nice man. He didn't deserve this.

"How do you know that?" Mikah asks.

Stevens shifts uncomfortably in his chair. "We, uh..." He looks to Officer Ruiz then back down at the table. "Forensics came back on Vivienne's apartment. We found a t-shirt that wasn't Vivienne's. It was white, and it had several spatters of blood on it. We found three types of blood." I flinch. "Vivienne's, Mr. Crowley's, and what we can only assume is Riley's, as it doesn't match any DNA in our system, but it matches DNA on a couple of hair fibers we found in Mr. Crowley's apartment as well as-" He pauses again, looking at me. "-on Rebecca."

I can feel the tears sliding down my cheeks. "That asshole," I spat. "I get it, I get me, I get why me, but damn it why them?" The tears are flowing harder. I bury my head in my hands and start to sob.

I vaguely hear Chrys. "I think we're done here. If you have any more questions for her, contact me. Or when you capture him and need an identification, let me know."

"Come 'ere, Viv." I feel Mikah's hand across my shoulders. His other hand snakes under my legs as he pushes the chair back and picks me up. "Here or downstairs?" he whispers.

"He-" I can't finish, but he catches my words and he turns toward his room.

SEVENTEEN

For two weeks Mikah barely steps foot out of the building, staying with me no matter what comes up. We talk, watch movies and take naps, and when he needs to do some work-related things, I indulge in his library. About a week into our self-imposed seclusion, I finally start to feel more like myself. I have a little trouble with being tired, but sometimes I think it is because I'm not doing much. Mikah and I start taking morning walks along the river, when the weather is decent.

Connor, Andrew and Red are ever-present in and around the two apartments, and I take it upon myself to get to know Connor and Andrew a little. They are really nice guys, and I get the distinct impression that they are naturally protective.

Zirah hasn't made an appearance since the Sunday I was released from the hospital, though, strangely, I keep having the same recurring dream about the white hallway and Mikah. I always seem to wake up right before we kiss, and it is getting to the point of frustration. I want to know what's going to happen next.

Mikah and I grow close, but he hasn't so much as kissed me - well at least on the lips - and it's starting to feel like my dream: so close and yet so far away.

Then he has some pressing business to deal with in Phoenix, and he leaves me alone for the first time since bringing me here.

I miss him like crazy, and it doesn't quite feel like home without him here. The house is far too quiet; I leave the iPod he gave me - loaded with music and hooked up to the stereo system – on all the time. When he first gave it to me, of course, I rebuffed the gift, telling him it was too much and there was no need to spend his hard-earned money on me. He wouldn't hear it. Eventually I relented and kept it.

I'm in my bedroom, getting dressed for my appointment with Dr. Alston, when I realize for the first time that my breasts seem very swollen and tender. I was never well-endowed in that department, but holy crap, these things are getting huge. My nipples are puffy and turning a dark, almost cherry wood color.

I turn around to look in the full-length mirror on the back of the closet door. I'm a little shocked by what I see.

My eyes are a bright blue, bluer than I've ever seen them before. I turn completely sideways and look toward the mirror. Of course I've noticed my belly getting bigger physically, but I've never really looked at it like this. Okay, it's not huge, but it is definitely there, and it looks....

Tears prick at my eyes. Good tears, but damn. This whole thing is really sneaking up on me.

I face the mirror head on again, and now I can see why I really hadn't noticed it much; from this angle it looks cute and tiny, small compared to my breasts.

I notice too that my hips are softer, the bones no longer as defined as they once were. All the food I've been eating, plus the vitamins that Mikah has been making me take three times a day, have no doubt been helping me put on some weight. But it appears to be really good weight.

My face has completely filled in, rounded, and there is a flush to my cheeks, no doubt because I've been looking at myself in the mirror. My collarbones are still visible, but in a very healthy, almost sexy way.

"Sexy?" I say. I've never thought of myself as sexy before.

A knock on the bedroom door causes me to jump, like I've been caught doing something I'm not supposed to do. I cover myself instinctively as Andrew's accented voice comes through the door. "Vivienne, we have about five minutes before we need to leave."

"I'll be right there," I holler back and slip the bra on. It's a little bit snug in the chest and made from a thin, sheer material. My nipples poke through like nobody's business.

Standing here in my sheer black bra and black yoga pants, I cannot help but admire myself. For once in my life I actually look and feel pretty. I flush at the thought and reach for a black tank top, then I grab an old Boston College hoodie I inadvertently "borrowed" from Mikah a couple of days ago. It's soft, huge, and warm. I throw it on and head out the bedroom door.

EIGHTEEN

Within a matter of moments we're out of the apartment, down the elevator and into the lobby. Connor is standing next to a sleek black SUV, something I've never seen before. The windows are tinted really dark, and it looks mildly intimidating. Andrew opens the rear passenger door for me just as Connor slides in behind the wheel. I clamber in, noticing that the window on the driver's side is down, wiping out my anxiety of tight spaces. Andrew shuts the door behind me. He is quick to slide into the front passenger seat, and we're off.

I take a deep breath. "What's the big rush?" I ask.

Connor peers at me through the rearview mirror. "Safety precaution, ma'am."

I roll my eyes, whether at the safety comment or the fact that he called me "ma'am," I'm not sure. "Call me Vivienne, please, Connor?"

"Yes, ma'am."

I scowl at him.

"Vivienne," he corrects himself.

"Thanks."

He turns back to the road, driving at a speed I'm not entirely sure is legal. I watch out the window as we make our way through downtown. It is Friday morning and the traffic is moving quickly.

A few minutes later we pull into the parking garage at H.C.M.C. Connor steers the car up the ramp to the third floor of the structure and pulls up at a door.

Andrew climbs out of the car, moving a little slower now. Is that deliberate?

He opens my door and I climb out. I expect Connor to drive away to a parking space as soon as Andrew shuts the door behind me, but the SUV doesn't move. Andrew walks with me through the automatic doors into the hospital.

"Do you know where we're going?" I ask Andrew.

"I do." He looks down at me with his bright blue eyes, and his thin lips stretch into a friendly, reassuring smile.

I smile back. Andrew has been really nice to me these last couple of weeks.

We round a corner, and it's practically a dead end except for a door to the right. Andrew goes straight to it and knocks.

"Come in," I hear a woman on the other side of the door say.

Andrew opens the door. "Hi, Dr. Alston," he says. "Vivienne is here to see you."

"Of course. Come on in."

Andrew steps in and stands with his back to the door, holding it open for me. I sneak in between him and the jamb to see Dr. Alston sitting behind a desk.

"Is there any other way into your office?" Andrew asks.

"No, just the room behind you, but no outside access," she says, looking at the same door Andrew is leaning against.

Andrew quickly figures it out and checks the other room. Then, turning back to me, he says, "I'll be right outside if you need me."

"Thanks," I say, and he slips out, closing the door behind him.

"Hello, Vivienne, how are you doing?" she asks as she looks me up and down.

"Great," I say, but I feel a little uncomfortable at her gawking.

"You look amazing," she says with a bright smile on her face, and I relax. "You've put on some weight. Good job."

I blush a little bit. "It's all the food Mikah's been feeding me."

She laughs. "I'll bet. Come in, have a seat."

"Thanks." I do as she says and take a seat in the chair across from her. Then I look around her office. It's decorated in warm browns and tans, not sterile at all, but rather homey looking. She has a few landscape pictures on her walls, but nothing clinical. Though there are no windows, the room is well lit by lamps. The florescent lights overhead are off.

"So, you've been eating okay?"

"Yeah. I have some issues with meat, particularly red meat. The smell turns my stomach," I say, making a face.

"That's not all that uncommon. When we're pregnant, our bodies tend to crave the things it thinks it needs and reject the things it doesn't, or at least doesn't like. What about white meat? Like chicken or pork?"

I notice that as she asks these questions she isn't very doctorly – if there is such a word. She's talking to me like I'm a person, not a patient, and I warm up to her a little bit more.

"If I don't smell it in raw form, I'm okay, though mixing it into pastas or soups makes it easier for me to eat," I tell her.

"What about vitamins, have you been taking them?"

I nod. "Three times a day." Partly because Mikah is insistent about them, but I leave that part out. "The one in the morning makes me a little nauseous, but it doesn't last for very long."

Her cell phone rings. I don't expect her to answer it, but she picks it up. "Dr. Alston." She listens for a moment. "Hi, Mikah." Oh, fabulous. He's checking up on me. "I don't see why that would be a problem, but have you asked Vivienne?" She pauses again. "Well, she's right here. Want to ask her yourself? Alright, hang on."

NINETEEN

She reaches across her desk to hand me her phone. "It's Mikah," she mouths.

I take the phone from her, shaking my head in disbelief. "Hello."

"Hi, sweetheart. Look, I wanted to be there but I can't. I'm still in Phoenix taking care of stuff, but I'm wondering if it would be alright if I video conference in on your appointment?"

What? "Why?"

There is a pause on the other end of the line. I'm about to say *hello* again when he pipes up. "I really wanted to be there to support you today, and I can't, so...well...I was hoping this would be okay."

I take a deep breath - not in anger or frustration, but at the fact that this is one of the many signs he's shown over the last couple of weeks that there is more than friendship between us. His persistence in making sure I'm well taken care of extends to the baby, and I don't want to deny him this.

"It's fine, though I have no idea how-"

"Don't worry about it, Dr. Alston knows. Hand the phone back to her and I'll see you in a minute."

"Ohhkaaay." I hand the phone back to Dr. Alston, my stomach flip flopping with excitement at the idea of seeing Mikah. Sure, I'd talked to him on the phone last night, but it's not the same. Speaking of which: Why didn't he bring this up last night?

"Sure, okay. Call me back in about ten minutes and we should be ready." She pulls the phone away from her ear and presses a button. "Are you sure you're okay with this?"

"Yeah, it just took me by surprise. I talked to him last night and he didn't mention anything about wanting to be here."

She shrugs. "I'll set him up so that he can't see much more than a little bit of you and the monitor. I'd like to do another ultrasound, just to check on progress. After today, we will wait a couple of months for another one."

I nod, a little excited at the prospect of seeing my baby again.

"Did you open the envelope I gave you last time?"

"Envelope? What..." I think back for a moment. "Oh, you mean the one where you wrote down the baby's sex?"

She nods and smiles wide, hopeful.

"Um, no," I say shyly.

"Do you really not want to know?"

I think about it for a minute. What are the reasons to not know? Other than the surprise when it's born? "I guess I kinda forgot about the envelope. I haven't seen it since you gave it to me. But yes." I smile wide. "Yes, I want to know."

Dr. A., in a very uncharacteristic manner, starts clapping excitedly. I can't help but laugh at her reaction.

"Come on, let's have a look." She stands, comes around her desk, heads toward a door next to the main door into her office and opens it.

I stand hesitantly, not sure where she's taking me.

"I have a private ultrasound and exam room in here."

Oh.

I follow her into the room. This room is a little bit more clinical, but it's still decorated in the light tans with red as an accent color, and it looks nice. There are a couple of monitors near the head of a short bed that has stirrups coming off of the end.

"I'm going to step back into my office. I would like you to remove your pants and underwear." She hands me a blanket, similar to the one that was on my hospital bed. It is far from warm, but it beats sitting here naked. "Climb up and cover yourself with this when you're done. Once we're done with Mikah and the ultrasound, I'd like to do an internal examination, if that's alright."

I nod and she turns to leave.

TWENTY

After just a minute or so I hear her knock. "You all set?" she asks through the door.

"Yeah," I call back, and she comes in.

"Go ahead and lie back," she says as the thing in her hand starts ringing. It's not a phone; it's similar, but bigger, white with the Apple logo on the underside. She pushes a button and waits. "Hi, Mikah," she says and then turns the machine toward me.

"Hi, beautiful," he says to me, and I can see his smile, big and bright.

"Hi," I say, blushing at his words.

"Mikah, Vivienne has decided that she wants to know the sex of her baby. Do you want to know, too?" Dr. A. asks.

Mikah's face lights up. "If she wants to know, then I'd like to know, too." The whole time he says this, it's as though his eyes are boring into me, searching, seeking, wanting. Similar to the way he looked at me when I first met him at the diner.

"Okay then," Dr. A. says. She walks around to the other side of the bed from the ultrasound machine and places the device into a holder of some sort that is attached to the bed. "How's the view, Mikah?"

I now notice the little image in the corner of the screen that shows what Mikah can see. It isn't much, really: a little bit of my bump, but more of the machine that Dr. Alston is now standing at. She turns the monitor toward us. "This might be a little shaky on your end, Mikah."

"Alright. Viv, you okay?"

"Yeah," I say to Mikah.

Dr. A. proceeds to push my sweatshirt and tank top up so that my belly is exposed. Once that's done, she goes for the bottle and squirts nice, warm gel along the lower half of my belly. Then she brings out the small, flat-headed wand and gently presses it to my stomach.

Everything is very quiet as Dr. Alston does her thing with pushing buttons.

I can see the baby's heart pumping wildly. She pushes another button and the echoing sound of a heartbeat fills the room.

She moves the wand around a little more and the head comes into focus. It looks similar to last time, but this time it's bigger; there isn't as much black surrounding the baby as the first time.

She points to the monitor. "There are the eyes, nose, lips and chin. See this string of pearls? That's the baby's spine." I watch as the baby moves. "Oh, I see. A little showoff." She laughs and moves the wand again. "There's an arm, and the other one is...right there." She moves her finger up on the screen, pointing at a faint, translucent white line in the background, leading up to a cluster of shorter white lines. "The other hand."

She moves her hand down further on the screen at the same time she moves the wand. "A leg," she says.

I'm starting to be able to see what she's pointing out. She moves the wand again to my right side, and I can see feet. Two of them with little tiny bones. As if on cue, the baby spreads its legs, and one foot goes off the screen.

Dr. Alston laughs. "Yup, she's quite the showoff."

"She?" Mikah and I say together. I smile.

"Uh huh. Look." She points to the apex of the baby's thighs. There is nothing there to look at, just some more semi-transparent lines.

"There's nothing there," I say.

"Exactly," Dr. Alston says, pride in her voice. "You have a baby girl."

I smile and tears roll down my cheeks.

"A girl," I hear Mikah say through the device over my shoulder. His voice is soft, quiet, reverent.

I look over toward him and I see him staring at something. I'm assuming it's the monitor. Though he's not actually crying, I can tell by the look on his face that he is in awe.

I turn back to Dr. A., and she is back to pushing buttons. Sometimes the image freezes momentarily as she pushes a button.

I'm about to ask what she's doing when she says, "I'm assuming you'd like some more pictures."

"Yes, please."

After a few more clicks she pulls the wand away.

I turn back toward Mikah. He's wiping his eyes, not like he's wiping away tears, but rather like he's rubbing at them. I notice now that he looks very tired.

"How are you doing, Mikah?" I ask.

His hands come away and his head pops up a bit. "Thank you for letting me join you both for the ultrasound."

"Anytime," Dr. A. says. "I'll give you two a minute, and then I'll be back in." She walks around the bed, pulls the device out of its cradle and hands it to me.

I sit up and take hold of it.

As soon as the door clicks closed behind Dr. Alston, Mikah asks, "You okay?"

I nod. "It's just all so overwhelming sometimes. I wish you were here right now," I say. There is definite sadness in my voice, but also excitement. "How are you doing?"

"I'm fine. Was just up late last night dealing with some stuff." He smiles. I can tell that he's not wanting to go into details, which is okay with me. He quickly changes the subject. "A girl, huh?"

I smile. "I guess so." I can't stop the smile from spreading wider. "I was hoping, but you know..." I trail off. I had been hoping for a girl, but I didn't want to be let down.

"So you're happy?"

I cock my head at him, puzzled by his question. "Yes, though regardless, boy or girl, I'd be happy, so long as it were healthy."

He smiles. "Good. If I'd known that you wanted to know, I would have given you the envelope."

"No, it's okay. I'd forgotten about it until she brought it up again. Besides, she seems more sure now than she was when she gave us the envelope."

"True. What else has she said?"

"Not much. We talked about my aversion to red meat." He laughs at that. "She said it was normal for me to not like everything I may have liked before. She also asked about my vitamins and if I was taking them, and that was about as far as we got when you called."

"Okay, no more red meat. Got it." He laughs, teasing. "Can I call you tonight?"

My heart pounds. "When are you coming home?" I pause momentarily at what I've just said about home.

Mikah, on the other hand, doesn't quite catch it. "Tomorrow, in the morning. Early. I think. It's been pretty chaotic around here."

"I can tell, you look exhausted."

He snorts. "Yeah, I didn't sleep very well last night."

My brows knit together. "Why not?"

"We can talk about it later. I'm going to let you get back to your appointment. I'll call you when I'm done here, okay?"

"Okay. Thanks for joining us."

"No, thank you for letting me be a part of this."

I smile a little wider. "By the way, what is this thing that I'm talking to you on?" I ask.

"It's called an iPad. It's like your iPod, only bigger and a bit more sophisticated. Do you like it?"

"It's pretty cool, though all I've done is talk to you. Not sure what else it can do."

"I'll show you when I get home. Actually, I'll ask Celeste to show you the FaceTime app on your iPod. We can video chat tonight, if you'd like."

My heart patters a bit at the thought of seeing him again when we talk tonight, and I smile wide.

"Good. Alright, I wish you luck with the rest of your appointment, and I will talk to you soon."

"Okay, bye."

"Bye," he says.

The iPad beeps twice and he's gone.

Within a matter of seconds Dr. A. is back in the room.

"Thank you. For letting him call and join us." I say to her.

"You're welcome," she says and smiles.

I hand her back the iPad and she sets it down behind her. "Shall we finish this up?"

I nod and lie back down.

TWENTY-ONE

After about ten minutes, she's done doing whatever she needed to do down there. It didn't hurt exactly, but it was very uncomfortable.

"Everything looks fine. You're closer to eighteen weeks along and everything looks great."

I sit up. "Can I ask you something?" I say and blush.

She shakes a little in silent laughter, and an all-knowing smile spreads across her lips. "Of course."

"I'm wondering..." I can't seem to find the words I want to say.

"You're wondering about sex?"

Oh, God, is it really that obvious? The idea has crossed my mind once or twice over the last couple of weeks. I nod slowly, certain I've turned cherry red at this point.

"Don't be embarrassed, Vivienne. It's a perfectly natural question to ask, and every expectant mother asks the same question. The answer is yes, you can have sex."

I let out the breath I've been holding. "Can I ask you something else?"

"Anything, Vivienne."

"I'm not sure I want to know the answer to this, but I have to know..."

"The answer is no. When you came in the last time, I was deeply concerned about it too, so I checked almost immediately. There were no signs of trauma to indicate that."

I feel a tear streak down my face. I'd wanted to ask before I left the hospital two weeks ago, but it wasn't something I felt comfortable enough to ask. I'd healed so fast that I wasn't sure I would have noticed if Riley had succeeded in...

I can't even think the words.

"Thank you," I say quietly.

"Have you talked to anyone yet?"

I shake my head.

"It would probably be a good idea if you-"

"No, I don't want to talk to someone. I don't remember much about what happened to me, and I don't want to relive the memories that I do have over and over again while someone analyzes me. My past is my past. I can't change that fact. And I truly seem to be better about my reactions to certain things." I take a deep breath. "Andrew, the man outside, for example, doesn't scare me. Neither do Red or Connor, for that matter.

"Mikah is cautious, sometimes too cautious, but he'd figured out a lot of my triggers before. I've talked to him about it. Even a little bit about my past with Riley." I cringe internally at the name. "What happened with my mother is old history."

She is watching me carefully. "You're a strong woman, Vivienne. Don't ever let anyone tell you differently. I admire your courage and even your determination. But know that we can't always solve things on our own."

"I know, and Mikah has offered the same thing. I really just think that I've managed to process this all on my own, in my own way. Something I've always done."

She nods. "Okay then. I will leave it be, but know that I'm only a phone call away. If you need me for anything, all you have to do is call."

I smile and nod. "Thank you."

"You're welcome. How's your shoulder? And your wrist?"

I smile again at the change of subject. She knows when to stop, and I really like that about her.

"They're great. I don't have any problems moving my arm, and my wrist has been fine since I left here."

"Good. I will allow you to stop wearing the brace." Considering that I haven't been wearing it, until this morning, I try not to smile as she continues. "If you can, I'd recommend some light exercise, like walking. Or even yoga could be good for you. I will also allow you to return to work. However, I don't want you doing anything that requires you to be on your feet for long periods of time. So no waitressing."

Jeez, I hadn't even thought about the diner. Partly due to Mikah's vehement refusal to let me go back to work there.

"Talk to Mikah," Dr. Alston says. "He might have something for you, if you feel it's important to work. I would like to see you back here in a month. We will start regular monthly visits from here until closer to your due date."

"Speaking of due dates?"

She reaches into a drawer behind her. "Forty weeks is total time of pregnancy, give or take a week or two." I watch as she twists and turns the cardboard wheel in her hand. "April thirteenth."

I smile. "April thirteenth," I repeat. "I like it. But please tell me that's not a Friday?"

She laughs. "Superstitious?"

"Not really. But you know, it doesn't hurt to be cautious."

She laughs again and pulls out a calendar. "No, it's a Saturday."

"Good," I say and laugh.

TWENTY-TWO

When I emerge from the exam room, clothed and ready to go, Dr. Alston says, "All set?"

"Yeah."

She hands me a bag with a couple of things in it. "I've included another copy of the book I gave you, since you don't have the original one, and a few additional things about diet and such. To help with the lack of red meat." She winks at me.

I look in the bag. It's the book about how the body changes with pregnancy, the one left behind at my old apartment. "Oh that reminds me," I say. "I noticed this morning that, um, my breasts are swelling. A lot. To the point of painful."

"How painful?"

"Achy, really."

"That's pretty normal. A little early, but normal. Your breasts are beginning to produce colostrum. It's a form of breast milk. It's a thicker, creamier substance that is generally higher in fat and very good for the baby when she's born. Sometimes you can begin to leak early, which is okay. A good, supportive bra or sports bra can help alleviate some of the tenderness. Even wearing one at night can help. There are some tips in that book that might help. Plus..." she says as she turns back to her desk. She grabs a couple of pamphlets and brings them over to me. "Here are a couple of good information sources on some things you can do to be more comfortable. They will better explain that part of pregnancy."

I take them and slip them into the bag. "Thank you. For everything."

"Anytime, Vivienne. Anything. I'll see you in a month."

"See you then." I reach for and turn the knob on the door.

Andrew is standing in front of the door, but he moves away quickly as I step through.

"Thanks again, Dr. Alston," I say over my shoulder.

She waves and Andrew whisks me down the hall. He reaches for his phone. "On our way," he says as we round the corner back toward the parking garage.

TWENTY-THREE

I hop into the shower shortly after arriving home from my appointment. When I come out, Celeste is in the kitchen. She is standing over the sink, washing dishes. The first couple of times she was here cleaning and doing dishes and such, I offered to help, but she would hear none of that.

Celeste is awesome to be around. She's very funny and down to earth, and I'm comfortable with having her here. She talks about her boyfriend all the time, and I get the distinct impression that they are head-over-heels in love with each other.

"Hi, Celeste," I say as I take a seat at the breakfast bar.

"Hi, Vivienne. How was your appointment?"

I smile because she remembered. She really misses nothing about what's going on around her.

"It was good. Mikah called in and we used...an iPad?" I say, puzzled. "He was able to watch the whole thing."

"That's awesome. Those iPads are amazing."

"I'd never seen one before. But it was nice to have him there without him being there. He said he was

410

going to get in touch with you, ask you to show me how to use FaceTime?" I think that's what he called it.

"That was nice of him. I haven't heard from him yet, but I can certainly show you on your iPod," she says sweetly. "So did you find anything out?"

"Like?" I say, confused.

"Did you find out what you're having?"

"Oh, yes." I smile. She looks at me expectantly and I laugh. "It's a girl."

She bounces up and down, clapping, excitement radiating off of her. I can't help but laugh at her girlish behavior.

"You're having a girl. Oh, Viv, I'm so excited for you."

I smile. "Me, too." And for the first time, I really do feel deep-down excitement about being pregnant and the fact that it's going to be a girl.

She settles down some, but I can tell that she's still really excited. "What would you like to eat?" she asks.

I roll my eyes, but my stomach growls. "Peanut butter and jelly?" I say.

She smiles. "Alright, coming right up."

"I can make it," I say, knowing full well that she will shoot me down.

"Oh, no. That's my job."

I shake my head as she gets busy. I climb off of the chair and head toward the living room.

One of the things that I hate about not working is the fact that I just sit around doing nothing. Celeste handles all the cleaning in my apartment, all the laundry, and even the majority of the cooking. What she doesn't cook, Mikah does. Well, he heats up things that she's made, but his easy manner in the kitchen tells me that he is more than capable of cooking a meal on his own.

I wonder idly about the diner. About Laura especially, and how she's doing. I haven't thought about any of that since the attack because, well...the dream I had right before leaving the hospital. I don't know if that's now or in the future, and it scares me. I haven't called the diner because if Nyssa really is in cahoots with Riley, the less they know, the better. I make a mental note to ask Mikah if he ever told them about what happened to me.

I grab my journal off of the coffee table and take a seat on the couch. I'd been avoiding this since Red brought it back to me from my apartment. It's just another reminder of my old apartment and what happened. I guess it was my way of dealing with the whole mess.

At the push of a button on the remote, my iPod flickers to life in its cradle. A beautiful instrumental piece starts to play as I open up my journal. The money I stored in it falls out. I'd forgotten all about this being in here. Plus there are the food stamp vouchers. Jeez, and W.I.C., too. Dang it, what am I going to do with all this stuff? I could give it to Celeste to use when she goes shopping, but I hardly see that as necessary.

I tuck the vouchers into the back of the journal and decide to put the money in my purse.

Where is my purse? Wow, I really hadn't thought about a lot of this stuff.

"Celeste?"

"Yes, Vivienne?" she calls back from the kitchen.

"Do you know where...or, if Red managed to recover my purse from my apartment?"

She stops what she's doing, almost as if she's recalled something she hadn't intended to remember. "Um, Red found it, but..." She pauses, looking at me, concern etched in her features. "I threw it out because it, um..."

Well, shit. "It's alright. What about my wallet and the stuff inside?"

She lightens up a little at my response. "That I do have. I'll run up to Mikah's and get it for you." She hurries to finish making my lunch.

I loved that bag and I'm sad to see it go, but I'm happier that I've been sheltered from seeing it covered in blood.

I shudder.

"Here you go." Celeste is standing behind the couch with my sandwich on a plate.

"Thank you," I say as I reach up and take it from her.

"You're welcome. I'll be back down in a bit."

"My wallet is no rush," I say, assuming that's why she's rushing upstairs.

"Okay, but I need to go take care of a few things upstairs, anyway. I'll let you eat in peace, and I'll be back down in a bit. Would you like to go shopping for a new purse this afternoon?"

Normally I would reject the idea, but I have the money from my journal. "I'd love to," I say with enthusiasm, and her face lights up.

"Perfect. I'll let the guys know, and when you're done eating, come on upstairs, if you'd like, or I'll be back in about an hour."

"Okay." I nod.

She turns to leave and is about a third of the way to the door when I stop her. "Celeste?"

"Yes?" She stops and turns toward me.

"Can you help me find something for Mikah while we're out?" I ask shyly. I'd like to give him something to thank him for all he's done for me, though I have no clue what.

She smiles. "Of course."

I smile back and she heads for the door. As she opens it, I can see Andrew and Connor in the hallway, talking. They turn to Celeste as she shuts the door.

TWENTY-FOUR

About halfway through the second half of my sandwich, the phone rings. I expect it to be Celeste from upstairs, but when I look at the handset I see Mikah's name and my heart flutters.

I swallow the bite that's in my mouth and click the green button. "Hello."

"Hey, beautiful," he says with enthusiasm.

I smile at his endearment. "Hi, Mikah. How are you?"

He laughs a little bit. "I'm good, how are you doing?"

"I'm great. Just finished eating a sandwich."

"Peanut butter and jelly?"

I laugh. "How'd you know?"

"Because it's what you always eat." He has a point there. "Listen, Celeste sent me a text. You want to go shopping?"

Uh, crap. "Yes, I just found out that she threw out my purse because it, um, was in my apartment." I don't need to say any more. "Though the shopping was her idea."

He chuckles. "I know it was. At my urging, though she didn't expect you to be enthusiastic about it."

415

"I'm not sure that I'm excited about it. I'm not much of a shopper. But I..." I debate with myself about whether to tell him about my own money. In the end I decide to be honest with him. "I finally opened my journal, and I had money stashed in there. So I'd like to get a new purse." I brace myself.

"I think you getting a new purse is a great idea. But-" Yup, here it comes. "-I've already arranged for a shopping budget for you-"

"Mikah, that's not necessary. I have some money-"

"Please, Vivienne, can I explain?"

I sigh. "Yes."

"I arranged the budget about a week ago. I wanted you to be able to..." He pauses. I hear him take a deep breath. "I wanted you to be able to buy things for yourself. And for the baby. I knew that your not working would mean you couldn't buy the things you need or want without my or Celeste's intervention."

I think I'm maybe starting to understand. He continues, "There are certain things that I know you're going to need or want that wouldn't have been the easiest things to ask for, so I thought if I arranged a way for you to get them on your own, you wouldn't have to ask."

I immediately think about the conversation that Dr. A. and I had this morning about sports bras and such. Surely a budget from Mikah isn't necessary, though. A sports bra and a purse can't really be that expensive, right?

"Vivienne?" he says quietly, bracing for my reaction.

"I...I'm just processing this. Give me a moment. I'm really trying to not be angry at you."

"My cute little tiger," he says coyly.

I smile at his tone. "What's that mean?"

"You're like a tiger trapped in a cat's body, just waiting for the moment to strike."

There is a undertone of adoration in his voice that surprises me. I actually laugh. "Well, Mikah, I've learned to expect the unexpected with you. No, I'm not happy about it. No, I don't really plan to use your money. But sometimes I feel that the argument is old because you know how I feel about it." I sigh. "You've given me so much already - a place to live, food, clothes - and it is very hard for me to accept those things from you when I have nothing to give you in return."

"That's not true. You give me everything, Vivienne."

"What's that supposed to mean?" I ask, surprised.

"I- Look, I really don't want to have this conversation on the phone. I would much rather do it in person. Can we discuss this when I get home tomorrow?" His voice is shaky, betraying nervousness.

"Yeah, we can talk about it tomorrow," I say, but the reluctance I feel is obvious in my voice.

"How did the rest of your appointment with Dr. Alston go?"

I roll my eyes at the sudden change in subject, but I also smile. "She's giving me clearance to go back to work, and I no longer have to wear the wrist brace."

"That's good." He pauses, from the past encounters we've had, when he's wanted something, this happens. I play with the hem of my shirt, waiting patiently for him to decide what he wants to ask me. "What if...what if I asked you not to go back to work?"

I try very hard not to roll my eyes. This isn't the first time we've had discussions about working, though he's never been so blunt about it. "Mikah, that's kind of important to my own sanity and survival. What am I going to do around here all day long? Celeste cleans and cooks everything, and I get bored easily. The only reason I've managed to stay sane so far is because you've been here. With you gone, I'm going stir crazy."

He sighs. "I know. But what if I could give you something to do all day, or at least part of the day?"

"What are you getting at, Mikah?"

"What if you could go back to school?"

"What?" I say, shocked. Going to college has always been something I've strongly desired - doing something with my brain - but it's always been out of reach. "What makes you think that's something I want to do? And even if I did want to, I can't afford it." I immediately regret that last part. I know dang well that he intends to pay for it.

"I'd take care of that, and I'm pretty sure that you'd be very good at school."

"What makes you think that?"

He takes a deep breath. "You're brilliant and..." He pauses. "I know what you scored on your SATs."

I roll my eyes again. "What *don't* you know about me, Mikah?" I knew from the first time he took me to the hospital that he'd pried into my past so I'm not entirely surprised that he knows my SAT scores, but it still bugs me that he's done this kind of research on me.

Then again, I researched him. Just not in as much detail.

"I don't know you," he says, "though I'm learning more and more each day."

"Can I think about it?" I reply.

"Of course. But if you don't want to go to school and you insist on going to work, would you allow me to offer you a job at my firm?"

"Doing what, Mikah? I have no skills or experience working in an office." Honestly, what could I do at his office that I would have even clue one about doing?

"Well, I have a couple of intern and entry-level positions open that I could offer you. You could learn. I have no doubt that whatever you put your mind to you will be brilliant at." I can hear the excitement in his voice. "Listen, we can talk about this some more this weekend. I don't expect you to decide right now. Okay?"

"Alright." I sigh. "When are you coming home?"

"Do you miss me?"

"Yes."

I hear his sharp intake of breath at my words.

"Why does that surprise you?" I ask.

"Because. I miss you, too."

I smile.

"I will be home tomorrow, hopefully in the morning. Viv, I wanted to ask you something else."

"What's that?"

"Tomorrow night there is a charity gala that I'm supposed to attend. I'd like it if you would be my date."

"Uh..." I'm taken aback by his question, surprised that he would want to take me to something like that. "Mikah, I've never been to anything like that before." I pull my feet up, cross my legs and lean back into the couch. I place my hand on my belly and begin rubbing it.

"I know, but it's really no big thing. We go, have dinner, there is an auction, and dinner is followed by a dance. It's a stuffed shirt, black tie kind of thing. I am not a fan of going to them, but this one is for an important charity that I've been a part of since its inception, so it is really important that I be there. I just don't want to go without you."

I'm pondering his words as I continue to stroke my belly. "I have nothing to wear," I say, and he chuckles.

"Does that mean you'll go?"

I roll my eyes at his enthusiasm. "Yes, Mikah, I'll go."

"Yes! Okay, I will have Celeste make some arrangements for you to have a nice, relaxing day tomorrow, get your hair done, be pampered a little. And when you guys go out today, you can find yourself a dress." The excitement in his voice is infectious, and I can't help but smile.

I splay my hand across my belly, and as I do, I feel something, almost like bubbles under my hand. "Holy crap."

"I'm sure you'll-"

"No, not that." I cut him off. I rub at my belly again, placing a little more pressure on it, and it happens again. "Whoa."

"Vivienne, what's the matter?"

I feel tears on my cheeks. "I-" It hits again. "I think she's moving. It feels like little bubbles."

"Vivienne, are you serious?" he says with major excitement in his voice.

I laugh a choked laugh. "Yes, I'm serious. It feels so..." I can't think of the words.

"Viv, that's so...wow."

My thoughts exactly.

TWENTY-FIVE

Not long after I get off the phone with Mikah, Andrew comes into the apartment, hands me an envelope and tells me that Celeste will be down shortly. The envelope has some papers and something flat and hard inside. I open it up.

Inside is a letter and a black and silver credit card that says *American Express Elite* and has my name on it. Holy shit, his damn shopping budget involves a credit card.

I open up the letter. At first I think it's handwritten, but when I run my fingers over it I realize it's been printed in a font that looks just like his handwriting.

Dearest Vivienne,

In this envelope you will find your very own credit card. Please do not be mad at me, but after our conversation today, I wanted you to be able to go out and go shopping with Celeste with your own credit card.

Andrew and Connor will accompany both of you, and I've reserved some private shopping time at Neiman Marcus to cut back on security concerns. Please make sure that you also pick up a coat or two, one for tomorrow night and one for everyday use. While I love seeing you in my Boston College sweatshirt, it is hardly warm enough for the weather.

I hope you enjoy your shopping. Once again I'm awed by the fact that I've been able to be a part of yet another milestone in your pregnancy.

I cannot wait to see you tomorrow.

Be Safe,
M

By the time I'm done reading the note, I'm over the fact that he insists on paying for my shopping. He's actually given me a list of the things he would like me to buy, which makes it a little easier to take the credit card, though I'm not sure I'll feel right using it for anything other than what he's outlined.

Neiman Marcus turns out to be a beast of a store – huge and full of everything and rather overwhelming. However, I do manage to find a dress for tomorrow night. I'm shocked beyond measure when I see it. It's too perfect and I'm able to wear it, pregnant belly and all, without purchasing a maternity dress. Celeste comments at one point that, despite my belly, my small frame will allow me to wear regular style clothing for some time before I really have to get into the maternity styles. I'm relieved to hear it because I'm not all that impressed with the maternity section in the store.

I also manage to find shoes and a coat for tomorrow night that actually match the dress, as well as a coat for everyday use. I also pick up two bras from the maternity section; when I try them on, the soft, supportive fabric brings nearly instant relief.

Purses are a whole other issue. Neiman Marcus doesn't have a single purse that I like within my price range, but when I ask Celeste if we can just go to Target or Wal-Mart, she looks at me like I've lost my mind. Eventually I find one that I really like for day-to-day use. Then I find a second one that's white and matches my dress for tomorrow night. It's smaller and fancier, definitely not for everyday use. I refuse to look at the price tags on them as we head toward the register.

Celeste does her best to encourage me to buy more things, but I'm determined to use Mikah's credit card only for the things that he's pointed out.

When we're done, we head home. I'm exhausted from all of the day's events and very thankful that Celeste is making me dinner because I don't have the energy.

Just as I sit down to eat, Mikah calls my iPod using FaceTime, and Celeste shows me how to use it. Mikah's exhausted, too. We cut the conversation short because his flight out of Phoenix is leaving early in the morning.

After dinner, I curl up on the couch to watch a movie, but before I know it, my eyelids become heavy. I manage to turn off the TV and stumble into the bedroom before falling into a deep sleep.

TWENTY-SIX

The next morning I wake up early, around seven, rub the sleep from my eyes, and shuffle into the bathroom to take a shower. As I shed my clothing I notice something strange about the way I'm moving, but I can't quite place it.

That's when I catch a glimpse of myself in the mirror and start to scream. I quickly clasp my hand over my mouth, remembering that one of the men is standing outside the door to the apartment.

"Calm down, angel."

"How in the hell am I supposed to calm down? Look at me!"

"I know. Breathe. We will handle this together," the female voice says calmly.

I don't even bother to look around; I know she's not in the room to be seen. No, she's in my head.

What the hell was I dreaming about?

"Elysium, and, erm..."

Well, crap, so dreaming about Elysium is now causing my wings to sprout? I thought I only had wings while I was in Elysium, not...

I trail off. It's obvious right now that my assumption was incorrect, as I'm staring at wings - smaller than

424

those in Elysium, but still wings - sprouting from my back. They are about a quarter of the size of those in my dreams.

I'd already managed to shed my tank top before I'd realized that these beautiful white wings with silvery trim were pushing their way out, and my naked torso, framed by my flaming red, curly hair and white wings is, well, breathtakingly beautiful. The image is actually quite-

"Angels do not think such things."

I blush at her catching the direction of my thoughts, but I say, "Can you blame me?"

She laughs, the sound like a chorus of angels singing and bells ringing. "No, my child, I do not and cannot blame you for such thoughts."

I suddenly have a mental image of her fanning herself, and I shake my head.

Looking back into the mirror, I almost don't want the wings to go away. But I'm not sure how on earth I will explain this to Celeste, let alone the men and Mikah.

"Mikah knows."

"Wait, what? How?" I've suspected that we share the dreams together, but not that he actually knows.

"Well, he has an idea. He is the one that noticed your back first. In the hospital."

"Why hasn't he said anything?"

I feel her shrug. "More than likely, he is trying not to scare you. And he isn't the only one aware of what you are."

"Wait a minute. Who else knows?"

"Your guardians know." She's playing coy and it's starting to piss me off.

"Spill it, Zirah. Who the hell else knows about this?" As I say this, I watch my wings flare, almost like they're taking a big breath.

"Celeste."

My eyes bulge and my mouth drops open.

"Andrew, Connor, and..." She stops.

"Red?" I whisper the last name.

"Yes," she says.

"Does Mikah know this?"

"No. He suspects, but he doesn't know for certain that he is not the only one protecting you. The others are something different. They are not angels, but guardians of Elysium. They have abilities of protection that you and Mikah do not. They act as shields, especially for you. They are more like assistants to Mikah. They are able to regenerate and to morph into anything that you may need for protection, though they also have their limitations."

I take a deep breath, trying to take all of this in. Since stepping out of those hospital doors two weeks ago, I've been more protected than I ever could've thought possible. Having guards outside the door was one thing, but knowing that those guards are really doing more than I can imagine is...

"They've been able to hide you from detection. While the ones who wish to harm you cannot detect you, your being alive has prevented the *foinse olc* – or source of evil, the devil - from returning to his full strength. This is the reason that Riley tried to kill you. Though he has his own personal reasons for wanting you dead, he is operating on the command of the devil. He has failed, and is failing, and it is only a matter of time before *he* has his way with him."

"How so?" I breathe.

"He will take Riley into the inner circles of Hades."

I'm reminded of our earlier conversation about Dante's *Inferno*. There are levels of hell in that book.

"You're not far off. That story is surprisingly accurate. Killing you was to be Riley's rite of passage. He was to be one of the devil's minions, part of his demon circle. Riley's failure is your gain, and he will soon be doomed to relive torture day in and day out."

I shiver and watch as my wings shimmer in the light of the bathroom.

"Okay. Can you make these things go away?" I manage to mumble.

"Yes, my angel, but I would like to teach you how to bring them in. It's actually rather simple. All you need to do is visualize them coming back in, and they will retract of their own accord."

I close my eyes to avoid being distracted by the sight of them in the mirror. I flex my shoulders and can feel them move from deep inside. I focus on that feeling and imagine pulling them in. The process is slow, but little by little I feel them settling in on my back.

Once I feel that they are back in place, I slowly open my eyes. They're gone. All that is left in the mirror is me. I sigh. I rather enjoyed seeing my wings in person for the first time, but I'm glad to have them tucked away.

TWENTY-SEVEN

After my shower, I put on one of my new bras and am excited by the fact that my breasts are not as sore. I still feel the tight heaviness and it's mildly uncomfortable, but it's manageable.

Once I'm dressed, I head out into the living room. Surprisingly, Celeste is nowhere to be found, but on the breakfast bar is a bagel, spread thickly with strawberry cream cheese, and a card.

I shuffle toward it and take a seat. Picking up the card, I read:

Good morning, Vivienne. I've left this bagel for you. I will be back around 9:15 to collect you. Mikah has arranged a day at the spa just for you.
Enjoy! Celeste.

The spa? What the hell is that? I shrug and pick up my bagel, taking a huge bite.

When I'm done eating, I still have about twenty minutes before she will be back. I take to transferring the minimal contents of my old wallet to the new one, which matches my new black purse. It is round on the bottom and flat at the top. Celeste called it "bucket style." She was careful to remove the tag so I wouldn't see the price, but it is covered in silhouettes of the letter *C*. The wallet is the same material and color. She tried to convince me to get another color, but I preferred the black one.

I also put my journal in my new bag, along with a few of the other things, chapstick, a tattered picture of my mother and a gentleman, whom my mother said is my father and a small package of Kleenex, that Celeste saved from my old one. I pause a moment to look at the picture again. There is something strangely familiar about the man next to my mother, but I can't place him. I take one last look at my old wallet, I toss it into the garbage under the coffee table. I won't need it anymore.

I grab my new bag and set it up on the breakfast bar, waiting for Celeste to show up.

The phone rings. My heart pounds as it occurs to me it might be Mikah. Then I scowl, remembering he was leaving early this morning and should be on a plane. But when I pick it up off of its cradle and look at it, I see that it is Mikah.

"Good morning," I say enthusiastically into the phone.

There's no answer on the other end of the line.

"Hello?" I say again. Nothing. For reasons unknown the wings on my back buzz. "Mikah, are you there?"

Still no answer.

I turn toward the door to the apartment and jump, dropping the phone. Standing in the doorway is Mikah with his phone to his ear.

"Gah! Don't do that to me," I say, but he's just standing there.

My back is ablaze. Fear strikes through me, and I suddenly understand that this is not Mikah. My wings begin to push out from my back and into my top, straining against the material. I hear the seams starting to rip, and the next thing I know, the shirt is no longer tight but shredded and falling away from my body.

Whatever is standing in the doorway is staring hard at me, its gaze intense.

Inside my head I start yelling for help, but what I'm screaming isn't English.

Suddenly, out of nowhere, Andrew is standing between me and the figure in the door. He is poised and ready to take on whatever it is, but he's puzzled by what he's seeing.

"Blake," Andrew says.

The man's eyes do not waver from me.

My wings flap hard, once, twice, harder and faster each time, sending waves of air past and around me. I feel lighter on my feet, but before I can actually take off, Red appears in front of me.

"Do not take off. You are safe, no harm will come to you."

He turns around, and suddenly all the air my wings have produced is pushing back at me, almost like I'm in front of a wall, and Red has disappeared. The scene in front of me shimmers and ripples as if I'm looking through a fishbowl. I can still see the room, though, and I watch the eyes of the man at the door as they shift, searching.

Connor appears behind him. So quickly that I can't follow it, Connor has his arms around the man's neck and Andrew attacks from the front.

Andrew strikes, throwing a punch at the man's gut, not once but three or four times. Then he spins him out of Connor's grasp and into his own.

"Who are you?" I hear Andrew growl. His voice is deep, scary and demonic. The muscles in his back shift as he strains harder against the man in his arms.

Connor is on him fast with a blade at least six inches long pointed at his chest. "I will run you through. Who are you? What are you doing here?"

The figure in Andrew's arms shifts and morphs. His skin takes on a darker tone, almost black, mixed with green. His hair disappears and...horns?

"Jesus, a shifter." Connor spats. "Who sent you?"

"Who do you think? I've come for her. I've come to take her to Him," the demon snarls the last word.

"I don't think so," Andrew says, and in one fast move he's turned the shifter around and pushed him to the floor. Andrew's legs are entangled with the intruder's and his hands are pressing hard into his shoulders.

Before I can even worry about the fact that the demon's hands are free, Connor is on them, holding them down as Andrew reaches inside his boot and withdraws another six-inch knife. This one looks like it's made out of gold.

"Take her, now!" Andrew shouts at Red.

In an instant I'm engulfed in a bubble-like shell, and then I'm standing in a solid white room, much like the room from my dreams. Elysium.

TWENTY-EIGHT

My heart races and blood pulses behind my ears. I can't even begin to imagine how I've managed to get here, let alone so quickly.

I pinch my arm. "Ouch!" Nope, I'm not dreaming.

"What the hell just happened?" I nearly scream.

"Calm down, Vivienne, no need to get worked up. That was a shifter."

"How did he get past Andrew and Connor?" Come to think of it: "And how did you get here? You're supposed to be with Mikah."

Red takes a seat on the white couch. His face wears a soft expression that I find comforting. "I'll explain it all," he says. "Have a seat, take a breath. You're alright, and we'll discuss it."

I start to pace.

"Vivienne, please, sit. Everyone is fine. No one is harmed." I try to sit, but I can't, at least not in a chair. My wings are still in full extension. I take a seat on the bench opposite the couch.

"Shifters are something of an in-between. They are not exactly human, but they are not demonic, either." I never noticed Red's accent before, but the more he talks, the more I hear it. "They have the ability to travel between realms, but the catch is that they can only project themselves. They are not actually present until they complete their transition. They project to an area where they want to be, which in this case was the end of the ringing line. Where you were. When you answered the phone he honed in on your position and projected to it."

"But he looked like Mikah," I say, completely breathless.

"He took the shape of something you wouldn't run from." He twirls his wedding band around his finger. "He needed you to keep the connection open long enough for him to fully teleport into the room. That's when Andrew and Connor intercepted. There's an alarm system in the house to warn us of intruders, but it doesn't always detect shifters when in their projected form. He pauses to take a deep breath. "When he tried to complete his teleport, it set off all the alarms and connected to my phone. When it went off, I came as fast as I could. I shielded you so that the shifter couldn't see you when he teleported into the house. He'd be confused, allowing us to take him down as we did."

I look up at him, confused. Then Zirah's words from earlier come back. "Shields?" I whisper.

"Yes, darlin'. All of us - Andrew, Connor and myself - have the ability to create a camouflage of sorts that will turn anything behind it invisible."

I put my head in my hands. "This is all...it's too much."

"Breathe. You're safe, and your location is still undetected."

My head snaps up. "You're joking, right? He was in the apartment."

"No, his image was. All this one saw was the inside of an apartment, but the location of that apartment is covered up by the securities we have in place. Think of him as a hologram."

"A what?"

"It's like a three-dimensional picture. You can see it, but if you touch it there is nothing there. Shifters are different from holograms in the sense that they shift into the dimension they're after, and though they are not solid, certain supreme beings have the ability to touch - or make physical contact with - and control them. Myself, Andrew and Connor are three of those people.

"The location is safe because your shifter was unable to move, unable to fully shift into the apartment because of the protection we have in place."

"So now I have to worry about holograms showing up in the apartment."

"No," says a voice behind me. I turn to the sound and it is Andrew.

"Gah! Jesus, stop that, would you?"

"Sorry." He looks from me to Red. "We're in the clear." He looks cautiously at me then back to Red. "It's been taken care of."

I need no more explanation from him; I know what he is saying without him actually saying it.

"We've added additional protection to the building, especially the apartments."

"Aaron?" Red says.

"Aye, he's taking care of it."

"Wait a minute, who's Aaron?" I interrupt them.

Andrew kneels down next to me. "Are you okay?"

"Who's Aaron?" I repeat.

The way he shakes his head gives me the distinct impression that Mikah has done a thorough briefing with him about my stubbornness.

"Aaron is another one of us, but he has the ability to provide an additional protection, the ability to stop shifters from coming into an area that's protected by him. He's placing protection on the building, as well as on you. No matter where you go, you'll be safe."

I feel a knot of stress form in my back and my wings respond by quivering.

"Can you pull them back in?" Red asks.

I look at him and my wings twitch. "I think so. Though I've only done it once."

Red cannot hide the shock on his face. Obviously that was not something he was expecting to hear.

"I sort of woke up with them this morning. That's how I found out about what you guys are. Which is why I'm not so much shocked by what you've done, but rather by that thing finding me in the first place."

Andrew chimes in. "I'm not convinced he knows what he found for certain. Red was quick with the shield, and we've taken care of him so he cannot return and report."

"I just need to know that I'm safe and that this won't happen to me again."

"No, ma'am," Andrew says.

I scowl at him but I don't want to fight right now about him calling me Vivienne, so instead I focus on reining in my wings. I lower my head to my hands, placing the heels of my palms against my eyes and closing them tight, and I concentrate on my wings.

TWENTY-NINE

After I manage to pull myself back together, Andrew leads me to a door opposite where we were sitting and I magically walk back into the apartment. It looks exactly as it did when I answered the phone.

I need a serious amount of something to process all of this. It's just too much.

Connor and Celeste are in the apartment when Andrew and I walk in. Red doesn't follow us.

"Where's Red?" I ask.

"He went back to Mikah. They're on their way home," Connor says.

I nod. "Now what?" I say.

Celeste steps forward. "Now you have a spa appointment."

"You're kidding, right?" I retort.

"Nope. Come on, grab your stuff," she says.

"Please tell me you're joking. After that?" I say back.

Connor speaks up. "Mikah does not know about this, about you, or about us. Proceeding with the day as planned is the best way to keep it that way."

"Why is hiding who and what you are from Mikah so important?" I ask.

They all look at each other. Andrew is the one who answers. "Mikah can and will know about us, but him finding out about a shifter here will send him over the edge. We are just trying to take it slower on him." He pauses. "He is having a harder time adjusting to what he is than you are."

I look at all of them, puzzled. "I'm not sure I'm handling any of this, to be honest."

They all laugh, just a little.

"Yeah, you are," Celeste says. "You've yet to freak out."

I laugh. "I guess it is just a matter of accepting my fate. It is what it is, and until it affects me to the point of spending every day in Elysium or in fear of someone or something getting to me, I'm not sure there is much I can do about it." I also take into consideration that the one person I seem to want to spend all my time with is just like me. But I don't tell them that.

"That is a beautiful attitude. I wish we all had that kind of outlook when we found out." Celeste is still smiling as she says this. "That is how we know that you can handle this more than Mikah can. Eventually he will step into his own role. We just need to give him time."

I nod. "Okay, then. I guess we're going to a spa?"

THIRTY

A little over three hours later we arrive back at the underground garage of the condo. Andrew and Connor are both there to escort me into the elevator. However, neither one of them join me on my way up to my floor. When the doors open, Red is in the hallway.

"Good afternoon and welcome home, Ms. Vivienne."

"Thank you, Red. Is he home?"

"Yes, ma'am. He's inside waiting for you."

"Thank you."

I'm immediately surprised when I walk in: Lining the hallway are candles about every three feet. They've been placed so nicely that they almost look like they've been there forever.

I don't see Mikah anywhere, but I can hear the shower in the guest bathroom. He must be in there. I pause by the door, tempted to open it and let him know I'm here, but decide against it.

Instead I follow the path of candles to the breakfast bar. Sitting atop the bar is a vase containing two roses: a beautiful red rose in full bloom and a baby Fire and Ice rose. I smile. Next to the vase with the roses sits a

438

package that looks similar to the one that contained the original Baby Callahan picture. A note on top says *Open Me* in Mikah's script.

I pick it up and rip open the paper to reveal a black box. I pull the top off, and looking back at me is a silver frame engraved with the words *It's a Girl* along the top and *Baby Callahan, taken November 9th, 2012* at the bottom. The frame is empty. I remember the ultrasound pictures Dr. Alston gave me yesterday and I know the perfect one.

I head over to the coffee table, bypassing the other candles. I'd like to put the picture in this frame before Mikah gets out of the bathroom so he can see it.

Grabbing the envelope off of the table, I flip to the one of her beautiful profile and lift the frame from the box. I'm surprised to find another frame underneath, this one an exact duplicate of the one he gave me before, picture and all. He's given me back my picture.

I slide the picture into the first frame and stand it up next to the vase, then pick up the other frame and set it up on the other side.

I'm about to throw the box away when I notice that it contains another, smaller box, a black velvet one. It's a jewelry box. Puzzled, I open the lid hesitantly and gasp.

Inside is a silver bracelet. It has a small heart locket near the clasp. Hooked onto the heart is a pair of miniature baby booties with pink gems on them. It's beautiful.

I slip the bracelet onto my wrist and I'm instantly in love with the way it looks and the way it feels. It is, of course, too much, but it is something that he's actually thought about, like the frames. And it symbolizes our baby girl.

Whoa, did I...? Yeah, I did. But I'm surprised to find that, rather than feeling really awkward, I take comfort in the idea of *our*.

I look at the bracelet as it sparkles in the shimmering light of the candles throughout the apartment.

After a few moments I pull the box off the counter, again intending to throw it away, and this time I spot a card taped to the counter underneath where the box sat.

Leave the box. There is something else waiting for you in the bedroom.

I notice now that the shower has stopped, and I get a tingling feeling that Mikah has been watching me from the bathroom. I smile but don't turn around as I head off toward my bedroom.

THIRTY-ONE

Stepping over the threshold into my bedroom, I notice that there are no candles in here but that the lights are on and dimmed. Lying on the bed are three boxes: one huge, one about the size of a shoe box, and one smaller still.

"Mikah, what have you done?"

The biggest one says *Open first* across the top. I smile and pull the paper-wrapped lid back to find pink tissue paper.

I slowly pull the paper back.

And gasp.

Any doubts that Mikah has been sharing my dreams with me are swept away. Inside the box is the very same dress that I've been wearing in our dream: the white tank top dress with silver accents beneath the chest and atop my baby bump. The straps are accented with the same design at the top. These accents hold the flowing gossamer train. The back is wide open, allowing room for my wings if they were out.

Peeling my eyes away from the first box, I sidestep to box number two.

Tears prick my eyes as I pull the lid off the box. Inside is a pair of white ballerina slippers that have long ribbons attached, no doubt to wrap around my calves. They're very pretty.

Finally, box number three.

These belonged to my mother.

I cover my mouth to hold in my gasp. Why would he give me something from his mother? Do I really mean that much to him? Then I remember our dream. Yes, I think I do.

I slowly open the last box and slide back the tissue paper. Sitting upon a shiny material are two bracelets. The bands that I'm wearing in the dream. In the center of the swirls are the white pearls. Also sitting among the material is what appears to be a headband of sorts, or a tiara.

My fingers gently glide along the smooth silver.

"You don't need to wear it all tonight."

I don't jump because I've had a feeling he was watching me. "I don't know what to say."

"Say you'll wear it."

I nod my head enthusiastically. "Of course I will."

I turn around to face him. He is standing there barefoot, in dress pants, no shirt, and his hair is still wet and dripping slightly.

The sight of him has me weak in the knees, but a huge weight dissolves almost the instant that I look into his bright, brilliant blue eyes.

"Hi, beautiful," he says and smiles that gorgeous smile he has that no doubt has the ability to bring any woman to her knees.

"Hi," I breathe.

He makes no move toward me, so I cross the room to him and throw my arms around his chest. I accidentally touch the wings on his back, and a tremor runs through his body.

He wraps his arms around me and kisses the top of my head.

"I missed you," I mumble into his chest.

"I can tell. I missed you, too."

He rubs along my back, and my body shakes in response. A desire to be closer to him grows hot within my body and it frightens me. I don't have a clue what this means. I've never felt anything like it before.

"You look beautiful," he says quietly.

"Thank you."

"You're welcome. Now, we need to leave in about twenty minutes. Will you be ready?"

I nod into his chest once again and he pulls back slightly.

"Good. Now we both need to get dressed," he says, kissing the top of my head again and pulling free of my arms.

I reluctantly let him go.

He turns toward the other bedroom and I see his beautiful wings shimmering across his back, vivid and alive.

THIRTY-TWO

I change quickly, starting with the shoes. I slide them onto my feet and crisscross the laces up each calf. Standing straight again, I replace the tan bra I'm wearing - which would've worked well for the dress I'd planned to wear - for a white, lacy one. I also pull on a pair of white lace boy shorts to match. I'm relieved to notice that although the back of the dress is open, it will still cover up my bra.

I slip easily into the dress and guide one bracelet over each of my wrists. I cannot bear to part with the locket he gave me earlier, so I decide to leave it on, too.

I cannot help but smile at the beautiful woman staring back at me in the full-length mirror. She is elegant, graceful, and classically beautiful. With her hair pulled back off of her face and cascading down her back, she looks like Cinderella, ready for the ball.

I'm overcome by the idea of what people will think, seeing me on Mikah's arm. I will become the center of attention; I can feel it already.

"Get a grip," I say quietly to myself. I've never cared what anyone has thought of me. Why start now?

I feel a tingle of excitement right as the knock comes. "Viv, it's almost time to go."

"I'll be right there," I say back loudly.

I reach for the little purse I bought yesterday to go with the dress I'd originally planned to wear. That dress is similar to this one, but it will sit unused in the closet. I wonder if Celeste can return it for me.

I sneak one final sideways glance at myself in the mirror. My bump is more pronounced from this angle, but for some strange reason, it's a very welcome sight.

When I step out from the bedroom, I see Mikah standing at the breakfast bar with his back to me. The candles are still lit, but the light over the bar is on. He's changed his pants. He's now wearing white pants.

I take a few steps in his direction and he turns toward me. As he turns I see that a thick silver stripe runs up the outside of his pants and that he is wearing a silver vest and tie under his white jacket.

I can't help the fascinated smile that spreads across my face at the fact that we match.

"Hello, beautiful," he says, and I blush. Not from his words but because I actually feel beautiful.

He walks toward me, his eyes raking me up and down, taking me in. The dress covers my feet completely. Only he and I will know that I wear only skimpy ballet slippers on my feet.

"You look gorgeous," he breathes.

The desire to kiss him is burning through my body, and I can't help but look up at him, hoping that maybe he'll finally kiss my lips.

But he goes for my forehead instead. Ever the gentleman.

I smile.

I step back slightly and turn around so that he can see the whole dress. It is a lot lower cut than I'd thought, and the sheer material barely covers the top of my butt.

When I come back around he is staring, slack-jawed, breathing heavier.

Desire flares in me again.

He extends his elbow to me, an offer, and I take it.

"Shall we?" he says.

"Yes." My voice sounds husky to my own ears. I want to stay at home tonight with him, but I know that won't happen.

Andrew and Red are waiting for us when we emerge into the hallway, both of them dressed in black tuxedos with matching bow ties. Red is holding my jacket, but Mikah quickly takes it from him. He opens it up and presents it to me to put my arms in, and I do.

He offers me his elbow once again, and we're off down the hall toward the elevator.

THIRTY-THREE

After a short drive in the limo we arrive at the Millennium Hotel downtown. Outside are people standing around and what seems like a never-ending stream of flashbulbs going off. Press? Photographers? Why?

Then I see the bright red carpet that extends from the street into the hotel.

"Take a deep breath, Vivienne, you look beautiful."

I do as Mikah has asked and I feel calmer almost instantly.

"Good job. All you have to do is stay close and smile. I will handle the rest."

I nod, not sure of my voice right now.

Red is at Mikah's door, and I see Connor coming down the carpet to meet us. I would much rather have Andrew. Though I trust Connor, especially after today, I like Andrew better.

It's almost as if he's sensed my preference; instead of joining Red, Connor walks to the front of the car and Andrew gets out. I see them exchange some words, and Andrew comes around as Red opens the door.

Mikah steps gracefully out of the car, his long fingers buttoning up his jacket as he stands.

Then his hand comes back into the car, extended in invitation, and I take it, sliding across the bench seat. As I step out, Mikah is quick to wrap his arm around me to steady me.

He waves, and I hear people shouting his name. Through the wave of flashbulbs I try to focus on where I'm going and what I'm doing, but it's hard; all the flashing lights are disorienting.

"Breathe," Mikah says.

I take a deep breath and smile. He releases my waist in exchange for taking my hand. I would much rather be closer to him, but it's hard to walk that way. I follow him along the line of cameras down the red carpet. Red and Andrew are right next to us.

About halfway up, he leans into my ear. "We're going to pause, face left, smile, then turn around and do the same on the other side. Then we will go straight in."

"Okay," I say with a little more confidence.

Two more steps and he stops and turns left, his hand leaving mine and coming to rest on the small of my back. I smile, and a flurry of flashbulbs go off in my face. I find it hard to look straight ahead. After a couple of heartbeats, we turn around to face yet another onslaught of flashes and more people shouting his name.

After another heartbeat I hear Mikah say, "Okay, let's go."

We turn back toward the door and make our way into the hotel almost double-time. I'm blinking rapidly, trying to clear the dark spots in my vision.

"Good evening, Mr. Blake," a gentleman in full livery says. "Right this way."

He leads us toward a bank of elevators. The spots are slowly subsiding, but I don't really get a chance to look around at the entrance of the hotel.

We reach the elevators and someone else in full livery is standing inside, holding the door. We all step in, and the doors close.

I hear Mikah let out a huge breath. "Glad that's over," he says.

I giggle a bit. "That was awful," I say, and all three men laugh.

Mikah looks down at me. His eyes are a vibrant green tonight. He's excited about this for some reason. "You look gorgeous," he says and smiles warmly at me.

I nudge him with my shoulder. "You don't look too bad yourself," I say back, surprised by my momentary lack of filter.

He smiles wider. "Thank you, Ms. Callahan." Whoa, where'd that come from? But his eyes are alight with even more excitement at my words.

After a few more beeps the doors finally open into a reception area. Off to the left are several coat racks behind a table.

"May I take your coat?" he asks.

I nod, suddenly nervous.

I turn my back toward him as I undo the two buttons in the front. He gently slips the jacket from my shoulders. A shiver runs through me as his fingers gently stroke along my shoulder. He hands my jacket to the lady at the table, who takes it and hands him a ticket in return. Once the exchange is done, he grabs my hand and we turn around.

Ahead of us is a set of double doors and a sign overhead that reads *Ballroom* in gold lettering.

I notice very quickly that the majority of the guests in the ballroom ahead are wearing black. There are a couple of red and blue dresses scattered throughout, but Mikah and I are the only ones in white.

Mikah leads me into the ballroom, which is huge but not packed full of people. Round tables surround a small stage and dance floor, and I'm suddenly anxious; I have no clue how to dance. I secretly hope that Mikah won't ask me to.

We work our way through the crowd. There are waitresses walking around with trays of glasses full of what I think is champagne. Mikah stops one of them and takes a flute from the tray. "Would you please get the lady some cider?"

"Yes, sir," she says, and she heads off, making a beeline for a table at the far end that is covered in full glasses and champagne bottles.

"Thank you," I say to Mikah, and he looks down at me, a quizzical look on his face. "For the cider," I add.

"Of course. Don't want you to be thirsty." He smiles.

"Mikah." A woman's voice carries over the hum of conversation, and I turn my head in its direction. Walking toward us is a woman with medium blond hair, cut into a cute pixie style, and bright brown eyes. Her floor-length black dress shimmers in the light.

I look at Mikah, who raises his glass in her direction as she approaches.

"Hello, darling," she says and places her hands on his shoulders to gently kiss each of his cheeks. I watch in awe. "You look fabulous."

"So do you."

She looks expectantly at me.

"Sydney, this is Vivienne," Mikah says.

Recognition registers on her face and she smiles warmly at me. "Vivienne, it is a pleasure to finally meet you. I've heard a lot about you."

I'm at a loss, but Mikah doesn't miss a beat. "Vivienne, Sydney is my senior partner and my right hand. She's the reason I've been able to take these last couple of weeks off."

"Oh, hello." I smile and offer her my hand. "It's an honor to meet you."

She takes my hand and we shake.

I can feel the pride washing off of Mikah. I too am surprised by my own poise and confidence. It's not something I've ever had to do, but it seems to come naturally to me.

The waitress has returned with my cider. I take the glass from her.

"Likewise," Sydney says. "I will let the two of you mingle and I will see you at dinner."

"Thanks, Sydney," Mikah says, and she's off, just like that.

I can see by her confidence and the way she greets people along the way that she's very comfortable with who she is and what she's doing here.

I take a sip of my drink. It's good. Sweet, but not too sweet, and bubbly.

"Come 'ere, I'd like to show you something," he says.

THIRTY-FOUR

He guides me by the small of my back toward a room to our right. As we approach the doorway I can see that the room has a domed ceiling of glass and that there are tables scattered around the room.

When we enter, I notice that each table has something on it. I can see everything from bottles of wine to books to a computer, and then some of the tables just have signs on them.

"This is a silent action." Mikah pauses his steps and turns toward me. "All the items in this room have been donated by someone in attendance. So whatever the winning bid is on an item, that money all goes toward the charity for tonight's event."

"What is tonight's charity?" I ask, rather anxious to know.

He takes my hand and leads me to a small round table on the left-hand side of the room. Upon the table is a sign that reads:

The 5th Annual Hearts and Hands Charity Gala
Hearts and Hands is a charity specializing in helping battered women and their children.

Hearts and Hands is also the parent company for many women's shelters throughout Minnesota, including Hope House and Amber's Place right here in Minneapolis.

Tonight's event is sponsored by MSB Enterprises and MSBE International.

My eyes fill with tears. The overwhelming emotion I feel is beyond anything I've felt in a long time.

Mikah leans down. "Please, don't cry."

"Did you do this for me?" I say through the tears.

"I'd love to say that I did, but my company started this gala about five years ago. Hearts and Hands was the first - and remains the primary - charity that my company supports." He gets down on one knee so that he can look up into my eyes. "I brought you here tonight because I felt it was important for you to see that my caring for you extends beyond just helping you. I take pride in my company's sponsorship of not only this event, but at least two others throughout the year. However, tonight's event is the big one of the year and raises more than five million dollars for Hearts and Hands." He reaches up to wipe away a stray tear on my cheek and my heart flutters at his touch. "Every dollar raised tonight is matched by me." He takes a deep breath. "I also brought you here because I need someone to help me run and organize MSB's charity division. I'd like, in time, for that person to be you."

I'm speechless and, to say the least, freaked out by his proposal. "Mikah, I haven't a clue about any of this."

He smiles warmly. "I know. Which is why I made the offer for you to go back to school - to learn." It's all starting to make sense now. "Vivienne, you're a brilliant young woman and you deserve every opportunity I can give you. I'd love to see what you're truly capable of when you put your mind to something. I want to see your passion for something shine and carry you into doing something you will love. You don't have to answer tonight, but please tell me you'll think about it."

The idea of going back to school was so overwhelmingly exciting for me when he first mentioned it, and now that I see there is a real purpose behind it, the idea is even harder to resist. "I'll think about it," I say quietly.

"Good. Now, let's take a look."

He stands, takes my hand, and leads me over to the first table, where we look at each of the items being auctioned before moving on to the next table. It takes about ten minutes to make our way through the room. The stand-up display on the last table says *MSB* on it. I read it.

Portfolio review and adjustment provided by MSB on a portfolio size of up to $10 million.
Estimated value: $100,000.00

I look down at the bid sheet. Up until now, the bids have been very impressive, ranging anywhere from five thousand to sixty thousand, but this one surprises me most. The current bid stands at ninety-five thousand dollars. I gape at it.

"Holy cow."

"I told you," Mikah breathes, and I look at his beautiful bright blue eyes. Once again they've shifted colors, though the green lingers around the edges. He gestures around the room. "Did you see anything you like?"

I nod. A couple of tables back, there is a cool iPad and a laptop that looks similar to Mikah's, but both the iPad and computer have a special matching design on them done in the most beautiful deep purple with a rose in gold inlay. The center of the rose is created by a jewel - a diamond, I think. The tag said that they were specially designed and donated by some businesswoman out of Phoenix, and I wonder if she was the reason for Mikah's trip.

"Which one?" he asks.

"The iPad."

He smiles. "I thought you might like that one. Let's go take a look."

He turns us back in that direction just as an announcement comes from the other room. "Dinner is served, ladies and gentlemen. If you would please take your seats." Ironically enough, my stomach growls.

We approach the table and look at the bid sheet. It is up to thirty-five thousand dollars, and my eyes go wide as Mikah writes something on the sheet.

"What are you doing?" I squeak.

I see him shake with laughter at my tone. "What does it look like?"

He stands up, and I look down at the bid sheet.

THIRTY-FIVE

4. Vivienne Callahan $50,000.00

"Jesus, Mikah, I don't have that kind of money."

"Sure you do. You have a credit card, remember." He has a shit-eating grin on his face as he says this.

"No, Mikah, that is your credit card-"

"And you're free to purchase what you want with it. I told you that."

"But-"

"Don't argue, please. It's for a good cause, and there is a chance that you won't win," he says, but the confidence in his voice tells me that the bid he placed for me will win.

I know I'm going to lose this argument, but I have to at least try to help him see where I'm coming from. "Mikah, it's too much. I don't even know how to use it, or spend that kind of money on it. Surely there are cheaper alternatives."

"Of course there are, but I would rather see it go to a charity than to some business that will only use the money to further their profits. Besides, that is a one-of-a-kind design. Just like you."

He smiles warmly at me and my heart melts, at which point I lose any and all will to argue.

"Alright," I say, relenting even while secretly hoping I'll lose the bid.

He smiles wider and brushes his hand through his hair. "Shall we eat?"

I nod, and off we go toward the throng of people finding their tables. Mikah leads us straight to ours. Sitting in front of the beautiful place settings - china plates, silverware and crystal goblets - are tent cards with our names on them: *Ms. Vivienne Callahan* and *Mr. Mikah Blake*.

He pulls my chair out for me and I take a seat.

"Thank you," I say as he helps me slide in.

Instead of taking his seat, he remains standing behind his chair. Slowly the other eight chairs at our table are claimed, though half of the remaining chairs are occupied by women while their men stand behind them or behind their own chairs. Finally Sydney arrives, but she doesn't sit down, and I notice with curiosity that no one is with her, though there seems to be an empty chair next to her.

Looking around the room, I notice it is the same at every table: The women are seated - talking with the other women at the tables and drinking champagne - while the men stand behind them. Beyond the tables is a wall of floor-to-ceiling windows hung with elegant white and red curtains that are tied back with gold ropes, allowing the Minneapolis skyline to complete the room. An amazing view.

I look back at the glasses in front of me; there are three. One has water in it, another other contains what looks like champagne, and the third remains empty. I've never had champagne before, but I'm not about to try it now.

I reach for my water glass and take a sip. As I'm returning the glass to its place on the table, Mikah leans down and whispers, "The other glass is cider." I look more closely, comparing mine to Mikah's. The color of the liquid in my glass is just a shade darker. I smile.

After just a couple more minutes, a very attractive older gentleman with speckles of gray in his otherwise black hair comes to the table and pulls out Sydney's chair. She takes her seat, and he heads to the podium on the stage just across the dance floor from our table. I notice now that we are in the very center of the room.

"Welcome, ladies and gentlemen, to the Fifth Annual Hearts and Hands Gala. My name is Gary Harper, and I will be your emcee for this evening." He pauses to take a drink of water. "I'd like to start off this evening with a few announcements. The silent auction is over in the atrium, to my left. The bidding will remain open through dinner, and we will announce all of the winners during dessert. In the center of your tables you will all see an empty vase. Please feel free to place tips for your waiters and waitresses inside these. All of your servers tonight are here as volunteers and they are donating all of their tips to Hearts and Hands, so please, tip them well." He takes another sip of his water. "Now, without further ado, please, gentlemen, take your seats. Dinner is served."

And just like that, seeming to come out of the woodwork, are lines of servers, many of them carrying four plates at a time. They all head straight toward their designated tables. I am first to be served: grilled chicken breast, some vegetables and a spaghetti-style pasta salad. Chicken is far from my favorite, but I highly doubt peanut butter and jelly sandwiches are on the menu tonight.

Mikah's plate comes next, followed by the rest of the table's. I'm surprised to see that everyone else at the table has a thick, round cut of beef with the same sides as mine. And then my heart warms as I realize that Mikah has made special arrangements just for me.

I lean in close to him. "Thank you," I breathe.

He leans toward me and places his hand on my lap. I take it, and he squeezes my fingers gently. "You're most welcome." He holds my hand long enough for me to begin to wonder how I'm going to eat one-handed, but then he squeezes again and lets go.

THIRTY-SIX

Gary comes down from the podium to join us, sitting next to Sydney and kissing her on the cheek. They make a beautiful couple. He smiles at me and begins to eat, just like the rest of us.

Mikah, Sydney and Gary make small conversation throughout the meal. I get about halfway through my chicken before my stomach starts to turn a little, so I stop eating the meat and focus instead on the vegetables and pasta salad. I eat everything else on my plate and put down my fork and knife.

"The chicken too much?" Mikah asks me quietly.

"It was really good, someone just has better ideas." I smile at his grin.

"I can ask for something else for you."

"No, I'm actually pretty full. But thank you."

"Okay. Are you feeling okay?" he asks.

"I'm good." I smile.

"Let me know if that changes, okay?" he says, his tone sincere.

"I will."

He goes back to finishing up his meal. I notice that tonight, like most nights, he cleans his plate.

I watch as people get up and begin milling about. Many walk toward the silent auction or over toward the bar at the back of the room. Some stand around talking to people at other tables. A couple of times people come and speak with Mikah or Sydney, or both. I don't pay much attention to most of their conversation, as it is business-related.

As more and more people finish eating, the dull murmur in the room increases to a roar. Gary takes this as his cue and excuses himself from the table, heading toward the stage. Rather than stand on it, he grabs the microphone and says, "Ladies and gentlemen, the silent auction will be closing in five minutes."

Panic sets in; I hope and pray that someone else has outbid me. I couldn't even bring myself to look at the price tag of the purse I bought yesterday; how on earth am I going to manage paying fifty thousand dollars for something?

My stomach churns, more from nerves than anything, I hope, and I notice Mikah looking at me. "What?" I say quietly.

He grins. "Nothing. You're just so beautiful."

On cue I blush.

Then I move to stand up, and Mikah, along with all the remaining men at the table, do the same.

"Where are you going?" he asks, concerned.

"The ladies' room."

I can see the silent "Oh" on his face. "Are you alright?" he whispers.

I smile. "Yes, I just need to use the restroom."

He offers me his hand. "I'll show you."

I know where they are - I saw them when we walked in - but it's not worth the argument. I take his hand and he leads me between the tables back toward the entrance.

For the first time all evening, I notice Red and Andrew standing near the door. I take strange comfort in knowing they're here, and I smile at them as we pass.

Mikah escorts me right up to the bathroom door, and I step inside. The bathroom is just as elegant as the rest of the ballroom, with gold accents everywhere.

A couple minutes later I emerge, having freshened up just a bit. Mikah immediately takes my hand again and we head back toward the ballroom. Gary is back onstage, organizing pieces of paper - no doubt the auction bids - and my stomach rolls again.

On our way back to our table, Mikah stops to make small talk with some of the guests. He introduces me to most of them, and I hope there won't be a test; I can't keep them all straight.

Then Gary takes up the microphone and asks everyone to return to their seats. Mikah and I head over that way to find that our desserts are already on the table. It's some tan-colored pudding; it almost looks like caramel or butterscotch. I'm suddenly eager to find out.

Again, Mikah is a gentleman, pulling my chair out for me and helping me scoot in. This time, though, he doesn't wait before he, too, takes his seat.

Just as he sits down there is a flurry of bubbles in my belly, in the same area as yesterday, and my hand flies to the spot.

Mikah is quick to notice the shift in my posture. He leans in. "Are you okay?"

I smile wide. I don't respond, but I grab his hand and pull it toward my bump. His eyes widen as he realizes what I'm about to do.

I gently push his palm against my stomach. His hand is huge - it covers nearly the entire lower half of my bump - and I can feel the heat from his skin radiating through my dress.

Nothing happens. I remember that yesterday when I applied more pressure she moved again, so I press his hand a little tighter against my bump and look at him.

He seems confused, like he can't feel anything, which is understandable because she hasn't moved again.

Gary is talking at the podium, but I can't stop staring into Mikah's eyes. I'm lost in them. Consumed by his beautiful gaze. I pull his hand in a little tighter, and just like that, the bubbles return.

Mikah looks down and then back up at me, his expression changing from confusion to wonder. His eyes are alight with excitement as the bubbles continue for a few more beats, and then they are welling up with tears.

I reach up and gently cup his cheek. He kisses my palm as I do and then leans into my touch. The bubbles have stopped, but I can tell he doesn't want to move his hand, and I'm not sure I want him to, either. I place my right hand over his on my belly and pull my other hand away from his cheek. I can't be sure, but I think he actually pouts briefly.

THIRTY-SEVEN

Gary is talking about how Hearts and Hands has grown over the last fifteen years, and with each passing year they are able to help more and more women leave abusive relationships.

"This year alone, Amber's Place has taken in more than two hundred women, and each and every one of them have either found jobs or are seeking stable employment and stable places to live.

"Currently there are more than twenty thousand women in Minneapolis alone that are living in abusive relationships. With this year's gala, Hearts and Hands hopes to expand Amber's Place to accommodate another one hundred women and their children, bringing the total up to two hundred and twenty-two rooms.

"Women who visit Amber's place are allowed to stay as long as they need to in order to obtain a job and to secure housing and financial assistance from the state to get them started and on their way to a better and brighter future.

"Tonight, we are proud to welcome four women, our guests of honor, who were once residents of Amber's Place."

Am I one of these women here tonight?

"Ladies and gentleman, please give a warm round of applause to Sydney Harper, my wife and Vice President of MSB Enterprises."

Whoa, what?

I watch as Sydney stands, tears in her eyes, and makes her way to the podium. She hugs Gary, then she stands beside him and begins to speak. "Thank you, Gary, and thank you, ladies and gentlemen, for your generous support tonight. I would also like to recognize the three other women who are guests with us here tonight, though I will not name them as I have been named.

"I knocked on Amber's door about seven years ago. I had just walked out - with my daughter, who is now eight - of a physically and emotionally abusive relationship. One day, after hearing about Hearts and Hands, I found the strength to walk away.

"When I arrived at Amber's Place, I was bruised and battered, but I was welcomed with open arms. Once I was inside the safety of their walls, and through their encouragement, I was able to call the police and have charges pressed against my attacker.

"Had it not been for Amber's Place and their willingness to help me get back on my feet, I would never have been able to find a job that put my hard-earned degree to good use. I am forever thankful to Mikah Blake and his staff for their support and endless patience when I began to learn the ropes."

I immediately understand all the pieces of who Mikah is and the things that he's done for me and it becomes clear that this is who he is.

"It is through strong will and determination that I stand here before you today. The idea behind Hearts and Hands is to give the women who go there a real chance at life, to give them a fresh start not only in their jobs but with themselves, as well.

"I am proud to tell you that tonight's event has been our most successful ever. We have raised three million, two hundred and twenty-one thousand dollars. I am also honored to be a part of MSB, who will be matching every dollar raised for a grand total of six million, four hundred and forty-two thousand dollars."

Mikah's hand comes away from my belly, as does mine, and we join the rest of the guests in a standing ovation.

The tears overwhelm my eyes as reality hits me. I'm one of those two hundred women who've been through Amber's Place this year. Two hundred is such a small number when compared to the thousands still out there suffering. How can I even begin to say no to Mikah's offer to help me become a part of their solution?

The applause continues as I gently wipe away the tears that have spilled from my eyes. Mikah hands me his handkerchief, and I take it. He wraps his arm around my back and pulls me close.

I look up at him, and he is looking at me, his eyes full of emotion.

"Yes," I say.

He cocks his head to one side.

"Yes, I'll work for you. I'll go to school. Whatever it is you want me to do, I'll do it."

He smiles, wide and bright, and pulls me in tighter to kiss my forehead. Once again, I'm left with a strong desire to kiss him.

The applause finally dies down. Gary has taken back the microphone.

"Does Sydney know about me?" I ask Mikah as he helps me to sit once again. I expect him to say yes, but he doesn't; he shakes his head.

Once Sydney has returned to the table, Mikah sits back down. I'm in awe of her speech and her openness about having been a victim of domestic violence.

Mikah leans in and whispers in my ear, "I thought it would be more appropriate if it came from you. That is a part of your life, and it is your story to tell, not mine."

I reach for his hand and squeeze, my silent reassurance that I've heard him. My heart swells at the overwhelming amount of respect I now have for him.

THIRTY-EIGHT

Gary begins announcing the winners of the silent auction. I'm thankful that the dollar amounts are not being announced. Mikah and I have been holding hands between each announcement and the clapping that follows. My palms are starting to turn red.

Gary seems to be going in random order, so I'm completely surprised when it has been some time since it began and neither Mikah's donated lot nor the one he so graciously bid on have been announced yet. But given that Mikah's was by far the highest valued item, it would make sense if Gary saved until last.

"And now, for our second-to-last item of the evening, we have our Escaping with Technology package. Donated and designed by CTM Capital out of Phoenix, Arizona, this item contains an iPod, an iPad, and a MacBook Pro laptop, all inlaid with various gems and fully loaded with business-grade software. The package also includes more than one thousand dollars in gift cards, a set of matching bags and cases, and ten hours of tutoring time, and it is valued at more than seventy-five thousand dollars."

I'm not sure I can breathe right now. I look at Mikah, who is looking at me with the biggest cat-ate-the-canary expression on his face.

"And the winner of this impressive package is..." Dramatic pause. Does he not know that I can't breathe right now? "Ms. Vivienne Callahan."

The entire room erupts in applause. Mikah is clapping and staring at me. My mouth drops open and I feel like a fish out of water, fighting to suck in air in order to breathe.

When the applause finally dies down, Mikah's still looking self-satisfied, but there is a warmth about it, too. "Way to go," he says.

Seriously? Did he seriously just say that? "I'm kind of angry with you right now," I say through gritted teeth.

He leans back dramatically, pretending to be appalled, and I cannot help but laugh at his expression. He smiles back, leans over, and places his arm along the back of my chair. His hand begins to play with a strand of my hair. "Please don't be angry. I would not have made a bid of that size if it wasn't alright. Okay?"

Gah! Why does he do this? "I feel guilty for using your money."

"Don't. It's alright. And besides, it will help you with school." He smirks at me, but the reminder that I've agreed to go to school and help him with the charity work makes me feel excited again.

Bubbles flit in my belly as the baby moves around once more, and I tense, just a little.

Mikah notices. "What's wrong?"

I smile wide at him and he knows.

"Again?"

I nod.

He smiles as Gary announces the winner of Mikah's donated lot and the room applauds.

Mikah pulls his hand back and we both join in.

"Ladies and gentlemen, thank you again for coming and for your generous support of Hearts and Hands. Please be sure to see the table in the auction room to claim your winnings, and enjoy the band." The room applauds once more, and the band that I hadn't notice set up behind us starts to play.

"Dance with me?" Mikah says.

Oh, no. My worst fear of tonight, aside from the auction, is being realized. He wants to dance.

I look at him, no doubt with overwhelming fear in my eyes, but his expression is warm and soft.

"It's easy, come on."

He stands, pulls my chair back from the table, and offers me his hand. Instinct sets in and I take it.

I look at the dance floor. There are already several couples dancing, which instantly makes me feel better; at least I won't be on display. Well, not the center of it, anyway.

"I don't know how to dance," I say as he takes me in his arms.

"It's easy, just follow my lead."

I position my hands like his and he starts off slowly, left to right, and then he's off.

The gentle pressure against my back and squeezes of my hand tell me what direction he is going to go, and all in all, it's not that bad. I'm not going to win any trophies for dancing, but it is fun just the same.

THIRTY-NINE

About halfway through our second song, my back comes alive with a zinging fire. Mikah, too, stiffens, and we stop dancing. He's looking around rather frantically, searching for something.

That's when I see it. Over at the door, near where we came in, a man is trying to come inside, but he is quickly headed off by Andrew and Red. They are pushing him back and away from door toward the elevators.

"Mikah," I say and nod my head in the direction of the door.

He turns to see. "Shit," he growls.

"What's going on? Who is that?"

"Come on. Come with me."

He takes my hand and we head toward the hall opposite the emcee's stage. There are several other people standing there, so we don't look out of place, but that doorway is our only way out.

We're out of the intruder's line of sight and well-hidden behind a rather large planter. I'm pressed up against Mikah, and I feel a vibration in his pocket.

He reaches his hand in and pulls out his phone. "Yeah." His tone is clipped. "Make sure he is gone off of the property, and we will wrap things up here. Send Andrew back up to escort us down." He pauses. "Are we sure he was alone?" He listens. "Yeah, okay. Thanks, Red."

He pulls the phone away from his ear. "It's time to go."

"Mikah, what's going on? Who was that?" There was something about that man that was familiar, but I couldn't place him. He was dressed up in a tux and looked like he belonged here with the others.

"We're going to square away your auction winnings, say good-bye to Sydney and take off. I don't know about you, but I'm tired."

I grip his arm tightly and pull him back toward me. He leans down slightly so that we are eye to eye and I don't have to talk loudly. "Don't you dare shelter me, Mikah. Who in the hell was that man?"

I see resolve in his features. He doesn't want to tell me. But then something changes and he leans in a little closer to me.

"That was Elton Bennett."

FORTY

"Riley's father?" is all I can manage to whisper.

"Yes. He is an ex-business partner of mine. Our ties were severed the minute I discovered who was after you. My staff has done a pretty damn good job of damaging his reputation. He's pissed and wants revenge on me."

"Does he know about me, who I am?" I'm trying to wrap my brain around all of this.

Mikah takes a deep breath. "He knows of Vivienne Callahan, but I don't know that he is aware that you are her. He may or may not make the connection. I'm guessing by your reaction you didn't know him, either?"

I shake my head. "No. Riley never introduced me to his father." I don't go into the reasons why that is with Mikah, but I think Riley's words were that I wasn't good enough for the upper class and that I was "a good-for-nothing whore." I shiver at the memory but move past it quickly.

Mikah turns as someone approaches. "Hi, Sydney."

"Hello, you two. Vivienne, I would like to thank you so much for your generous bid and to

473

congratulate you on winning," she says. She is very friendly, awkwardly so.

I smile. "It was really Mikah's doing."

She smiles, bright and warm, giving me the distraction I need from what has just happened. "I know. I saw the handwriting."

She and I both laugh. Mikah has a look of mock disgust on his face, and we laugh a little harder.

"Either way, thank you. And thanks for coming." She takes me by the shoulders and kisses each of my cheeks. "I look forward to seeing you again." She steps back and turns toward Mikah. "Will you be in on Monday?"

He looks down at me and shrugs. "Let's see how the weekend goes."

She smiles. "Sounds good to me. Enjoy your evening." She waves and heads back toward Gary.

Mikah leads me toward the table that now separates the two rooms.

"Good evening, Mr. Blake," the elderly woman behind the table says.

"Hello. This-" His long fingers casually gesture in my direction. "-is Vivienne Callahan. She-"

"Oh, of course. Thank you so much, Ms. Callahan, for your bid and your donation." She stands and turns to a gentleman behind her, and he goes toward the tables where the last few remaining prizes are sitting. There is a beautiful deep purple case on the table with the same rose pattern on it as the laptop.

"How would you like to make your donation tonight, Ms. Callahan?" the elderly woman asks.

I look to Mikah briefly, trying desperately not to look completely freaked out.

Mikah smiles and turns to the woman. "Credit card."

"Perfect," she says and reaches for something on a table behind her.

I reach into my purse, glad that I didn't take the credit card out of my wallet when I switched bags this afternoon. I pull it out and hand it to her. She does a couple of things and hands me a receipt and a pen. Having just done this for the first time yesterday with Celeste, I'm suddenly thankful for the shopping spree. I sign my name with a shaky hand and give her back the receipt and pen.

"Wonderful, you're all set," she says as the gentlemen hands me the case. Mikah grabs it before I can and slings it over his shoulder.

"Thanks so much for all your help this evening," he says to both of them, and off we go toward the door.

Andrew is waiting with my coat in hand. Mikah takes it from him and offers it to me. I turn, slip my arms inside and quickly button it as Andrew hits the call button on the elevator.

The doors open immediately and we step inside.

FORTY-ONE

We make it to the limo in what feels like record time, helped by the fact that the reporters and photographers who were here when we arrived are gone now. I also note that, though the windows are up, every light in the back half of the limo is on.

"Thank you for a fabulous evening," I say once we are settled and in motion.

He looks at me, tenderness in his eyes. "You're most welcome, Vivienne. I had a wonderful time."

I slide a little closer to him and he wraps his arm around me, holding me close.

Sitting here next to him, after seeing Elton in the ballroom, I realize how safe I feel. I know that, no matter what, he will protect me from anything and everything that can be thrown at me. Even though Riley is still out there and the possibility of his finding me sends a chill through me, what Zirah said about Riley's fate has me feeling more and more certain that Riley will likely never be coming after me again. I'm finally starting to see that over the last couple of weeks my mind, too, has been healing, and Mikah is responsible for that.

I'm also hyperaware of the fact that the feelings I have for Mikah in the dream are becoming reality.

"I'm sorry that I ever accused you of bad intentions when you offered to help me," I say quietly. He pulls back a little and I look up at him. He's puzzled. "In the hospital. Well, the first time we were there. Every time I've jumped to conclusions, I've been wrong, and I apologize."

He takes a deep, thinking-style breath. "You had every right to think and even express those things. I realize now that I came at you pretty strongly without knowing your circumstances." He smiles slightly. "So for that, I apologize."

"You're forgiven," I whisper as I snake my arms around him and hug him tight.

He lets out a breathy chuckle. "Thank you for your forgiveness and..." He pauses long enough for me to pull back and look up at him expectantly. His eyes are soft, filled with something I'm not sure I recognize. "I don't know how to express to you what it meant to me tonight, when she was moving around. I've never felt anything like that before. It was..." He doesn't add anything more to that statement, but I know what he's trying to say.

I lean back into him, and a sudden vision fills my mind: Mikah with a beautiful baby girl with curly red hair. Though this baby is not his biologically, he feels some deeper connection to her than I ever could have expected from anyone.

The idea of Mikah stepping into her life as someone she can look up to brings new tears to my eyes. I succeed in blinking them back so that they don't drip onto his shirt. I don't want him to know what I'm thinking about right now.

We pull into the underground garage and are met by Connor at the elevators. He opens Mikah's door, and Mikah slips out. I follow right behind him when he offers his hand again.

We ride up with Connor and Red in the elevator. Their presence makes me a little nervous because they don't usually ride with us. But after tonight's events with Elton and this morning's events with the shifter, their caution is understandable.

Jeez, could today have been any more of a mess?

FORTY-TWO

After I've washed my face and changed into one of Mikah's t-shirts, I stand in the doorway watching him work on his laptop. I notice that my iPod is playing quietly in the background and the TV is off.

He's rid himself of his jacket, vest and tie. I can't see if he's changed his pants, but he is still wearing his dress shirt, so I think not.

"You don't have to stand back there and watch me," he says, surprising me. "Come here."

I smirk, totally busted. I push away from the doorway and walk around the couch. He puts down whatever it is that he's been looking at and opens up his arms.

I go stand between his legs, and he puts his hands on the backs of my thighs. When he gently rests his head against the upper curve of my bump, that surge of desire returns. Once again the urge to kiss him comes over me, this time stronger than before, nearly overpowering.

Though he hasn't actually made any moves toward advancing our relationship, he's shown me no reason to fear rejection. On the contrary, everything he's done tells me that he needs me, too.

I run my hand through his hair and he holds me tighter, closer to him. When he does this I'm instantly reminded of the dream - our dream - and how he took so much care in preparing my outfit for tonight. He, too, must feel and see the same things as I do in that dream.

"Are you ready for bed?"

I yawn. "Yes."

I step back, and it's there in his eyes - that look I saw earlier - and in this context it strikes me as desire.

I take his head in my hands and lean down. He doesn't flinch or say anything. But as I move my lips closer to his face, fear washes over me, and I end by kissing him on his forehead.

"Good night, Mikah. Thank you for a wonderful evening."

"Good night, beautiful. You're most welcome, and I'm very glad you were there with me." He smiles. "See you in the morning."

I nod and head off toward bed.

FORTY-THREE

I'm back in the white room. Mikah is down on his knees with his eyes closed, wings fully extended. It's right where we left off the last time I had this dream, and here I have no inhibitions about doing anything to him.

I reach up and place my palm against his face. He leans into my touch. "Give me your hand," I say, and he does. I bring it up past my face and place it on the top of my wing. Pleasure surges through me, hot and rapid, pooling between my thighs.

I take his head in both my hands, and he mirrors the gesture on my own cheeks.

He rises, bringing me with him, tilting my head upwards. I feel my belly bump into him, pressing gently into his stomach. His eyes open, and they are the purest blue I could ever imagine.

Steadily, he brings his face closer to mine. The motion is impossibly slow and I ache with anticipation. I stretch upward a little in an attempt to meet him faster, and he smiles.

Just like that, his lips are on mine. All my angst and anguish dissolve in an instant, and I'm lost to the soft, warm touch of his lips.

His tongue lightly traces the outline of my lips, teasing me, tempting me to open them. Desperate to feel his tongue on mine, I open my mouth. The touch is electric. It surges, hard and hot, straight to my innermost desires of love and lust.

Desire. He's awakened a need stronger than anything I've ever felt before.

His kiss grows more urgent, and his hands move slowly and lightly down my neck to my shoulders and then along my arms. I shiver at the contact from wanton need.

My nipples, which are already tight and tender, harden and ache. An ache that can only be soothed by something warm and wet.

His fingers trail back up my arms as my hands slowly slide down his neck, along his chest, then follow the line of his ribs. I bring my arms around him, desperate to be closer to him, to be touching him.

His ragged breathing matches mine. We're both practically gasping for air as our kiss deepens. Nothing else matters; there is nothing in the world but him and me. Us.

A loud grunt. It comes from behind me and is followed by a moan, but it is not from me or Mikah. It's something else...

"Ahh."

This is real, different. It's not my dream. I'm awake, and someone is moaning, but not in pain.

"Mmmm."

My eyes fly open. There is light in the room, but from where? I sit up and look behind me, thinking it's the bathroom, but no, it's coming from the corner, near the closet door.

It's.... What is that?

"Ahh!" it comes again.

I jump to my feet and turn around. My eyes are adjusting to the light. It's not bright, but I can see now that it is coming from the kitchen, but at a very strange angle.

My hand flies to my mouth. "Holy shit," I mumble.

I pull my hand away and take a deep breath.

It's Mikah. He's on his knees on the kitchen floor. But that's not what has my attention. Spread out in full, awesome splendor are a pair of brilliantly white wings.

FORTY-FOUR

I walk quietly toward him. I can't tell if he's awake or sleeping. He's not looking at me, but down toward the floor. As I get closer I see his wings flare and twitch slightly.

When I'm about five steps away from him, I shed my shirt so that I'm down to my bra and lacy boy shorts. I don't want to destroy his shirt.

I concentrate extra hard and, after a beat, I feel them pushing out, spreading outward. The sensation is strange, almost like arms emerging from my body. I smile at the fact that I was able to bring them out on my own.

Once I feel as though they are fully extended, I open my eyes and peer over my shoulder. They are as brilliant as they were this morning, but bigger, and I gasp as I watch them shimmer in the faint light of the kitchen.

I test the muscles in my back, flexing them. My wings move slightly and a thrill of excitement washes over me.

I turn back toward Mikah. He hasn't moved, but his breathing has grown strained, ragged like in the dream.

I take the five small steps I need to reach him and stop.

I reach down and gently stroke the stubble along his jaw. He leans into my touch. I lower myself to my knees; they slide along his as they come to rest on the floor.

"Keep your eyes closed," I whisper.

He nuzzles into my touch a shade more, and with my other hand, eager to see if the sensation is the same, I reach for his wing. When I make contact, his mouth goes slack, his breathing stops momentarily, and the feathers of his wings flare. He moans: a warm, sensual sound.

I pull my hand back and cup the other side of his face. He does the same with my face.

"Kiss me," I breathe, and he rises up, bringing me with him.

I'm looking up at him, and slowly, even more slowly than in the dream, he lowers his kiss to mine. I stretch, hoping to meet his mouth faster, and he smiles.

The next thing I know, his lips are on mine, soft and warm, hot and needy. The moment we make contact, satisfaction and desire sweep through me. I can feel his need in the touch of his lips, in the trembling of his fingers against my face, a need that matches my own.

His tongue lightly teases my lips. I part them. In an instant, his tongue is on mine, teasing and tasting.

My hands slide along his neck, down his sternum, and then follow his ribs. I slip my arms around him, bringing him closer and tighter against me. His chest touches mine. My belly presses into his taut stomach and his hands trail along my neck, shoulders and arms.

I shiver, causing all my nerve endings to come alive.

Sliding my hands up his back, I find the tips of the feathers on the bottom of his wings and I lightly stroke them. His erection comes to life against my belly. I moan into his mouth as my eyes roll back into my head.

I open my eyes again and he is looking at me. His bright blue eyes are warm, filed with need and with something else, that emotion that I can't quite name.

Then, confusion.

He pulls back, trying to gain his bearings, unsure of where he is. The vision in front of him hits him. I can tell the moment that he realizes that my wings are spread wide. He flexes his shoulders, and his eyes grow wider still as he understands that his wings are open and visible, too.

"How..."

"The dream. We've..." I take a deep breath, trying hard to calm my breathing. "We've been sharing the same dreams."

He sits back on his feet, but he doesn't release the grip he now has on my hands.

"Mikah, I want this. I want you," I say breathlessly.

He doesn't need any more encouragement from me. He stands, steadying himself as he realizes the full weight of his upper body with his wings fully emerged. He pulls me up by my hands and I stand with him. He's quick to cup my face, and once again his lips are on mine.

His kiss is urgent and my body responds, desire pooling stronger deep inside of me. I put everything I have into our kiss, pulling him tighter and closer against me, and he does the same. I feel his fingers weave into my hair as he gently urges me to take a step back. I do, and he nudges again. And again. I refuse to open my eyes as he continues to urge me backwards; I'm completely lost to his kiss, his lips, his hands in my hair.

Then I feel the bed against my knees and I stop. His kisses wander from my mouth to my jaw, behind my ear, down my neck, along my shoulder, his lips soft against my skin, leaving a trail of blazing hot nerves in their wake.

His hands glide down my body along the outside swell of my breasts, down my ribs. Feather light, his fingers trail the sweet curves of my bump, and I'm lost to the purest pleasure I've ever felt in my life.

His kisses continue, and the need to have him grows hotter, stronger. My legs begin to tremble, but still he runs his hands up my back toward my wings, and I shiver in anticipation of his touch along my feathers. But he stops when he reaches the clasp of my bra.

He pauses, waiting for permission.

"Yes," I breathe.

His breathing spikes. He shakes slightly, as though nervous, but he hasn't stopped his kisses along the swell of my breasts. I raise my hand to his hair and run my fingers through its soft texture. It tickles against my palm.

With my fingers I urge him to pull back slightly. He does so and looks at me. His eyes are hooded with desire and something deeper, some stronger emotion trying desperately to spill through.

"I. Want. You." I emphasize each word. "I'm ready."

"I...I don't know if I am," he whispers.

"What do you mean?" I cock my head toward him.

He sinks to his knees in front of me, looking into my eyes with an intensity that's almost frightening. "If we cross this line, everything changes. We-" He swallows. "I will never be able to be apart from you. Everything between us will be different."

I sit down on the bed. Then I reach my hands around my back, reaching for the clasp of my bra. As I unhook each tiny hook, one at a time, he watches me, eyes wide but excited.

Finally I reach the last one and I look at him, pleading with my eyes, trying to show him just how much I need him. We're face to face, and as I unhook the last of the clasps, I bring my arms tight against my sides so as not to allow my bra to completely fall away.

I bring my hands back around to cup his face.

"I'm tired of fighting the urge to kiss you." I lean in and kiss him. Softly, gently. "I'm no longer able to resist being closer to you. I can't stand that we sleep in separate rooms, or that I feel as though I can't touch you." I splay my right hand wide and run the tips of my fingers down his beautiful face from his forehead to his chin. As I reach his lips they part, and I feel his hot breath caress my hand.

"Bring our dream to life. Show me that you cannot resist me." I straighten my arms, pull them away from my body, and let my bra fall down, fully exposing my breasts. The cool air hardens my nipples further.

I hear his sharp intake of breath. "You are so beautiful. An angel. My angel."

He reaches up to cup my face and brings his lips to mine. I feel him push forward, pushing me onto my back, and by some miracle, I manage to pull my wings in as he lays me back on the bed.

He hovers over me, the skin of his tight stomach gently touching mine as our lips continue their slow, sensual assault, lighting up my senses.

He trails his fingers down my neck, along my chest, across my nipple. I moan as the ache is relieved by his touch. He continues down my ribs to my stomach, and the sweet touch along my bump once again sends delicious shivers through my body.

He begins to kiss me along the same path his hand has just taken, and goose bumps begin to radiate across my skin.

I'm lost to my desire.

CHAPTER FOUR

Give Me Love

ONE

"What have you done to me?" His voice cracks, the effect like gargling gravel. The last thing he knew, he'd come to the cave to tell him about Vivienne. There was a girl with him, but all he can remember is a flash of light and the pain.

The growl comes from across the room. "I have given you life anew! Do not make such inquiries of me again!" From deep in the shadows emerges a man – no, not a man, something far more sinister than anything any man has ever laid eyes upon. Skin the color of charcoal and flame. Two horns at the peak of his skull, and wide, black and red wings even taller than he is flared out behind him.

Understanding immediately that he is once again in the presence of the devil himself, the human kneels in submission. "I'm sorry, my lord."

"Your apologies are weak and unnecessary. A servant of mine does not express remorse." The devil takes two more steps. With each step his body changes, morphing into a body like any other man's. He is tall with long, black hair and deep, dark eyes.

"Rise!" he growls, and the human rises, still looking at the floor. "Look at me."

He raises his head, and shock etches his features. He knows by his voice that the man standing before him is the same demon, but now the demon's features are, well, normal. But the human is not fooled; he knows the demon is still just as menacing as he was a moment ago.

"What I've done to you is bring you back to life." The devil laughs. "I've brought you back because your drive is unparalleled to anything I've ever seen before." He takes another step toward his lesser. "I'm giving you one chance, and one chance only, to bring her to me, dead or alive. If you fail you will spend eternity with the ghouls, who would love nothing more than to torture you after I kill you."

TWO

Mikah has found his own personal heaven on earth: There is nothing sweeter than kissing Vivienne. Her scent is like flowers on a warm summer day. It's heady, and he can't stop himself from kissing her as if his life depends on it.

His hands roam, slowly and gently, up and down her body while his mouth moves along her jaw, down her neck, onto her shoulder. Her head falls back and she squirms under his touch. Her desire for him has grown hotter with each passing touch of his lips. She's never experienced anything so sweet and kind. She understands that what he's doing is proving that she is all that matters, right here, right now.

Her breathing begins to spike as his mouth moves down to her breasts, skirting her nipples. The ache in them is scorching hot and she wants his tongue to ease her need.

Instead, his mouth moves lower still, over her bump to the junction of her thighs. He kisses her there. Licks, and then teasingly drags his teeth along the flesh, and she moans at the sensation. He's yet to make any real contact with any intimate part of her;

he's only showing her and her body what he's capable of.

Then his wings blaze at the same time a knock on the door interrupts their heavy breathing. "Mikah. Vivienne. Please, we need to go. Now."

"What? Where?" Mikah moves off of Vivienne, and she instinctively reaches for the covers.

"We need to go into Elysium. Now." Red's voice is stern, unwavering, as Mikah scrambles to his feet.

His eyes meet hers, wary. He wants to explain to her what is going on, but then he sees in her eyes that this is unnecessary; she knows of Elysium and knows more than he thought she knew.

"Mikah, it's alright. Red, give us a moment, please?" She turns her head toward the door but never breaks eye contact with him. "You have nothing to be afraid of. Let's get dressed, okay?" she asks, nodding at him.

Though he's looking at her, he's not entirely sure what he's seeing.

Only a few moments ago they were in the heat of passion. Both their wings have made an appearance, and while he understood then that she knows what he is, he didn't fully understand what he was seeing. Confusion had wracked his brain as he tried hard to decipher whether he was awake or dreaming. But now reality hits him: This is no dream, and she fully knows and understands who and what he is.

He'd noticed when he laid her down that she was without her wings. Asking her seemed like the appropriate thing to do. She'd be his best teacher to show him. "How do I, um…" His voice is gravelly and unsure. "How can I pull these back in?" he manages to finish, and she smiles.

"You concentrate, then visualize them locking back into place. Give it a try."

He steels himself, afraid of what might happen if he isn't able to pull them back in. Then he flexes so that he can feel the point where his wings and body come together.

She watches his wings flare slightly and flap while his face shows that he's concentrating.

Steadily his wings pull in, shrinking moment by moment as he concentrates. Then a furrow appears on his brow, and his wings stop retracting and instead expand.

"Relax, you're doing great," she encourages him.

The furrow softens and he concentrates again. This time he doesn't stop until he feels the click and his wings are locked down.

Opening his eyes, he sees a bright, warm smile on her face. Then his gaze drifts downward and he realizes that she is still topless. The sight of her looking up at him causes his breath to hitch. She really is beautiful; her fair skin, bright red hair, beautiful blue eyes and luscious pink lips drive his desire deeper than it was only a few minutes ago.

The knock on the door comes again, and Vivienne stands and reaches for her shirt. He takes it from her and helps her into it.

She senses his worry, but it's unclear to her whether it is coming from the fear that he thinks she doesn't know about Elysium or if it stems from the fact that Red also seems to know more about what is going on than he does. She tries to ease his worry. "Please Mikah, it will be alright."

He doesn't say anything right away, but he knows deep down that she is right. "I don't have any clothes in here," he says. "Are you good to go in what you're wearing?"

"Yes, I just want to pull my hair back," she says as she slides past him toward the bathroom.

"Don't, I like your hair down."

She smiles and turns toward him.

Tonight they've reached a turning point in their relationship. Everything from here on will be different. That invisible barrier separating them has dropped, and somewhere inside she knows that Mikah is who she wants and what she needs, and that everything is falling into place.

Mikah smiles at her as he heads toward the door. His smile is warm, genuine. That hint of something she's seen before slides over his features again, that something she's yet to figure out but he knows to be love.

He opens the door to find Red standing about two feet away.

"We must hurry," he says, his eyes avoiding Mikah's.

Vivienne comes to stand on the threshold of the bedroom door.

"How is it that you know about Elysium?" Mikah asks. He's not sure he wants to know the answer, but the question will bug him until he knows.

"Mikah," Viv interjects before Red can answer, "I think it is best if we do what he says. I'm sure you can get the answer to that question while we're there."

Mikah strides past Red toward the other bedroom, his body language betraying a mixture of determination and frustration. Vivienne can understand why. He thought he knew all the secrets of those surrounding him, and that is proving to be wrong. Vivienne was the primary secret; he never expected Red to be part of it too.

As Mikah enters the other room, Red says, "Mikah, we will explain everything to you, but right now, we need to go to Elysium."

Vivienne and Red exchange a look. Vivienne starts to follow Mikah, but just before she makes it to the doorway, he comes back out, wearing a black t-shirt and his pajama pants.

"Lead the way," Mikah says.

Red turns and heads back toward the front door, but he stops short at the guest bathroom. He swings open the door to reveal not the expected bathroom but rather the room in Elysium where Vivienne and Mikah have spent so many nights in their dreams.

Mikah stops dead in his tracks. "What the hell is going on here?" he says, confusion radiating off him. The only way he's known how to get into Elysium is through dreams; now all of a sudden his bathroom has been turned into a portal.

Vivienne turns to him and takes a hold of his upper arm. "Mikah, look at me."

He looks at her, his face screwed up with confusion, seeking comfort and explanation.

"It's alright. Let's go do this, and then I will explain everything I know about all of this to you. Okay?" Her voice is sternly sincere.

"Okay," he says, his resolve setting in.

She can see the shift in him as the protector he was born to be returns. She completely understands his reaction; it's similar to her own yesterday morning, when everything she thought she knew was twisted into something else.

He takes her hand from his arm. But rather than brushing her off, he intertwines their fingers, and together they step through the doorway into the white room.

THREE

In front of them is a bank of windows, only this time they can actually see through them into a luscious green garden. In front of them are two couches, one longer and one shorter, that form an L shape around a empty space where a coffee table would normally be.

Off to their right is the outline of another door, only there is no handle or knob to open it. Every other wall in the room is solid white, broken up by small windows.

They come to stand behind the long couch, and on the other side of it is a woman. As they approach, she turns toward them. She is beautiful in a youthful way, with long hair and soft features.

"Hello, Mother," Mikah says with a curt nod in her direction. The tension in his body is visible.

Vivienne recalls that Mikah's mother passed away some years ago, but it is obvious that this isn't the first time he's seen her since then. She wonders why he's so cold toward her.

"My son," she says. "Vivienne, I am Elizabeth," she says and moves a step forward, though she appears to be floating more than walking. "It is an honor to finally meet you." She reaches out her hand and Vivienne steps around the couch to take it. Mikah follows her.

"The same to you," Vivienne says, unsure how to greet her, but Mikah's mother doesn't seem to take any offense.

Elizabeth looks over to Mikah. "It is time for you to learn and to understand all that is going on around you. What I need to tell you is no doubt going to make you angry, but I need you to be calm and listen."

"I cannot make any promises. I'm already upset and confused. How in the world does Red know about all of this?"

Elizabeth's eyebrows shoot up, and she looks at Vivienne with a question in her eyes. Vivienne shakes her head.

"Vivienne?" Mikah says with a hint of menace in his voice.

Vivienne turns toward him. "Maybe you should sit down."

Mikah's eyebrows draw together and his lips purse.

"Don't be mad at me. I've only just learned all of this within the last twenty-four hours or so. Hardly enough time for me to tell you about it."

His features thaw and he takes a seat.

Vivienne lets out a breath, and her shoulders relax.

"Yesterday morning when I woke up, the dream I'd been having filtered into reality, much like it did earlier tonight." She blushes as the memory of Mikah on his knees, his wings spread wide, and the—

She stops the thought but not before she sees his eyes light up with excitement as he too remembers what happened. She blinks, desperate to concentrate.

"When I woke up, I went into the bathroom and caught a glimpse of myself in the mirror and I almost screamed. Once I began to realize what had happened, Zirah, my teacher—" His eyes snap up to hers; he, too, has a teacher. "—came to me and explained what had happened and how to fix it. She also told me that those closest to us are our greatest allies and protectors. Red—" She gestures behind Mikah to the man standing behind him. "—Andrew, Connor and Celeste are all guardians of Elysium." She pauses to give him a moment soak up the information she's giving him.

While he processes it, Vivienne, too, is struck by how strange this all sounds. Now that she hears herself say it aloud, the thought that none of this is real flits through her mind.

"How... Why?" he says.

Vivienne turns toward Elizabeth.

"When you chose the business path you did, you put yourself in the public eye. I had no choice but to help protect you, not only from evil, but from yourself." Elizabeth starts to pace. "When I died, Shannon knew nothing of angels, knew nothing of what you were or were to become, so the stories stopped with me. We feared that, should your inner angel make himself known, we would be exposed to the world. But it would also expose you to the demons who wish to harm you." Elizabeth continues to pace. "Demons seek out angels on Earth to either destroy them or convert them."

Mikah has a flash of intuition that this information is important, but before he can ask about it, Elizabeth goes on. "When you started looking for bodyguards, we sent Red in. Then the rest of your staff. Andrew and Connor are just as he is, and Celeste too."

Elizabeth continues to pace around the room. Viv looks to Mikah, who is sitting still as can be, his head in his hands. The tension in his shoulders could shatter a boulder to a million pieces. This is not what he was expecting to hear tonight.

"Mikah?" Vivienne says quietly as she comes to stand next to him. Looking down at him, she sees his shoulders relax and the tension wash out of him. He lazily raises his head, and when their eyes meet, everything seems to stop. Nothing matters but him. She senses that need he feels for her, and her heart swells.

Their connection is broken by a clicking sound, like a door closing behind Vivienne, and she turns quickly in that direction. A momentary fear causes her heart to start racing. Striding toward them are two women more beautiful than anything Vivienne has ever seen before. The woman in front is blond with hair that flows out behind her. The second one is red-haired and fair-skinned, much like Vivienne. They wear matching white dresses befitting Grecian goddesses.

The red-haired one smiles at Vivienne, who takes an involuntary step back. "Do not be frightened," she says, bells for a voice, and Vivienne immediately recognizes her.

"Zirah?" Vivienne asks. The redhead nods enthusiastically at her, and a warm smile spreads across Vivienne's face. Vivienne feels Mikah move behind her, and her eyes go to the blond woman, whose face lights up.

"Hello, Mikah," the blond woman says. "I am Seraphina."

Though he doesn't smile back at her, Mikah's eyes register recognition. "Hello, Seraphina."

Once again there is a click behind them, this time from the door they'd entered through a few minutes ago. Mikah and Vivienne watch as Zirah and Seraphina quickly look past Mikah and Vivienne toward the noise.

Standing in front of the door are Andrew, who is smiling of course; Connor, who looks pissed off as usual; and Celeste, who gives her usual impression of Mexican jumping beans bouncing around inside their shell.

"Now that we're all here it is time to discuss the real reasons I've called on you. Vivienne, I have some rather sad news to share with you. Your mother—"

Vivienne's ears begin to ring, and she does not need to hear more to know that Elizabeth is trying to tell her that her mother has passed away. Her body goes limp, but Mikah catches her quickly and carries her to the sofa.

"Vivienne." Elizabeth tries again to gather her attention. "Vivienne, your mother, Rebecca, did not die of natural causes."

"What?" Mikah and Vivienne say in unison, his more of a growl.

"How?" is all Vivienne can manage to say, but then she realizes she already knows the answer to that question. He's back.

"Riley."

FOUR

"I always knew that little shit wasn't done," Mikah snaps.

Vivienne's body begins to shake with silent sobs, and Mikah does the only thing he thinks he can do to console her: He gently strokes her hair. She leans deeper into him. Her gesture is silent assurance that she needs him as much as he needs her.

Vivienne always knew that this day would come, but she never expected it to come at the hands of Riley Bennett. Vivienne had been sure that Riley knew nothing of her mother. In fact, he never so much as showed an inkling of interest in her. So how had he found her?

"We're not entirely sure it was Riley," Elizabeth says, and Vivienne and Mikah both look up at her.

"How are you not sure?" Mikah asks the question that Vivienne can't.

"Well, we simply haven't had the time to investigate what happened, and Rebecca has been no help."

"What do you mean?" Vivienne asks. Her voice is full of emotion and the words are hard to understand.

"We mean yes, we suspect as much, but we are unable to confirm it just yet. We have a small team on their way to investigate and report back," Elizabeth is quick to answer.

"But you said something about Rebecca being of no help," Vivienne says, a little clearer now.

"We've brought Rebecca to Elysium."

"She's here?" Vivienne and Mikah both say at the same time in nearly identical flat tones. They both look to each other.

Mikah can see the fear in her eyes, and he squeezes her hand slightly, just to let her know that he's here for her no matter what.

"Yes, she's here and we're trying to talk to her. However, it takes some time for the departed to adjust to what's happened, and I'm afraid she hasn't been much help." Elizabeth begins to pace back and forth again in front of the bank of windows near the couches. "We also have to take into account the fact that your mother was not of sound mind prior to her death. We're not sure if we will get any information from her at all. But we're going to try."

There is a moment of silence while this news sinks in, and then Elizabeth stops pacing and speaks again. "Vivienne," she says, "I'm wondering if you could help us?"

Vivienne looks to Elizabeth, a quizzical look on her face. "I'm not sure what help I can be," she says finally.

Mikah leans in a little, curious as to what his mother is asking.

"I'm wondering if you would try talking to your mother, see if she will tell you what she knows about her death."

"Elizabeth, I—" Vivienne looks to Mikah, confusion on her face, and then back to Elizabeth. "I don't think that's a good idea."

Mikah looks to Vivienne, trying to read her reaction, but he can't. Too many emotions are playing out on her features.

"I think it might be the best chance we have to get her to talk."

"I'm pretty sure that won't work." Vivienne's heart is pounding, making it impossible to think straight. Nothing good can come from seeing Rebecca, at least not anything that won't result in more heartache.

"Vivienne, we should at least try," Elizabeth says.

Mikah moves to stand behind Vivienne and places his hand on the small of her back. He leans down and whispers in her ear, "You can do this."

It's strange how his words have calmed her almost instantly.

Vivienne smiles slightly, takes a deep breath and says, "Bring her here."

FIVE

Two heartbeats later, the door behind Zirah and Seraphina clicks again. Zirah and Seraphina part, allowing Vivienne a full view of the woman who has just entered the room.

Vivienne feels trepidation fly through her veins. She stands and takes a few steps toward the woman. Mikah is close behind her; she can hear the shifting and footsteps.

The woman is modestly dressed in a white nightgown-style, sleeveless dress and has long reddish-brown hair framing her heart-shaped face. Her green eyes stare wary at the scene laid out in front of her, but she is doing her best to pretend she's not looking. Though the woman looks lost and confused, it doesn't take but a few moments for Vivienne to recognize her.

"Rebecca?" Vivienne says, and the woman, who is the focus of the entire room, jerks her head in Vivienne's direction. Vivienne knows it's her mother, but the woman before her appears much younger, as if she is about Vivienne's age.

The woman looks at Vivienne, her eyes squinting for a moment before widening as she realizes who

507

she's looking at. "Vivienne?" She takes a few steps toward Vivienne.

Vivienne takes a step back. She realizes now she wasn't ready for this. Needing support and reassurance, she tears her gaze away from the her mother and turns to see Mikah right next to her. She feels oddly comforted by his look of confusion. Behind him, the same look is on the faces of her guardians and she can sense their tension.

Mikah isn't entirely sure what to say or how to interpret what he is looking at. He'd expected an older woman.

"Is that...?" Mikah says aloud.

"Rebecca, Vivienne's mother," Elizabeth answers.

Mikah hears a sharp intake of breath behind him and looks over his shoulder to see Red, who is white as a ghost. Mikah follows Red's gaze back to the woman standing in front of them. She appears dazed, obviously in shock.

"Vivienne?" the woman says again, and Viv takes another step back toward the line of people standing behind her.

Mikah cocks his head, trying to understand how this woman, who is no older than Vivienne, could be her mother.

Elizabeth answers his unasked question. "When those who die on earth are brought to Elysium, they take on the appearance of their younger selves, when they were happiest and when they were their healthiest."

Behind Mikah, Red has started mumbling to himself. Mikah turns his head to look, and his forehead creases in confusion. Red is staring intently at Vivienne's mother as if he knows her. Mikah strains to hear what he is saying, but it's incomprehensible.

"What is going on here?" Mikah says.

Vivienne looks at him, confused, but then her gaze follows his to Red, and Red's back to Rebecca, who is still staring at Vivienne.

"Red?" Mikah says, watching Rebecca closely.

She doesn't disappoint him. She raises her eyes to Mikah, and then her gaze shifts from Mikah to the man standing to his right.

Vivienne takes a few more steps backwards, putting distance between herself and everyone else. She can't stop staring at Red.

"I always thought there was something strangely familiar about you," Vivienne says, "but I could never place it. The picture. The one I carry in my purse." Vivienne looks from Red to her mother and back again. "It's you in that picture, isn't it?"

"Vivienne, what are you talking about?" Mikah says.

He takes a step toward her, and she steps away from him. He reaches out for her, but she doesn't see it. She's still staring at Red.

"You—" She squints and cocks her head to the side. Red squints back at her and there is no doubt in her mind. "You're my father."

SIX

Red can only stare at Vivienne, looking confused. Something is passing between them when someone breaks the silence within the room.

"Impossible," Seraphina says. Her voice isn't angry, but rather sweet and breathless.

"Vivienne, I—" Red stops. Something in his voice and the way he is looking at Vivienne suggest that he had no idea.

Suddenly Vivienne understands. "Mother, is there something you'd like to tell us all?" she says sternly.

"Yes, please do." This time it's Mikah.

Vivienne finally pulls her eyes away from Red to look at Mikah. The concern is clear on his features, but his eyes are alight with curiosity, too, as this twenty-two year old mystery unfolds.

"I...I don't know," Rebecca says, but Vivienne isn't fooled. Her mother is notorious for avoiding the truth.

Vivienne turns toward her mother, who is still staring at Red. "For the love of Christ, Mother, now is not the time for games or jokes." The wings on Vivienne's back flare in frustration. "This is it, isn't it? Despite the fact that you're here, you're still going to continue to play games. Stop it. I've had enough. Is he or is he not my father?"

Rebecca starts to sob, and she crumples, as if in pain, to the floor.

Andrew and Connor rush to help her, but Vivienne puts her hand up. "Stop, leave her be. She's still up to her same old tricks. Resorting to tears to get her way or avoid dealing with something she knows she needs to explain. She doesn't want to discuss this, so she is going to play the blubbering fool on the floor." Vivienne notices Mikah out of the corner of her eye. He is gaping at her, slack-jawed, and she realizes he's never seen her like this.

Vivienne is also surprised by her tone. Growing up, she could never be cross with her mother. But now, after all this time, the anger and frustration have reached a boiling point, and she resolves to be done with her mother's games.

"Red?" Mikah says.

"I honestly don't know. I met Rebecca some years ago, and—" He stops again.

Vivienne looks toward him. He seems to be doing some math in his head.

"It would've been about twenty-three years ago. I was pulled away, brought back to Elysium by—" He looks toward Elizabeth. "—Alexandria. About the time Mikah's wings were discovered."

"Wait, what do my wings have to do with— I've only known you for a few years." Mikah looks to his mother for an explanation.

But it's Red who answers. "No, I've known you since you were a lad, since shortly after your family came to Boston. Though neither you nor your mother ever saw me, I was sent to keep watch over you. To protect you." As Red talks he is trying desperately to understand and put all the pieces of this together. "As I said, I was pulled away from Rebecca by Alexandria, who was dethroned to make way for you, Elizabeth. She told me that I was to stay away from Rebecca, that I could never return. I questioned her, but she wouldn't explain it to me. Then I met Kelly. Though I never truly forgot Rebecca, I was — and am — so taken with Kelly that I never regretted the way things turned out."

Vivienne's eyes scan the room, unseeing, as she tries to understand everything that Red is saying. There is a connection here, something between Elizabeth, Red, Alexandria, and herself that she doesn't understand.

"I was pulled away in late February. That would have been twenty-two years ago." Red looks to Rebecca. "Were you pregnant when I left? Were you pregnant with Vivienne?" he asks, his voice low.

"Yes." Rebecca sobs, still kneeling on the tile with her head in her hands.

An eerie silence follows, finally broken by Mikah addressing Elizabeth. "Mother, did you know about all of this?"

"Yes and no. I knew that Vivienne's father was of angelic descent, I just didn't have the details. Our archives are incomplete or missing," Elizabeth says, and she doesn't elaborate further.

SEVEN

"Rebecca," Vivienne says, her voice strong and determined. She's finally recalled the reason Elizabeth brought Rebecca here, and she's going to get answers.

Her mother looks up at her, tears still streaming down her cheeks.

"We need to ask you a few questions." Despite the fact that every muscle in her body is tight and her hands are shaking, Vivienne's voice sounds confident. She feels Mikah's hand on her back and she relaxes just a little bit more.

"I need to ask you about what happened tonight."

Everyone in the room takes an added interest in Rebecca and what she has to say, but Rebecca's face only shows confusion.

"Uh..." Rebecca's features goes through a series of different emotions: confusion, concern, thoughtfulness. Finally she says, "The last thing I remember is hearing a girl scream."

"Girl scream?" Vivienne repeats. Now the same puzzled look on Rebecca's features is displayed on Vivienne's.

"Yes, and there was a lot of noise – fighting or arguing – then a loud crack and a door slamming shut." She pauses, thinking harder about what she remembers. "There was a man. He was pushing her around, but I couldn't see him. I was sitting on a couch. After the door slammed shut, I heard scraping noises and then pounding."

Vivienne begins to shake uncontrollably. As her knees give out, Mikah is quick to catch her. Her heart is beating harder and faster than anything she's felt in a long time. Her breathing becomes quick and shallow.

"The man comes to me. He's dressed in blue jeans. He's taking off—"

"Enough," Mikah snaps, and Rebecca falls silent. "Vivienne, look at me. You're safe, no one can hurt you." He brushes a few stray strands of hair out of her face. She's clearly petrified, scared out of her mind, but Mikah can't even begin to understand where this is coming from.

Vivienne's heart rate is slowing, little by little. With each passing beat the memory begins to fade away and she can feel her strength returning.

"Vivienne," says a sweet, soft voice a little distance away. Vivienne recognizes it as Zirah's, but she can't turn away from Mikah to look at her. The sadness in his heart can be seen through his eyes.

"That wasn't a memory of what happened to her tonight," Vivienne whispers to Mikah.

"What is she talking about then?" he says back to her, wishing he knew how to comfort Vivienne in this moment.

Vivienne moves to sit up, stand up, and Mikah doesn't hold her back. She gets back to her feet, wobbling a bit, but Mikah is there to support her.

"She's talking about a night that happened nearly seven years ago."

Rebecca is trying to understand what Vivienne is saying, but she can't seem to remember anything.

"She's talking," Vivienne says, "about what happened the night she had her stroke. When I was locked in the closet for three days." She turns to her mother, eyes flashing. "Three days until the police showed up," Vivienne says, glaring at Rebecca. "The last night that you stood by while your *pimp*—" The word drips with anger and pain. "—beat me and locked me away so that he could do whatever it was he wanted to do."

No one in the room says a word, unsure of what to say, including Mikah. He knows that she needs to say what she needs to say and he can't stop her.

"Vivienne, I—" Rebecca says. The look on her face says more than her words can; she is scared and unsure.

"Don't," Vivienne snaps. "You have no idea what you've put me through, nothing you say now will change that." Everyone can see how her words cut into Rebecca, but Vivienne doesn't want to hear her apologies. "I need to know if you remember anything at all from *last night.*"

Rebecca tries to think, tries to remember, but she's so confused. She comes up empty. "I don't remember."

EIGHT

"What are we supposed to do now?" Mikah says after Seraphina and Zirah have escorted Rebecca out and come back to stand with the group once again.

Surprisingly, it is Red who steps forward. "You were about to receive a call from the rehab center. We believe the phone call was meant to be a trap to lure Vivienne to whoever killed her mother."

"Okay, so we don't go to the funeral home. Got it. Now what?" The irritation in Mikah's voice is heard by all. The secrets and the vague descriptions and explanations are really starting to piss him off.

"Do not take that tone."

"What do you expect me to do, Mother? You've thrown all of this at us at lightning speed. I will not sit here idly as everything Vivienne's ever known begins to crumble." His statement would've been more effectively delivered if he'd been standing, but the second he started speaking, Vivienne's arms had wrapped harder and tighter around him, reminding him that she was there with him. "I need to know what I need to do to stop that madman from—"

The look on Elizabeth's face forces him to stop talking.

"If it was that madman, as you call him, then you need to know that he has become the left hand of the devil himself. He was brought out of whatever circle of hell he was in to come after her. Though it is not truly Vivienne that he is after. It is her child."

Mikah's heart pounds hard against his ribs, and Vivienne's head jerks off his chest. They both stare at Elizabeth.

"What does he want with my baby?" Her voice cracks with a strength of emotion unlike anything Mikah's ever heard from her before. It's that deep-seated level of emotion only a mother could express. Mikah has heard it many times from his own mother.

"Riley's initial attack on you, when you told him you were pregnant, was driven by vengeance. But when he did that, the devil saw in him something he could use: a weapon of hatred that could be used to destroy that which could destroy the devil himself." Elizabeth looks at both of them with worry and sadness in her eyes, but lying underneath is something else, something that Mikah doesn't quite understand.

"Go ahead, explain all of this," Mikah says sternly.

"Vivienne is the sole remaining descendant of *Dia*."

"What? How?" he whispers.

Vivienne looks to him in confusion.

"Those stories are long and better told by a *scéalaí*," Elizabeth says, "though they are very hard to find. Alexandria, the matron who preceded me, was dethroned because she refused to relinquish the location of *Dia's* heir. She believed that if no one knew of Vivienne's existence then Vivienne would always remain safe. But *Dia* knew that in order to protect his heir, we all needed to know where she was."

Mikah and Vivienne's eyes meet. But Elizabeth doesn't pause for questions.

"For thousands of years we've believed that a full-blooded angel could only be male, as there were no records of females of full-blooded ancestry."

"What about you?" Mikah asks. "Given your position within Elysium."

"One would assume, but no. I am only half angel. Your father, on the other hand, is full-blooded." She pauses momentarily, but Mikah doesn't feel it's appropriate to take the opportunity to ask about his birth father. Elizabeth continues, "Vivienne's mother is the closest thing to a full-blooded female that Alexandria knew of. When Rebecca met Vivienne's father—" A strange look crosses Elizabeth's face and there is some uncomfortable shifting around the room. Vivienne shifts in her seat and starts to play with her fingers. "—Red, who is also full-blooded, and they conceived Vivienne, she became the next closest pureblood. Even so, Vivienne is only about fifteen-sixteenths angel."

Vivienne's hand gently caresses the swell of her stomach, finally understanding the importance of her baby.

"Yes, my child. Your daughter is of the purest angelic blood that we know of, and possibly the closest we will ever come to a full-blooded female."

Vivienne opens her mouth to say something, but words fail her, and Elizabeth drives home what Vivienne already knows.

"Riley too is a full-blood. He, however, is of the demonic bloodline."

"SHIT!" Mikah exclaims.

NINE

Seraphina is quick to speak. "Calm down, Mikah, this doesn't mean anything is wrong. We have several angels here in Elysium that have more demonic blood than angelic. Just because demon blood runs in their veins does not make them a demon."

Mikah looks to Vivienne, who has a wary look in her eyes.

Though Vivienne's heart rate spikes at the confirmation that Riley is of demonic descent, it is also something she's suspected since all of this angel stuff was brought into her life.

"Vivienne." Zirah is vying for her attention. Vivienne pulls her eyes away from Mikah to look at her. "Your daughter will be full-blooded angel. There is nothing in this world that could pull her away from that path."

"How can you be so certain?" Vivienne breathes.

This time Elizabeth is the one to speak. "Why, child, would she be anything but? She will be taught our ways, live amongst the purest of angels. She will know no different. Take a look at your life, Vivienne. You've dealt with far more than any one person should have to endure in a normal lifetime, and look at yourself, what you've turned into. You've never followed the path of evil, why would your daughter?"

Though Elizabeth sounds confident, it is hard for Vivienne or Mikah to be certain of the path her daughter will take.

"Some of the devil's demons are full-blooded angel, as well," Zirah says. "The path we choose dictates where we will spend our lives. Those who choose the path of evil stay evil, and those who choose the path of good stay good. Their goodness or evil is heightened by their blood, but their blood does not dictate their path."

Vivienne is trying to process Zirah's words.

"Take your mother for example, and we've already talked about this, but while she never did anything to earn herself a spot in hell, she's done enough away from the good that she cannot live in Elysium and is considered one of our fallen."

The reality of her mother's banishment from Elysium is slowly starting to sink in. Vivienne wipes tears away from her cheeks as Mikah softly rubs his thumb along her back. She wonders if she'll ever see her mother again.

When you're ready to see her again, we can bring her back here, Zirah says quietly inside her mind.

Vivienne looks to Zirah. Vivienne's heart rate spikes, she fights the urge to let the revulsion play out on her face.

Only when you're ready.

Vivienne realizes she doesn't know if she'll ever be ready to face her mother again. Suddenly she feels overwhelmed by everything that's happened in the last several hours, and exhaustion overtakes her.

Mikah senses a shift in Vivienne. His ability to feel and read her emotions has him sliding closer to her.

"I'm not sure how much more of tonight I can take," Vivienne whispers, and Mikah wraps his arms around her.

The guardians exchange urgent glances with Elizabeth, silently pleading with her to let them all go for tonight.

"Go and rest. We will have more information soon, and when we do, I'll bring you back here," Elizabeth says.

Vivienne leans into Mikah, and the rest of the guardians are quick to lead them to an exit.

When they walk back through the door, they are no longer in Vivienne's condo, but in Mikah's.

"Until we know what's going on, I think it would be best if you both stayed here," Red says as he turns back toward Vivienne and Mikah.

Vivienne nods, and Mikah holds her a little tighter.

"Thank you," Mikah says.

Red nods at him, but his eyes fall to Vivienne. She can see the sadness in his eyes.

"Vivienne, I—" But he falters. Red, usually so sure of himself, is at a loss for words.

Vivienne breathes. "It's a lot to take in. I'm exhausted. Can we talk about this later?"

Red's lips form a half smile. "Of course. Get some rest. I'll come if there is news."

"Please wait until at least tomorrow afternoon, no matter how urgent you think it might be," Mikah says.

Red nods, and he and the others leave.

TEN

"How are you?" Mikah asks as soon as they are alone.

"Tired, scared, concerned, tired, confused. What about you?" she asks as she leans into him.

He gently kisses the top of her forehead. "All of the above. Let's go to bed."

They both start toward the bedroom. "Are you okay with staying here?" he asks her, knowing how she feels about her independence and not wanting to upset her by forcing her to stay.

"I'm happy to be wherever you are."

Mikah's heart swells at her words and he stops, gently taking her cheeks in his hand, and kisses her, softly and tenderly.

She returns his kiss, this time without any hesitation. Knowing that tonight they've crossed a line that can never be recrossed, she puts everything she feels into their kiss.

Mikah pulls back and looks deep into her eyes. She recognizes that underlying emotion. Similar emotions are running wild through her veins, she takes his hand and he leads her into the bedroom.

As she steps across the threshold, the dream image of her and Mikah in this bed comes back into her mind, and she's reminded of how ready she is for their relationship to move forward.

"I'm going to use the bathroom," she says as she heads in that direction.

Once inside, she takes stock of herself in the mirror, runs water over her face and tries to take a deep breath. She doesn't understand why she's suddenly so nervous.

When she steps back into the bedroom, Mikah is standing on the opposite side of the bed, pulling back the covers.

He looks up to see her standing in the doorway. A brief moment passes between them, and then he gestures for her to come to him.

He watches her as she walks quietly around the bed. Her hair bounces across her back, and she smiles at him as she comes closer. The desire he felt for her earlier tonight grows deeper within him and he wants her. After all the mess in Elysium, he needs her close to him.

He reaches for her hand and gestures toward the bed, and she takes her cue and climbs in. He bends down and kisses her forehead.

"I'll be right back," he whispers as he steps back and goes around the bed toward the bathroom.

Vivienne snuggles into bed, turning to face the other side, where she expects Mikah to lie down when he returns.

While she waits for him, her mind begins to go over everything that has happened in the last twenty-four hours: the shifter in her apartment; learning about who and what Red, Connor, Andrew and Celeste are;

the news of her mother's passing; the new information about Riley. She has no doubt that he is behind her mother's death, and she wonders how much more destruction he will create in his haste to get to her. And then her confrontation with her mother and the discovery of who her father is.

What is she supposed to do about Red? Is she capable, after all this time, of embracing that relationship? What will Red think if she doesn't know what to do?

"Easy," she whispers to herself. "You can deal with that tomorrow."

Just then Mikah steps out of the bathroom. He's wearing the same pants, but he's shed his shirt. Seeing Mikah standing there shirtless, his inky black hair falling onto his face and those liquid eyes vibrant and blue, has her desire for him growing hot and fast throughout her veins.

Vivienne's beautiful. Her soft cheeks are flushed, and a hint of a smile plays on her lips. Seeing her in his bed brings back the memory of seeing her with his other self in that dream so many weeks ago.

He'd wanted to stop earlier, unsure of what she was really feeling for him, but seeing her now leaves no doubt in his mind that they are both on the same page, both wanting and needing each other in a way he's never felt before.

But he won't push it. She needs to come to him when she's ready.

Resolving to be patient, he walks the ten steps to the bed. As he does, she pulls the covers back to receive him. Excitement spreads like wildfire through his veins. Just the idea of sleeping in the same bed as her is enough to send his heart racing.

But his mind is running wild with what happened earlier tonight and everything that's happened between them in just the last few hours. He needs a chance to collect himself and bring his overwhelming need for her under control.

She watches as he turns to sit down on the edge of the bed. He puts his elbows on his knees and rubs his face. She reaches over and lightly runs her fingers down his back along his wings.

He shivers with pleasure at her touch, and he can feel his wings unlocking themselves. Closing his eyes, he hopes to keep them in check. She does it again and he turns toward her.

She's so beautiful, unlike anything he's ever seen before. He can no longer resist; he climbs into bed facing her.

"Hi, beautiful," he whispers.

She slides closer to him, brushing his hair out of his eyes. He kisses her palm and she shivers.

He wraps his arms around her, holding her close, trying to understand her mood, or her need. Having her close to him, knowing that she's safe in his arms, helps to bring his racing heart back to normal.

Relief washes through Vivienne as she settles into his embrace and feels his heartbeat slow. While being with Mikah is what she wants more than anything, she's too tired.

Before they can even consider anything further, exhaustion claims them and they both fall sound asleep.

ELEVEN

"Your plan isn't working. We have to get out of here before we get caught."

"No. We wait for her."

"Why, she's not showing up here. You said it yourself, you never even knew she had a mother until Link told you. If her mother didn't mean enough to her to tell you, what makes you think she will show up here?"

Riley turns away from the window in Rebecca Callahan's old room. He looks the same as he did before the devil killed him in that cave, but he's far more powerful now. "I just know," he snaps. He runs his hand across his buzz cut hair and looks back to the window

Derek, the idiot Link made him bring along, has been pacing the floor on the other side of the bed since they got here. Riley's six-foot-one frame is big enough, but Derek dwarfs him. His military-short hair is jet black, and his features are hard. His eyes are a solid black, something Riley guesses he's gained from all his years of service to Link. Derek is also someone Link trusts, otherwise he wouldn't be here now. Link had made Riley fight Derek before he left hell, and the idiot had somehow managed to kick his ass. The last thing Riley wants to do is admit Derek might be right, that Vivienne might not come after all.

He'd succeeded in taking care of Rebecca so that no one would think she'd died of anything other than natural causes. Then he'd read her chart. Vivienne, no doubt, drove her to the madness she suffered from. Vivienne isn't good for anything other than pissing everyone off.

"I wouldn't be too sure about that. Let's go."

"You go then, if you're so damn concerned about the humans."

"Let me explain something to you, Riley. You don't call the shots here, he does. You will follow orders or you will end up back where he pulled you from. You get me?"

Riley shivers at the memory of hell. He vowed to complete his task just so he wouldn't have to return to the pits he was pulled from. Anything is better than being sliced open and left to bleed out, only to heal back up and go through it all over again.

All Riley wants to do is be done with this mess. He could've sworn up and down that when he'd left Vivienne in her apartment she wasn't breathing and didn't have a pulse. Once this is over, Link will see that he means business and let him keep working for him and, more importantly, let him keep working with the amazing powers the devil himself has given him.

"Fine," Riley spats finally. "I'm going to see my father."

"I wouldn't do that if I were you," Derek says as they leave the room.

They walk down the hallway toward the exit door at the end of the hall. It has a warning on it that an alarm will sound when opened, but they crash the bar and go right through, and no alarm goes off.

"What the fuck do you care?"

"The cops are watching your dad's place."

"What do I care about cops?"

Derek slams him up against the brick wall of the building they've just left. "You better start caring. If you fuck this up, get caught or get yourself killed, you will be tortured, and believe me, you don't want to have to deal with that again."

But Riley shoves him off, straightens his jacket, and takes off as fast as he can toward his father's house.

TWELVE

A few hours later, Vivienne stirs in his arms. Opening her eyes, she can see that it is still early; it's very dark in the room. Unsure of what woke her, she snuggles closer to Mikah.

This isn't the first time she's woken up next to him, but this is the first time since she came to understand all the hidden emotions she's been fighting. She squirms slightly and he stirs.

"What's wrong?" he asks, and she can hear the concern in his voice.

"Nothing, I just woke up. That's all."

"Oh."

She pulls herself closer to him, pressing their bodies tighter together. She can't stop what happens next; it comes so natural to her now. She leans in and softly places her lips to his.

Her heart begins to race, desire shattering the nerves that have built up since they stepped into the room. Last night, seeing him on the floor on his knees with his wings extended had brought out her deepest desires for him, ones that were, at one time, only felt in their dreams, and she couldn't stop herself.

She can't stop herself now.

He kisses her back, letting go of all his inhibitions, and he lets her take the lead.

She hitches her leg onto his hip and pushes him onto his back. Rolling with him, she now sits atop him, her hands sliding down his cheeks, down his neck. Their kisses grow more and more passionate with every touch.

She runs her hands down his chest and back up to his shoulders, then down along his arms until she finds his hands. She lifts them to her body, encouraging him to touch, to explore, and he takes the not-so-subtle hint.

While their soft, warm tongues continue dancing, he ever so lightly runs his hands from her hips up her sides and down her arms. Her desire for him skyrockets to a fever pitch.

She shivers, and that need she feels for him grows hotter, stronger, making her bold and brave. This is it. This is what she's been needing: to know that she can have him as completely as he has her.

Until a moment ago, kissing Mikah was all she could think about, all she ever wanted to do, and she wants more. She trails her fingers down his chest and over his abs, lightly tracing the bumps with her fingertips until they reach the point where their bodies meet. She can feel it between them, his erection growing stronger.

His hands glide down her body once again, but she longs to feel his fingers against her bare skin. She grabs the hem of her shirt.

His hands cover hers, stopping them. Through their kiss he whispers, "Are you sure?"

"Yes," she breathes back, and he lets go of her hands.

"Can I?" he whispers again, and she nods.

At a slow, measured pace, he pulls the hem of her shirt up. Once the t-shirt rises higher than her breasts, the cool air of the room hardens her nipples into tight, painful peaks, and desire explodes. It causes her wings to unlock and spread.

She raises her arms to allow the shirt to come off, but in order for it to come off, she has to stop kissing him. She doesn't want to stop kissing him.

Mikah pulls away from their kiss long enough to bring the neckline of her shirt over her mouth. Then he is instantly kissing her again. He stops pulling on the shirt, but it still covers her eyes. She smiles as she kisses him again; she's trapped slightly by her shirt.

His hands are on her bare skin, leaving goose bumps in their wake. She shivers again and her wings rustle. She pulls her shirt off the rest of the way, and as soon as she tosses it aside she hears Mikah's sharp intake of breath. His touch radiates through her wings and is felt deep down there. She moans into his mouth.

"You're so beautiful," he breathes as his hands continue their exploration.

He sits up, taking her with him so they are nose to nose, lips against lips. His hands slide up her sides to the swell of her breasts, tickling along her heated skin until his fingers brush her nipples and she moans again.

He pulls his lips away from hers and begins to kiss along her jaw, down her neck. Vivienne is lost to his touch; nothing matters but the two of them. His mouth continues down her chest to her breast — licking,

kissing, nipping lightly as she writhes in his lap —
until finally his tongue makes brief, searing contact
with her nipple and she trembles.

He feels the tremor along the shaft of his throbbing
erection, and suddenly he's on the verge of losing
control.

Sensing his distress and pleasure, she flicks her
hips against his erection once again. This time he
responds by running his hand along the front part of
her wing. She stops as the pleasure locks down all of
her muscles in a delicious tease. The moment his
hand comes away, she is released.

"Not fair," she says.

She smiles and breathes. Bringing her own hands
around to his back, she brushes her fingers along the
edges of his wings, which are still locked away, but
the touch has the same effect: He is locked down with
desire.

He turns, pushing her onto the bed, but before she
makes contact, her wings disappear. He laughs at how
quickly she pulled them back in.

"Now it's my turn," he says.

He slides his body between her legs and she wraps
them around his hips, holding him tight. He kisses her
again, then slowly licks and kisses his way down her
body, between her breasts, and further still. Her legs
fall slack and she runs her hands through his hair,
urging him to keep going.

His lips come to the top of her bump, and he kisses
it ever so tenderly. She fights the urge to cry as the
emotions swell inside her. Something deeper spreads
within her, a feeling she's never experienced before
and never wants to lose, as he softly kisses her belly
along the waistband of her yoga pants.

He's never felt this way about anyone before – at once nearly overwhelmed by his desire for her but also desperately needing to take things slow.

His hands slide into the waistband of her pants, and she responds by lifting her hips so that he can remove them. But he doesn't pull them off immediately. Instead he continues to kiss along the lower swell of her belly.

"I will always protect you," he says, his lips brushing against her belly while his eyes never waver from hers.

She knows that his declaration is not just for her, but is for her daughter too. All the raw emotion boils over, and this time she can't hold back the tears.

THIRTEEN

"I will always be here for you," he breathes against her belly. "Never doubt that." He can feel her emotion pouring into him. It is the emotion that he needs to feel in order to continue.

Vivienne is not just a girl in his bed; she is the woman who has his heart. Her emotions tell him that he has hers and lets him know that what he's been fighting for for weeks is finally going to be his.

In agonizingly slow fashion, he begins to slide her pants down her legs. She doesn't stop him. She needs this. She needs him. She fought for so long to prove to herself that she needed nothing and no one, but right now, she realizes that she was wrong. She needs him like she needs air to breathe.

As he's freeing her legs, he can't stop his eyes from wondering up her beautiful body. He slowly moves up her body, sliding his hands along her legs to her hips, and he watches as she closes her eyes to savor the sensations. He needs to worship her body, show her what she means to him.

She senses his need as he gets closer to her lips. He pauses to flick his tongue across one nipple, then the other, and she moans with each contact. Then finally he reaches her lips.

Throwing aside all resistance, he kisses her with more passion than he's ever felt in his entire life.

She wraps her arms around him and pulls him against her as tight as she can, needing to feel his skin on hers.

Using her feet, she tries to push down his pants. He smiles, knowing that she wants what he wants just as badly. He pulls back from their kiss and rears up, which allows him to slide his pants down his legs. She surprises him by maintaining eye contact; he can't pull his eyes away from hers.

He manages to liberate his raging erection from the constraint of his pants. Then he leans back down and kisses her once again.

She wraps her legs around him again, holding him to her. She can feel his erection pressed against her pelvic bone, so close, and her growing need for him can be felt in the warm wetness between her legs.

When his erection makes contact with that wetness, he cannot hold back anymore. "Are you sure?" he breathes against her lips, needing her reassurance.

"I've never been more ready for anything than I am right now."

That's all he needs to hear. He pulls his hips back, lining up the head of his erection with the warmth of her sex.

"Please," she breathes, and slowly he pushes into her.

She can feel her body giving way to his sensual invasion, feel when the crown makes it past the tightness of her entrance. He's bigger than anything she's ever felt before.

He moves unhurriedly, not wanting to hurt her, knowing that he is larger than most men. Vivienne writhes beneath him as he pushes himself inside.

Vivienne has never felt anything like this before. Her body is stretching and contracting in ways she's never experienced. Just when she thinks she can't take anymore, he pushes in a little deeper, filling her a little fuller.

He finally stops pushing when he feels significant resistance. He pauses, looking deep into her eyes, waiting patiently for her to adjust to him inside of her. When she starts to move, he takes it as his cue that she's ready.

He pulls back and then slides in a little faster. The pleasure within her starts to fire through her veins like lightning. His hands roam her body from her hips to her belly to her breasts. Her eyes close, the better to feel his touch and savor the sensations flying through her body. She moans and runs her hands up his body from his hips up his sides to his neck, where she tugs on him, pulling him down toward her.

He gives in and follows her lead, arching his back so he doesn't put his weight on her, and she kisses him, slow and sweet. He can't help the moan that escapes his own lips as he feels her tighten and respond to the pleasure he's providing her.

"I want to see you," he says as he pulls back from her kiss.

Her eyelids are heavy, but she opens them to meet his eyes, vibrant and blue. Pleasure and desire pass between them at the same time she feels herself building, climbing toward something beyond anything she's ever felt before. The intensity is too much and she moans again, her eyes rolling up and closing just as her sex clamps down hard.

He picks up his pace, moving inside of her faster and faster with each short breath they take. Sweat covers both of their bodies.

She opens her eyes again to see him: His eyes are closed, immense pleasure on his face. His hair is a mess and falling down over his forehead.

Just as she reaches up to brush his hair away, he opens his eyes, and that emotion, the one she couldn't identify before, is there again, only this time she knows it for what it is. She can feel the same emotion building up inside of her. Love and adoration.

With each thrust of his hips, Vivienne's pleasure builds and builds, climbing higher and higher. Then, just like that, the pleasure peaks. Her eyes close and she moans louder, arching her back to the pleasure she feels deep inside.

In a second they both come unraveled, lost in the climax, and Mikah pours himself into her.

FOURTEEN

They are both breathing heavily, and neither one says anything for some time. Staring deep into each other's eyes, they know nothing needs to be said. It's there, between them, everything they've been fighting emotionally since they met.

Vivienne's never experienced anything like this before, has never known what real, raw desire and love truly feel like. Somewhere along their journey, she's fought it, fought to embrace it, to accept the fact that she could be deserving of more, but he makes it clearer to her now; it's in his eyes.

Destiny. That's what this feels like to Mikah. And the look in her eyes now is all he needs. He will do anything for her, anything to protect her, no matter what the cost.

Once their breathing finally returns to normal, Mikah slowly slides out of Vivienne. She winces and shivers at the loss.

"Did I hurt you?" he whispers.

"No," she says back to him as he rolls to her side.

He snakes his arm in under her head and she snuggles into him. He pulls the covers up to cover them and brings one hand to rest on her belly.

She smiles.

"Are you feeling okay?"

She blushes. "I feel great," she says and kisses his chest. She puts her hand over his.

He smiles at her. "Good." He kisses the top of her forehead and settles in with her. He knows now what all of this emotion has been building toward.

That first night, in the diner, he found a woman who wasn't helpless but who maybe needed a little bit of help to get through. There was something special about her; he felt it in places that he'd long since forgotten. When his mother died, he built up walls of determination that made loving another woman nearly impossible. He'd tried, but there'd been nothing like what he feels right now.

He'd gone back the next night with no prompting from his wings. He'd just wanted to see her again. He kept going back because the wanting became needing. He knew it then – that she was something special - and now...now she's here, in his arms and in his bed. He meant what he said: He will stop at nothing to protect her, to make her safe, and no matter what, he will always be here for her, for both of them.

Vivienne tilts her head toward him. His eyes are closed, but his hand rubs lightly along her belly, sending goose bumps across her skin and a warmth into her heart. Her life has changed so much in such a short time; she can't imagine going through all of this with anyone but him. To have him here to help her, to protect her and to guide her is exactly what she needed.

She pulls her hand away from Mikah's and begins to trace the lines of his chest. Doing so reminds her of his chest in their dreams, the tattoo that runs over his right shoulder. She wonders where it comes from.

She hears his breathing hitch a little with some of her strokes, but she doesn't stop, and when she looks up at him he's smiling.

He begins to do the same, trailing his fingers along her belly, down over her hips, across her pelvic bone and up the other side. His fingers are light against her skin, and her nipples harden.

He continues tracing the lines of her body, carefully avoiding all of those spots that would send her over the edge. Her caresses have stirred his erection once again, but he's not sure how she'd feel about a round two. He's content to touch her in any way he can.

She writhes beneath the slow, sensual patterns he is making along her skin, which has been made even more sensitive by the explosive orgasm she experienced not all that long ago. The desire she feels for him is building once again, and she can feel his erection pressed against her thigh between them, but since he hasn't made a move to intensify the contact between them, she's not entirely sure what to make of it.

She can't see his body and he can't see hers, but their touching continues until the pleasure closes their eyes one last time and they fall asleep in each other's arms.

FIFTEEN

Around noon, Vivienne begins to stir in Mikah's arms. One of his legs is draped over her, and his arms are both wrapped around her. She takes a deep breath, breathing in his scent: sweet and heady and simply Mikah.

She fights the urge to squirm. She really needs to go to the bathroom, but he's sleeping so peacefully – something she's never seen before because he always manages to wake up before her - that the idea of waking him nearly breaks her heart. He looks so innocent. The beautifully tanned skin of his bare chest begs her to touch it.

Last night feels like a dream and miles away from right now. She'd come home from the spa trip with Celeste to find her apartment lined with candles, the pictures, the bracelet, and then the clothes, that dress, the one she always seems to be wearing in Elysium. Then taking her to the charity gala. Did she really tell him that she'd go back to school and eventually work for him? She smiles at the memory of the evening and where it had been going...at least until Red had interrupted them.

Going to Elysium and having Mikah find out about nearly everything makes her a little anxious. She knows that she still needs to tell him about the shifter.

She also knows that at some point she wants to speak with Elizabeth about talking to her mother in private. This, Vivienne knows, will not be an easy thing, but it is important. Vivienne would never have gotten to talk with her mother while she was still alive, at least not with any real conversation or comprehension. Maybe this is her chance to tell her mother how she feels, at the very least.

Her bladder finally overcomes her desire to let Mikah sleep, and Vivienne squirms involuntarily.

Mikah stirs. His blue eyes meet hers and a smile spreads across his lips. Vivienne swallows the thoughts of her mother and smiles back at him.

"Good morning, beautiful." he whispers, his voice groggy from sleep.

She smiles wider at his vulnerability. "Good morning," she says back.

"How'd you sleep?" he says as he slowly peels himself off of her.

There is both joy at being free so she can use the bathroom and sadness at the loss of their connection.

"What's wrong?" he asks.

She blushes. "I have to use the bathroom."

"Oh," he says, and he pulls back to free her completely. "Sorry." He smiles sheepishly.

She runs her finger along the bridge of his nose. "Don't be." She climbs out of bed and heads for the bathroom.

Weeks ago, when Vivienne crawled onto Mikah's cot in the hospital room that night, he savored it, afraid it was a momentary weakness on her part and that it would never happen again. But this morning outshines anything he felt that night.

Her bright blue eyes, messy, bright red hair and beautiful smile stop his heart. He'd tried so hard to control himself, to not rush through being with her the first time, but being with her was exquisite in the most delicious way he could've ever imagined. After last night he was worried about how she'd feel toward him this morning, but she is here with him.

The morning-after bliss clouds his memory of the other events of last evening. So much happened in Elysium, but it will be dealt with tomorrow. Today he wants to spend with Vivienne, whether in bed all day or out of it. Today is their day.

He rubs his eyes, getting rid of the crusty sleep, and stretches. He looks over at the nightstand. The clock says 12:33p.m. He smiles. It has been probably ten years since he's slept until after noon.

Vivienne steps into his field of vision and he smiles at her. Her answering smile is warm.

"How are you feeling?" he asks.

"Good. Still tired, but I feel great."

"You look amazing," he says, his hungry eyes roam over her naked form standing at the foot of the bed. He laughs a little when she realizes that she's naked.

"Jeez, thanks for reminding me." She scurries into the bed and under the covers.

"Never cover yourself for me. I think you're beautiful." He kisses her on the forehead and pulls the covers back. "My turn."

He quickly jumps out of bed, giving her a view of his beautiful, well-sculpted ass as he disappears into the bathroom. She blushes and buries herself under the covers.

Mikah emerges from the bathroom and leans on the doorjamb, watching to see if she'll emerge from her hiding place under the covers. When she doesn't stir, he decides to play with her. He creeps to the foot of the bed. When he lifts up the comforter, she giggles. The sheet is still between them, but looking up her body, he can see the swell of her belly. It's one of the most beautiful things he's ever seen.

He climbs onto the bed under the comforter and snakes his way up her body, kissing and breathing hotly through the sheet between them, and she giggles again. When he reaches her belly he kisses it, then reaches up to pull the sheet back. She helps him lower it.

Still underneath the comforter, she stares down into his beautiful blue eyes. He looks so sweet and boyish hiding under the covers, his hair all mussed up. The image is breathtaking, and the now-familiar ache from last night returns.

Mikah senses her shift in mood. He slides up a little further until his mouth is even with hers. His kiss is filled with passionate promises of what's to come.

SIXTEEN

Sometime later they emerge from under the comforter, sweaty and breathing heavily. Neither one of them speaks until their heart rates calm down and their breathing returns to normal.

"Are you hungry?"

Vivienne laughs a little bit. "I'm starving," she says, and he smiles back at her.

"We can't have that. How about breakfast in bed?"

She laughs a little harder. "Breakfast? Mikah, it's nearly two in the afternoon."

He laughs with her. "You're right, but it's never too late for breakfast."

He flings the covers aside, sits on the edge of the bed and looks around for his pants. "Hmm," he says when he can't find them. He gives up, deciding instead to give Vivienne another show. He stands and walks toward the closet. When she realizes that he's walking around naked, she hides under the covers again, giggling.

Mikah grabs two pairs of pants, one for him and one for her. He also grabs one of his Boston College t-shirts for her to throw on.

"Here you go, sweetheart," he says, emerging from the closet. "I'll have Celeste and the boys bring your stuff up from the condo downstairs, but in the meantime, here's a pair of my pants and a t-shirt for you."

She peeks coquettishly out from under the covers and giggles again.

He laughs. "You silly girl."

She smiles and he leans down to kiss her. She kisses him back, remembering all too clearly the last hour or so spent under the sheets.

But he doesn't linger.

"Mind if I take a shower?" she asks.

"Never ask me, my home is your home. Please, make yourself comfortable. I'll be back in a bit with food," he says as he reaches the door.

As soon as he leaves the room Vivienne is desperate to see him again, but instead she climbs out of bed and takes the clothes Mikah's laid out for her into the bathroom.

Mikah isn't in the kitchen very long when he hears the running water of the shower. Smiling at the idea of Vivienne in his shower, he opens the fridge. He's moving a few things around when Celeste comes around the corner.

"Can I help you, Mikah?"

He jumps at her voice and grazes his head on the door of the fridge in his haste to stand and turn around.

"Good morning, Celeste."

"Afternoon, sir," she says with a grin.

He laughs. "No, I think I can handle some bacon, eggs and toast."

"Of course." She hesitates a moment. "Mikah, I just wanted to apologize. For last night."

He cocks his head at her.

"Neither Red nor I nor any of us had any intention of having to spring who and what we are on you like that. We wanted to wait until you were comfortable with being an angel before we sat down to discuss it with you."

"Stop. Though I don't appreciate being kept of out things and I'm not certain I've grasped all of this angel stuff yet, I'm not angry. But I am curious as to how Vivienne found out before I did."

Celeste looks uncomfortable for a moment. "I suggest you ask Vivienne about that. It's not my place to explain it."

"Fair enough."

"Do you need anything else?" she asks, changing the subject.

"Can you and the boys clean out the apartment downstairs? Bring up whatever you need from down there, plus all of Vivienne's things?" he asks, his voice gentler than when they first started talking.

"It's already been done. Her stuff is in the second bedroom. I will move it over to your room, if you'd like, when you're not in the bedroom."

"Please?"

She nods.

"Thank you, Celeste."

"Anything, anytime. Anything else?"

"No, I'm good. I think we're going to spend the day in bed or in the TV room."

"Sounds good."

The shower turns off and Celeste takes that as a cue to leave. She heads down the hall toward the door, and Mikah goes about starting their breakfast.

Vivienne towels off and gets dressed. Her hair is still soaking wet, so she wraps it up in her towel and piles it on top of her head. She smells like Mikah – well, at least his body wash – and she savors the scent.

The last twenty-four hours have been a whirlwind of events, and when she woke up yesterday, she never imagined that this morning she would wake up with Mikah. She smiles into the mirror as she throws on Mikah's Boston College t-shirt and turns to leave the bathroom, knowing that Mikah is probably waiting for her in bed.

When she steps out of the bathroom, though, he isn't there. She can smell bacon frying, so she heads for the kitchen.

When she opens the door she hears shifting and plates being set down, followed by the popping sound of the toaster. She comes around the corner of the kitchen to see him standing over the stove stirring something. She smiles because he's still shirtless and his wings are shimmering in the light over the center bar.

"Smells wonderful," she says, and Mikah jumps just a little bit. She giggles. "I didn't mean to scare you."

He turns toward her, taking in the beautiful sight of her in his t-shirt, her hair up in a towel, and the beautiful smile on her face. "Feeling better?"

She nods. "The shower felt great, thank you."

He comes around the counter and wraps his arms around her. "I said we'd have breakfast in bed." He kisses the top of her forehead. "So why don't you go lie back down, get comfortable, and I will be in in just a couple of minutes."

"But I like watching you cook," she grumbles against his chest.

He laughs. "There's plenty of time to watch me cook. Go on. I want to serve you breakfast in bed."

"Hmph," she huffs.

She stalks off toward the bedroom and he laughs at his fiery tiger.

Guessing the direction of his thoughts, she can't help but smile to herself as she crosses the threshold into the bedroom.

SEVENTEEN

"What would you like to do today?" he asks as he wipes his mouth and hands with a napkin. He places the napkin back on the tray he's brought into the bedroom, and then his hand seeks hers.

"Do you have work to do?"

He scowls at her question. "Today is just for us. I'd had plans to take you shopping today, get some more clothes for you, but I think it would be better if we stayed in the condo."

She thinks about this and finds that she's not at all upset about the idea of him buying her more clothes. Everything's different between them since last night, and suddenly it feels okay. Though perhaps part of the reason it feels okay is because they won't actually be going shopping.

"I'd like to get my stuff from the condo downstairs," she says.

"Already done. Celeste had it all brought up and placed in the second bedroom while we were sleeping." He winks at her and she blushes. "I'd like to have her move your clothes over here into my closet, if you'd like that?" The question is already out before he can stop himself, and only then does he begin to feel uneasy. He didn't mean to ask her to make a decision about whether to stay with him and live out of the same bedroom so soon.

His question surprises her, but she can see in his face that he is a little concerned about her response, so she smiles at him. "Is there room in there?" She points toward the closet.

He laughs. "No, but they can make room. There are a lot of clothes in there that I no longer wear. I'll have them removed and donated, and you can have space in there too."

She likes the idea of him making room for her and is pleased that it doesn't seem to come at a personal cost or inconvenience, such as having to go into the second bedroom for his own clothes. "Alright," she says.

He leans over and kisses her, this time square on the lips. "Now that's resolved. But we still haven't answered the question about what we'll do today."

She smiles and shakes her head. "Did you have something in mind?"

He wiggles his eyebrows at her and she blushes.

Then he says, "Want to watch some movies? Play around with your new laptop?"

Vivienne had forgotten about the super expensive laptop until Mikah mentioned it and it's not something she wants to mess with today, maybe tomorrow. She thinks for a moment, then says, "How about we watch a movie, then see what we feel up to after that?"

There isn't a TV in the bedroom, which will make what Mr. Wiggly Eyebrows Suggestive Glances hinted at more difficult. Though, now she thinks of it, she's not sure she doesn't want him to succeed, either.

"You got it, sweetheart. Let me take the tray into the kitchen. Do you remember where the TV room is?"

She thinks hard for a minute, trying to remember from the first time she was here. "Down the hallway on the left?" she says.

He smiles and nods at her. "Why don't you go in there and get comfortable. I will put this stuff in the kitchen and be there in a few minutes."

"Okay," she says, and they crawl out of bed together.

EIGHTEEN

Just as the closing credits begin to run on their movie, Mikah's wings buzz in a warm, familiar fashion. It's the same sensation he's felt when Red makes an appearance, but something about him charging into the house warns him that something's happened.

Vivienne notices Mikah's change in demeanor and she too senses Red coming into the house.

Both of them relax until Mikah takes in the look on Red's face.

"We have a bit of an issue," Red says quickly. "I didn't want to bother you today, but can you turn the TV to channel eleven?"

"Uh, sure," Mikah says as he sits up. He takes up the remote and presses a button to change the channel.

The TV flickers with images of a building. Remnants of a fire, it looks like, smoke still billowing off of the roof. "We are live at the home of Elton Bennett, a prominent local businessman in Minneapolis. Police received a call from the home's security system and responded to find the house going up in flames. Despite the internal sprinkler system, the home appears to be a complete loss.

"Police are currently looking into the situation. However, fire crews found what appear to be human remains inside of the home. Now, it is unclear whose remains they are, but Mr. Bennett's security team says that Mr. Bennett was home alone at the time of the fire. All security footage from within the home has been turned over to Minneapolis Police, and they are asking anyone with information to come forward.

"They are also on the lookout for Elton Bennett's son, Riley Bennett, who is wanted for questioning in a triple homicide and attempted murder case from about a month ago. Police are asking for any information on his whereabouts—"

Mikah hits the power button on the TV "Why would he kill his own father?" he asks out loud.

"I'd wager a guess that his father probably pissed him off. More than likely he went to his father to seek refuge, but with everything Elton's suffered as a result of Riley's choices, I'd like to think that Elton wasn't very welcoming."

"I'd hope not, but we all know how they work. Elton has defended his son for years, protecting him, finding him the best attorney. Why would he stop now?" Mikah counters.

Vivienne is silent, not entirely understanding the situation but feeling vaguely and irrationally guilty. Yet another life lost at the hands of Riley.

"Elton's never lost so much as he has in the last month," Red says in response to Mikah's question. "With his son labeled a cop killer and wanted for murder of three people and the attempted murder of another, Elton's political career is over. No amount of damage control can right that ship. Couple all of that with you backing out of the condo project that was set to make him millions and give him the financial power he needed to proceed with his political ambitions, and I'd imagine that he'd be pretty pissed."

Mikah can feel a shift in Vivienne – not just physically, but emotionally too – and he remembers he hasn't told her about his confrontation with Elton at the hospital, nor about all the behind-the-scenes things that MSB has done to destroy Elton's career. But her mood is not one of anger, as he'd expected, but awe.

"You—" The words are difficult for her to get out. "When did you pull out of Elton's condo project?" she asks, her voice weak. She needs to know if it was in retaliation for what Riley did to her.

"The night you were attacked."

Vivienne flinches, remembering.

"The cops came here to the condo," he continues, "questioning me because of the car Red was in when he drove by your home."

"It wasn't you in the car?" she says, a little disappointed.

"All the other nights, yes it was. I was caught up at a dinner function that night, so I sent Red in my place."

A sense of relief washes over her. Knowing that he backed out of his business deal before he knew what had happened to her gives her new insight into Mikah and what he was thinking or feeling before she was attacked. But a sense of guilt still plagues her heart: She was so mean to him, rejecting him, and look at what he did for her.

"When the police left, I immediately went searching for a connection. That was when I discovered that Elton Bennett, who was a business partner, is Riley's father. As soon as I found out, I severed the connection. Pulling all my funding for his condo project caused all the other investors to back out, and Elton lost just about everything he had.

"He retaliated, of course. He showed up at the hospital to confront me. We argued, I punched him, and that was the last I heard from him, other than last night, when he showed up at the gala. But his intentions remain unclear. The office has been dealing with it through the legal channels."

Vivienne doesn't say anything, and Mikah is silent as she lets all that he's just told her soak in.

If it hadn't been Vivienne, Mikah might not have pulled out of his business deal with Elton, but the fact is, it was her, and he never thought twice about it.

Vivienne continues to stay quiet, unsure what to say to him, but she is quickly beginning to understand that she means more to Mikah that she could've ever imagined.

"So what do we do now?" Mikah asks Red after a minute.

"We need to go back into Elysium with what we know. I'm sure they're already aware, but I think that we need to discuss what to do next. It is becoming clear that Riley is behind Rebecca's death, and we need to plan our next move." Red looks to both of them. Mikah and Vivienne's confusion and concern are obvious to him, but he can also see in Mikah's eyes that he understands what needs to be done.

"Andrew picked up on some additional activity regarding search efforts for Vivienne, but before we can go after Riley, you need some training, Mikah."

"Training in what? I already know how to fight."

The statement surprises Vivienne, but she doesn't say anything. She's wrestling with a heavy sense of guilt. All of this is her fault, and she doesn't even know how to stop it.

"You do, and you fight well," Red says. "But those that you'd be going up against will not fight in the traditional ways. Which is where Andrew, Celeste, Connor and myself come into play."

Red looks at Vivienne. "Perhaps it is time to tell him the rest and explain what you know."

NINETEEN

Vivienne's eyes meet Red's. Hers are wary. She is worried Mikah might be upset that she hasn't told him about the shifter yet. But Red gives her an encouraging nod, silently telling her that it's alright.

Vivienne nods and turns to Mikah, who is visibly irritated that once again something has been kept from him.

"Yesterday morning, as I was getting ready to leave with Celeste, the phone in the condo downstairs rang. When I looked at the number it was yours."

"I didn't call yesterday morning."

"I know you didn't, but I didn't know that at the time. When I picked up, no one was there, but when I turned around you were standing in the doorway." Mikah's face scrunches up, puzzled. "Only it wasn't really you. That's when Connor and Andrew appeared. And, within a matter of a few heartbeats, so did Red." Vivienne watches as Mikah looks from her to Red and back again, no doubt wondering how Red could have been on the plane with him and in Vivienne's condo at the same time. "When Red showed up, he protected me while Andrew and Connor took out the shifter."

"Shifter?" Mikah says.

"In a minute," Red replies.

"Red then pulled me into Elysium, where he explained it all to me. However, I'd already had an idea what they – the guardians – were because Zirah had told me earlier that morning." Vivienne begins fidgeting with her hands. "Red, Andrew, Connor and Celeste all have the ability to protect us in ways I've never imagined. Red was able to camouflage me so that the shifter couldn't actually see me even though I was there."

Mikah looks to Red, confused. "Why am I only finding out about this now?"

The irritation in his voice sends a shiver through Vivienne.

"We wanted the time to be right." Red's voice is stern, but there is an underlying understanding that Mikah picks up on quickly. "You've had such a hard time adjusting to what you are that we felt it best not to inundate you. Vivienne's introduction to what she is took place more subconsciously, and her overall attitude toward it has made it easier for her to understand. You like control, Mikah, and being an angel is something you can't control."

Mikah knows that Red is right. He does like control, and finding it in himself to believe that he is an angel has been one of the hardest things he's ever had to do.

"I accepted being an angel because I felt that, somehow, I always knew. Or maybe my blind hope that there had to be something better for me had me believing that anything is possible." Vivienne's voice is soft and she continues to fidget with her fingers.

Mikah reaches over and takes her hand in his. "Anything *is* possible," he whispers to her. Still holding her hand, he turns back to Red. "Now what?"

"I'll go to Elysium, talk to Elizabeth, discuss it with them, decide what to do next. But now that we know the who, we just need to try and figure out the why and the where."

Mikah nods at Red. Red gives them both a half smile and departs the condo.

As soon as Red is gone, Vivienne sags into Mikah's embrace, deflated and defeated by the turn of events. She knew last night that it was Riley who killed her mother simply because it was something he would do, and it proves that no matter what, he is coming after her. That Mikah or Red, or any of them, might end up in harm's way puts a lot of unwanted, but necessary, weight on her shoulders.

"Mikah, I never meant to keep anything from you," Vivienne says a moment later. His eyes meet hers and she knows that he's not angry with her. "I just wasn't sure how to tell you. Up until last night, neither one of us talked about anything angel-related."

He raises his hand to caress her cheek, and she leans into it. "I didn't know you knew," he says. She gives him a quizzical look. "I didn't know you knew that you are an angel."

She smiles at him. "I guess we both had our secrets."

"I wouldn't put it that way. I think it was more that both of us were waiting for the right time to talk about it." He pulls his hand away from her cheek and rubs it along his thigh, contemplating something. Then he stands up. "Or maybe I wasn't ready to face it." His voice drops, becoming heavy with emotion. He runs his hand through his inky black hair. Vivienne watches him intently, trying to decipher his mood. "I'm pretty sure I still don't understand it," he says, running his hand over his face.

"Mikah," she says looking up at him. He's standing a few feet in front of the couch, looking toward the door Red just left through. "I'm pretty sure that neither one of us had a choice in all of this. Maybe that's why I'm having an easier time, but the bottom line is that we are who we are." She takes a deep breath. "It doesn't mean it has to change who we are. Besides..." She stands up and comes to stand in front of him. He looks down at her and their eyes meet. "I wouldn't change it for anything."

Her arms snake around his waist and she pulls herself close to him, still looking into his eyes.

"I'm scared," he breathes.

"Of what?"

"Anything happening to you." His eyes glass over. "I nearly lost you once, and I will never forget what that felt like. I will do anything and everything I can to never feel that kind of pain again." He thinks but doesn't say that he's pretty sure the pain would be worse today than it was a month ago.

Vivienne squeezes him tighter and he wraps his arms around her. She's at a loss for words, unsure how to comfort him. It's unclear what the future holds for anyone, she just wants to enjoy this moment, right here right now.

TWENTY

Around nine the next morning, Red and Andrew come into the condo, and Mikah knows where they're headed. He half expected Red to come for them last night, but he and Vivienne had been left alone to just be with one another for the evening.

"Elizabeth wishes to see us all," Red says as he comes to stand in the dining room.

Vivienne and Mikah, who had just finished cleaning up from breakfast, stop what they're doing and both nod. The four of them head for the hallway that leads to the condo's foyer and there, at the end of the hallway, is a portal straight into Elysium.

"No smoke and mirrors this time?" Mikah teases Red.

"No, there's no need. Portals can be opened anywhere."

"Huh," Mikah huffs as they all step through, back into Elysium.

Nothing has changed in the white room since Saturday night except that Elizabeth, Zirah, Seraphina, Connor and Celeste are all already in the room.

When they come in Elizabeth gestures toward the couch, indicating that Mikah and Vivienne should take a seat. "Listen, I know a lot has transpired over the last couple of days, however, we now know that a trap was laid out for you by Riley. He killed your mother in an attempt to bring you to the funeral home."

Mikah's heart rate rises quickly, and Vivienne can feel the tension in his embrace. She looks to him, hoping to comfort him.

"Riley went to great lengths not only to kill Rebecca, but also in his attempt at laying a trap for Vivienne. He's yet to discover that Vivienne is with anyone. At least from what we can tell. Riley figured that if Rebecca was dead, Vivienne would run straight to the rehab center and she would go alone, therefore giving him the opportunity to complete his task."

"Which is what exactly?" Mikah asks the question everyone is thinking.

"At this point, from what information we've received, we believe he intended to kidnap her and take her back to the devil."

"So what are we supposed to do about him?" Mikah asks. "Can we call the cops and have—"

The look on Elizabeth's face says it all: The police can't stop Riley.

"*We* need to..." Mikah doesn't finish the sentence. He doesn't have to. His heart beats even faster.

"Yes, this is a matter for the guardians to handle."

Vivienne is overcome with guilt; if it hadn't been for her meeting Riley in the first place, they wouldn't be here today.

Mikah can feel her worry and the pain she is feeling in his wings; they begin to burn.

"Vivienne, do not blame yourself, this is not your fault. You see, your daughter— Have you thought of a name yet?"

Vivienne responds by shaking her head.

Elizabeth half smiles but continues. "Your daughter will have the power to overthrow the devil, and the devil knows that. He is so blind to the truth that he will stop at nothing to ensure his survival."

"What do you mean 'the truth'?" Vivienne asks.

Elizabeth starts to pace again. "The battle between good and evil will never end. It can't end."

Everyone in the room looks to each other, confusion written all over their faces.

"There are two reasons for this," Elizabeth says. "One being that the devil, like *Dia*, can appoint an heir. So even if we overthrew Link, his heir would take over."

"Does Link have an heir?" Mikah asks.

"No, though if he fails to capture Vivienne, he will seek one as quickly as possible."

"Why would capturing me be to his advantage?" Vivienne asks. The question that has been bugging her since Elizabeth first mentioned it.

All eyes are on Vivienne, and it seems to her that the others already know the answer.

Zirah steps forward to answer. "Capturing you means that your daughter, though of the purest angelic blood, would be raised by the devil himself, therefore giving him the weapon he would need to overthrow *Dia*. You see, the path an angel takes is based on how they're raised and the choices they make. If your daughter were to be raised by Link, he would have control over her and she would learn no other way but his."

565

Everyone is silent for a moment.

Vivienne can't think of anything to say. She knows that no one in this room would ever let that happen, including herself and Mikah, which means that Link will have to find his own heir. She guesses Link wouldn't be the type to settle for second best; he'd want one of his own. He'd just need the right woman to help him along in that scenario.

One name runs through Vivienne's head, a name she hasn't thought about since that dream in the hospital. "Nyssa," she whispers.

TWENTY-ONE

"Whoa, who?" Mikah says.

"When I was in the hospital, right before we left—" She glances at Mikah. "—I had a dream. A dream where I was in a dark cave. I couldn't see anything or anyone, but I heard voices. Riley was there, though based on what I heard, he was either dead or unconscious. And someone, I'm assuming it was the devil, was talking to a girl who said her name was Nyssa."

Mikah recognizes the name but doesn't understand the significance behind Vivienne's realization.

"Do we know who Nyssa is?" Elizabeth asks Vivienne.

"No, I never saw her face, but I know a Nyssa from the diner I used to work at."

Elizabeth stops in her tracks and turns toward Vivienne.

"Do you think they are one and the same?" Elizabeth asks.

"I can't say for certain, and I'm not sure I want to find out. But I'm also not sure when in time this happened. Or will happen. In the dream I was pregnant, further along than I am now, so I'm guessing it hasn't happened yet."

Ideas begin turning in Elizabeth's head, and she turns to Red. "Can we figure out who this person is?"

Red takes a step in Elizabeth's direction. "We will do whatever we can to try and find out. Though I'm not convinced she's significant."

"Good point, but I'd rather try and figure it out before Link does."

Elizabeth goes back to pacing. "As far as Riley is concerned, we're aware that he is not acting alone. Though Link has a lot of confidence in Riley's ability to complete the task he's been sent to do, he doesn't trust Riley enough to send him out on his own. Which is why I believe that Riley is meant to kidnap Vivienne and bring her back to Link. But again, it's speculation."

Vivienne takes a deep breath and places her head in her hands. Exhaustion begins to overwhelm her. "How do I stop him?" she mumbles.

"You, my dear? No, *you* don't stop him. *We* stop him." Red says, and Andrew, Celeste and Connor step forward.

"You cannot do it with the four of you. You will need Mikah too," Elizabeth says, her voice a whisper that resonates throughout the room as if shouted through a megaphone.

Vivienne begins to sob. She understands what the potential consequences of Mikah helping are, and she can't even begin to process the idea. "There has to be another way," Vivienne cries.

Elizabeth kneels down in front of her. "Vivienne, believe me, I wouldn't send him to fight if there was any other way. I don't know what kind of fight this will be, but I can assure you that we have the advantage."

All eyes immediately turn to Elizabeth, and Vivienne raises her head to look at her.

"What do you mean?" Mikah says hesitantly.

Elizabeth smiles slightly. "Well, for one, we've taken away their element of surprise. With the level of protection that is in place around both of you, Riley cannot find you until we're ready for him to do so. That is why he tried to get you to the rehab center."

Mikah stands and takes a few steps away, trying to figure out where his mother is going with all of this.

"Mikah, I suggest you both plan to stay in your apartment, versus the one downstairs, for the foreseeable future. Though both are protected, your penthouse has more layers of protection, along with fewer access points."

"Alright, but please tell me that's not all we have in our arsenal. I don't know if that will be enough." Mikah's pessimism drives a valid point.

Andrew chimes in for the first time. "Do you honestly think that whoever was sent with him will leave Riley alone, unsupervised?"

"No, Andrew, I don't think they will leave him alone, at least not intentionally. And no, the penthouse is not your only weapon, though that may be the wrong word for it." As Elizabeth speaks, Zirah and Seraphina move to stand alongside her.

"Please stop with all the vagueness." Mikah's patience is wearing very thin.

"I cannot tell you how your battle will end because we do not know. I can only give you some strategic help. With any luck, that will be everything you need to survive. Our first advantage is being able to control when and where Riley sees Vivienne. We will know they are coming and we will set them up, luring them into a trap of our own. Vivienne herself is the second advantage."

TWENTY-TWO

"Wait, I don't understand. How am I the second best thing we have to beat these guys?" Vivienne stands and walks toward Elizabeth. "I'm nobody, I haven't got a clue how to fight and wouldn't even consider it."

"Though you will need to be the one to lure Riley out and into the trap, you will not need to fight. Your talent lies elsewhere. Over the course of the last month or so, have you ever wondered how you were able to heal so quickly from your injuries?"

A flood of images runs through Mikah's mind: Vivienne nearly dead in her apartment; her lying in that hospital bed; her body healed, almost as if the attack hadn't happened at all.

Though Vivienne was unconscious through the entire ordeal, she recalls that, other than exhaustion, she felt no pain. She was unable even to determine the level of injury she incurred during Riley's last attack, so much so that she had to ask Dr. Alston whether Riley had raped her.

"Yes, I've thought about it, but what does that have to do with us trapping Riley?"

571

Zirah joins the conversation. "Everything, Vivienne. It means that no matter what happens during the fight, or whatever happens with Riley, you can save your guardians. Your extraordinary ability to heal doesn't stop with you."

Mikah remembers Seraphina telling him that he helped Vivienne heal. But if she's the one with the healing ability, she didn't really need him, did she?

Yes, she did. She needed your strength, your encouragement, and your need for her in order to pull herself through. Seraphina's voice rings clearly inside Mikah's mind and he understands. *You gave her hope.*

"How?" Vivienne breathes. She hadn't healed herself consciously; how was she supposed to heal anybody else?

"We will teach you," Seraphina says aloud to Vivienne. "Just like we will teach Mikah what he needs to know. Though Andrew and Connor are pretty deadly, so there may not be much he needs to do."

"Do we have that kind of time?" Mikah asks from behind Vivienne.

"You do. As I said, you're fully protected within the apartment, and when you go out the same applies. We can drop the protection anytime and expose you to Riley when you're ready."

"But if we're fully protected, why do we even have to expose ourselves to him at all? Or to anyone for that matter? What is the point of all of this?" Vivienne is rather upset. "Why can't we just leave it alone and forget about it?"

Mikah takes a deep breath. "I think I can answer that one, Vivienne. If we don't fight, you will never be in the clear."

"Mikah is right," Elizabeth says. "Riley is not all you will have to worry about in your lifetime, however he is the one who poses the biggest threat to you now. The devil knows that he's found something in Riley. The anger that, for whatever reason, Riley holds against you is a very powerful tool, and Link will do whatever he can to exploit that. If you, Mikah, and the guardians eliminate Riley, you send a message to the devil that even his best men will be unsuccessful." Elizabeth paces again. "Link is too blind to see that evil will always exist, that it has to. There has to be a balance in the world of good and evil. When Riley fails, he will turn to his next tactic."

"Which is what exactly?" Mikah says flatly.

"An heir." Zirah steps forward. "The devil will seek an heir to his throne so that when your daughter comes of age and if she decides to defeat him, the circle of hell continues with that heir."

"What happens, hypothetically speaking, if my daughter defeats the devil and there is no heir?"

Elizabeth, Zirah, Seraphina and Red all look at each other, but no one seems about to answer.

"I don't recommend ignoring that question," Vivienne says, a warning note in her voice.

Elizabeth looks at her, anger in her eyes, but she softens when she realizes who it is that she's talking to.

"If the devil has no heir when he is defeated, a state of anarchy will break out within the walls of hell. When that happens, hell on earth will be born and the destruction of mankind imminent." All eyes are on Elizabeth, fear and understanding radiating throughout the room. "You see, again, it is about the balance of good versus evil."

No one says anything. Vivienne takes a few steps back to sit back down. "We have no choice." Her voice is weak and quiet.

"Believe me, I wish there was." Elizabeth's voice has taken on a somber tone, and Vivienne places her head in her hands again, deflated and exhausted.

"Is there anything else we need to know?" Vivienne says through her hands.

"No, not right now," Elizabeth says. "You, Mikah, Red, and the other guardians can work on your plan. Mikah, when you're ready, speak to Red and you two can discuss training. Vivienne, you will need to come to Elysium for yours. Zirah and Seraphina will be more than happy to help you. I suggest that you don't wait too long to get started. The sooner we can end this, the sooner it will be over." Elizabeth, sensing his determination to be done with this, approaches Mikah. "But you do not need to do this alone, my son. Those in this room will help you, and you will have Elysium on your side when you go."

Mikah takes his mother by the arm and kisses her cheek. He whispers in her ear so that only she can hear it. "I know. And you know that I will do anything to keep both of them safe."

"Do not be a martyr. Protect them *and* yourself," she whispers back. She knows how much Vivienne and her daughter mean to him, though he may not yet realize it himself.

He kisses her cheek once more, and she goes to Vivienne and kneels in front of her. "I knew from the very first moment I saw you, so many years ago, that you were special."

Vivienne raises her head to look at her. Elizabeth's eyes are soft, warm and a comfort, but they are wary too.

"Your strength, your determination, and most of all your heart are pure. Call on me at any time if you need to talk." Elizabeth kisses Vivienne on the cheek. "Go now and rest."

TWENTY-THREE

"What do we do now?" Mikah asks. He, Vivienne and the guardians are back in his penthouse, standing in the dining room.

"We need to establish some type of daily routine for Vivienne. Like walking along the river or going to a store nearby. And while she's engaged in this activity, we have to drop her protection." Red says.

"No. Absolutely not. She cannot go out unprotected and alone."

"Mikah, she will not be alone. We will all be there with her. But she has to appear alone. We need to be able to draw Riley out, get the attention of Link, who will send Riley in to do whatever it is he wants him to do. But in order to do that, we have to lay the trap, and in order to do that, her presence needs to register with the devil's watchers. They need to know at what time of day they can expect her to show up. Once they've identified her pattern, they will pass the message along. Exposing her one time will not draw out what we're after."

"I don't like the idea of using Vivienne as bait," Mikah says, but his tone is more plaintive now than commanding.

Vivienne looks at Mikah. "We have no other choice."

She's right of course, and Mikah knows it, but fear grips him; he is putting her in danger, something he swore to himself he would never do again.

"She's right, Mikah, we have no other choice," says Red.

"I know, it's just...it's so dangerous. He got to her once and I couldn't live with myself if he gets to her again." He looks to Vivienne, on the verge of tears at the idea of anything happening to her.

"We have a plan in place," Red says, "we just need you two ready and willing to make it happen. No harm will come to Vivienne, we will make sure of that. We will do everything in our power to make sure no harm comes to anyone, but Vivienne's protection is our main concern."

Red's commitment to keeping Vivienne safe makes Mikah feel a little better about the situation, but still he's not convinced.

"You don't think I worry about you?" Vivienne whispers to Mikah, aware that his concern for her safety could drive him to try and stop this from happening. "All of you? It would kill me if anything happened to any of you."

"We know," Red says, compassion in his eyes.

Something occurs to Vivienne. "I'm not sure that I'm understanding all of this," she says. "If the devil likes control, why doesn't he handle things himself?"

"The devil doesn't do his own dirty work because he knows that there is always a chance that someone could defeat him. He uses 'tools' like Riley to keep himself out of harm's way."

"Okay, so where do we come into all of this? How does our defeating Riley change any of that?" Mikah asks. It is the same question that's weighing on Vivienne's mind.

"The devil killed Riley, thus making him a tool at his disposal to do his work. Until the demon Riley is destroyed by something other than the devil, Link can continue to use him as he sees fit. When he is destroyed, Link has no choice but to send him into hell."

Vivienne recalls the stories of Dante and the circles of hell and wonders idly which circle Riley will fall into once he is destroyed.

"We destroy Riley," Red says, "and Riley is no longer a threat to either one of you, and the devil goes about his task of finding an heir."

"I'm willing to do anything if it means that Riley never bothers me again and I know that my daughter is safe," Vivienne says with more confidence in her voice than what she's had since Red knocked on the bedroom door.

"That, my dear, is why you are an angel," Red says.

"When do we start?" Mikah asks.

"Tomorrow morning around nine. We will have Vivienne go for a walk, and we'll drop her shields, putting her on the radar. My guess is that it will take at least three or four days before the watchers report back to Link. They will be certain that this is a daily thing before they report. If there is anyone they don't want to piss off, it's the devil."

Mikah and Vivienne nod as Red, and the guardians turn to leave. Neither one of them says anything for some time as they consider what comes next.

TWENTY-FOUR

The next morning the guardians arrive around 8:30. All three men are wearing black cargo pants and black hooded pullover sweatshirts. But what catches Vivienne's attention the most is what's attached to their legs. Strapped to Red's and Andrew's right thighs, and Connor's left, are black guns.

Mikah notices Vivienne's unease. "Are those necessary?" he asks them.

"They are." Andrew steps forward and hands Mikah a bag. "Inside you will find pants, a sweatshirt and a pair of boots."

Mikah takes the bag from him. It weighs more than what pants, boots and a sweatshirt should weigh, and Mikah knows that there is a holster and gun inside for him. The gun doesn't bother Mikah – he knows how to shoot; it's just been a long time.

"Why don't you go change? We're going to explain some things to Vivienne."

"I'd like to be here for that."

"No need, lad," interjects Red. "We're just going to discuss what she's going to do and how she's going to do it. Go change."

Mikah nods hesitantly, then looks to Vivienne and smiles. He heads into the bedroom just as Andrew starts talking to Viv.

"Okay, we're all going to walk out the front door toward the river. Once you're on the riverside path we will lower your shields."

"Will I be able to notice the difference?"

"Not likely, but you might. Here," he says as he hands her a tiny black sphere that's about the size of a blueberry. "That goes into your ear. You will be able to hear us, and we will be able to hear you if you talk. We will be walking with you, but you won't be able to see us. You may, depending on your skills, be able to sense us with you."

"I'm pretty good at sensing Mikah," she says, thinking about how sometimes she knows he's there even when she can't actually see him.

"That should be enough then. Today we're going to have Celeste walk with you."

Vivienne nods her understanding and looks at Celeste, who smiles back at her.

As if to prove what she said about sensing Mikah, Vivienne turns to Andrew. "He's behind me, isn't he?"

Andrew laughs. "Well done. Yes he is."

Vivienne turns to look. The sight of Mikah in the black pants and sweatshirt send her heart fluttering like crazy. He looks tough yet so normal. Then she notices that he, too, has a gun strapped to his thigh, and her excitement over seeing him turns to anxiety.

"Are those really necessary? Will they even work against anything that might be coming after us?"

"Actually, yes. They're gold-tipped bullets. Though we're not sure how effective they'll be against the likes of Riley, they should be enough to at least slow him down."

Andrew's confidence is comforting to Vivienne and even a little to Mikah.

"Vivienne," Andrew continues, "once you hit the river path we're going to walk north, to your right, for about fifteen minutes and then turn around and come back toward the house."

"That's it?" Mikah asks.

"Yup, that's it."

"What happens if someone shows up?" Vivienne's voice is halting and Mikah can feel the fear that she's feeling.

"Unlikely, but should it happen, you're Celeste's first priority, even if it means transporting you to Elysium. If it is anyone other than Riley, Red can transport Mikah, and Connor and I can handle it. Better to keep the two of you safe."

Vivienne reaches for her jacket, which is hanging on the back of the stool at the breakfast bar, and Mikah notices her hand shaking. He doesn't say anything as he walks up behind her.

She leans into him. "I'm scared."

"Don't be, sweetheart, you'll be safe. You've seen these men in action already. You know what they're capable of."

Mikah's words calm her significantly, and he helps her into her jacket.

"You'll do great," Mikah reassures her, despite his own reservations. He knows that he needs to be strong for her.

She nods as she zips up her jacket, turning toward the line of men. "I'm ready," she says, her voice surprisingly confident given the fear raging through her veins.

Celeste grabs her own coat and goes to stand next to Vivienne.

"Alright, let's go," Red says and leads the way.

Once they reach the lobby Celeste and Vivienne take point. Vivienne takes great comfort in the fact that Mikah is close behind her. It makes it a little easier to walk out the door.

Celeste leads them toward the river. It's only a couple of blocks away, but there is not a whole lot between the condo and the river. The north side of the condo complex is paved walkways and manicured lawns, trees and bushes. Winter has left the trees bare, but the color of the evergreen bushes stands out against the brown grass. It hasn't snowed much yet.

As soon as Vivienne's feet hit the asphalt of the river path she feels the strangest sensation, like a shimmer across her back. Andrew announces in her ear, "Shields are down."

As Vivienne and Celeste walk side by side Vivienne can feel the presence of the guardians and Mikah in her wings. "Are you surrounding us?" Vivienne whispers.

"Yes. Why?"

Each sensation in her back is a little bit different. She immediately knows Mikah's because his is the warmest and softest, more like a caress than the other three spots. "Mikah is to my back and left. Celeste is next to me, obviously. But..."

"Go on, Vivienne," Red says. When he talks, a spot on her back stings and she is quick to determine that his voice, or whatever he is doing, is registering.

"Ah, Red, you're to my front right."

"Well done." Connor's voice is oddly comforting, though her back's response to him is a little sharper.

"Back right?" she says back to him.

"Excellent, Vivienne," Andrew says.

"Front left," she says. "But how can I feel you guys?"

"Can you feel Celeste?" Andrew asks.

"Not the way I feel you guys, but I can sense her, despite the fact that I can see her."

"You can feel us."

"Whoa. That tickles." Her ear is filled with soft chuckles of the four men around her, and suddenly the sensations have all shifted. "You moved."

"We did. You can feel us because you're in tune to us. When we lowered the shields you became more aware of the things around you. If you concentrate hard enough you may be able to feel more than us, but we will worry about that another day."

TWENTY-FIVE

They finish their walk without incident, and then Mikah, Andrew, Red, and Connor all head downstairs to Vivienne's condo to begin Mikah's training. Vivienne isn't sure what they will be doing and she doesn't have time to dwell on it because Celeste opens a portal to Elysium and they both step through.

Standing on the other side of the room are Seraphina and Zirah, both wearing white haltered pantsuits. Next to them, Vivienne feels self-conscious in her yoga pants and t-shirt.

"Hello, Vivienne." Zirah steps forward, then turns to Celeste. "Celeste, you may go."

Celeste doesn't hesitate; she walks back out the door they just came through.

"Are you ready to learn how to protect your guardians?" she asks Vivienne.

"I'm ready, but I haven't a clue what to do."

Seraphina steps forward. "That is why we are here. Fighting, in your condition, is not going to be your strongest skill, so we're going to teach you how to heal and use some basic protection techniques."

584

"Okay," Vivienne says uncertainly, but she's eager to know what it is that she needs to do – or can do – to protect Mikah.

"Come with us."

Zirah and Seraphina both turn toward a door. Through the windows on either side of it, Vivienne can see green grass and flowers. A garden.

Vivienne follows them out the door and into the vast garden. It is probably one of the most beautiful sights she's ever seen. Stone paths lined with all different types of flowers crisscross the garden, and between the paths is lush green grass that is soft under Vivienne's feet. Two benches surround a brick walkway around a fountain in the center of the garden, and four pathways lead away from the fountain to arches in the bushes and hedges that mark the borders of the garden. Beautiful white flowers peek out from the hedges. Vivienne can't see what lies beyond that.

"In order to show you what you need to do, we first need to teach you what not to do," Seraphina says as she plucks a white rosebud from a nearby bush. She brings the bud to Vivienne. "Hold out your hands."

Vivienne does as she says.

"Now bring them together to make a bowl."

Vivienne brings her hands together pinky to pinky and cups them, then Seraphina places the rose bud gently in her palms.

"Now, I want you to close your eyes and visualize the rose in your hands. Let it become a part of you." Vivienne closes her eyes. The flower is light and soft against her palms.

From somewhere behind Seraphina there is a loud noise like two pieces of wood slamming together. Vivienne starts. A white-hot flash kisses her palms and she drops the rose.

Opening her eyes, she looks at Seraphina, then down. The rose is no longer a rose but a pile of black ash on the ground.

"What happened?"

Zirah says, "You lost your concentration, and instead of healing the rose, you burned it."

"But—" Vivienne is confused. She didn't even know what had happened until after it was already done.

"This was to show you what can happen when you lose focus. Your ability to heal also has a negative side. You cannot have the ability to heal without the ability to destroy. Balance," Zirah says, and Vivienne understands immediately.

"So let's try again," Seraphina says. "Only this time, once you find the rose within yourself, imagine it opening." She holds up another rosebud.

Vivienne braces herself by widening her stance so she feels both more relaxed and more stable. She brings her hands up and cups them, and Seraphina places the rose against her palms once again.

Vivienne closes her eyes, concentrating on the bud in her hands. She finds the rose – she can see it, touch it, smell it within herself. She watches as each of the rose's petals slowly begin to fall open.

In front of her, another loud clap, but this time she is expecting it and she doesn't flinch. She can feel Zirah and Seraphina surrounding her, watching her.

As the final petals unfold, exposing the center, Vivienne is awed by its simple beauty. She opens her eyes to see the rose, open and beautiful, no longer resting against her palms; it's suspended above her hands.

She looks up to see her teachers' reactions, and that's when she sees her. In the distance, across the garden on the other side of the fountain, Rebecca stands in an archway in the hedge. Vivienne's concentration breaks. The rose flashes and turns to ash in her palm.

"What happened that time?"

Vivienne isn't sure which of her teachers asks the question because she is staring too intently at her mother. "I thought she wasn't allowed in Elysium without an invitation," she whispers to the angels standing near her.

"Who?" Zirah responds and follows Vivienne's gaze. "She's not—" Zirah is cut short by the arrival of Elizabeth.

"She's not. I brought her here to further discuss what happened. I'm sorry, Vivienne, she wasn't supposed to be here in the garden."

Vivienne peels her eyes away from Rebecca to look at Elizabeth. "Have you learned anything further?"

"No, not really, other than she seems pretty certain that Riley wasn't alone. But we already knew that."

Vivienne nods. Two cloaked figures appear behind Rebecca, commanding her attention, and she goes with them willingly.

TWENTY-SIX

For the next two weeks, Mikah and Vivienne train during the day, Vivienne in Elysium with Zirah and Seraphina and sometimes Celeste, and Mikah with Andrew, Connor and Red in the condo downstairs, which now looks more like a karate studio than an apartment. The tension builds as each day passes and they continue wait for Riley or one of the devil's other minions to make a move.

Vivienne's bump is no longer just a bump. Now, at twenty-one weeks, she's grown quite the belly, and Mikah spends every moment he can talking to or playing music for the baby. Her kicks get stronger everyday.

In order to ensure that Vivienne and the baby will have everything they need in the event that something happens to Mikah, he talks to Red and Andrew about his wishes. This is not an easy conversation for any of them.

Every morning they take their walk along the river, each day a little longer than the day before. About three or four days into the routine, they add an evening walk.

Every night, and sometimes between training sessions, Mikah and Vivienne make love. Each time it's a little more intense and emotional for both of them. Mikah knows he loves her and is confident that she loves him in return, but he senses her hesitation to say it out loud. He also knows it has nothing to do with him.

Then, finally, she tells him her story about her mother and about Riley. Her confiding in him is the turning point; he knows she's learning to trust him.

One night, with an hour or so to spare before their evening walk, Mikah leaves Vivienne to eat and heads into his office. Only his office is not where he is going. Once he's shut the door behind him, he transports himself to Elysium, something he's been taught how to do over the last two weeks.

He walks through the great room and passes into the sanctuary, where he finds his mother standing at the altar.

"Hello, my son."

"I need to see her."

"Who?" His mother turns to him.

"Rebecca."

"For what purpose?" Her tone is forbidding, but Mikah will not back down.

"I need to talk to her." Mikah had decided a couple of days ago that he needs his own answers so that maybe he can figure out what he can do to help Vivienne.

"Is that really your place, my son?"

"No, I'm sure it's not, but I need to anyway."

"Are you going to marry Vivienne?"

"What? What does this have to do with my request?"

"Everything, my son. Do you plan to marry her?"

"She has to learn to trust and love me before I can propose marriage to her. I'm sure you can understand that."

"I do. But when she finds that she already loves you and trusts you, will you marry her?"

"Yes." Mikah watches a smile spread across his mother's face.

"Good." She gestures toward the door to her right. "Rebecca is outside."

Mikah steps through the door and into the garden. Despite all the white inside of the sanctuary, the garden is green and full of color and life.

Rebecca sits on a bench opposite him, looking right at Mikah as he walks toward her. Her features as he approaches are devoid of emotion.

"Mind if I sit?" he asks her, not really intending to give her a choice.

"No," she says, and she goes back to looking around the garden.

"Why?" It's all he can ask.

"Why what?" Rebecca looks at him, trying to read him.

"Why did you do to Vivienne the things you did?"

Rebecca stands and starts to walk away. Mikah follows, catching her quickly by the arm and turning her around. "She deserves an explanation, Rebecca. You owe her that much."

"It's none of your business." She tries to turn and he stops her again.

"You're wrong about that," he says, emotion raw in his throat. "You see, I care about her. Deeply. But your inability to show her love and affection has her terrified to admit to herself that it's okay to fall in love. She deserves better than that."

"You want to know why? Fine, Mikah, I will tell you why. I loved Red with all of my heart. When I found out I was pregnant with Vivienne, I couldn't wait to tell him. I was dying to tell him. I knew that he would be happy and that we would all be happy together. But I never got that chance. He never came back."

Mikah's grip loosens on her arm. She pulls free but doesn't run away.

"When I finally realized he was never coming back, I was too far along to do anything about it. Being a single mother was the hardest thing I've ever done. I found it much easier to handle her and life with the bottle. I blamed her for Red leaving, I blamed her for my being a single mom, I blamed her for everything."

Mikah's knees weaken and he sits alongside the fountain in the center of the garden.

"I had to live with that choice every day of my existence. I had to live with it inside of my own head at the rehab center, and I had to live with it every time she looked into my eyes. I gave up on her, but she never once gave up on me. Now I have to live with my choices for eternity and beyond. There is nothing I can do to make things right with her." Rebecca takes the bench opposite Mikah.

"I wouldn't be so sure about that."

Rebecca looks up into his eyes.

"You said it yourself, she never gave up on you. Maybe that is still true today. Elysium is not about repenting for your sins, it is about forgiveness and life. Start a new chapter with her."

"I can't," Rebecca says, standing again and turning to walk away.

This time Mikah lets her go.

"She is hopeless, Mikah. She will never change."

Mikah stands and spins around. Vivienne is standing opposite the fountain from him. "Vivienne, I—"

"Shh. She's right. I never did give up on her, but my reasons for hanging onto her were selfish. I wanted her to apologize to me, tell me that she didn't mean it, tell me that it wasn't my fault. I know now that it wasn't my fault and maybe it is no one's fault, but—" Vivienne walks around the fountain toward Mikah. "—but I know that the choices she made were hers and hers alone. I cannot change the past, and I am who I am today because of her. I don't need her apologies to move on with my life." She reaches her hand out for him to take. "Thank you."

"For what?"

"For getting her to say it out loud. Everything she said, I've suspected but never had the courage or the opportunity to get her to say. But now, I know."

"How did you know I was here?" he asks as they head toward the door that leads back to the condo.

She smiles at him. "I'm more attuned to you than to anyone else. I knew the minute you left the condo. I just gave you some lead time."

TWENTY-SEVEN

"You're one lucky son of bitch, you know that, Riley? You're lucky he hasn't sent you to be tortured."

The man in front of Derek groans. Tied up, gagged and bloody.

"Well, any more so than you already have been." His sinister laughter fills the room. "He obviously has something else planned for you."

"Leave us!" A grave and growly voice.

Derek turns toward the voice. Standing behind him is none other than the devil himself, a menacing look in his bright red eyes. Derek leaves the room quickly.

The air in the room warms to feverish temperatures as the devil draws closer to Riley, who is bound to the wall. With a small gesture, the devil cauterizes Riley's wounds one by one, and little by little the bleeding stops. But Riley's grunting, screwed-up face indicates that the pain is excruciating.

"The task I gave you remains unfinished. We know how and where to find her."

Hearing those words gives Riley newfound strength, and he begins to thrash against his bindings.

"Stop that. Why should I let you finish your task? You've done nothing but defy me from the moment you showed up here. Your latest stunt, killing your own father, gives me renewed confidence in your potential, but I don't trust you. If you defy me once more, I will happily watch your balls be ripped off again and again, day in and day out."

Riley squirms.

"Not your idea of a good time, is it?"

Riley shakes his head.

The devil continues closing up Riley wounds. As each wound closes, Riley feels as though a new one is forming.

"She is vulnerable. You will capture her and bring her back to me. If you kill her..." There is a sudden pulling and ripping sensation in Riley's groin and he screams, the sound muffled by the gag in his mouth. "If you harm her in any way..." Again the pain returns and Riley screams, sweat pouring down his face and body. "If you fail in your task..." Riley screams again, this time louder.

The pain is so intense he thinks he is going to black out, but before he does the pain stops.

Riley briefly wonders why his orders have changed and the devil has to have Vivienne alive now, but the fact that his balls are still throbbing with each pump of blood that passes through them reminds him not to question it.

"You will find her walking along the river, near the bridge. Sometimes she is alone and sometimes she walks with another female. You can destroy the other female, but bring Vivienne back to me alive. I will deal with her once she is here. Do you understand me?"

Riley's body is still ringing with pain and he doesn't respond.

"I can't think of any good reason not to destroy you right this second. I do not ask questions twice."

The stabbing pain returns once again. Riley screams out a garbled "Yes!" and nods his head. Immediately the pressure stops. His bonds loosen and he drops to the floor.

"Get yourself together. You're leaving soon."

Suddenly Riley is the only one in the room. He gropes with his hands, making sure that his balls are still intact, and then he removes his blindfold and gag. "One day," he mutters, "you're going to be sorry you did that."

If the devil hears him, he doesn't bother to respond.

TWENTY-EIGHT

Christmas approaches, and to take their minds off Rebecca and Riley and focus on more pleasant thoughts, Mikah tries more than a few times to get Vivienne to go shopping for the baby with him. But she refuses, so in the end he goes on his own.

And boy does Mikah go shopping. He enlists Celeste's help to keep it all a surprise for Vivienne, but it's all he can do to keep the secret himself. He's giddy as a schoolboy.

When Christmas morning arrives, Mikah is up before Vivienne. He brings her breakfast in bed, buying a little more time for everyone so they can get things set up the way he wants them.

Finally, Vivienne finishes eating. The moment has arrived.

"I have something I want to show you," Mikah says as Vivienne crumples her napkin and puts it on the breakfast tray.

She cocks her head at him. "Mikah, we talked about this. No Christmas presents."

He doesn't say anything, just smirks and climbs off of the bed, grabbing the tray before he walks toward the door. "Come on," he says with a smile and a wink.

Vivienne can't help but roll her eyes and smile at him. He's like a kid at a candy store, waiting impatiently for someone to open the door for him. She climbs out of bed to follow him into the dining room.

He opens the door just as she comes up behind him, and what she sees takes her breath away.

Covering every inch of the dining room table is a mountain of things, and it is obvious to her, even from the doorway, that everything on the table is a baby-related item.

She looks from the table to him and back again quickly.

"We agreed nothing for us, but I never said I wouldn't get her anything," Mikah says.

Tears fill her eyes as she takes in the scene before her. There are clothes, bottles, toys, and what looks like bedding. And beyond the table are three large boxes standing in front of a very modest Christmas tree.

As she steps into the dining room to investigate the boxes, Mikah watches her intently, afraid she might get angry with him. He notices how her eyes glass over while she takes it all in. He follows her slowly, placing the tray on the kitchen island as she goes around the dining room table.

The labels on the three boxes reveal them to be a crib, a matching dresser, and what looks like a rocking chair. Vivienne wipes the tears from her eyes.

"There's more."

"More?" she says, turning around to face him, shock on her features. "What more could there be?" she says.

He lets out a chuckle and smiles wide. "Well..." He walks around to her and holds out his hand. "I'll show you."

Vivienne looks at him skeptically, not sure what he's getting at, but she takes his hand and goes with him willingly.

He leads her to the door of the second bedroom and opens it.

"Mikah, it's empty," she says, puzzled. She remembers that there was furniture in this room the last time she saw it, and now there is nothing but bare white walls and tan carpet.

"Exactly. I'd like to turn this into her room. Vivienne, I'd really like it if both you and your daughter would stay here with me." His breath hitches. The way that they've been going these last two weeks, one could assume that her staying here was implied, but Mikah is afraid that once the Riley situation has been handled, she will want to move back downstairs. He doesn't want her to do that. He wants her to stay here.

"Mikah, I..." She turns to look at him. She can see the worry in his eyes. "I'd love to stay here."

He watches as her face lights up. He wants to say it, he wants to tell her, but—

"Thank you," she says into his chest as her arms come tight around him.

He can't help but hold her to him. He plays with her hair, kissing the top of her head. Seeing it all in her eyes, he knows she doesn't need to say it out loud. She only needs to see it, feel it, and understand it for herself.

"Of course. Anything, anytime," he whispers.

TWENTY-NINE

The weather has grown cold and the wind has picked up. Vivienne is huddled inside of Mikah's Boston College sweatshirt and her jacket as she and Celeste walk down toward the river. The closer she gets to the river, the larger the pit in her stomach feels. Everyone seems a little more on edge tonight; their normal walking conversation is absent.

When her feet hit the path, the now-familiar shimmer spreads across her skin and she knows she's exposed. She feels her guardians around her: Mikah and Red behind her, Connor and Andrew in front. Celeste walks beside her, also exposed. With the shields down, she can sense an unfriendly presence nearby, but she doesn't think it's Riley.

After a hundred yards or so, Andrew says in her ear, "Let's pause up here near the dock, but stay on the path."

"Alright," Vivienne answers.

The closer they draw to the dock the more anxious Vivienne grows, her heart beating faster though she doesn't sense danger. Regardless, she's not letting her guard down.

They pause at the dock.

"Are you feeling okay?" Celeste asks.

Vivienne can feel a little of Mikah's anxiety, too, though it's muted because he is protected.

"Yeah, I feel fine, it's just..."

"Just what?" Celeste asks.

"Something doesn't feel right."

"We're all feeling it tonight, Vivienne," Andrew says in her ear. "Let's keep moving."

"Alright."

The air grows colder the longer they walk. Tonight they make it to the bridge – two hundred yards beyond their normal stopping point - before they turn around and start to head back. Vivienne can't quite figure out why Andrew wanted to go on further, but she doesn't question his intentions.

Vivienne slows down.

"What's wrong?" Mikah says in her ear, and she can feel him moving toward her.

"Stop, keep your position. I just want to drag this out a little longer. Slow down a little," Vivienne says back to him. "Something tells me that this is the night. I want to give him his chance to show up."

"Alright, let's—" Andrew stops talking.

The air shifts, and Vivienne senses a force unlike anything she's ever felt before. An evil force. Though it's unfamiliar, there's no doubt in her mind that it's Riley.

"He's here," she whispers.

"Where?" A chorus of voices rings in her ear.

"Ahead of us, along the path. But he's not coming toward us, he's staying put, hiding in the shadows just before the dock."

Mikah's breathing spikes and his wings blaze as Vivienne continues toward Riley's hiding place.

"This is way too easy," Riley whispers to himself as he watches the two women approach.

They're walking casually along the river, talking and seeming to have a good time, though neither one of them is smiling or laughing.

He runs through the possibilities in his mind. Killing Vivienne's companion would be exciting. Killing her slowly in front of Vivienne would be even more exciting. But he's not sure he can kill the woman and still capture Vivienne. Ah, but it would be fun to make Vivienne watch her friend die in front of her. Watch her squirm just a little bit, since he can't touch her; the pain in his crotch is a constant reminder of that.

Vivienne's training had all taken place in Elysium, and when she asked Zirah about it she told Vivienne that Elysium was the best place to learn about herself and what she was capable of because it is free of distraction and the protections she has on earth. The more Vivienne could understand about her abilities in Elysium, the easier they'd be to use on Earth.

Immediately after beginning her training in Elysium, Vivienne had begun practicing around the condo, and she quickly realized what kind of barrier their protection places on her abilities. But the more she practiced, the easier it became to work through those invisible protections.

"Breathe, you'll do fine," Celeste whispers to Vivienne. "Remember what I taught you."

Vivienne had been surprised when Celeste showed up in Elysium about a week ago. She'd come to show Vivienne some basic self-defense moves. Moves that came really easily to her, and it left her bereft and wishing she'd learned them sooner.

"It's strongest right here," Vivienne whispers as they pass the point where she believes Riley is hiding. Her eyes flicker in the direction of a deep shadow between several boats that are land-docked about fifty feet away.

As they pass the last boat, Vivienne can feel the men shift positions: Mikah and Red move in front of her, Andrew and Connor behind.

In a flash, arms wrap tightly around her, a knife at her throat. "I knew I'd get my hands on you again. Did you miss me?"

"Not really," Vivienne answers.

THIRTY

Vivienne struggles in Riley's grasp, distracting him so that Celeste can disappear unnoticed. Then Vivienne feels the shimmer of Celeste's shield wrapping around her.

"You're coming with me," he growls into her ear, and she can feel him tugging on her, but he's not going anywhere.

"What the fuck?" Riley groans as he realizes that getting away with her isn't going to be as easy as she'd made it seem. His grip on Vivienne tightens.

With one hand Vivienne continues to struggle against his grip around her chest. Though panic is washing through her, she feels remarkably calm as she reaches into the front pocket of Mikah's sweatshirt, where the gold-plated butterfly knife that Celeste gave her rests against her belly, reminding her that her little girl is what she fights for.

Mikah watches in horror at the scene playing out before him and struggles against Red, who is holding him back.

"She's fine. Let her do this. She needs to do this. And he can't get away with her. We've locked him down."

Vivienne grips the handle of the knife and pulls it free of her sweatshirt. She adjusts her grip and then jams it straight back into Riley's thigh, twisting it. At the same time, her wings burst free, pushing him backwards.

Riley screams as the gold blade burns his flesh.

As soon as she is free, Vivienne turns around to look at him, to watch him writhe on the ground in pain. "Not this time, asshole."

He looks up, and his eyes tell her that he's nowhere near done with her. But then he squints, finally seeing what stands before him.

She's an angel! Link had failed to prepare him for this, but suddenly he understands why the devil wants her alive.

"No!" he grunts as he staggers, struggling to stand up.

Vivienne watches his movements carefully, seeing what he intends to do. She can feel them, all of them, surrounding her, letting her have her moment of revenge.

Then, one by one, her guardians drop their shields and appear. Mikah, Andrew, Connor and Red all stand behind her in a semi-circle. Celeste, however, does not reappear. Just as soon as Vivienne thinks her name, her vision shimmers, and she understands that although Riley can still see her, Celeste is providing protection.

Riley's eyes widen as he takes in the scene before him. Unsure what to make of the four extremely tall figures dressed in black that have suddenly appeared behind Vivienne, he tries to shake himself loose and disappear back into hell. But he can't; something or someone is blocking his exit.

Riley pulls the knife from his leg and tosses it aside, glancing at the wound Vivienne's created.

Vivienne watches Riley's anger build, anger at the fact that she's finally managed to fight back. The bloodlust in his eyes is the same as it has always been, but this time it's backed up by the devil's powers, and suddenly his hands are on fire. Fireballs roll maliciously in his palms.

Neither Vivienne nor the guardians can prevent menacing grins from forming on their own faces, and Riley becomes even angrier that they are laughing at him.

He throws one fireball, then another, straight at them. Vivienne holds her breath and watches each of the fireballs bounce back toward Riley and explode. The first one causes him to flinch, the second one shatters as it hits the shield.

"Now it's my turn," Mikah growls, reaching for the knife tucked into his belt. He unsheathes it quickly and walks toward Riley. Red disappears and takes a protective form around Mikah.

Another fireball forms in Riley's hand. Mikah's eyes focus on it, anticipating, and when Riley throws it, he dodges. The fire bounces off of Mikah's protection and explodes somewhere over the docks.

Mikah lunges forward. Riley scrambles to run away, but Mikah is on him, bringing his arms around Riley in a bear hug. Riley manages to get one arm free. Feeling confident again, he goes for the other. Which is exactly what Mikah wanted him to do. Mikah brings his arms up around Riley's upper arms and interlaces his fingers behind Riley's neck, effectively immobilizing Riley.

Andrew moves toward them, gun in one hand and the other formed into a tight fist. Riley manages to conjure up another fireball, but Mikah's grip on him gives him the worst aim. Andrew laughs as the fireball whizzes past him.

Connor begins advancing on Riley too. Vivienne realizes that both he and Andrew are unprotected. Riley launches several more fireballs, but they dodge them easily. Vivienne flinches as one bounces off of the shield Celeste has created around Vivienne. Connor and Andrew seem in no hurry to take Riley down.

Why are they playing with him? Vivienne wonders.

Andrew's fist connects with Riley's gut. Riley doesn't even flinch at the contact, and his foot comes down hard on Mikah's instep.

"Shit!" Mikah growls.

Vivienne can see the bloodlust growing in Mikah's eyes. "Drop my shield," Vivienne says as she realizes that Celeste has immobilized her.

"No," Mikah growls back.

Andrew has Riley by the throat. "Who's with you?"

"I don't need anyone with me," Riley sneers. He brings his hand to Andrew's chest, and Vivienne sees streams of crackling white lightning coming off of his fingertips.

THIRTY-ONE

"No!" Vivienne screams.

Just as the jolt is about to make contact, Andrew releases Riley and disappears. It bounces off Andrew's screen, hitting Riley square in the chest and sending him flying backwards ten feet.

The distance is just what Riley wanted; he starts to fling fireballs and bolts of lightning toward Mikah, who is still protected by Red, and Connor, who is now protected by Andrew. The lightning bounces off their protection and back at Riley, but he's not giving up.

Mikah and Connor advance quickly on Riley, and then suddenly all four of the men are standing in front of him.

"Having fun?" Connor growls at Riley.

Riley laughs. "Of course I am. You idiots don't stand a chance against me."

Andrew laughs this time. "Really? Looks to me as if you're losing this one. But then again that is what he wanted. He wanted you to be destroyed so he doesn't have to deal with your ridiculous ass anymore."

"What are you talking about?" Riley spats, but Vivienne can see his determination waver.

"We know who and what you are, Riley. When you killed your father you pissed him off, didn't you?" Mikah says.

Riley's eyes dart toward him. "How do you know that?" The lightning stops.

"We know a lot more about you and what the devil's motivations are than you do," Andrew says.

"I don't believe you." Suddenly the lightning starts up again.

Mikah rears back and brings his fist around in a right hook straight to Riley's jaw. The contact is so hard that Riley's face jolts to his right, but then he smugly swings his head back to look at Mikah, bringing his own right hook with him. Mikah dodges the punch and connects with a kidney shot to Riley. This time Riley crumples a little bit.

"You see, Riley, we know that you came here to kidnap her and take her back to Link," Mikah growls.

Riley's eyes widen.

"He wants her so that he can lay claim to her child. Raise Vivienne's daughter in hell as one of his own. But you see, we're not going to let you do that."

All four men move at once, knocking Riley flat onto his back. Riley's head cracks against the pavement, but it doesn't stop him from fighting to get back up.

At the same time that Andrew raises his knife toward Riley, Vivienne is nearly knocked over by a force greater than Riley, and Andrew's knife is knocked out of his hand.

"He's not alone," Vivienne breathes. She senses something else in the area, something coming from the same spot that Riley stands.

Mikah and Andrew look around.

"Not a physical presence."

Andrew and Mikah recognize what she is implying. While Riley was already empowered by Link, the devil is now imbuing Riley with the last of his power.

Riley is on his feet in no time flat.

Everything at this moment starts to move in slow motion. Mikah's wings burst through his sweatshirt while Red disappears completely for a brief moment, and Vivienne watches as he surrounds Mikah.

Andrew and Connor stalk toward Riley; their rage can be felt ten feet away. They move lightning fast, and Vivienne watches as Riley's shirt shreds. Then Riley is fighting back, throwing punches and erratically launching lightning bolts and fireballs that Connor and Andrew dodge. Riley's blood drips from the cuts he's sustained from Connor and Andrew. The blood begins to pool at his feet.

Though time feels suspended, Andrew's and Connor's movements are nearly impossible to track, and Mikah stands back and watches, blade in hand and ready to strike when the time is right.

But three things happen at once. Andrew and Connor come to a halt, one on each side of Riley. They have Riley's arms and legs intertwined with their own, holding him still, preventing any movement from him, and Red comes away from Mikah, morphing back into his human form with his gun pointed straight at Riley.

The blood runs down Riley's body as he stands trapped, unable to move, but he manages somehow to throw a fireball at Red. Red, realizing he doesn't have time to dodge it, begins to morph just as the fireball makes contact. Red is knocked to the ground in his human form. He coughs and staggers back to his feet.

Riley's blood loss is causing him to fall weaker into Andrew's and Connor's arms, and the necessity of having everyone here becomes clear to Mikah. He lunges forward, knife raised and ready to strike Riley in the heart.

At the instant contact is made, right through Riley's heart, there is a flash of bright white, and Vivienne watches in horror as Mikah's wings suck in and he drops to the ground.

"Mikah! NO!"

THIRTY-TWO

"God dammit, Celeste, let me go!" Vivienne screams as she struggles against Celeste's immobilization.

Another flash pops near Andrew, Red and Connor, only this time it's on the ground. A massive puff of smoke rises, and ashes go flying in the breeze.

All trace of evil presence is gone. Riley has been destroyed.

"So help me God, let me go."

Suddenly the bonds holding her back are gone and Vivienne takes off running toward Mikah. "No! No! No!" she screams as she runs.

Andrew, Connor and Red all surround Mikah, and Vivienne has to fight to get through them. Finally she breaks through the wall of men and tumbles onto him.

"No, Mikah, not like this." She places her head on his chest, listening, hoping to hear something. But the rushing of her own heart makes it impossible. She can smell burnt cotton.

She raises her head up to see a hole in his sweatshirt. There is no blood, but she can see scorch marks on his chest. Vivienne takes ahold of either side of the hole and pulls apart the sweatshirt, widening the hole enough for her to see five points, charred black, on his chest.

"No, no, no. Mikah, no, you can't do this. You can't leave me."

"Vivienne. We should get him to Elysium."

"No, not yet," Vivienne argues.

The guardians look at each other, wondering how to get Vivienne to let him go so they can get him to Elizabeth, who is his best chance for survival. Just then, a bright white light rises up between them. Everyone looks down, confused.

Vivienne kneels over Mikah, her hands over his chest, over the scorch marks. The light is coming from her.

They watch and listen as Vivienne recites an ancient healing prayer. All five guardians kneel down, surrounding both of them as Vivienne continues to recite the incantation. The men look to Celeste, who nods and mouths, "She knows what to do."

The longer Vivienne recites the prayer the more labored her breathing becomes. Tears streak down her cheeks, and the light begins to die out. But the marks fade from Mikah's chest and a beautiful, intricate Celtic tattoo begins to spread across his shoulder and down his arm.

But he still isn't breathing, and his heart, when she again lowers her head to his chest to listen, doesn't beat.

"Mikah, no, you can't. Please, Mikah."

Failure washes over her. She couldn't save him.

"I love you," she whispers.

THIRTY-THREE

"I'd be lying if I said I was surprised by you coming back through the death channel."

Once again Riley stands before the devil. This time, though, the room is different. It's hotter, and there are screams – haunting screams that echo off the walls.

"Death channel?" Riley realizes all too clearly that the men on the path were right all along.

His inquiry is met with laughter. "I always knew your arrogance was going to get you into trouble. Yes, the death channel. You're dead. Again. And you're mine. Or rather, you belong to the pits of hell, and I have just the person to torture you for all eternity."

Riley could never have predicted what happens next.

Striding into the room is a woman. She's confident, maybe even a little smug.

"Yes. She will do wonderfully," Links says as the woman comes to a stop in front of Riley.

Her hand slides down his stomach as she struts around him, down past his dick, heading straight for his balls. She wraps her fingers around them and starts to pull.

Riley lets out a blood-curdling scream as he looks into the eyes of Rebecca Black.

JANUARY

FEBRUARY

THIRTY-FOUR

"Madison?" He breathes against her belly.

They're sitting on the white couch in the big white room in Elysium. Mikah is lying across the couch with his ear pressed to Vivienne's belly. She's dreaming of him once again, as she has every night for the last two months.

She laughs and nods.

"I like it. I think it's a good, strong name."

Vivienne runs her hand through his hair as he gently caresses her belly. "Madison Callahan-Blake," she says.

His head comes up off her belly and he stares deep into her eyes, not even trying to hide his surprise. "Why?" is all he can manage to breathe.

"Is it not what you want?" she asks him, returning his gaze.

"I love it, but..."

"But she's not really your daughter."

Vivienne moves to sit up. Mikah lets her, then he lays his head on her thigh. She goes back to playing with his hair.

"No, she's not. But I want her to be, just like I want you to be my wife."

She rolls her eyes at him. This isn't the first time he's brought up the subject of marriage with her. "My opinion on marrying you hasn't changed, at least not until after she's here. Then we can talk about it." She rubs her tummy as Madison moves around.

Mikah notices Vivienne's wince.

He also notices that her image is flickering like a bad channel on the TV, and he knows that she's going to wake up soon.

"I want your name on her birth certificate," Vivienne says, bringing the conversation back to the original subject. "I don't want hers to look like mine."

She flickers again.

"I'd be honored to have my name on her birth certificate."

He sits up and turns so that they're face to face, then leans in to bring his lips to hers.

She kisses him back, but the kiss doesn't last as long as either one of them hoped.

Tears streak down her cheeks as she climbs out of bed and shuffles toward the bathroom. Being eight months pregnant keeps her dreams a lot shorter than they used to be. But it is the same every time: Vivienne wakes up crying, bereft, and the ache of loneliness courses through her veins.

Mikah is gone, stuck in Elysium. She'd fought hard to save him that night, but the damage had been too much for her to handle. Despite Elizabeth's reassurance that there is a chance that Mikah can return home, the longer he stays away and Elizabeth refuses to let Vivienne see him during her waking visits to Elysium, the more hopeless Vivienne starts to feel. Her dreams are the only place she can see

Mikah, and when she wakes, she misses him that much more.

She believes in her heart that this is not the way it was supposed to end.

THIRTY-FIVE

"How are you holding up?" Celeste asks as they walk by the river.

Vivienne sighs. "I'm alright, just very ready for her to come out. Beyond ready." She rubs her hand along her extended belly.

Celeste and Vivienne have continued to take their daily walks since that day in December. It's become a ritual of theirs, and they have become very close since that night, what seems like eons ago.

They approach the spot on the blackened pavement where Riley was vanquished back to the devil. Vivienne doesn't look at it very much anymore. However, the mark next to it is another story. That's a mark she touches every day.

Though now it is nearly impossible for her to touch it with her fingers anymore. Bending down has become a thing of the past. She's lucky if her socks actually make it on her feet. She's thankful that the cold Minnesota winter is coming to an end.

"What would you like to do today?" Celeste asks Vivienne.

"Sleep." She laughs. It's a sound that has become more common in the last few weeks, but the ache in her heart is still there.

They continue until they reach the bridge and then turn back, smiling as the runners fly past them without a clue that they're there. Ever since that night, whenever Vivienne wants to take a walk along the river, she goes under complete protection, invisible to everyone outside of the shield.

"Have you decided on her name? Last we talked about it you were tossing around Madison and...what was that other name?"

"MaryAnne."

"That's right. See, all the more reason to name her Madison, I can't remember the other name."

The vision of Mikah stretched out on the couch as they discussed her name last night helps bring a smile to her face. "Madison it is." Although she told Celeste some time ago that she was seeing Mikah in her dreams, she doesn't keep her updated on what they talk about.

"How's your relationship with Red?"

"Strained. We're both trying very hard. I think when he looks at me he sees a lot of wasted years, and he's not sure how to get them back. Couple that with— He has a hard time with it.

"Kelly is great, though. She is so excited about the baby. And Andrew and Connor have finished the baby's room."

"I know what we can do today." Celeste says, a little too excited.

"No. We're not going shopping. I'm so tired of shopping, and you know damn well I don't spend any money. You always just go back and buy anything that I had my eye on." She laughs. "Besides, Aubrey is coming at one."

"Oh, you can skip yoga for one day."

"Nuh uh, nope, won't do it. Not to go shopping with you." She laughs again as they turn onto the walkway that leads home.

THIRTY-SIX

"Red asked me to stop by his condo when we came back," Celeste says as she pushes the elevator call button. "Are you okay to go up on your own?"

"Absolutely. I'm going to lie down for a while." She absently rubs her belly as the elevator door chimes.

"Alright, I'll come wake you when Aubrey arrives."

Vivienne nods, and the elevator door closes. She inserts her keycard into the slot and presses the button for the seventh floor.

Standing alone in the elevator makes it seem like it takes forever. Finally it reaches the seventh floor, and the elevator bell dings and the doors slide open.

Lit candles line the foyer walls.

"What?" She remembers when Mikah laid out candles the day he returned from Phoenix, and her heart rate spikes to a fever pitch.

She races to the door and pushes it open. More candles line the hallway, and the floor is strewn with rose petals leading into the dining room, where she can see that every surface is covered in candles.

She walks as fast as she can manage without slipping on the rose-covered floor. The hallway seems like it's ten miles long.

Finally she comes around the corner to the kitchen. Her eyes follow the line of candles to the opposite side of the kitchen.

"Mikah," she breathes.

But he isn't there. Her knees grow weak.

Her head falls into her hands and she can't stop the tears from pouring down her cheeks. She's so confused. She doesn't understand why anyone except for Mikah would do this.

But he isn't here. She can no longer hold herself up as the pain of realization washes through her body.

He wraps his arms around her and catches her before she hits the floor. The scent of everything Mikah fills her nose.

She pushes at him, pushing him away. "I'm tired of dreaming. It hurts too much."

"You're not dreaming. I'm here, Vivienne, I've come home."

Her head lifts out of her hands, and she looks up into his beautiful, vibrant blue eyes. She touches his arm, his neck, his face, his chest.

"It can't be real. I fell asleep, I'm dreaming. I—" She slumps down again and he catches her once more.

"I told you, I will always catch you. I will always be here for you."

All the strength goes out of her and she crumples into his arms, tears streaming down her cheeks.

Mikah has never seen anything more beautiful than Vivienne with her red hair and bright blue eyes. She truly is an angel, and he's been waiting for this sweet reunion for far too long.

"I'm here and I'm here to stay."

"But...but..."

"Shhh, sweetheart." He touches a stand of her hair. "You saved my life. Our life. I couldn't have born to watch you leave Elysium. To see the pain in your eyes every time you knew you had to leave."

"But you left me here. Alone. Losing hope. Losing faith that they'd let you return to me," she sobs into his chest. "To wake up every morning crying because what we had was gone and I had to face another day alone, without you."

"I can't even begin to put into words how sorry I am that you had to suffer like that."

He takes a deep breath, pulling back, hoping to look into her eyes. She tries to look up at him, but it's too painful. It's too hard to look at him.

"It was selfish. I was selfish. I thought that being in your dreams would be better than you having to walk out of Elysium without me. I'm sorry. I was wrong." He kisses her forehead. "I love you."

She pulls back to look him in the eyes. "I love you," she breathes.

He brings his lips to hers: strong, needy and passionate.

She has missed the taste of him, and part of her is still afraid she's dreaming, that she'll wake up and he'll be gone. Tears continue to slide down her cheeks.

As if he's read her mind, he says, "I'm not going to leave, I'm never going to leave you. Let me prove it to you?"

She nods, weak and helpless in his arms. He reaches under her legs and stands up, bringing her with him.

"I've missed you so much," she says. "I could never wait to get to sleep so that I could see you."

He smiles and kisses her forehead. "I know, but now you'll never want to sleep."

He carries her into the bedroom.

"Let me love you," he says as lays her out on the bed.

The look in his eyes gives her hope that he speaks the truth, that he isn't going to leave her again. She begins to let herself believe.

"Are you comfortable?"

She laughs through her tears. "No. She's practically sitting on my lungs."

He smiles wide and tears form in his eyes.

She slides her feet off of the bed and sits up. She reaches for his hand and tugs him down onto his knees in front of her. "Please, Mikah, don't cry."

He smirks at her. "Me, what about you?"

"You know this is real. I'm only starting to believe it."

He leans forward, sliding his hands under Vivienne's sweatshirt and placing them gently on her belly. His thumb grazes her belly button and she squirms. "That's like a hot button straight to my bladder. Be careful with that," she laughs.

Her laughter is carefree and he loves the sound of it. He rubs his hands along the curve of her stomach, and underneath the surface he feels Madison move. His eyes dart to Vivienne's and she nods.

"That's her. That's Madison."

He leans forward and presses his ear to her belly, not really to listen, just to be closer. To Vivienne and to Madison.

"I'm sorry. I'm sorry I haven't been here. I'm sorry I had to stay in Elysium and that I couldn't tell you when I was going to be able to come home. I couldn't bear it, to see it in your eyes every time you looked at me. To know that I was hurting you nearly killed me everyday. I knew I had to heal fully before I could be what you needed." He lifts his head, and their eyes meet. "I love you so much it hurts."

She takes his head in her hands. "As I love you."

She urges him up, bringing her lips to his.

THIRTY-SEVEN

Mikah's hands roam around her body as his lips meet hers. In an instant their breathing becomes heavy and sweat begins to bead across her skin.

Mikah senses her slight discomfort and reaches for the hem of his Boston College sweatshirt. He couldn't help but notice it the minute she rounded the corner. She'd been wearing it that night, and when he caught her earlier tonight he felt the new stitching on the back where her wings had burst free.

He begins to lift it up over her belly, and she raises her arms. He pulls back from their kiss to pull the shirt off and takes a peek at the white tank top she's wearing. It is stretched thin over her breasts and belly. He smiles. She looks amazing.

"Can I?" he says as he reaches for the hem of her tank top, and she nods.

She is wrapped up in the fact that he's here, really here, and despite her fear, she knows he is here to stay.

He pulls up her tank top and her nipples harden. He reaches around to undo her bra at the same time she goes for the hem of his shirt. He unclasps each hook as she pulls his t-shirt up higher.

She waits patiently for him to finish before tugging, wordlessly hinting to him to lift his arms. He does. She removes his shirt and he immediately starts to kiss down her shoulder, slowly pulling her bra strap down.

He switches to the other side and her head falls back. His touch is so soft and warm. He urges her arms up and pulls her bra away from her body.

Her nipples are hard, dark brown peaks. "Do they hurt?" he asks, his hot breath caressing her skin.

"They're tender, but no, they don't hurt."

He smiles and licks the tight bud.

Her head falls back again and she moans.

His erection strains against the zipper of his jeans, but she is more important in this moment. He sucks her nipple into his mouth and is rewarded with another delicious moan. He continues to kiss, lick and suck his way over to the other nipple, which is equally as big and hard as the first. He can't help his tongue from licking softly against her skin.

Her hand is in his hair, holding him to her, encouraging him to continue what he's doing. She squirms under him and he reaches for the waistband of her pants.

His silent command for her to lift her hips has her eager for so much more from him.

He slides her pants past her hips, down her legs, and leans back to allow room to free her.

"Stand up," she whispers and he looks at her. "I haven't been able to look at you for two months. I need to see you."

The plea in her eyes has him rising to his feet.

She reaches for his belt buckle, undoes it quickly, then reaches for the button and zipper. Once they're open, she places her thumbs in the waistband and slides his jeans down his legs to his knees.

When he realizes that she can't bend over much further, he smiles and helps her by pushing them the rest of the way.

"Slide back," he says, looking at her with a mountain of promise, and she slides back onto the bed. Pulling her legs up, she lies on her back.

"Here," he says and climbs onto the bed, grabbing a couple of pillows. "Give me your hand." He helps her sit up then lays the pillows down behind her and she lies back down on them. "Better?"

She smiles, overcome again by the care he is taking to make sure she's comfortable. "Much."

He crawls between her legs.

She needs him so bad, but he lies down and flicks his tongue across her clit. She moans, squirming under his touch, but he doesn't stop.

She can't see his head, which is disappointing, but she can touch it. She runs her fingers through his hair as he continues to lick and suck her clit, and then writhes beneath him as he slides one finger inside. She begins to grind against his tongue and finger. The feeling pooling deep in her core is a reminder of everything she's missed these last couple of months.

Fireworks start to explode behind her eyes and her heart is pounding as she grinds harder, pushing his head downward and tighter against her sex.

He loves every minute of it as he feels her unraveling around him. Her legs begin to shake and then stiffen, and she moans, harder and louder than she ever has before. With her orgasm comes tears – tears of joy, tears of love.

He kisses his way up her belly, careful to avoid her belly button, to her nipples, and then to her neck, jaw and lips. He arcs his body over hers so that he's not pressing on her at all.

When their mouths meet, she tastes her own arousal on his lips and tongue, and she does what she can to kiss it off of him.

After a few more flicks of his tongue against hers he pulls back to sit on his heels. He urges her to lift her leg and she does, though unsure of what he's doing. He brings it around him so that she rolls onto her side. The pressure on her lungs and back eases immediately.

"Better?"

"Much."

He lies down behind her, kisses her shoulder and reaches down to lift her leg.

"What are you...? Oh."

She can feel his erection lying against her thigh. She reaches down to hold her leg up for him, and he positions the head of his cock against the entrance of her sex. She scoots her butt back toward him, eager to feel him inside her once again.

He senses her desire and gently slides himself inside. His need to be in her takes over and he slides in and right back out, again and again.

She can feel every throbbing inch of him enter and leave her. Her eyes roll back in her head and she relaxes.

Mikah keeps ahold of her hip as he slides himself in and out from behind.

The full feeling is so amazing that Vivienne starts to cry, and although he can't see her face, he somehow knows and he can't stop the tears that form in his own eyes.

Having Vivienne back in his arms means so much to him that he realize he loves her even more.

THIRTY-EIGHT

Mikah and Vivienne stay spooned on the bed for some time after they've finished, he still resting inside her. They let their breathing return to normal and he wraps his arms tight around her, holding her close.

After a while she rolls onto her back, dislodging him from her sex, and he groans at the loss.

She smiles at him and moves the hair from his eyes so she can look into them. Her fingers trace the black lines on his right shoulder, down his arm and across his chest to where the scorch marks were originally.

"I'd often wondered where this came from. I wish I'd known beforehand," he whispers.

"Me too. I'm so happy you're home."

"Me too. Have I missed anything?" He smiles at her. "Well, besides you?"

"No, I managed to keep you pretty well up to date. I do have an appointment with Dr. A tomorrow. It's the third of our weekly check ups until she—" She places her hand on her belly. "—decides it's time to show up."

Mikah's hand covers hers. "I'd like to go with you."

"Please? Those were always the hardest days. I knew that you wanted to be there."

"I did, and in a way I was." His hand moves up to rest against her chest, against her heart.

"Why did you have to stay in Elysium for so long?"

"I had to heal. It was unclear what would happen if I crossed back over if I wasn't completely healed. I didn't want to take the chance. Better to be locked in Elysium than never to come back at all. At least that was the way I saw it. But every day that I was away from you was harder than the day before. By the end, I was driving Seraphina crazy."

"I haven't heard anything from Zirah since before that night."

"You won't. You've learned all you need to know. And Zirah is not the best with secrets. Elizabeth was afraid she'd let it out that I'd be coming home. A part of me was scared, when I crossed the threshold, that I'd be kicked back into Elysium. I didn't want to get your hopes up if I couldn't come back."

Vivienne thinks about that. "If I'd known that you were going to come back and then suddenly you couldn't, I think that would've been worse. I guess I had more hope than I thought that you'd return."

He brushes a strand of hair out of her face.

"I know you were only trying to protect me," she says.

He kisses her forehead. "You give me more credit than I deserve. You were left here to suffer alone, just so that I didn't have to see and feel your heartbreak."

"But didn't you have your own heartbreak to deal with? You had to watch me vanish when I woke up."

His face falls and his eyes glaze with tears.

"It killed me every day."

She reaches up to cup his face, her thumb wiping away a stray tear. "See, we both suffered in our own way. But it's over now. You're home, and in my arms."

She stretches up to kiss him and he meets her halfway. Their kiss is passionate and heartfelt, all the anguish over the last two months pouring into this one kiss.

THIRTY-NINE

"What time is it?" she asks him.

"It's ten minutes to one."

"Crap. Aubrey will be here soon."

Mikah cocks his head at her.

"She's my yoga instructor. At Dr. A's urging, Celeste found a personal trainer for me. She comes three times a week. Ironically, Celeste wanted me to cancel today and go shopping with her. Did they know?"

He shakes his head. "No, no one did. Let me call downstairs, have them tell Aubrey that you've had to cancel. I want to spend today with you."

She smiles at him. "You can't hide in here from everyone all day, you know that, right? Besides, I have a couple of things to show you."

"Sounds great to me. Let's take a shower, then we can get dressed."

She nods her agreement and he sits up.

While Vivienne crawls off the bed he reaches for the bedside phone and calls the front desk. Now that she mentioned the yoga classes, he can see it in her arms. Though she's gained weight since the last time he saw her in person, it's good weight and he likes it very much.

Vivienne heads toward the bathroom and turns on the shower. After a minute more Mikah joins her.

Celeste returns to the condo to find the foyer and hallway lined with candles. She hears the shower kick on and she can feel that Vivienne is not alone. Remembering when she'd set up the candles for him back in November, she realizes quickly that Mikah has come home. She whips her phone out to call Red.

"Come on, pick up."

"Hi, Celeste," a woman's voice answers.

"Kelly, is Red there?"

"He is, one second."

There is a pause while Kelly gives the phone to Red. "Celeste, you just—"

"He's alive. He's here. In the apartment."

"What? How?"

"I don't know, but get your butt up here quick. Bring the boys, I need your help."

"On my way."

The phone clicks dead and Celeste goes about blowing out all the candles. She wants to clean them up before they come out. Dressed, she hopes silently.

Red, Andrew and Connor arrive in no time, having taken the stairs.

"Help me clean these up. They're in the shower."

"Have you seen him?"

She shakes her head as she continues blowing out candles.

"How do you know it's him?" Connor says.

"You know, you can stop being a pessimist now. What is your deal anyway? You're always so grumpy. You didn't used to be like this."

"Lay off of him, Celeste," Red steps in.

"I just don't understand it. You scare Vivienne sometimes and I don't like it."

"I don't try to scare her intentionally. I just don't like to get attached. Sometimes keeping my distance is the best way to avoid that." That's the easiest explanation he can come up with; the rest of that story is a lot harder to tell and not worth the effort. Suffice it to say, he could relate more to Vivienne these last two months than anyone else could.

"That's a load of bullshit, Connor, and you know it. You ran up here just as fast as these two knuckleheads when I called Red," Celeste bites back. "Now, help me." She smiles at the three men just standing there.

About five minutes later they hear the water shut off in the shower and they scramble to finish picking up the candles.

When Celeste bends over to pick up the last of the candles, Andrew is quick to notice. This isn't the first time he's looked at her over the last couple of months. Before, he was too occupied with the task of protecting Mikah and Vivienne, but there've been no sightings of Riley or any of Link's other minions since the night of the battle, and since things seem to have settled down, all the worry has settled too, allowing for other emotions to bloom and blossom.

After the battle, Celeste had become so emotionally closed off that her longtime boyfriend had broken up with her. It hadn't helped that she couldn't explain anything to him. She thought she would be destroyed by it, but in the end it had been the best thing for her.

"Now what?" Andrew whispers.

Celeste looks at him. He's practically bouncing in his skin. She stops for a minute, just to look at him. She's never really looked at him before. Such a professional relationship they've had, but something is different about him today. Maybe it's the beard he's grown over the last month or so. As she moves to put the candles in the hall closet, she smiles at him.

FORTY

"You know they're all in the condo, right?" Vivienne whispers as they get dressed. Right before they'd stepped into the shower, she sense Celeste entering the condo, and while they were in there she felt the other three come in too. "All your candles were a dead giveaway to Celeste. She helped with them the last time, remember?"

He smiles. "I remember, and it's okay. Like you said, I can't hide from them all day, though I want to."

"They've missed you too."

"I missed you more."

"Come on, let's go say hi." She smiles at him as she leads the way to the door.

"Let me get that." Mikah comes around her and reaches for the knob. When he swings it open, standing near the breakfast bar are Celeste, Connor, Andrew and Red.

"The candles gave me away," he teases, and Celeste comes running, bounding into him. Mikah hugs her back, though he refuses to let go of Vivienne's hand, which makes for an awkward hug.

"Come now, lass, let the man out of his room." Red smiles, but Mikah can see the tears in his eyes.

Next comes Connor, surprising both Vivienne and Mikah by giving him a hug. "Welcome home." He backs off but then punches Mikah in the shoulder. "You could've given us a warning." He steps aside.

"And ruin the opportunity to get a hug from you?" Mikah laughs.

Andrew comes up to him and hugs him next. "I never gave up hope that we'd see you here again. Welcome home."

"Thanks, Andrew."

"Anytime, sir," Andrew replies.

"No more of that. Mikah is just fine."

Vivienne can't help the smile that spreads across her face at their exchange. Andrew has been like a big brother to her, especially these last few months. She also senses a change in Mikah's demeanor. He's happier than he ever was before. At least when it comes to these four. Maybe fighting Riley together changed the dynamic of their relationship. She smiles again at the idea.

Red comes a little more slowly, and Mikah meets him halfway. Finally releasing Vivienne's hand, he takes Red into a big hug.

"Welcome home, lad. Things haven't been the same since you left."

"I know, but I had no choice."

"I know. I always hoped, but as time went on and your mother got more and more insistent that you couldn't be seen, it became harder."

"I know, Red. I made her do that. I'd have never been able to live with myself if she or I made a promise we weren't sure could be kept."

"I understand. Glad you're home."

"I'm happy to be here. Let's all have dinner tonight." He turns to Celeste. "That okay with you?"

She smiles so wide it spreads to everyone in the room. "Absolutely."

The guardians all leave the condo, giving Mikah and Vivienne a little more time to themselves, with the agreement that Celeste will be back in a couple of hours to start making dinner.

"Sydney will be happy to hear from you," Vivienne says.

"You guys didn't tell her I was gone?"

Vivienne shakes her head. "We all felt that telling her would make it final, and none of us were ready to do that. We all held out a little hope, hope that you would be allowed to return. Red and Andrew have been communicating with her via email, dealing with what few important business matters needed addressing. I'd imagine she'll be excited to have you back in the office again."

They both go into the TV room. The couch is more comfortable.

"Red has been handling the finances," Vivienne continues. "I didn't feel I had the right to do it. Not only that, but I would probably pass out from the amount of money spent each month."

Mikah laughs. "Maybe," he says.

"Except for morning walks with Celeste and sometimes one of the others, I never leave the condo unless she drags me, usually kicking and screaming, to go shopping."

"How are things with Red?"

She takes a deep breath. "Strained, but I imagine that things will get better between us now that you're home. Kelly is ecstatic over Madison. She'll make an amazing grandparent. Red will too. I think he sees Madison as a chance to redeem himself for what he missed with me, and that's okay. It wasn't fair to him what my mother did, and I don't blame him at all. It's just hard to go from no father, no parent, to now there is one. Same for Red, he has a twenty-two-year-old daughter that he didn't know about."

"So you'll give it time?"

She nods. "I will."

"What about your mother?"

Vivienne shrugs. "I haven't decided yet. Nothing she can do or say will make it right. She won't be able to stay in Elysium, and I can't cross over to see her in heaven, so it seems a little pointless to try and build a relationship now."

"No, you can't, but at some point she might want to apologize to you."

"When that times comes, I'll listen to her. But I came to accept who she was and what she did to me a long time ago. I don't know that I need her apology like I thought I did."

"That's my girl."

"Come on, I'd like to show you something." She gets up awkwardly from the couch and heads toward the door.

He grabs her hand. "I didn't say it enough before, so forgive me if I make up for lost time." He kisses her forehead. "I love you."

"I love you too, Mikah." She touches her other hand to his cheek, enjoying the feel of the light stubble against her palm, and he leans into it. "Never doubt that."

As they walk toward the second bedroom, the one closest to theirs, Vivienne tells him, "Red, at one time, asked if I wanted to move back downstairs, asked me if it would be easier, and I told him no, I wanted to stay here. So one day at the end of January, Celeste dragged me out shopping, and when I came home, this is what I found."

Vivienne turns the knob, pushes the door open and hits the light switch. Two soft lights kick on, and Mikah gets an eyeful of soft pink, purples, and white. Directly in front of them is the sleigh crib he bought her for Christmas. The matching dresser is to his right and a changing table is to the left of the door. Beyond the changing table is the rocking chair Mikah bought her for Christmas.

"We still need a few things for her," Vivienne says. "I've been putting it off, but we're running out of time."

"We are, so after your appointment tomorrow, I'd like to take you shopping."

She wraps her arms around him. "I'd love to."

"Kicking and screaming?"

She laughs. "Kicking and screaming."

FORTY-ONE

Vivienne falls asleep around three, and Mikah sneaks downstairs and knocks on Red's door.

"Hello, Mikah. What can I do for you?" Red says as he swings the door open, inviting Mikah into the condo Red shares with his wife Kelly. Mikah can see Kelly at her desk and he waves to her. Kelly is small-framed like Vivienne, with shorter brown hair and brown eyes. Her age is only apparent in the laugh lines that frame the corners of her eyes.

She stands up and comes over to him.

"Welcome home," she says as she hugs him. "Glad you're back."

"Me too. Thank you, Kelly."

She pulls back from him.

"Everything alright upstairs?" Red asks him.

"It's perfect." He smiles to both of them. "I wanted to thank you for all your help these last few months, and for taking care of Vivienne. I'm not sure what I would have come back to had it not been for you and everyone else. So thank you."

Red puts his hand on Mikah's shoulder and squeezes slightly. "Anytime. I know how much she means to you. It seemed appropriate."

"It was, and I can't thank you enough. However, there is one more thing I need to ask of you."

Red pulls his hand away and ushers Mikah toward the living room. "Come in, sit down," Red says to Mikah.

"I can't stay. I want to be there when Vivienne wakes up."

They take a seat in the living room, Red and Kelly on the smaller of the two couches. Just from the way they look at each other, their love for one another is more obvious to Mikah than it ever was before, now that he looks at Vivienne the same way.

"What can we do for you?" Kelly asks.

Mikah fidgets a little with his hands, much the way Red does when he plays with his wedding band. "I'd like to ask for your blessing to marry Vivienne."

Mikah watches Red as his eyes portray a deep-seated sense of love and protection, something that comes natural to a father. In conjunction with what Vivienne said earlier about Red trying, it is obvious to Mikah that he trying but is lost as to how.

"Mikah, I..." Red pauses. "I'm not sure I'm the one to ask that question. Perhaps you should ask her."

"I plan to, but I'm hoping for your blessing as well."

"Of course, lad. I could never deny you your true love."

"Thank you, Red. Kelly."

"Anytime, anything. I just wish I knew what to do to get closer to her."

Mikah smiles. "It will come in time. Be patient with her. She doesn't know how to handle having someone in a parental role caring about her. Give her some time." Mikah smiles again.

"I can do that."

They all stand. Kelly goes back to her desk and Red escorts Mikah to the door.

Mikah turns to him. "Please, bring Kelly to dinner tonight. I'd love to have her join us."

Red smiles and nods. "See you later."

FORTY-TWO

"Dinner was great, Celeste, thank you."

Celeste looks to Mikah, a warm smile on her face. "You're most welcome, it's great having you home."

"Hear, hear," Andrew says as he raises his glass. The others follow his lead. "To new beginnings," Andrew says, and they all drink.

Mikah is overwhelmed by Andrew's candor and it warms his heart. In the two weeks before the night of the battle, the four men had spent a lot of time in close quarters, and as they all sit around tonight, talking about the things that have happened over the last two months, he is reminded of that time. At one point, to Mikah, Celeste, Andrew and Connor were simply a housekeeper and a couple of bodyguards. But that's all changed now.

Vivienne watches Red lean over and kiss Kelly. Despite Red's graying hair, he has a very youthful appearance. Especially when he's with Kelly. She knows that he was being honest when he said he didn't know. If he'd known about Vivienne – or any child of his, for that matter – the efforts he's made now tell her that he wouldn't have stayed away, and she takes comfort in that. But although Red may be her father, she also realizes that maybe a father-daughter relationship is not what they need. Or at least it may not be what she needs.

"How are you feeling?" Mikah whispers to Vivienne as she yawns.

"Great. Stuffed, but great."

"Good." He kisses her temple, and Vivienne watches as Andrew smiles at her before his eyes wander toward Celeste.

That could be rather interesting, Vivienne muses.

"Umph," Vivienne grunts. "Ouch." She's not sure what to make of what's just happened. All eyes are on her.

"What's wrong?" Mikah asks.

Vivienne can't help but smile at the concern in his voice.

"I don't know. It feels like Madison just flipped over and took my intestines with her." She lets out a chuckle. She doesn't want to concern anyone until there really is something to be concerned about.

Mikah leans back and puts his arm across the top of her chair. She can feel his fingers brushing lightly on her shoulder. She looks at him and smiles while the conversation around them continues, and the chatter fades into garbled static as she stares into his eyes. Nothing in the world matters but him, for right now at least.

"Well, I think it's time to call it a night," Red says as he and Kelly stand, effectively ending Mikah and Vivienne's staring contest.

"It's early," Mikah says.

"Yes, but you haven't seen her in two months. You don't need us keeping you apart any longer." He smiles warmly at them both.

Their other friends stand and start to clear their dishes from the table. "Leave the dishes. I'll take care of them." He looks to Vivienne. "In the morning."

They all laugh and place their dishes on the breakfast bar, and they take their leave of the condo.

"That was a lot of fun," Vivienne says as she rises from the table. Mikah comes to stand in front of her, wrapping his arms around her and pulling her toward him.

"That was a lot of fun. We should do that more often," he says into her hair as he kisses the top of her head.

She snakes her arms around him, holding him close. "At least once a week?" she says and he smiles.

"At least."

"The five of us ate a lot of meals together while you were gone, and tonight was the most interactive an animated we've all been for months. It was nice to let our hair down, so to speak." She hugs him tighter.

"Good, it should be like that all the time. Are you ready for bed?"

She nods into his chest. He pulls back. Their eyes meet, and again, nothing in the world matters more than each other.

FORTY-THREE

"Marry me?" he breathes into her ear. They're both sweaty from their roll between the sheets.

Vivienne's breath comes shorter and faster than it did just moments ago when they finished. "Mikah, we've talked about this."

"I know," he says, and she can hear the slight disappointment in his voice. "I just thought that maybe you were brushing me off because I was in your dreams, or that you were uncertain of our future. Do you feel that way?"

She twists toward him, dislodging him from inside of her, and his breath hitches.

"I never felt that way," she says. "I really don't want to have Madison in the middle of our wedding ceremony."

He brushes the hair from her face. "I didn't say we had to get married right away. We can wait, I just want to know that you will be mine forever."

"You need a ring to know that?"

He smiles. "No, sweetheart, I don't. I just enjoy the idea of you wearing my ring, telling everyone that you're taken and reminding you that you're mine."

She smiles at his logic. "Ask me again," she breathes.

"Vivienne Alison Callahan, I promise to care for you, cherish you, and love you for the rest of eternity," he says.

Tears well in her eyes.

"Will you do me the honor of being my wife?"

Seeming to come from out of nowhere, a ring appears between his thumb and forefinger, a beautiful heart-cut diamond ring with two smaller stones on either side. The band is braided. It's beautiful in its simple elegance.

"Yes," she breathes, and the tears spill over.

"Do not cry, sweetheart," he says.

He takes her hand and places the ring on her finger. Once it is in place, he lifts his lips to meet hers, strong and passionate. "Thank you," he says between kisses, and she smiles at his excitement.

His hands begin to roam her body once again, and she is instantly lost in his touch. Desperate to have him inside of her again. To show him that she loves him, unconditionally.

This time, though, he skips the fanfare, eager to slip back inside of her.

FORTY-FOUR

"Okay, three things," Dr. Alston says as she removes the gloves from her hands. "First, her lungs look great, maybe even a little ahead of the predicted due date. Which ultimately means that you could go into labor any day now."

Vivienne's eyes widen fractionally, but then a smile of relief washes over her face.

Mikah feels it too.

"Which leads me to point number two. If at any time you feel pain or tightening in your abdomen, check the clock, see if another one comes. If it does, start timing it. Once they start coming about ten minutes apart, give me a call." She hands Mikah a business card.

"Ten minutes apart?" Vivienne asks.

"Yes. Sometimes you can experience what are called Braxton Hicks, otherwise known as false contractions. Those are usually random. If they fall into a regular pattern, try moving around or taking a shower. If they stop, you're okay. If they continue even though you're moving around, odds are they're real contractions."

Vivienne nods her understanding.

"Don't play down the pain. If you feel something, don't hide it," she says, looking at Vivienne.

"Okay, I will say something," Vivienne says, and Mikah squeezes her hand.

"Lastly, your blood pressure is a little higher than I'd like it to be, but it is still within the normal range. So I'd like you to take it easy. Soak up the chance to lie around in bed, watch TV, read a book or two. Don't do too much," she says, raising her eyebrows at Vivienne.

"I don't do much now. Walking and yoga, sleeping, and that's about it."

"Good, though I'd cut back on the yoga to once a week. Twice a week only if you feel it is helping you to relax. Otherwise, walking is okay, just take it slow."

"No problem," Mikah says.

"You've already started to dilate. Only about a centimeter or so, and that's perfectly okay at this stage. Other than that, we will see you back here next week. Same time?" she says.

"Perfect," Vivienne says as she tries to sit up. Mikah helps her up.

"Okay, I'll let you get dressed and you're free to go. Is there anything else?"

Vivienne shakes her head. "No, I don't think so."

"If you think of anything, just call me."

FORTY-FIVE

"Jeez, Mikah, she has more clothes than I do," says Vivienne, taking stock of their purchases. Mikah had a little more fun shopping than she expected, but it was so much fun to watch him.

"She deserves it. And it's not just clothes." He kisses her as he passes on the way to the dining room table, where all the other bags are. "There's still about six more bags downstairs."

Before he even finishes his sentence, Andrew and Celeste are halfway out the door.

Vivienne rolls her eyes. "You're too much," she says. As Mikah stalks toward her, she giggles.

"But it was so much fun." He smiles at her.

"Yeah, I suppose I didn't kick and scream too much."

Mikah laughs at her. In fact, she hadn't kicked or screamed at all. "You had fun."

She smiles at him. "I did."

Before too long, Andrew and Celeste return with the last of their shopping spree.

"I'll pull all the tags and get everything washed up," Celeste says to Vivienne.

"I'd like to do it. If that's alright with you?"

Celeste smiles at Vivienne and nods. "Of course. But make him lift all the laundry." Celeste points her thumb at Mikah.

Vivienne laughs. "I will, don't worry." She smirks at Mikah, who seems all too eager to dig into what they bought today. Andrew and Celeste take their cue and leave.

Mikah starts to pull things from the bags. "We got clothes in different sizes. Should we separate them by size?"

"That sounds like a plan." She walks over to Mikah and wraps her arms around his midsection from behind. "Thank you."

Mikah turns in her arms to look at her. "Of course. Hey, what's wrong?" He asks in response to a shift in her demeanor; she almost looks sad.

"I'm scared."

"Oh, sweetheart, of what?" he says as he takes a seat in a chair, pulling her toward him. He places his hands on her hips and kisses her belly.

"Of everything. That she won't be healthy, or that she'll come too soon, or that something will go wrong, or that I'll do something wrong." By the time she's done talking her tone is nearly hysterical.

"Oh, sweetheart. You'll do amazing. And anything that could happen, we will deal with when the time comes. But don't stress yourself out over something you have no control over. When she's ready, she'll come." He kisses her belly again and reaches up to brush the back of his knuckles against her cheek. "It's been a long day for you. Why don't you go lie down for a while. I can work on getting this stuff sorted out." He stands, taking her hand. "I'll separate everything and then, when you wake up, we can go through it all."

She nods and he leads her into the bedroom. He turns down the bed and she climbs in.

She reaches over for one of the other pillows and tucks it underneath her belly and between her legs. He smiles, realizing that last night she slept the exact same way, only it was him she wrapped herself around, not a pillow.

He tucks her in and kisses her.

"I love you," she breathes against his lips.

"As I love you."

FORTY-SIX

Vivienne and Mikah spend the next few days dividing their time between laundry, organizing, and putting everything away to get ready for Madison's arrival. Mikah notices that Vivienne has less and less energy each day and is taking longer, more frequent naps.

One afternoon she wakes up and all she can seem to do is organize and reorganize Madison's room, and he realizes that she's started nesting. He watches her work, mainly because she refuses his help and insists on doing it herself. After a few hours of reorganizing, she stops and takes a break to have lunch with Mikah.

"You okay?" He asks her as they sit down to eat her favorite, peanut butter and jelly sandwiches.

"Yeah, why?"

He doesn't want to embarrass her, but he looks down and her gaze follows his.

"Well, crap," she says, and he busts out laughing. "I guess it's time to get the pumping thing going." She smiles.

"I could help with that." The tone in his voice is suggestive.

"Wha—? How would...?" She wrinkles her nose, trying to understand what he's implying. "Isn't that kind of gross?" she says innocently, and his eyes dart away from her. "Mikah!" she says, laughing, and she throws her napkin at him.

"What? They're just so much fun to play with, it just kind of happens when I suck on them."

"Oh, for Pete's sake, why didn't you tell me?"

He laughs harder. "And spoil my fun? Never," he says as he places a potato chip in his mouth.

"How in the world did I not notice that?"

He wiggles his eyebrows at her and she blushes. You're usually otherwise..." He clears his throat. "Occupied."

She has no argument for that.

Mikah watches her as she mulls over what he's just told her. It's rather cute to watch the little furrow appear in her brow when she's thinking about something.

The rest of their lunch is filled with playful teasing. Mikah notes that when he pointed out the fact that she was leaking, she hadn't jumped right up to change. He also notices that she isn't wearing a bra. He finds it very distracting.

As she stands to clear their plates, he stops her. "Leave those and come here," he says as he reaches for her hand, pulling her closer to him. When she's standing next to him he rubs his hand over her belly and breathes hotly across her nipple. She squirms as her nipple cools and peaks.

"You're so bad," she breathes as she feels him tug on the hem of her t-shirt. He lifts it to expose her belly, which he kisses sweetly before continuing to lift her shirt higher. She raises her arms and bends forward so that he can pull it off.

Now she stands before him completely topless. Her breasts are swollen, nearly double the size they were yesterday, and his erection throbs. He leans in, takes one of her nipples into his mouth and sucks hard. She moans, and he is treated to a warm gush of milk across his tongue.

"Okay, I felt that," she says with a Cheshire grin.

He releases her nipple with an audible pop. Then he stands, takes her hand and leads her into the bedroom.

While she's still standing he slides her pants down, and she quickly returns the favor.

"Grab a pillow," he says, and she does. "I'd like to try something. Crawl on the bed." She smirks, already knowing what he wants.

She climbs onto the bed, staying on her knees, and leans forward to hug her pillow. She can feel the bed shift as he climbs on behind her, and then his fingers stroke her clit and then up her sex.

It doesn't take much to get her worked up when it comes to Mikah. She is already ready for him.

Seeing her like this is almost too much.

Vivienne can feel the excitement growing in anticipation of feeling him inside her once again.

He doesn't disappoint her. Before long she can feel the head of his erection testing her entrance. She smiles as he carefully enters her.

The sensation is so much she nearly explodes into orgasm before he's even finished sliding into her. She notices that she is much more sensitive down there than usual. She slides forward and then back onto him, encouraging him to move his hips.

But he doesn't need the encouragement. The second he enters her, he is overtaken by desire and begins to slide slowly in and out of her on his own accord.

FORTY-SEVEN

"Ow."

Mikah's eyes fly open, unsure of what's woken him up, to see that Vivienne is sitting up in bed.

"What's wrong?"

He watches as she slowly exhales and breathes back in through her nose. She doesn't respond to him as she concentrates on breathing.

"Contraction?"

She nods.

He can tell the moment it stops because her whole body just kind of sags.

"I think so," she says. "It's the second one."

"When was the first one?" he asks, a little bit of panic in his voice.

She gives him a half smile. "About fifteen minutes ago. I didn't catch the exact time, it woke me up."

Mikah looks over to the clock. It's two in the morning. It has been a week since his return from Elysium, and today is their next scheduled appointment for Dr. Alston.

"What can I do?" he asks.

She turns to him, brushing his hair from his eyes. "Nothing. Yet. Let's see what happens."

662

She lies back down, turning toward him and wrapping herself around him, much the way she does with the pillow when she naps alone.

He starts to play with her soft, gorgeous red hair. She wraps her arms around him, and in a matter of moments her breathing settles into a calm rhythm, and he knows she has fallen asleep. He anxiously looks at the clock and watching the time tick by and waiting to see if she wakes up again with the next one. If there is another one.

Two oh five.

Two ten.

Finally two fifteen comes and goes without any sign that she's having another contraction.

He continues to play with her hair, thinking about what's coming in the next couple of weeks. Madison. He's never been more excited about anything in his entire life. Not even his return from Elysium can compare to how he feels about Madison's arrival.

Suddenly Vivienne stirs. She squeezes him a little tighter. He looks at the clock. It's two twenty. She doesn't wake, but he hears her groan and feels her squeeze him tighter still.

Twenty minutes, that's not too bad, he thinks to himself as his eyes begin to close once again.

"Mikah."

He stirs in his sleep.

"Mikah, wake up." It's Vivienne.

His eyes jolt open and he sits up rather quickly, but not before noticing that there is something wet and warm in the bed. He pulls back the covers to find a patch of clear liquid.

"Mikah, I think my water broke."

He rubs his eyes and looks at the clock. It's eight in the morning. "How are your contractions?"

"They're about thirteen minutes or so apart."

"When was the last one?"

"About ten minutes ago. It hurt, and shortly after it, I felt the water. That's when I woke you up."

She stops talking and her face scrunches up.

"Breathe, sweetheart."

He takes her hand and she squeezes it. With his free hand he reaches for his phone on the bedside table. He presses two buttons and the line starts ringing. "Hey, Red. Can you get the car ready? Vivienne's water broke."

"It's nearly ready for her appointment. I'll have Andrew bring it around front. Do you need help up there?"

"No, I think we're alright. We will be down shortly."

"Sounds good. Call me if you need us."

"Will do." Mikah hangs up the phone. "I'm going to call Dr. Alston. How are you?"

"That really hurt."

"You're doing great. Can you get up out of bed?"

"Yeah, once it's over I feel fine, just a little weak." She takes a breath. He can see the worry in her eyes.

"You're doing great."

He calls Dr. Alston's number and she answers on the second ring.

"I had a feeling you'd be calling me this morning. How is she?"

"Her water broke."

"Well, okay then. Where was she when it broke?"

"Sleeping."

"Good, was the fluid clear?"

"Yes."

"Okay, bring her on down and I will get them moving on a room for her. We'll see you in a bit. How far apart are her contractions?"

"About twelve minutes."

"Okay. Don't panic, get dressed, grab her stuff and come to the hospital. See you soon."

"Thanks, doctor." He hangs up the phone.

"Shall I get you some clothes?" he says to Vivienne, and she smiles.

"Unless you want to show me off to the world naked."

He snorts and climbs out of bed. "I'll find you some clothes.

FORTY-EIGHT

"I can see the top of her head, so now, Vivienne, I want you to tuck your chin to your chest and push for about ten seconds. Then lie back, take a couple of deep breaths, and do it again. Okay?"

Vivienne nods.

Mikah's hand is lightly rubbing Vivienne's shoulder in encouragement.

For her part, Vivienne is ready to meet her daughter. She continues pushing. Mikah and Celeste are holding up her legs, but she can't really feel that. After about five more pushes, Vivienne can finally see, in the mirror, the head and hair of her daughter.

"Okay, Vivienne, I want you to push for about ten seconds, relax briefly to take a deep breath, and do it again." Dr. Alston nods in encouragement at Vivienne, who takes a deep breath and pushes.

Mikah helps her by counting softly to ten and then she relaxes, takes a deep breath, and pushes again.

On the third push, Vivienne watches in the mirror as Madison's head comes free of her body.

"Stop pushing," Dr Alston says. She goes to work with a mucus sucker on Madison's nose and mouth, and then looks to Vivienne. "One more big push."

Vivienne takes a deep breath. Amanda places something on Vivienne's chest, and Vivienne pushes as hard as she can manage. As she watches the mirror, just like that, Madison is born.

"Five oh six p.m.," Dr. Alston says as she brings Madison up and lays her on Vivienne's chest. Amanda wipes the baby off and wraps her up.

Vivienne looks to Mikah and he, like her, is crying. He bends down and kisses her forehead.

Then he leans over Madison. "Hello, baby girl," he says and kisses her forehead, too. Vivienne is now holding Madison in her arms, tears pouring down her cheeks.

The beautiful baby girl that she'd been fighting for from the beginning is now finally here.

"Hi, beautiful baby girl," she coos.

Madison yawns, and Vivienne's tears continue to stream down her cheeks. Mikah leans down to give Vivienne an awkward hug and to get into Madison's line of sight.

He places his hand very lightly on Madison's head just as a flash goes of.

"Seriously, Celeste." Mikah laughs and wipes the tears from his eyes.

Celeste laughs.

Amanda comes to stand next to Vivienne, opposite Mikah. "I'm going to take her, weigh and measure her, then clean her up."

Vivienne nods, reluctant to give Madison up, but Amanda smiles at her. She takes Madison with one hand under her neck and the other under her butt. "Hello, little one," she coos as she turns around. She places Madison on a bed under a lamp, off of which Vivienne can feel heat radiating.

Amanda walks around to the other side and pushes a few buttons. "Seven pounds, two ounces," she says.

Vivienne watches as she tugs a little on Madison's leg.

"Nineteen and half inches. You're a big girl," she coos at Madison, and Vivienne and Mikah look at each other, smiles and tears in their eyes.

They both turn back toward Amanda and Madison. Celeste is busy snapping pictures.

Dr. Alston, who has all but been forgotten at the foot of Vivienne's bed, says, "There you go. I had to stitch you up a little bit, but you'll be fine in no time."

Mikah remembers all too well how quickly Vivienne healed the last time she was here and wonders if the same will apply now.

"Thank you," Vivienne says to Dr. Alston.

"It's my pleasure, Vivienne. She's a beautiful baby girl." Dr. Alston brings the foot of the bed back up and covers Vivienne. "Kathleen," she says to the nurse who handed her instruments during the birth, "let's get Vivienne some new sheets and blankets and then have the anesthesiologist come back and remove her epidural." She turns to Vivienne. "Amanda will take things from here, help you get started on breastfeeding and get you settled in. I will come back later this evening to check on you." She winks at Vivienne. "You did an amazing job."

"Thank you, doctor, for everything." Vivienne smiles at her, and she leaves the room.

Mikah and Vivienne both turn back toward Amanda and Madison just in time to see Amanda lift her up and pull the icky blanket out from under her. Madison's back is to them, and they both see it, plain as day. On her back are the most beautiful wings in light and dark purples.

FORTY-NINE

No sooner does the door click closed do they look at each other.

"How is it possible?" Mikah is the first to ask the obvious question.

Suddenly, out of nowhere, Elizabeth appears before them, as if in answer.

"Mom, how?"

"Shh, my son, it's alright."

"Do you know what's on Madison's back?" Mikah asks her and she nods.

"She is special. She is an angel from birth, something we weren't sure of until she was born. Only the purest of angels are born with their wings." Elizabeth says matter-of-factly, and Mikah and Vivienne look to each other, their eyes expressing the same sense of worry. "You needn't be frightened. Though she has the markings, it will be at least a few years before they will start to show, at which time we can put a suppression spell on her to keep them locked down. But we will worry about that later. I just came to see her and to check on all of you."

Though Vivienne's worry isn't eased by Elizabeth's words, given that Madison is still an infant it is not a cause for concern right now. All the people around them are aware of who she is, and the overwhelming level of protection on Vivienne tells her that no harm will ever come to Madison.

Elizabeth comes over to the bed so she can have a clearer look at Madison. "She's beautiful," Elizabeth says, and in an uncharacteristic manner she leans down and kisses Vivienne on the forehead. "Well done, Vivienne."

Elizabeth smiles at Vivienne, then Mikah. And just as fast as she appeared, she's gone.

FIFTY

Two months later.

"Vivienne, you look amazing." Celeste fusses over Vivienne, who is standing in front of a full-length mirror tucked into a room off of the main chapel in Elysium.

Her dress, which consists of a beautiful corset top and a free-flowing skirt, is pure white. Over it she wears a sheer, full-length overcoat trimmed with an intricate gold design that comes together in a clasp just under breasts. The back of her corset hangs a little lower than most, and the overcoat is specially designed to accommodate Vivienne's wings. The dress was a gift from Elizabeth, and as per the information she got from Elizabeth, her wings will be a part of today's ceremony, as is tradition when two angels marry.

"Are you nervous?" Celeste asks.

Vivienne smiles at her. "No, he is who I want to spend my life with, and I know deep down that he is truly my soulmate."

Celeste hugs her gently, not wanting to disrupt her dress. "I'm so happy for you guys," she croons.

"How are things with Andrew?" Vivienne asks.

"Oh, for heaven's sake, let's not talk about me. Today is your day," Celeste says as she straightens Vivienne's overcoat. "Okay, ready when you are. Remember what we practiced, nice and slow."

Vivienne smirks and closes her eyes to concentrate. She can feel her wings pushing out slowly, and she pauses long enough for Celeste to adjust the back of her coat over her wings. When her wings reach their full extension without mishap, Celeste claps excitedly.

"Yay, we did it," Celeste says. "Though getting it off will likely be harder." She laughs.

Vivienne stands in front of the mirror, taking in the whole effect. Her hair, bright red and curly, is pull up in a messy bun. Hooked into her hair is a simple but elegant circlet made of gold with a white pearl in the center. Above the stone, a Celtic knot forms a heart.

Her makeup is subtle, her lips a soft pink.

Around her neck is something that Red gave to her after they came home from the hospital the evening after Madison was born. It is a special locket that holds on one side a picture from the hospital of Vivienne, Mikah and Madison, and on the other side a picture of Madison and Red.

She is, as she likes to be while in Elysium, barefoot, though you can't see her feet below the dress.

"Are you ladies ready?"

Vivienne turns to see Red standing in the doorway, looking extremely handsome in his black tux.

Vivienne smiles at him. "I'm ready, are you?"

He smiles back, and she can see the emotion in his eyes. The same one that was there when she'd asked him to walk her down the isle.

"I am," he says.

Celeste squeals with excitement, and Vivienne turns around. Celeste is wearing a beautiful burgundy halter top dress that comes to her knees. She too is barefoot, only because she insisted on not towering over Vivienne with their height difference. Celeste was the perfect choice for Vivienne's maid of honor. She's seen Vivienne at her best and at her worst, and they've grown very close.

Celeste hands her a beautiful bouquet of three red roses, two larger than the third. Each one represents a member of their family: Mikah, Vivienne and Madison.

"How's Madison?" Vivienne asks.

Red laughs. "Being eaten alive by Kelly, Seraphina and Zirah. She's perfectly fine and happy too."

Vivienne smiles. Since her return from the hospital, she has always had someone to help support her in taking care of Madison, and Red, surprisingly, has been there the most often.

"Okay, I'm ready." Vivienne says as she walks toward Red.

FIFTY-ONE

"Nervous?" Andrew whispers to Mikah.

"Not in the slightest."

Andrew laughs. "You're full of sh— crap."

Mikah snorts. "I'm more excited than nervous."

He looks out over the small gathering of people they've got with them. Andrew is standing with him next to his mother. Well, where his mother is supposed to be. Right now she is loving on Madison in ways Mikah remembers she loved on his younger brothers.

Speaking of his younger brothers, they too are here. Elizabeth insisted that they be allowed to come today, for which Mikah is thankful.

Zirah and Seraphina are here too, both vying for Madison's attention.

Rebecca, on the other hand, refused to come, which was no surprise to Mikah, though he was sorry for Vivienne's sake. Vivienne said that it was alright, though, and she remained adamant that the people who would be here today would be the people who mattered.

Andrew nudges him in the arm. Mikah looks to the back of the sanctuary, and standing in the middle of the entrance is Celeste. From somewhere nearby a beautiful chorus of soft voices begins to sing.

Elizabeth refuses to let go of Madison as she takes her place next to Mikah.

Celeste makes her way down the isle. She looks beautiful in her burgundy dress and bare feet, but Mikah is practically bouncing in anticipation of seeing Vivienne come down the isle.

She doesn't make him wait much longer. As she rounds the corner he sees only a silhouette, backlit by the lights behind her, but it's clear that her wings, like his, are out. She takes a few steps forward and the doors close behind her.

Now he can see her clearly. She is standing there next to Red, and she looks amazing. Mikah can't help the tear that escapes his eye. He smiles at her and she smiles back at him.

Her dress is gorgeous and something he hasn't seen until right now. He watches as Vivienne and Red make their way to the altar.

When they reach it, Red leans in to give her a kiss on the cheek and then places her hand in Mikah's.

As soon as they make contact, nothing else matters, nothing else but them.

They walk a few steps and kneel before the altar.

Elizabeth begins the ceremony in fluent Gaelic. Neither Vivienne nor Mikah can catch everything she is saying, but it doesn't really matter. All that matters is that they're joining their lives together forever.

Elizabeth motions for Vivienne and Mikah to stand. Vivienne hands Celeste her flowers, and Celeste gives her Mikah's ring. Mikah takes Vivienne's ring from Andrew, and they begin to speak their vows in unison.

"I choose you for life. I promise you my deepest love throughout the pressures of the present and the uncertainties of the future.

You have shown me what love feels like, and for that I thank you. You are everything I need, and at this moment I know all my prayers have been answered and that all my dreams have come true.

I promise to be here forever and always. From this day forward you shall not walk alone. My heart will be your shelter and my arms will be your home. As I have given you my hand to hold, I give you my life to keep."

They slip the rings onto each other's fingers, shutting out the world around them.

"You may kiss your bride," Elizabeth says.

Clapping erupts behind them, and Mikah dips her and she laughs.

"I love you today and forever," he breathes.

"As I love you."

He plants a warm, beautiful kiss on her lips, and thus their life together begins.

an Deireadh
(The End)

EPILOGUE

Two years later.

It will have been two years ago tomorrow that Mikah married the woman of his dreams. Literally. Since then, they've lived in that beautiful honeymoon stage. At least that is what Celeste says all the time. Though she can't complain too loudly, as she too lives in her own wedded bliss.

About six months ago, they relocated to a two-story house in a suburb of Minneapolis. The house is far larger than the condo was, and Red, Kelly, Andrew and Celeste are close by, in their own homes on the same property. Connor moved on about a year ago; his services were needed elsewhere, and he happily took the job and is enjoying his new assignment. About once a month he stops by to see all of them.

Mikah stands in the doorway of Madison's room. She's just over two years old and she is the most beautiful person he's ever laid eyes on. Well, with one exception - his wife will always hold that place in his heart. He watches her for a while from the doorway as she sleeps peacefully – much like she does every night, which is a blessing to both Mikah and Vivienne

– and then he quietly walks into her room and leans down to kiss her on the forehead one last time for the night.

Stepping quietly out of Madison's room, he turns toward the room he shares with his wife. Here too he pauses in the doorway to watch her sleep. She is so beautiful.

He goes into the bathroom, brushes his teeth and pulls off his t-shirt. As he watches himself in the mirror he has the strangest sense of déjà vu, but he can't quite place it. He runs cool water over his face, dries off and turns off the light on his way out of the bathroom.

The déjà vu washes over him again as he walks into the room. He seems to remember doing this before, only from a different angle. He shrugs it off and walks around the bed to crawl in behind Vivienne. She stirs a little as he climbs in.

"Hi, baby," she whispers.

"I didn't mean to wake you."

"No, you're okay." She turns her head toward him and kisses him awkwardly.

He runs his hands up her beautiful body. He hears her breath hitch as he touches the underside of her breast, and his thumb grazes her swollen nipple.

"You can wake me up like this anytime," she says.

He pushes the covers down her body, exposing her already hard nipples to the cool air, and she shivers and rolls into him. His hand slides along her swollen belly as she climbs clumsily on top of him, facing his feet.

Somehow, she doesn't know how, he's managed to rid himself of his pajama pants, and she slides her sex along his raging erection. She reaches behind her and places her hands on his chest to steady herself. She lifts up, he quickly and smoothly aligns the head of his cock with her entrance, and she lowers herself onto him.

His hands roam her body, which is swollen and eight months pregnant with their son. Neither one of them could be happier than they are right now.

Lost in complete and total bliss, as he is whenever they are with one another, Mikah has a clear enough mind to realize where the déjà vu comes from. The dream from the hospital all those years ago. Their dream has come true, just like all their other dreams have and will continue to come true.

Sliding herself up and down his erection, she begins to shake as her orgasm begins to overcome her, and Mikah knows that she won't be able to hold herself up anymore when she comes. He gently rolls, bringing her with him so that she is on her side and he is spooning behind her. Grinding his hips against her he feels her tighten around him, and his own climax takes him.

They fall asleep intertwined with one another, like they have for many nights before and will for many more nights to come.

Thank You!

Thank you, from the bottom of my heart, for your amazing and continuing support of my stories. Especially Vivienne and Mikah's.

Acknowledgements

This story wouldn't be in your hands if it wasn't for the amazing support of my wonderful friends and my family. You're all the best and I couldn't have done this without you.

I would like to thank my Street Team - The Z Team. Ladies, you're the best an Author can ask for.

Sione, my fabulous editor, thank you for keeping with me, keeping me going, and for putting up with me. This last year has been amazing and I can't thank you enough.

Rachel and Barb - Thank you for putting up with me, and for bring my biggest fans.

And to my AMAZING FANS! I couldn't do this without you!

Find More Zoey

Other Works By Zoey Derrick

Finding Love's Wings

CAMERON ENDERS seems to have it all: a brand new condo in a city she loves, a top executive position at an international entertainment firm, an insane amount of money, and a gorgeous boyfriend. But when Cami catches the boyfriend in the act with another woman, it triggers all the anguish from years of neglect by her parents, and she realizes she never learned how to love or be loved. Cami flees to the remote tropical island of Tarah, but she can't avoid facing her problems any longer when she meets the man of her fantasies...

TRISTAN MICHAELS, one of Hollywood's hottest new stars, has come to Tarah to ride out a storm. His girlfriend of five years has been caught on camera cheating, and she's determined to make Tristan stop the story from breaking. But Tristan's done cleaning up her messes. He needs to escape all things Hollywood for a while--and especially the firm that represents him--until the whole thing blows over. What he doesn't count on is meeting an irresistibly beautiful woman, a woman who just so happens to be the CEO of the firm he's trying to avoid.

Can Tristan and Cami help each other learn to trust and love again, or will their histories of betrayal tear them apart?

This story contains Tattoos, Piercings, a Hot Movie Star and a Sexy Heroine. No rich guy poor girl story here, just a story of what it's like to learn to love.

The Struggle

27 writers. 29 original stories and poems. A single theme:
The Struggle.

Proceeds from the sale of this anthology will go to helping writers in need.

From horror and humor to love and loss, each tale reflects the struggles we all have to face – in life, and within ourselves. They are as varied as the array of talent who united to create them, spinning the threads of storytelling together to weave an extraordinary anthology unlike any other.

The Struggle features works by Delilah S. Dawson, Michael Birchmore, Bobby Salomons, Sue Birchmore, James R. Tuck, Corey Seeley, Sheila Hall, Lily Luchesi, Karina Cooper, Mari Wells, Andrea Wheeler, Sarah Broadley, J. Luis Licea, Zoey Derrick, Aly Morlock, Casey Harris-Parks, Samantha Lee, Trevor Neale, J. Elizabeth Hill, Romantic Dominant, J. Hewitt, Christopher Liccardi, Caroline Rainbow, Gabi Daniels, Peter Davis-Parker, and Rick Austin.

About Zoey

Amazon Best Selling Angels, Demons & Devils and Paranormal Author of Give Me Reason - The Reason Series Book One comes from Glendale, Arizona. Zoey, was a mortgage underwriter by day and is now a paranormal, romance and erotica novelist full-time. She writes stories as hot as the desert sun itself. It is this passion that drips off of her work, bringing excitement to anyone who enjoys a good and sensual love story.

Not only does she aim to take her readers on an erotic dance that lasts the night, it allows her to empty her mind of stories we all wish were true.
Her stories are hopeful yet true to life, skillfully avoiding melodrama and the unrealistic, bringing her gripping Erotica only closer to the heart of those that dare dipping into it.

The intimacy of her fantasies that she shares with her readers is thrilling and encouraging, climactic yet full of suspense. She is a loving mistress, up for anything, of which any reader is doomed to return to again and again.

www.ingramcontent.com/pod-product-compliance
Lightning Source LLC
Chambersburg PA
CBHW030837030726
47495CB00005B/1269